TRIAL in the UPPER ROOM

BOOKS BY PAUL SANN

AMERICANA

Pictorial History of the Wild West (with James D. Horan)   1954
The Lawless Decade   1957
Fads, Follies and Delusions of the American People   1967
American Panorama (revised from the above)   1980
The Angry Decade: The Sixties   1979

SPORTS

Red Auerbach: Winning the Hard Way
   (with Arnold Red Auerbach)   1966

CRIME

Kill the Dutchman! The Story of Dutch Schultz   1971

FICTION

Dead Heat: Love and Money   1974
Trial in the Upper Room   1981

TRIAL
in the
UPPER
ROOM

A heavenly novel
by the defendant
PAUL SANN

cop. 2

A HERBERT MICHELMAN BOOK

CROWN PUBLISHERS, INC.   NEW YORK

Inquiries should be addressed to Crown Publishers, Inc.,
One Park Avenue, New York, New York 10016
Printed in the United States of America
Published simultaneously in Canada
by General Publishing Company Limited
Library of Congress Cataloging in Publication Data
Sann, Paul.
Trial in the Upper Room: A heavenly novel
by the defendant
I. Title.
PS3569.A54T7 1981   813'.54   80-22106
ISBN: 0-517-542846
Design by Camilla Filancia
10 9 8 7 6 5 4 3 2 1
First edition

This one is
for my other
family—
Lisa
and
Robert Steele
and my friend
Gabrielle Gillian,
age one

PAUL SANN
Leather Stocking Farm
Easton, N.Y.

Love's not Time's fool, though rosy lips and cheeks

Within his bending sickle's compass come;

Love alters not with his brief hours and weeks,

But bears it out ev'n to the edge of doom.

  If this be error, and upon me proved,

  I never writ, nor no man ever loved.

—WILLIAM SHAKESPEARE

Day I

Chapter 1 ••••••••••••••••••••••••••

I could have had a lot more years. Good Ira, who was not just a cardiologist but a jogger like myself, told me it was a sure bet after I had that heart attack in '75 when I was only a kid brushing past sixty-one. No more smokes, three ounces of gin a day, *every day,* no more 'round-the-clock bits on the paper and plenty of sleep, alone or with somebody. But that wasn't much of a heart attack. It was only what they call a myocardial infarction, which cuts off the supply of your blood (or your gin) to the heart. Who but a doctor would translate a thing like that into a big thing for a runner, three-on-three basketball player and seven-day-a-week editor who also wrote books?

Once I had all that worked out, I said the hell with it, although a smashing Italian woman had something to do with it. You see, I laid off the Camels for two years but then one night in my favorite restaurant in Manhattan's Greenwich Village that woman lit one of those mile-long MORES and, oh, how that cigaret looked in that mouth. A shy sort, I asked the lady I was with to go over and bum one for me. Well, I never had a stick of grass—or a woman, for that matter—that tasted that good. After my second martini (CLASSIFIED: I was up to nine ounces a day then on my shorter days), I went over and borrowed another MORE, and the next day I bought a pack in the discount store near my brownstone. I thought I would be a good boy, especially since my so-called heart attack had been followed by an equally ridiculous incident—the extra beat with the name hardly anyone can spell. I figured I'd have one after breakfast and one after lunch and a couple with the dinner martinis and then one more to wrap it up. Don't ask me why, because I was never anything worse than a three- or four-pack-a-day smoker but pretty soon anytime I dropped into that discount place the Ms. at the counter would just hand me a whole carton of MORES and ask for six dollars, which I always had even though I had left the newspaper trade by then to become a full-time author.

Anyway, as '79 was winding down I had a five-hour dinner with a nun—Sister Margaret Mary of the Dominican order, who was a classmate of my ex-secretary in an M.A. course in psychology at The New School. I never ran much with nuns but I made that date because I wanted to do a book on Edith Stein, the convert from an Orthodox family in Breslau who had gone into the Carmelite order and then before the Holocaust was spirited off to a Dutch convent in Echt only to be scooped up there after the occupation of Holland and returned to Germany to perish in one of the ovens at Auschwitz. Sister Margaret Mary, who was about forty, had spent years dipping into that story herself, but when I raised a question about a bride of Christ killing time in a gin mill with a guy like me my old helpmate brushed it.

"Paul, this is not anybody in a habit," Helene told me, noting that the Dominicans were miles away from the rigidly sequestered Carmelites. "She dresses the same as I do and you don't even have to call her Sister Margaret. We all call her Mimi. Just try to watch your language. Would that be too hard for one night?"

Of course not.

So there we were, the sinner and the saint masquerading in a plain brown dress. I thought I knew a good deal about Edith Stein, who became Sister Teresa Benedicta of the Cross, but Sister Margaret Mary knew a helluva lot more. We talked for two hours about the fabled but never adequately celebrated convert. How back in April 1933, teaching philosophy then and not yet in the Carmelites, she wrote to Pius XI imploring him to denounce Hitler's anti-Semitic course. How that letter, warning that the drive against Germany's Jews inevitably would extend to other faiths unsympathetic to the Hitler goals, earned Edith Stein a postcard from the Vatican secretary thanking her for her concern and wishing her and her family well. How even in that Netherlands sanctuary nine years later, wholly unconcerned for her own life, that brave nun made no secret of her contempt for the occupying *Gauleiters* and so, along with a sister of hers who was a lay nun, had been collected by the black uniforms. Talking about all this, we stumbled into the hereafter when I said the Edith Stein story had been in my head twenty years and what a terrible shame it was that the Nazis had killed her.

"I wouldn't look at it that way if I were you, Paul," my companion told me. "Sister Teresa is not dead at all but still in her ministry because her soul is in Heaven. A man of your intelligence must understand that."

What intelligence? Not in that ballpark.

Well, Sister Margaret Mary could not have been more tolerant when I said sorry, Mimi, for this nonbeliever there's no Heaven, up or down, only Hell and no second chance. I said I knew all that even before I knew there was no Santa Claus and it was too late to switch, whereupon that sweet nun took a swig of her ginger ale.

"Paul," she said, "I won't argue with you that all of us weren't put on this earth for a given purpose, let's say as in your case to edit a newspaper and also strive to set down some words between hard covers, as you have mentioned, which future generations might profit from. That's all well and good, but it is not the end of it, only the beginning. It is the *first* life, *not* the last. We must all believe that to sustain ourselves. Otherwise, life would not be worthwhile at all."

"Mimi," I said, on my fourth martini now, "with me it's each to his own. I'm mostly a reporter. I just can't believe in anything I can't see or touch, and the last thing I can believe, the very last, is the all-loving Man up there, because I've been to the funerals of too many good people. I've seen my wife and the best guy I ever ran with, the two at the head of my own list, dumped into the ground in their prime. All the Mafia dons lived longer. Hell—sorry, I mean heck—Hitler and his idiot pal Mussolini lived longer. Now nobody can tell me there's somebody upstairs looking after *us*, because if there is, an awful lot of people would have had the dirt shoveled on them long before this."

I didn't hear any sales pitch or sermon from that nun. When I walked her over to the bus for the long ride back to her convent in the Bronx lest she get mugged and tossed into the rain-swept gutter by some night worker from the legions of the town's "disadvantaged," she told me ever so softly that if I thought about it some more I would see the light, and I said I would do that—I didn't mean it, of course—once I finished the novel I was half way through.

This is where this thing gets interesting.

I went home to my IBM Selectric and got back to my thing. Wrote about twelve hours, some good words and some maybe not so bad, slept about three and returned to the attack with an occasional booster from the oversized bottle of Beefeater in the Frigidaire. Ran the MORES down, hopped around to the discount store, managed about two more hours' sleep and started banging away again.

It happened the next morning around four or so after I fed the cats and went up to take another nap.

I got hit.

I mean hit.

I never took a shot like that before, not even when I was a street fighter or squaring off with stronger men in basketball.

It started with a karate chop (black belt) to the chest, actually, but that didn't sting so bad. It was the one which tickled the lower back, coursed up and down my left side and then whacked me in the head that put me down, although I think I still had my senses for a little while. I know I thought about that first incident, when I made believe it was indigestion and waited ten hours before calling my doctor. I know I thought about calling the woman who was with me the night I fell off the cigaret wagon—she was the wife of a friend but a Yalie and writer and helpful with my more serious books—but the last thing I thought about before the darkness closed in was Sister Margaret Mary.

Man, was that nun ever right.

When I came to I was up there, very high.

The Pearly Gates—except that there were no gates that I could see. There wasn't anything. It was more like those TV shots of Neil Armstrong and Buzz Aldrin on the moon back in '69 but I didn't have the feeling that there was any ground under me, not even anything like the mush on the Sea of Tranquillity.

But there was a very tall man at the invisible portals, leaning on a staff.

Peter, a/k/a Saint Peter, I assumed, and damned if he wasn't expecting me.

"Good day, Mr. Sann," he said in the most mellifluous tone, "and welcome to you. There's always room for one more here." Pause. "That is, of course, if one is able to meet the required standards for permanent residence. I am sure you understand that."

No, I didn't understand at all. Either there was room at the inn or there wasn't. If there wasn't, I could check in somewhere else.

"How the H———er, excuse me, I've got the granddaddy of all hangovers. How do you happen to know my name, Pete?"

"Saint Peter, if you will. All the names are known to us here, and yours happens to be something special."

"Special? I don't dig that."

"Your name was mentioned in the morning prayers of a certain nun within recent hours."

"No kidding," I said. "Well, Pete—I mean Saint Peter, sorry—I owe a publisher a book I'm writing in a cellar in Greenwich Village, New York, New York, Zip Code one oh oh one four. Maybe you can tell me how I can get back there. I'm on the half fare."

"Let us not squander any time on frivolity, shall we?" said that fabled personage. "You have made a long and surely tiring journey and there is much to be done before you proceed to your new regimen."

"Look, man," I said. "I just told you I owe a publisher—it's Crown, by the way—a novel or some lawyers come after me to get back the advance, which I've already blown."

"Blown?"

"That means spent, gone, like I used it all up."

Now there was the gentle tinkle of a bell and a very short party in a very short white shroud appeared at my side.

"Brother Hector here will take you first to the tonsorial quarters, where you will be relieved of your Vandyke and . . ."

I had to break in.

"I don't get this. You've got that white beard running down to your knees, or darn near them, anyway. What's so wrong with my Vandyke?"

"Mr. Sann, I shall brook no further interruptions. You will go with Brother Hector now and thence you shall be taken to the supply depot to be issued your G.I. accoutrements."

"G.I.?" I shot back, stunned. "I'm a few years overage for the trenches."

"I believe you have reference to Government Issue. On these premises G.I. is to be read 'Godly Issue.' You will go now."

Since I didn't know what to make of this bit and wasn't going to flatten a gent that old even if I could reach his chin, I put it all down to some idiotic, gin-ridden dream and followed the half-pint.

The barber shop had no walls but was a pretty tricky piece of work just the same. While there were no shelves either, the thing was enfolded on all four sides, as far as the bloodshot eye could see, with the kind of shaving mugs they had downstairs when I was a small boy no bigger than Brother Hector.

"This is Mr. Sann, Brother Francis," my escort said, whereupon the barber turned around and produced a mug with the name P. SANN in gold-leaf block lettering. Either a mute or just plain unfriendly toward new clients who arrived with liquor on their breath, that uniquely silent professional, using a straight razor made of plastic, had the Vandyke off in a few deft strokes. This man surely was a master at his craft, because I barely felt the razor, so I made him out as the kind of guy who must have worked in the Waldorf-Astoria and commanded such high respect that any permanent houseguest like "Mr. Ross," who was really Mr. Charles (Lucky) Luciano or Frank Costello, a regular, had a lock on his services. With the beard off, I asked about a trim, since my pepper-gray mane was kind of shaggy. All that came back was a glare and a shake of the head. The glare got even glarier when I reached into my heavy tan corduroys.

"There is no tipping here, Mr. Sann," said Brother Hector, somewhere down near my knees even though I was only five-ten, as he motioned me to follow him before I could ask Brother Barber whether he had any aftershave lotion. With my wristwatch down at the house, I had no idea how long it took before I found myself facing a potbellied gent of five-six or so.

"This is that writer person, Henry," Brother Hector said, whereupon the other party whipped a tape measure off his collar, and while I wondered what he stood on when he had to work on a real tall type, he had me measured in seconds—except for a problem he ran into.

"Mr. Sann," he said. "I have to keep you here a few minutes. Your left arm is almost half an inch shorter than your right."

"Oh, don't go out of your way," I said. "I stopped worrying about my shirt sleeves after I quit my job and went off the dress-up circuit. It doesn't matter to me."

"It matters to me," came the firm but softly spoken answer and now, looking harder at that face, I knew who the man reminded me of. Peter Lorre, the weasly little helpmate of the weasly big Sydney Greenstreet trying to do in Humphrey Bogart in Dashiell Hammett's *The Maltese Falcon*. I remembered that Lorre had put on a lot of weight before he died.

"All right," I said. "I'm not looking for an argument in my shape but don't fool with the sleeves on my account. Hardly anybody ever noticed my uneven arms back home."

Brother Henry—and I had a feeling it might be Hank and Paul after a while despite his coldly formal manner—did not respond to that.

"You will remove all your garments," he said, reaching behind him and producing a shroud from a plastic hanger that didn't hang from anything but had a handwritten label affixed to it that said 32 REGULAR.

It was time to weigh in with a small protest.

"Look, mister. I'm not anybody they picked off some Skid Row—well, where I come from we call it the Bowery. These corduroys come from Miller's in Manhattan, and that's *the* store for the horsemen and outdoor types. Like it costs, I mean, and this heavy shirt comes from L. L. Bean up in Maine, which is no junk shop either and . . ."

"Please, you will remove them."

Well, I wasn't going to blow the whole morning in any tailor shop.

"The T-shirt and underpants now."

"Hold it, man," I protested. "This T-shirt isn't off any pushcart either. It's straight out of the equipment room of the Boston Celtics. I got it from Mr. Arnold Red Auerbach when he was coach of that basketball team and set the winningest record in the whole history of sports—eleven titles in thirteen seasons. This thing has a very strong sentimental value to me. I wrote Red's autobiography."

Another waste.

Off came the gray shirt with the giant kelly green letters bearing the name of my favorite NBA club.

And the Munsingwear shorts, and don't think I wasn't feeling a chill now with no walls to shield me from the December wind that had to be out there somewhere. If the sneakers came next, sneakers with the sainted Auerbach name on them, I was a cinch to blow my hung-over stack.

"I don't mean to bug you, Brother Henry," I said, "but you've got to let me keep these sneakers. I'm having trouble walking around here with no ground under me. That's on the level."

The tailor looked down, all the way down, at Brother Hector, who responded with a nod indicating that he could hold still for a small bend in the house rules.

"Very well, Mr. Sann," Brother Henry said. "They won't show under your shroud. You will have to remove your sweat socks, however."

"Do I have to? These are from the Knicks, the local pro club in my town."

"You will remove them."

I did that, not that it was easy standing up in my fragile condition, and put the sneakers back on. Then the tailor handed me my shroud, saying he would have to adjust that left sleeve but it could wait since the first day up there was always so hectic for the newcomers.

"I appreciate that," I said. "You've been real swell, and by the way there are some bills in those pants. You're welcome to hold on to them, since I gather that this outfit you staked me to comes without pockets."

"Your possessions will be kept intact," said Brother Hector.

"Thanks a lot. I don't happen to care about the cash. It's not all that much and there's always more coming in—from my old paper, book royalties, the rent on my upstairs tenants and some odds and ends—but there are a few things in my wallet I wish I could hang on to if it's no big deal. I don't need my driver's license, I guess, but I do have a whole flock of credit cards and there's a color snapshot in there I'd like to keep on me."

Brother Henry:

"You won't need your credit cards."

"That figures, but I could get ripped off pretty good if they fell out of this place. I don't care about my American Express or Visa or Master Charge. There's a limit on how much you can get clipped for on those, but I've got an air travel card in there and a piece of gold-tinted plastic that gives me a line of five thousand in chips at the Sands in Vegas. See what I mean? I could have one bum flying around the world with some babe in my name—first class, no doubt—and a high roller blowing five Gs in Vegas with *P. Sann* on the markers. Man, the least you can do is slice those things up so I don't get written off as a deadbeat."

"There's no need for that, Mr. Sann, I assure you, but I can do something about the picture you mentioned—providing it is family, that is."

"Family? Brother, all I got left is a daughter and a son with a beard—and I never even carried any baby pictures. I'm talking about a woman."

"Your wife?"

"No, no. Her chips got cashed in eighteen years ago. This is some other guy's wife, but we're good buddies and she's the only one I ever let have a peek at any manuscript of mine. It's as simple as that."

Brother Hector now, up from the depths.

"Mr. Sann, you are in an area which rests in the hands of higher authority and there is no further time to waste here. I must return you to the entry area at oh eight hundred hours."

I didn't dig that reference.

"What's that?" I said. "You're talking navy time and there wasn't any navy time when this place was set up in business."

All that drew me was a nasty look, and now I knew where I had seen this mini-stiff before. He had to be the midget who tried to mother off

007 in *The Man with the Golden Gun*. I had seen that only a week ago on the "Late Late Late Show" after one of those title bouts with my IBM which left me so punched out I couldn't fall asleep without the help of Mr. Carvel the Ice Cream Magnate or Frank Perdue the Chicken Man or the cretin with those Crazy Eddie commercials or the blond Mrs. Potamkin of the Cadillac outfit. You know the midget died a flaming death in that movie.

I can't imagine what had taken me so long, probably this whole wacky scene I was suddenly in after that dandy time with Sister Margaret Mary which now apparently was paying its increasingly dubious dividend, but I suddenly realized that I needed a booster real bad and a cigaret even worse, so I thought I might as well go for broke.

"Brother Hector, sir," I said. "I know we're bumping some kind of deadline, but can I have a minute with Brother Henry on a personal matter?"

"That is most irregular," the runt said, "but I'll wait at the door."

I didn't waste any time trying to figure out where the hell that door was, especially since I wasn't wearing my bifocals when I took that sneak shot at the house, but sidled up to Brother Lorre called Henry.

"Listen, Hank," I said, "You've been goddamned decent. I mean about the sneakers. I think maybe you're a man I can do some business with."

"What business, Paul?"

Now I knew I had him. The use of that first name was the tip-off.

"Look," I said. "You have the sound of a guy that knows his way around this joint. I'm not looking to beat the price but I got some habits, you know, like drinking and smoking. What's the score up here?"

The answer couldn't have been more direct.

"Well, Paul, you look like somebody I can lay it on the line with. There *are* ways. I mean there are people around who moved some stuff on the black market in their other lives but I wouldn't push it if I was in your sneakers. You wanna take it slow, or else you could get jammed up pretty quick. The butts and a blast now and then is no big deal, but if you're into the hard stuff that's a horse of another color."

"You mean grass or the real horse or what, Hank?"

"Yeah."

"No problem. I was never into anything worse than marijuana—and damn little of that. Couldn't hold it down in what was left of my lungs."

"Fine, so it's not such a big deal. How much green you say was in that wallet?"

"I didn't say, Hank, but it's two dimes. I made a pretty good score on an NFL game last Sunday." I had no doubt whatever that Brother Henry knew a dime was a thousand dollars in the gambling fraternity. "I had all those C notes on me when this thing hit the fan, so I didn't make the shuttle up this way in any impoverished state."

"No problem. Just cool it, like I said. Cold turkey. You better scram now or the short fella might get some ideas—and by the way, watch yourself with that one. He's got more ears than balls."

How right that fine tailor would prove to be in time.

Now Brother Hector was on the way back in with an even meaner look on that ugly face than I had detected before.

"What's the next stop?" I asked.

"The gate." And there I was, too damn soon, back with Pete.

"Well, I must say, Mr. Sann," sayeth The Beard. "You do look considerably more presentable. Let us proceed."

"May I ask where?" I asked.

"To the Tribunal, of course."

"Aw, have a heart, Saint Peter. If I'm where I think I am there's some people I'd like to check in with. Can't this Tribunal, whatever it is, wait a while?"

"No, it waits for no man, and it is but a square away."

We made that square and I was directed to follow the bossman up the steps.

Were these the Golden Stairs described in the Koran? No. I wasn't aware of any steps but I found myself myself on another level with eleven other Saint Peters. I mean they all looked alike except that you could distinguish them from *the* Peter because their robes had no belts and were not embellished around the neckline with the same expensive corded fabric. But if this was a jury trial I was being led into there was something decidedly unkosher about it. Where were the two alternates? How stupid. Why would you need alternates in a courthouse where nobody ever got sick or died because everybody there already was dead?

"You may be seated, Mr. Sann," a pasty-faced attendant with a gaunt appearance to match his long gaunt frame said to me, pointing toward a witness chair I couldn't make out, and what I sat down on was a floor I couldn't make out any better, not that it didn't have its virtues for me. In a chair if I forgot myself and crossed my legs those Celtic sneakers would shine like green diamonds and I'd have Hank in a jam. Sitting with my legs folded in a yogalike position, my secret would hold.

The jury, way over my head, did seem to be seated, as if they had chairs, but if this wasn't a kangaroo court I don't know what the hell is. I had very mixed, or perhaps mixed-up, feelings about the spot I found myself in after an all but exemplary life. In that setting, I felt like a black man deep in the heart of Dixie in the old days sitting in a pickup truck between two beer-barreled, cigar-chomping slobs in white hoods with shotguns in their laps and a whole fleet of cars ahead of us and behind us. Destination: Endsville. The charge: whistling at some white woman outside the blacks-only barbershop. The burial ground: the soft red clay of some lonely hillside. I also felt like a soldier in one of my own town's five Mafia families plunked before a "sitdown" for going south with a load of pure heroin or, worse, having committed the even higher crime of getting nailed in a motel with some loftier *capo*'s bride. Destination: the furnace on some don's New Jersey estate, the bottom of the East River in a concrete casket or maybe some smelting plant where I would emerge as a piece of scrap metal. Between the two alternatives, the Klan or the nicer people of the mob, I had no special feelings. If you gotta go, I always said, coining a phrase, you gotta go. The only thing I had any real distaste for was any kind of torture during which I would be denied all my medication, like the gin and MORES, the yellow Procainamide for my heart, the Valium for my head, the Gelusil in case my ulcer kicked up or the green pill to keep my blood in proper balance.

But there wasn't going to be much time for that kind of dawdling.

Once I was sworn by the pasty-faced bailiff (I won't burden you with that description henceforth because everybody up there was pasty-faced and bloodless ash-white except perhaps the members of the Tribunal themselves; there was no way to make out what those gents looked like because of those identical beards), we were under a full head of no-steam.

Saint Peter opened up for the prosecution in terms so somber that I had trouble making him out from that great distance. It was almost as if this trial was in the Bronx County Courthouse with the Jerome Avenue El rattling by a few blocks away and a World Series game going on in the Yankee Stadium on the other side of the tracks.

"Mr. Sann, this Tribunal is laboring under the restrictions of an extremely heavy calendar. I assume you know why you are here. Is that correct?"

"No, sir," I said. "It couldn't possibly be more unclear."

"Very well then. We can rectify that quite readily. You are seated before this body on an indictment consisting of ten counts."

"Felonies or misdemeanors, Your Honor?"

"Why do you raise that question?"

"For a pretty good reason. Where I come from a misdemeanor is what we call a meatball rap, which means the possible sentence is so trifling you can do it standing on your head if you do happen to go inside instead of getting off with an SS, a fine or, say, nothing more than probation, and . . ."

"I am impelled to interrupt here, Mr. Sann. What is an SS? That terminology is not known to this body."

"That is a suspended sentence, Your Honor. I mean the judge imposes a jail term but rules that if you're going to be a good boy from that point on and not constitute a threat to your community then you don't have to do any time."

"Thank you. Proceed, please."

"Well, the felony bit is what worries me. That's a capital case, and in my state you're only allowed three to a customer. On the fourth one you go inside and they throw the key away, so to speak. I don't mean three felony counts in a single indictment, only that a man is better off without any of those on his yellow sheet."

"And what, pray, is that? The color here is all white, as you surely must have observed by now."

"The yellow sheet is your record in the New York Police Department files."

"The chair understands. Is there anything further which you may wish to convey to this Tribunal before the clerk reads the indictment?"

"There is, indeed, Your Honor, since I do possess some small knowledge of the law. What concerns me here, if I may say so, is the apparent nature of this proceeding. The Constitution and the Bill of Rights guarantee accused persons a number of things not evident to me in this chamber."

"You will enumerate them, please."

"Well, the Fourth Amendment protects me against unreasonable search and seizure except upon a show of probable cause, but I was emptied out awful fast in the G.I. depot this morning."

"Mr. Sann, you must be aware that you arrived in a condition such as to preclude any appreciation on your part of the situation into which you have placed yourself by your own conduct over a period in excess of six decades. You may continue."

"Thank you. The Fifth Amendment enjoins any effort to compel me to bear witness against myself. It says in so many words that I cannot be deprived of my life, liberty or pursuit of happiness without due process of law."

"Any further remarks?"

"Yes, sir. The Sixth Amendment guarantees me a speedy and public trial before an impartial jury of my peers in the district where the crimes ascribed to me are alleged to have occurred. I have a right to be confronted by the witnesses against me, to produce witnesses in my own defense and enjoy the right of counsel. I don't want to belabor all this, mindful of the crowded condition of your calendar—and by the way, in the city where I come from we're running around a hundred thousand felony arrests per year—but there's also an Eighth Amendment which prohibits excessive bail or fines or excessively cruel punishment. All of these amendments, I might mention, have withstood any number of challenges since the Founding Fathers propounded them."

"Are you quite finished?"

"I am, and thank you for your indulgence."

Saint Peter turned to the Peter on his left, evidently El Prosecutor.

"Sir," said that beard, "we are guided here by standards of fairness which also have withstood centuries of testing. With that preface, I shall take up point by point the issues which you have raised, and may I start by complimenting you upon your excellent presentation since, in truth, you are but a layman?"

"Well, I may have fooled around in my time but I have always done the homework required in my dual professions as a newspaperman and author."

"Splendid. The Constitution which you have cited appears to be a statutory document in force in the province from whence you have come, but you are now standing [standing?] before a worldwide forum operating as an entity unto itself under Divine Authority responsible only to the Supreme Being Himself. Accordingly, your reference to any 'unreasonable search and seizure except upon a show of probable cause' may be dismissed out of hand. You went on to discuss your 'right' to the pursuit of life, liberty and happiness shielded by due process of law. On that point, I counsel you that due process is precisely what you are now undergoing. Finally, you spoke of a Sixth Amendment guaranteeing you the right to a speedy public trial in the district of the crimes charged against you and a guarantee as well against any excessive 'bail,' whatever that may be, or excessively cruel punishment. Well, first, I daresay that you could not possibly find yourself facing a speedier trial. You arrived here at oh six hundred hours and were brought into this chamber at oh eight hundred hours, whereas a great many of the accused below have spent so much time in custody that your superior tribunals upon occasion have ruled that persons not tried within a twelvemonth of their incarceration must be forthwith set free.

"I come now to the matter of witnesses, pro or con. The evidence against you, Mr. Sann, is all on the written record and you shall enjoy complete freedom to seek out your own witnesses, solicit their testimony and make your own presentation of the facts adduced in that process. As for your mention of a trial within the jurisdiction of one's misdeeds as charged, that is wholly idle inasmuch as a rather sizable proportion of the falls from grace cited in the instant indictment occurred in widespread areas—all but worldwide, indeed. And as for your reference to 'excessively cruel punishment,' that is even more idle, since there is but a single penalty meted out in this Tribunal. Have I made all this adequately clear to you?"

Christ, talk about the steel-trap mind.

I couldn't believe that guy.

He had just quoted back to me damn near every word I had spake. I made that beard out for a Yale Law graduate *summa cum laude,* editor of the *Law Review,* clerk to a chief justice, professor emeritus at Harvard Law, author of all the texts in the field of criminal justice or, hell, maybe even Oliver Wendell Holmes, Louis Dembitz Brandeis or Felix Frankfurter reincarnated and all rolled into one ball of legal wax. I had gone head to head in my own time with some powerhouse lawyers and judges. The paper's own law firm was only Paul, Weiss, Rifkind, Wharton, Garrison and whoever. You know that Rifkind name. He adorned the federal bench before moving on to pick up the big bills in private practice, and there were no telephone booth lawyers or ambulance chasers in the three floors that outfit occupied on Manhattan's Park Avenue. I knew. I had dealt with them not only on libel suits but even occasional criminal matters since I was thirty-five. As a friend, I had spent countless hours with Irving R. Kaufman, Chief Judge of the Court of Appeals in my bailiwick. I had some tennis-playing buddies among a handful of the better judges in the state courts. I had covered some of the more towering defense lawyers as a reporter, went back to the time of Tom Dewey as Special Prosecutor, knew the more skilled district attorneys and a couple of the better U.S. attorneys, like Bob Morgenthau. Put them all together and they didn't measure up to the character I was now looking at. He had hauled me over the coals without taking a single note, you understand, because there were no quills and no legal pads in the joint.

I guess I let too much time pass in that painful reverie, because now that skeletal bailiff was tugging at my shroud.

"Saint Peter is talking to you."

I wrenched my glazed look away from the prosecutor and apologized for my inattention.

"That's quite all right, Mr. Sann," Pete said, peering down at me. "All of us appreciate the ordeal of self-examination which you very likely must be undergoing at this point. It is quite common here. You have been asked whether you had any questions before the chair adjourns this first session."

"I do, sir. I do indeed. How much time do I have?"

"For your questions, or your trial?"

"Well, I guess both while we're at it."

"You shall have ten days—nine after this day, pending adjudication."

Oh, how I was dying for a smoke and that blast, even some stale beer, but all I asked for was a glass of water to slurp over my caked lips. The attendant produced a Styrofoam cup from within the folds of his newly pressed shroud and handed me what had to be Perrier water at the very least. I knew it couldn't be any old tap water and put it down like the Deputy Marshal in the oateater who has ridden the dusty, sunbaked plains for nine days before running down the varmint he wanted. Or maybe the Gary Cooper type in the old French foreign legion epics where you're the last trooper in the fort after driving off the last Arab and the water's gone and you don't hear the happy sound of the arriving relief column's bugle until the last frame of film is shot.

Feeling renewed, I let my gaze wander over all my peers, a sheer waste since I've already mentioned that they all looked alike, and then came back to Saint Peter the First.

"I don't see any court stenographer, Your Honor. Does that mean there will be no printed record of this trial?"

"That is correct."

"Then I take it that there is no appeals process here?"

"Yes, there is no appeal," like the hit song from the twenties, "Yes, We Have No Bananas."

Another kick in the head, especially for a guy who had the big dollars to pay for a trial transcript.

"On the witness bit, sir, just how much time will I have to round them up?"

"These hearings will be set for oh eight hundred hours to oh twelve hundred hours daily to their conclusion. The intervening time shall be yours to dispose of as you may wish."

"Will I be free to talk to my witnesses in private?"

"No, you will be accompanied at all times by an officer of this Tribunal."

"I don't want to seem unduly argumentative, Your Honor, but wouldn't that put me at a serious disadvantage?"

The gent on the left picked up that ball.

"Not at all. Your officer-escort will not intrude upon your efforts in any manner, shape, or form."

"I dig that. I mean I understand, but you know people tend to be intimidated—less open, certainly—with a stranger present."

Now the sun dial struck the hour of noon, or something said it was oh twelve hundred hours, and Saint Peter, rising and looking about ten feet tall, closed it out.

"You have been furnished with all of your answers, Mr. Sann. The procedures of this Tribunal are subject to no variation and no exceptions regardless of one's previous station below."

As the main beard turned to make his exit, I took another shot between the eyes. The attendant swiftly fell into step behind him carrying a wooden-bound ledger almost wide enough for a half-court basketball game. It wasn't just its incredible girth that knocked me out. It must have been four or five feet thick. Christ, I hadn't been around long enough, or surely never had that many free hours when I was toting that barge and lifting all those bales for Dorothy Schiff's New York *Post,* to build up that kind of dossier. With the prosecutor and the other ten walking snowmen trailing noiselessly in the wake of Saint Peter and the attendant, who had to be a closet weightlifter the way he handled that ledger as if it was a paperback copy of Erich Segal's *Love Story,* I found myself alone with the bailiff.

"Where do we go from here, good buddy?" I asked.

"I am addressed as Brother Wilhelm," came the acid-tipped reply. "You will find Brother Hector waiting without."

Without what? In my time I had gone against some fast shuffles but this was the living end, if that's the way to say it. Man, with Sean

Connery's tormentor sticking to my tail like epoxy I was even deader than I thought.

But I got lucky.

The short one, cold enough to freeze the *coglioni* off those lions outside the Public Library on Fifth Avenue, led me to a new acquaintance. This was my officer-escort, Brother Vittorio—all of him—and I was home again, down in Manhattan's Little Italy in fact. No less than six-eight in his bare feet. Twisted nose. Scar running down the side of his faintly pockmarked face. I don't mean ugly, you understand. Just one tough looking hombre. Bushy black hair. Bull neck and—listen— the gentlest baby blue eyes. No fat, I guessed, but surely no shortage of muscle under that custom-made sheet. All that man had to do was say, "Hi, nice to meet'ya, pal," and that machine-tooled New York accent lifted my spirits clear up to Heaven, which I suppose sounds rather silly, since I knew all along that's where I was, especially with that tip-off from Sister Margaret Mary. I would have bet my Celtic sneakers against a secondhand shroud that I could operate pretty good with this guy, like with Hank the tailor, but decided not to push it coming out of the gate.

"What kind of timetable are we on, Brother?" I asked as El Shrimpo wafted away in the breeze or something.

"That depends onna shape you're in," I was told, "and the way the grapevine has it you got off the express on the wobbly side. You put away too much booze before you caught your cuffo flight?"

"Guilty," I said, enormously pleased because the big man had the sound of a party who might have been one of the boys in better times. "But I'm looking at a ten-count rap, so I'm not all that worried about my head right now. I'd like to get this horror show on the road as fast as I can, except that a stop at the mess hall wouldn't hurt."

"Mess hall?" A pitying look came with this one. "This ain't exactly the Atlanta pen, mister. There ain't no mess hall or no canteen either. Ever play golf?"

"No, I always made that a sissy's game. Why do you ask?"

"Well, you do know how them things are laid out, like the nine-teenth hole's your refreshment stop, right?"

"Sure."

"So it's the same way on the course up here—except that there's no golf and nothing to drink and the chow ain't to write home about."

"You're losing me, Brother Vittorio."

"Sorry. What I'm trying to tell'ya is as you keep movin around this trap you run into a stop here and there where you can get a bite. I ain't talkin about steak pizzaiola or linguine or scampi or even your kind of stuff, like deli, I imagine. It's all vegetables. Lettuce, parsley, cauliflower, parsnips, mushrooms, asparagus, onions 'n stuff like that. You won't put on no weight with it," the raspy voice went on. "I can guarantee you that. I came in under two-five-oh and I'm still there."

"I'm not worried about my weight," I said. "I never got more than ten pounds over the welters, say one-fifty-seven or so, so I don't expect to brood over the limited menu, although I was always real big for the Italian bit. Chinese, too. But you mentioned some junk I can eat warmed up, like the cabbage, or the onions fried a nice brown."

"Me, too. You bring a Sterno heater by any chance?"

"Why do we need it? The book of Revelation talks about all kinds of fire up here, not to mention the Golden Streets and a whole flock of goodies."

"Yeah, only them Bible writers was no better than you newspaper bums when it came to makin things up."

"Oh, the hell with it," I said. "I can make it on gin and cigarets and stay happy."

My guardian took a slow look around all sides of Nowhere and lowered his voice.

"You seen Brother Henry when you picked up your new threads, so you got an idea what the score is. This pokey with no bars is full of eyes and for all I know could even be bugged by that two-dollar horseplayer J. Edgar. We know the sonofabitch had a file on every living soul in the USA, so it figures he had some lines up here too, right? That means Mr. Hoover has his own suite in this joint if he ever kicked the bucket."

"The great man did," I said. "Four or five years back, although nobody thought that could ever happen to him."

"Sorry I couldn't make the services but that crowd probably woulda hung some old rap on me on account of I was always on the other side of the fence."

"You putting me on, Brother Vittorio? If that's the way it was how come you drew such a responsible job with the combination court and jury up here?"

"No sweat, Paul. They made me a trusty, like they're testin me because they knew who I ran with downstairs the most. The President Street boys."

"Crazy Joe and that whole Gallo tribe?"

"Yeah, till I switched to the Profaci Family because they had more brains and a helluva lot more artillery."

"Let's shake on that, Vito," I said. "I need your kind of company. I was afraid I would run into nothing but retired monks and Scoutmasters on this trip."

The grip that came back left a few of my knuckles stinging.

"Good to have someone with your savvy aboard," the big guy said, "even if that sheet of yours wasn't always too soft on my type. But you did lay it on that meathead Papa Colombo pretty good, so I figure that squared it."

"*Molti grazie,* Vito. Now can you point me to some of·that rabbit food and then start my rounds with me?"

"Sure thing."

"I take it you've got the whole layout, right? Where everybody is, I mean."

"Oh, yeah. Them high priests inna courthouse gimme the whole shmear. It's worse than with the feds, pal. The whiskers know your witnesses before you do. Whadd'ya wanna make your first stop after we put on the feedbag?"

"My wife, Vito. She went out in '61 but she's gotta be here. She was more like an angel."

"She is here, Paul." This came with an armlock which caused me to wonder how the walyo had kept his muscles so finely tuned on the health food diet which had now reached into the Great Beyond. "You're my kinda fella. That's the most important thing—the little woman. I miss my Rosario more than any goddamn thing I ever had downstairs. I'd give an arm and a leg just to glom that face and not even lay a hand on her. *After* that I'd go look for the creep who took me out with them dum dums."

"Maybe he'll show one of these days."

"No way. Not that scumbag. I always stood good with the church. Had the last rites 'n all. The other bum's gotta have a ticket punched for the hot place. You can bet your shirt on that."

I lifted my shroud and pointed to my sneakers.

"This is all I got on me for action right now, Vito," I said, "but Brother Henry's holding some Fuck-You money for me."

"What kinda money?"

"Milton Berle always said it that way when he talked about having a little extra loot so none of the TV wheels could push him around."

"I get it, pal. You're talkin about the two large you left with the tailor. That could go a long way around here. Wanna roll?"

Oh, did I ever wanna roll. I never figured to see my Birdye again, just to get dumped into the ground beside her on that green hill in Westchester, but from the moment I made that grudging trip through the nonexistent Pearly Gates I knew she had to be around. Alongside me, she had practically led the life of a Jewish nun. Hell, make that Jewish Mother Superior.

Chapter 2 •

Let's have a fat round of applause here for the afterlife, folks.

You wouldn't believe what my girl looked like in the Upper Room.

Well, you need to go back a step first.

A strong, perfectly molded five-four who was even-up with me on the tennis courts (and better, in truth, on the days when her sure, steady game threw me into racket-busting temper tantrums), she died of cancer at forty-seven after giving it a hundred-fifty-day battle that left her looking like a shopping bag lady pulled in out of some doorway off Times Square. The thing was so horrible I couldn't hold still and kept demanding that her lady doctor cut out the senseless blood transfusions and all the rest of it and let her go. I lost that argument. I was never sorry I made it. I wanted the blood given to some people who had a shot to live and the morphine slipped to some of the needier junkies so they wouldn't have to rob and kill for it. I know that sounds like sheer hysteria but that's the way it got to be after I could no longer recognize the woman I loved and wasn't always sure she knew me.

And now?

It was the other Birdye, the pretty one. The bright hazel eyes, the dusty brown medium hairdo, even—I could tell when we embraced— the same firm size thirty-six bust. This is the girl I went to high school with and saw grow into a whale of a wife and mother who could tackle anything and anyone, except the Big Casino which had taken her mother and two sisters before her.

She was not surprised to see me and did not jump for joy.

She knew I was there and was waiting in her open room in the women's dorm. I looked for tears, or perhaps just mist in those eyes, but there were none. What I saw instead were deep lines of concern on that perfectly round kissing-sweet face.

"Hey, baby," I said. "Where's the smile that made me your slave?"

"Paul, dear"—and this was ever so somber—"that will have to wait until your trial is over."

"You know about that? You get the *Times* delivered or what?"

"No, silly. There are no secrets in this place. You must know how serious your situation is."

Let's brazen this one out, huh?

"Come on, Birdye. What's so serious? It's a measly ten-count indictment. You know I can take those beards."

"Don't you know what those ten counts are?"

"What's the difference? They didn't read the indictment in the opener because I threw them so much stuff about the Bill of Rights they ran out of time. I stiffed them, baby. By the way, this flyweight here is my buddy Vito."

Birdye looked at the man mountain as if she had known him downstairs too. They were going to be good friends, but the amenities would have to wait. The lady wanted the whole score on the table and wasn't going to let me kid her for one minute.

"Paul, if you really don't know what those ten counts are then add up the Commandments, because that's what they are."

"Of course. What the hell's that got to do with anything, Birdye?"

"Why don't you ask your keeper here?"

Brother Vittorio disposed of that challenge nicely.

"Look, Mrs. Sann," he said, "I'm not supposed to let this husband of yours outta my sight, but I'm goin for a stroll so the two of ya can be alone a while, OK?"

"Thank you," Birdye said, and it occurred to me that I had never seen her quite so grim except toward the very end, so I lost no time returning to the attack.

"Hey, let's get off this silly trial bit, yeah? We're together again after all these lousy years. I know I must look pretty beat up but I thought you'd be climbing all over me. I'm here. I'm with you. Isn't that enough?"

Now the mist.

"Paul, you're not thinking straight. You got here with a hangover that would have knocked over any normal person. Fine"—and now that voice dropped to a bare murmur—"so we're together again, as you say, but for how long? Until that jury comes in?"

"So? Big deal. What's the worst that can happen, Birdye? Don't tell me the rack is still in fashion up here, or the guillotine, or the rope or electric chair. I happen to know there's no power lines in here. I checked it."

"Please, dear. This is hardly a time for your kind of humor. You have too much to do between now and eight o'clock tomorrow morning."

"Eight o'clock? Everybody else up here talks navy time."

"You know I could never follow that. You used to use it on me just to annoy me."

"OK. I'll never do it again. Now tell me how you ever know what time it is in this hotel where they separate the boys and girls so they won't mess around."

Birdye took her hands out of mine and lifted the left sleeve of her immaculate shroud—that kid always was one helluva clothes horse, especially after Dolly Schiff came perilously close to paying me like an editor who also doubled as a columnist and correspondent on the big ones—and my bleary eyes popped. She was wearing the Omega I had bought her for our twenty-sixth anniversary, not long before she went under the knife.

"You're the same tricky doll," I said, ever so elated. "How did you manage to hang on to that watch?"

"Remember the volunteer work I did at the Women's House of Detention all those years?"

"How could I forget? I think you even managed to get one of those hookers off the streets when she got out in your charge. Becky something, right?"

"Yes, Paul, it was Becky, one of our own people. Anyway, another one of those women I had spent a lot of time with was in charge of the supply room when I got here—Peggy Flanagan. She straightened out and went back to the church while I was sick, and she was so glad to see me she broke into tears and let me keep the watch."

"What else? No bra? All I got away with was a pair of sneakers I squeezed out of Red Auerbach a while ago."

Birdye looked around, bent her head toward me, and lifted her shroud to bare a gold chain I hardly remembered.

"Is that what I think it is, kiddo?"

"Yes, but there's no way I can show you the rest of it in this high-neck gown. It's the locket with the children's pictures. How are they? I never stop thinking about them. First you, then them."

"Oh, they're fine. Richie got his degree from Lafayette and worked on a little paper near Easton, the Pottstown *Mercury*, and then put in two years on the Philadelphia *Bulletin*, but I guess he couldn't stay with the business after seeing what a broken hulk it left of his father, so since then he's been free lancing and doing great except that his big thing is movie scripts and he hasn't sold one yet. And Leni got married not long after you were gone and had the cutest little girl. We named her Brandie because that was as close to Birdye as I could come up with. Now she's a real beauty, complete with her learner's driving permit and an Italian boyfriend who seems pretty nice, not part of the grass crowd."

Now that jump for joy? Hell no, and I think I knew why. Nobody ever made friends faster than my girl. Drew 'em like flies, and knew how to ask questions, too. She must have known that I was holding out on her. She must have known that Richie got busted for marijuana in Mexico in '68 and did a tough four months in Lecumberri Prison—the stinking, rat-infested hole called the Black Palace which we had visited as guests of the creepy Mexicans on a VIP trip back in the fifties. What else did she know about her son? Did she know I got rolled for eleven thousand Big Ones keeping him alive in that aboveground dungeon and then buying his way out of there and he was still bearing some of the scars of that time? Did she know her daughter's marriage fell apart right after the baby was born and Leni got custody but then messed up on speed and the kid went back to her father? Did she know Leni had gone through the mill in the Yale-New Haven Hospital facility for the druggies (down payment, eight thousand dollars), moved on to the Waterbury General Hospital and was just now getting back on her feet, doing volunteer work there with youngsters who also thought all the answers came in pills or the happy dust?

Whatever she knew, Birdye wasn't letting on, not on this day, anyway, because the last thing she was going to do was to tax me with anything that hurt. This day? You could make that any day, downstairs or, now, upstairs. It was always her style to do the bleeding for both of us if she could get away with it.

"Oh, I'm so glad Leni found the right man after those two broken engagements and settled down," she said, her face betraying nothing. "I wish you had brought a picture of her daughter, Paul."

If there was any ground under me I would have felt it rattling like one of the smaller San Francisco earthquakes. Did my girl know I had arrived in that haven with some other picture? She did indeed, so it was like Brother Vittorio said: there were no secrets where we were now.

"Who was that woman in the picture you had in your wallet?" she asked very softly. "I'm not prying, just curious."

"Nobody I was shacked up with, baby. We just talk good because she digs my prose. Real smart dame. Yale and about four other colleges before that. Her husband's a pal of mine too. You would love 'em both. They're good people. Name's Steele with an *e*."

"I know," Birdye said, "and her name is Lisa. Very pretty with those long black tresses, and sort of tall and slender. Have I got the right lady?"

How much inside dope did the girl in the form-fitting shroud have on any members of the opposite sex with whom I might have had, say, a more intimate relationship, like we went on Mr. and Mrs. vacations together and that sort of fairly close thing? If there was any way to sweat in the Elysian Fields I would have been standing there in a shroud that might have been hit by a cloudburst. It was time to get this tensely awkward reunion back on the tracks, but where the hell were the tracks?

I thought of something.

"Listen, baby," I said. "Let's not talk about broads. You know you were the only one who was ever going to count—and I'll come to some documentation for that in good time. You gotta be proud of the guy you walked out on. I've written six more books since '61. Had one on this year's list and another coming off the presses next month and a novel on the fire—Lisa's some help there, by the way, because she digs fiction better than I do—when the enemy caught up with me this morning. You see, I had a little thing with my heart four years ago and I guess there's only two to a customer nowadays."

"I hope you weren't alone when this one happened, Paul. I really do."

"I was, as a matter of fact. Had my own Last Supper with a nun, believe it or not, picking up some stuff about Edith Stein. Remember how far back I started yakking about doing the big one on that woman?"

"Yes. I surely heard enough about it, and I wish you had done it, because you're going to hear a few things about some of your other prose in the next few days."

"What do you mean, Birdye? Don't tell me I'm a hot item in the bookstores up here, because I haven't done all that well in the other place."

"You're a great one for the joke, Paul. You must know that everything you ever wrote is on the banned list in this place. Remember how Ernest Hemingway laughed when you reminded him about *The Sun Also Rises* being banned in Boston when it first came out? Well, anyway, what I'm trying to tell you is that you're going to hear some things about the language in your books, not to mention what you've written about a few large names who are very highly regarded by your judges."

"Like who?"

"Oh, just some people like Billy Graham and the other evangelists you always called Hell-robbers who were getting rich saving lost souls."

"Really? Talk about cheap shots. I must say you are one well-informed babe. You must have your own private intelligence operation even though they've got you salted away in this dorm."

"No, lover. I just keep up with things. You're not at the top of the no-no list with our friend Jackie Susann and Robbins and Wallace and all those other bedroom novelists, but you're on it just the same. That shouldn't come as any surprise to you, Paul. Didn't they have to caution you in advance about that mouth of yours when you were on those early news shows on Channel Thirteen and later with Mike Wallace?"

"Yes, ma'am. They sure did, but my own mouth's just in one little novel."

"It doesn't matter. Don't you understand? You're going to have to deal with it. I hope that doesn't break you up, especially since you mentioned that you haven't exactly made a fortune in royalties."

"Aw, hell, Birdye. That doesn't matter either. I would have blown it anyway even though I beat my gambling affliction once I quit the paper three years ago and lost my modestly fat paycheck, although I did pick up some loose change on a football game last Sunday because the point spread was too delicious to resist. They made the Pittsburgh Steelers only seven and a half points over some farmers. That loot's stashed with the tailor who relieved me of my city wear."

"I know," Birdye said, "and I wish it wasn't."

"Why do you say that?"

"Because I can imagine what you're going to spend it on."

"Hey, have a heart. I wouldn't get back into any heavy action even if I ran into one of my old bookies up here, which is hardly likely."

"You're wrong again. Big Sam has been here for years."

"You kidding me? He was a beautiful man but no candidate for this rest home. He had fourteen arrests that I knew of."

"He's here, I tell you. I don't know how, but he was religious, wasn't he?"

"He was indeed. Laid some of our money on his synagogue in Brooklyn. He had to have our brand of absolution, or extreme unction or whatever the Catholics call it, before he went out. I had no time—no rabbi either, for that matter—but even so how can I lose in what passes for a trial in that open air courthouse if Big Sam made it?"

"Paul, I don't know whether he was even tried." There was a growing impatience surfacing now. "Why waste time over him? You're the one with the problem."

I took my girl's hands again.

"There's something awfully wrong here, baby," I said. "My keeper was kind enough to leave us alone and we're talking nothing but nonsense. I never stopped loving you and now I'm getting the chill. We had the greatest marriage in all of history even though you had me on short rations in the hay when you had one beef or another. Don't you have anything left for me? I can't believe that."

"Then you shouldn't have said it. Paul, this will all hurt less if we don't get into it right now."

"Hurt less when?"

"After your trial, that's when. Now it's almost three o'clock. You should be preparing for tomorrow's session."

"What's the big rush? Is it lights out after ten, like on Rikers Island, or what? I've got nothing but time—and no place to lay my head either, for that matter, which gives me even more time. Of course, if Vito would let me stay here with my old girl . . ."

"Paul, you must have known when you got here that the sexes are kept separate."

"Didn't I, though. You can bet your sweet ass I had that figured, Birdye. The wonder is the word about Women's Lib hasn't got this high up. Downstairs the ex-weaker sex has taken over everything but our jocks. There are husbands doing the housework now, not just taking out the garbage like you used to make me do when I came home exhausted from the factory. There's a whole army of very angry dames on the march. Fat Bella Abzug, Billie Jean King, Gloria Steinem, Betty Friedan and dykes in regiment strength. Any one of them shows here and you're going to see all the barriers come tumbling down. Those sexy shrouds, too. The libbers are very strong for pants suits. Hell, they're very strong, period. I had nothing but trouble with those ball-breakers on the paper. Fired two of them for turning down what they call 'women's' assignments and got beat not only by the Guild but

Dolly herself, even though she wasn't any libber. Baby, I was lucky to get out of that one without having to go down on that pair in Macy's window, and one of them was a real dog."

"You haven't changed at all, lover. It's the same mouth."

"Look, I was just filling you in on something you missed, Birdye. I haven't been doing too good in the skirt-chasing department lately. Had trouble the minute you went away, in fact—and I mean trouble."

Those hazel eyes came ablaze.

"Oh, cut it out, Paul. You're insulting my intelligence. Don't you think I knew about that Italian you were seeing after I started to go?"

This must have been the first time I felt that scar on my duodenum —souvenir of a little surgery when my insides exploded one night in '45—talking back to me in maybe fifteen years.

We met Angela Lauritano at a screening of Otto Preminger's *Exodus* just before Birdye got sick, and afterward some of us went over to Shor's. Driving home later, Birdye threw in a friendly jab about all the attention I had lavished on that statuesque woman and I said something brilliant like hell, kiddo, that babe can't hold a candle to you, and besides if she isn't sombody's private property it's gotta be the upset of the century. Well, I had to check that out for the record, naturally, so the very next night I found myself staking Miss Lauritano to a somewhat more private dinner where I found out fast enough that my own home was in no peril at all. Daughter of a Sardinian import who had built a closet-sized bakery on Mulberry Street into a prosperous distribution operation, she had attended Iona, that Westchester college for proper Catholic girls, and emerged very proper indeed. She had a notion about modeling but had too much under her bra for the high-fashion beat and found herself decorating the reception desk at some ad agency with a promise of larger things in no time at all. When that didn't happen, apparently because she wasn't available for after-hours interviews with the brass, she moved on to Bergdorf-Goodman, where she was stepping up nicely in the promotion department when the "right" man came along. This was a friend of her big brother's who was a salesman for a printing company and enormously attentive. But that union was doomed to failure, although Angela drew the blinds right there as a piece of history she did not wish to discuss with a virtual stranger. OK, lady, how about a nightcap at your place? No. I could drop her at her door, but it was such a pleasant evening and perhaps we could do it again sometime.

And we did—under a very dark cloud.

Birdye went into Midtown Hospital a month after I struck out with the tall one with the bouffant hairdo. It was supposed to be a simple hysterectomy, but before the doctor was through he had cut out the uterus and ovaries and snipped some specimens from the peritoneum, liver and spleen. What my wife had was Krukenberg cancer, so new to me the name had to be spelled out. "This is a form of fibrosarcoma identified by a German pathologist around the turn of the century, Mr. Sann," the doctor told me while Birdye was in the recovery room. "It has a wholly singular metastatic characteristic. Wherever it has its origin, generally in the stomach or ovaries, it tends to drop seeds on all the organs below it, and when you come upon one of those it is almost invariably too late." We called in another surgeon more familar with that Nazi Krukenberg and went for a second operation even though I knew we were not only going against a million-to-one shot but running the risk of hastening the seeding process. Put that down as another bet I lost along the way.

During my six-months' vigil in and out of Midtown and into the crumbling old University Hospital on lower Second Avenue where Birdye finally gave up the fight, down to about eighty pounds from a hundred and fifteen, I saw Angela two or three times a week, never so much as making a small pass because I was dying too and there was no doubt anyway that I might have had a better shot at Marilyn Monroe or Ingrid Bergman or someone like that. I'm not putting those ladies down. I just mean to convey that Miss Lauritano was clearly off-limits for me.

With some persuasion, Angela came to the funeral, meeting Leni and Richie for the first time. It was an uncommonly warm, sun-splashed Thursday in November and at the time I was doing a Satur-day page which had started out as a *Times*-style review of the week for our magazine and degenerated into a fun thing off the newsbreaks and the more ridiculous junk in the syndicated columns, especially the lovelorn beat owned by Dear Abby and her twin sister, Ann Landers, along with the Hollywood and Broadway columns. In that process, I seldom let a week pass without throwing one soft jab or another at Birdye, often dressed up with a picture. The kids made the column as well, with Leni identified as Wednesday Sann on the pretext that she had been born the day after Tuesday Weld. I had all kinds of names for Rich, because he enjoyed the distinction of sharing a birthday with Mr. Hitler, and I don't remember the assortment I hung on Birdye. Titles, too, like the Duchess of Glenbriar after the house we lived in so happily. Anyway, I sat around with the family and a few friends after the funeral and then about eight o'clock decided I had to go and knock out a piece for the paper about Birdye, but first I called Angela and asked if she would stick around while I wrote it.

I started that piece by describing the way my girl and I met on a street corner in the Bronx when I was sixteen and she was fifteen and how neither of our socialite tenement families—her father drove a bakery wagon and mine was a garment cutter—was too thrilled by our romance. I said her parents wanted her to marry a doctor and mine probably wanted me to marry one too (a *woman* doctor, of course) but we shook them all off when we had the two dollars for the license and another eight for a one-night honeymoon (dinner and the Radio City Music Hall on a press pass) and I was all the way up to twenty-five a week as an editorial clerk on the *Post.* Then I described the battle that woman put up against Mr. Krukenberg and how when it ended there wasn't enough room in Campbell's for all the people who loved her and how neither of the kids shed a tear because they knew their mother wouldn't have wanted it that way. That was the heart of it, and I wound up with these two paragraphs:

> Now how do you say thanks? How do you thank little Birdye, who walked so tall? How do you thank her friends and yours? How do you thank the readers of this column who take the trouble to tell you they want a piece of your heartbreak? How do you thank the people who send money to the Damon Runyon Cancer Fund to fight a killer that strikes without asking for your credentials for death? You can't; there is no way, but I would like to say this much for Leni and Richie and Paul:
>
> Don't light any candles for our Birdye. She found the way when she was around. She lit up some of the dark places in the town. The question here is, will it ever be the same without her?

There were tears streaming down Angela's face when she handed that last take back to me and I wrote a head saying A GIRL I USED TO KNOW before carrying that piece of bloodletting out to the back shop and asking the night foreman to get it set by a printer who could find the keys on his Linotype machine and then corrected by a proofreader whose eyes hadn't been destroyed by too many years of poring over the agate in the *Racing Form.* Then I went back into my office to collect Angela and take her to dinner but she rejected that idea.

"Hell," I said. "You worried about those swollen eyes?"

"No," she said, ever so softly. "I would prefer to go to my place. I'll make a little bite for us."

"I can't believe this, Ang," I said. "I had to write my guts out to get invited into that steel vault of yours, but you must know it might not be the best idea tonight."

"I do know. You belong home with your children. I won't let you stay very long."

" 'Children'? You kidding? You know my daughter's twenty-two and set to get married and my son's in his first year at Lafayette, but I won't argue, lady. You set the ground rules and I play by them—tonight, I mean."

We had no dinner, just some prosciutto and crackers and a few drinks and then—Mama, pin a rose on me—I settled for a good night peck and did go home. I wanted to take that woman in my arms—oh, did I ever—but I was afraid if I ever did that she would have had to throw me out. For the next couple of months, except for my labors in the office and an occasional dinner with Angela, I spent most of my time with Leni once Richie went back to that college in Easton, Pennsylvania. Then one night I took the Italian to see Robert Morse, Rudy Vallee and Donna McKechnie in *How to Succeed in Business Without Really Trying*. At her place afterward, I embraced her and said that this time she had an overnight guest—or did she want to call over her brother and have me carried out of there?

Without a word, without a kiss, without a touch until I took her hand, Angela headed for the bedroom and I started to undress her. As I slipped off her black panties I kneeled down and ran my tongue along her thighs and then into that special place while she sank down on the bed and started to moan, "Oh, Paul, stop. Please stop." I did not stop until I felt those strong thighs straining against my temples and her body quivering and then exploding in a convulsion of ecstasy. Now it was, "Oh, Paul, Paul, what did you do to me?" and I got on top of her and smothered her words with a kiss that must have lasted ten minutes with some detours to the eyes, ears and breasts before she wiggled out from under me and, taking my face in her hands, demanded to know whether we were on a one-way street or if my clothes also came off.

"Yes, they come off," I said. "Now we're gonna make love."

And we made love, all the love anyone could make that I knew of.

Around the world in sixty minutes.

Then we laid back for a while, exhausted in a mutual release, until I got out of bed to get my Camels. When I came back I was asked whether I didn't really need to be home with the children.

"I am home, angel," I said. "The long way. It took me eight months to get here. I can't leave now."

"Would you put out that cigaret then?"

"Why?"

"You're too far away. I want you to hold me in your arms. Hold me tight. Kiss me and hold me tight."

Another hour passed before we fell asleep, and not just in each other's arms. I was still inside that treasure, surely the only person alive who could claim a hunger as voracious as mine. I don't mean a hunger for sex but that infinitely bigger word: lovemaking.

But we weren't destined to see our first dawn together.

Somewhere along the line Angela shook me awake, her hand coming away from my shoulder wet.

"Paul, darling, you have to get up."

I drew the woman to me but she pulled back and ran the powder-blue sheet over my sweat-dripping chest.

"Angel," I said. "Please don't tell me. I think I know."

"I will tell you. I must tell you." Now Angela lit me a cigaret, the first time I had seen one between those flaming lips. "Sit up. It's better to talk about it."

I sat back against the headboard.

"What time is it?" I asked.

"Three o'clock."

"Exactly what it should be," I said. "You can't knock my timing, big one. Scott Fitzgerald said it is always three o'clock in the morning—and this is my three o'clock in the morning. I'm for talking but you'll have to draw that sheet up first. I can't talk unless you're covered. We've slept about two hours, haven't we?"

"No, not quite, and I never closed my eyes. I couldn't. It's the way you've said it so many times yourself, Paul. I couldn't turn my head off, but you couldn't turn yours off either, even asleep. Do you really know why I woke you?"

"Yes, I'm afraid I do. I was having a dream. I think I can put it all back together for you."

"You don't have to. You were calling out Birdye's name, that's all."

"Is that all? I wish I knew how to ask you to forgive me, angel."

"Why should you?"

"We'll come to that. How long was I calling that name?"

"Long enough. Perhaps I should have awakened you sooner. You seemed to be in terrible pain."

I leaned over and stole a kiss but didn't dare get back under the sheets. I felt I had lost my pass.

"Angela," I said. "You saw how easily I wrote all those words after that funeral. Now I'm fresh out. I do have to ask you to forgive me and like I said I don't know how."

"Paul, I'm asking you again. Why?"

"Why? I'll tell you why. I make the most frantic kind of love to you—frantic, mad, bigger than wild, bigger than passion. I couldn't even stop. I think you had to roll me off before it was over—and then you hear me calling out like a baby for the woman I buried. There's something terribly wrong with that picture, like it's hanging crooked on the wall. Upside down, maybe."

"Don't say that, Paul." Those black eyes were so luminous I could make them out in the dark, mist and all. "You're trying to tell me it's wrong and you're sorry and I don't want to hear that. I'm not angry and I can't be angry with you, but this is not the night for me to tell you why."

"Maybe so, you doll, but it is a night for me to tell you something, and for this purpose I'll just pass on the kind of woman you are and what you are to me."

"Only if you feel you must."

"Well, I must. You know, I always had a thing with Birdye. Any time we had a bad argument over some silly thing I would split and go for a long walk, and when I came back it would all be over. That's what that dream was. We had a terrible row—I have no idea what it was about—and I walked for hours and hours, only this time when I got back there was no Birdye and nothing like that ever happened before. She was always there before, always waiting, and now she wasn't."

"Oh, how awful for you."

"Small word, Ang. I might as well get to the part that could really burn. I've had a thing in my head all these months that there was no way I could ever be good for any woman again, that I'd just roll in the hay with them like a teenager and wind up calling out some other name—Birdye, always Birdye. I was right, I'm afraid. What you just heard you're going to hear again unless you tell me to take my sad song somewhere else. You're going to hear it because we can all dream but we can't call back the dream. I don't suppose that makes any sense, but I'm going to tell you something else. Awake, together, this way, it's us two now. I mean it's us two if you can take it."

More mist in those eyes.

"Paul, I wish you wouldn't say any more now, because you'll make me say something I don't want to say on this. . . ."

"Sorry, big lady," I broke in. "I am going to say some more—without using the good four-letter word because I wore that one out in the column I wrote about Birdye. I'm hooked on you with everything, however much or however little I may have left. I mean hooked. I can't tell you how long because I don't know when it began to sink into this thick head. Some of the time I thought it was just because I was so mad at Birdye for getting so sick she had to leave me. Imagine that, leaving me. Practically a whole goddamn lifetime together and she was leaving me. That make any sense to you?"

"Why shouldn't it? I've known for a long time that one day we were going to have this kind of conversation, so I couldn't possibly have been more prepared for it."

"You stopping there?"

"Yes. It's the wrong night to go any further."

"Sold, but first I'm going to ask you something. It's just a few more words, OK?"

"Of course."

"Don't you ever leave me. Whatever happens, whatever the nights may bring, don't go away."

Angela eased that sculptured form down and nestled against my shoulder.

"I don't think I have to answer that," she said. "Don't you want to try to get a little sleep? You're due in the office pretty soon."

"So I am," I said, "but I need to know something first."

"What?"

"You rattled these walls before. I mean I had a notion somebody might call the cops between all the moaning and those screams. Tell me why it was that way for you, angel."

Angela turned around and a minute or two passed before I leaned over and said, "Come on now. Tell me. I haven't held anything out on you."

And then her story unfolded.

The dreamboat she married whisked her off to San Juan for the honeymoon, bought some champagne, took a quick gander at the action in the casino in their hotel and then they went upstairs. A virgin at twenty-seven, she was hung up with all those moth-worn notions about the groom carrying the bride over the threshold and then making the most tender love to her.

It hadn't happened that way for Angela.

The groom assaulted that bride. He was on and off in five minutes

and then dressed and on his way to the casino because it closed at 2:00
A.M. Angela got a towel, covered the blood on the sheet and cried
herself to sleep.

Well, didn't it get better after a while?

Not much.

Mrs. Vincent Viggiano, installed in a splendid East Side co-op, found
herself the legally wedded partner of a high-roller running to fat on all
the wine and pasta he was staking his clients to. And the thing he liked
the most next to writing orders with hefty commissions was the big
color TV set in the living room.

"Why did you hold still for that for three years, Ang?" I asked.

"Paul, we're not supposed to get divorced in my faith. I guess I was
just content enough not to bear any children with that monster."

"So how did it end?"

"Oh, that was a Sunday afternoon during the football season. My
lover was watching a game he had a bet on, stuffing himself with beer
and Genoa salami when I packed two bags and announced that I was
going home to my mother."

"And what did the football fan do?"

"His team must have been losing, because all he did was turn
around to tell me he would never give me a divorce. I doubt if he
missed more than one play. Maybe there was even a commercial on
then. I forget."

"How did you get out of it then?"

"Well, that was a bit touchy, Paul, but I am not really a divorced
woman."

"What's that mean?"

"Two things happened. First my brother took his old friend to dinner. I told you he was in the Golden Gloves and he's six-feet-six. So
they weren't quite into the main course when Mr. Viggiano agreed to
an annulment."

"I hate to ask, Ang, but it's the reporter in my soul. How was that
little thing arranged?"

"I don't know the details and never wanted to—except that the
grounds were that it was an unconsummated marriage, and I can't say
I'm all that ashamed, since that's exactly what it amounted to. Un.
Uneverything."

"Ouch. If you're telling me you never got it off with that animal
then you have to buy a tie or something for a reasonably clean dirty old
man."

"I'll do a little more," Angela said, and we made love again and I went down to the office to get the first edition out.

Oh, sweet memories. Love and death, all in the same day.

And here I was again—with the *only* woman, except that I had to be reminded that I was with her.

"Paul," Birdye said. "What on earth is going through your mind? I wasn't complaining. I didn't expect you to live like a monk all the time when I was so sick. I even told you in the hospital—I guess it was toward the end—that it would be all right. Don't you remember that?"

"Of course I do, doll, but let me tell you something. I gave that a pass. I didn't make it with that Italian—or anyone else, believe it or not—until months after it was all over."

"Did you stay with her after that?"

"Yeah—five, six years."

"And then?"

"That was all the lady could take, Birdye. She knew from the first night that she was stuck with a guy who was always going to love some other woman more."

"And since then?"

"Hell, by the time I made this trip I wasn't the four hundred hitter I was in that league when you were around. I'm not saying I quit scoring, only that I had my share of strikeouts because I could never get your face out of this crazy head. I got thrown out of a few beds for babbling your name in my sleep after rolling off—and, hell, I can't remember when I had a live-in roommate after that first one. It just came down to the weekend bit after a while."

"Oh, this is all so horrible. I don't want to hear any more. Where were we when I made that bitchy crack?"

"The absence of coed dorms, I think, but I don't really care much about that, Birdye. It's enough for me just to be able to see you and be with you again. I can skip the other nonsense, not that I expect you to buy that when you always put me down as the *numero uno* of all the sex maniacs."

"That's not fair, dear. I have no trouble buying it at all. Let's get back to your immediate problem, yes?"

"What's the problem? I told you hours ago I can take those beards. What do you want me to do? Go down all those counts one by one? What good would it do us? I gotta fight it out with them, not you."

"Paul, will you come to your senses?" There was some irritation now. "You know one of those counts has to do with adultery, and that's where I come into the picture. You don't want to kill any time on that one today."

"Christ, what a thing to ring in on me now, the spot I'm in. Don't tell me you're going to dig all those old demerits out of your memory book at this late date."

My girl looked as serious as I had ever seen her. Well, that's not quite so. She was pretty well shaken up when they bumped a naval officer off a military flight and flew her out to the Coast in the middle of the night after I had that ulcer operation, and she was grim as hell in the months before that when I was getting set to go to the Pacific as a marine combat correspondent to record General MacArthur's Homeric deeds.

"Look," she said now. "You can't expect me to pretend that anything didn't happen that did happen, even though I never could have hoped for a more caring and loving husband, but this isn't a place where you can rewrite any life stories."

I would have let Brother Henry keep that whole two thousand for just one little MORE and one double Beefeater martini at this point but I banished that notion and wrapped my arms around those strong shoulders.

"Birdye," I said. "You're not risking any perjury rap. You don't take the stand. Up here a wife can't testify *against* her husband and can't testify *for* him either. I can't believe what you just said if I heard it right."

"You heard it right. You never had any trouble with your ears, just your insides. I'm not trying to make it any harder for you. I'm only trying to get you to face the facts. We had so many glorious years together. You know I never expected you to play with yourself when you went off on all those long trips for the paper, and I was always satisfied that you never got yourself into any affairs when we were at home. You only stayed out all night one time, and I don't think I managed to stay mad at you for more than two days when that happened. And I never listened to the blabbermouths I kept running into, but can't we put this off, for God's sake? It's very painful for me and, more important, it's a sheer waste for you. You need the time, Paul. You really do."

That one had the sound of an oral eviction notice.

"Is it OK if I come around tomorrow, baby?" I felt like it was 1930 again and I was going up to that fetching teenager and asking for a date.

"Of course, silly. I want to know how it goes, every day. I'm sorry

I've been this way, but you must understand what I'm going through. What else can I do or say? I can't put on any kind of act while we're waiting for your trial and sentence."

Sentence? Not verdict? If there was a wall in the joint I would have banged my head against it. That girl could get along anywhere, not even excluding Devil's Island or a Manhattan street after dark. She must have been doing all right until I showed. I felt so rotten I was sorry I had quit to that second heart attack.

"Gee, kiddo," I said. "I didn't mean to mess up your day. Maybe I should have stayed away until I had this thing beat, but I couldn't. Like I said, I never stopped loving you. You can't imagine how many other women I've told that to—in writing, no less. If I could get a one-day pass I'd come back with a whole stack of letters to show you that it's all on the record. I'm loaded with carbons I kept because there were some things in them I thought might find a spot in a novel sometime. The one I was writing was about you, in fact, and the title I had on it was *Call Back the Dream.*"

Now there were tears streaming down the silken white skin so much cash had been invested in because one of my girl's few extravagances always was the beauty parlor, especially the once-a-week facial.

Birdye turned away.

"Please go, Paul," she said. "This has been so hard. You'll find me here tomorrow."

I hardly had to be told that but I guess my long lost love had to be absolutely shattered by then. The years up there must have taken something out of her, I thought as I patted her softly on the neck, drawing some desperately needed warmth from the gold chain under that shroud, and headed back to Brother Vittorio. The towering Dago might as well have sat—or stood—in on that whole session, because he read it all on my long face.

"Bad time, pal?" he asked.

"That's the mild way to put it, Tiny. How do you know?"

"No big deal. It's always like that the first day. All the married dames gab about how much they miss their husbands, even when you know they came out of real bummers, but the first time's always rough on 'em. I never seen it to fail. It's different with the guys, not that I could ever figure it."

"Vito," I said. "You are a veritable font of wisdom just the same. I can't believe you spent your whole life with the less highly regarded elements in our society."

"You can't, huh? Remind me to show you where the slugs landed sometime. The sonofabitch musta used a three-fifty-seven magnum on me—and that wasn't the only time I took some lead, pal, just the last. I still haven't been able to figure out why that two-bit torpedo hadda empty that whole barrel into me. His first shot took me out. I tasted the garlic and knew I was goin on a long trip. Wanna take a coffee break before your next stop?''

"My doctor knocked out the coffee after my first heart attack, *paisan,* and I'm one citizen who always listened to his doctor."

The big guy roared.

"I slipped that one past you, Paul. The java's not on the menu here either. I was talkin about droppin in on Brother Henry because I'm in possession of some inside information."

"Like what?"

"Just move 'em. I wanna stake'ya to a little surprise."

The walyo had to be talking about the nectar of the gods below, knowing how rocky I was, because I wasn't in that tailor shop more than twenty minutes before I was loaded like a Greek, which isn't all that easy for Hebrews.

On the house, and see what the boys in the back room will have.

The gin—my own brand and about ten bananas per fifth downstairs—had arrived while I was in that star chamber, and now old Hank was pouring. And pouring. And pouring. And what accounted for my good fortune? The sauce was the gift of an air crash victim who still had his carry-on bag with him once he got up above the blue. Don't ask me to explain that. I never believed in miracles but had no trouble switching on this very first day of my death.

Brother Henry, plainly no slouch at his earthly sideline, had the bottle stashed in a very tricky shroud that had a deep, heavily reinforced pocket on the inside. And I mean heavy, because there were three bottles of Beefeater in that bag. Thinking ahead, I suggested that we were mounting our assault on the liquid gold with a mite too much haste but the barkeep just smiled.

"There's always more where this came from, young fellow," he told me. "Don't ask me how the juice never gets ripped off by those thieves on the ambulances, because I've known them to dig the gold fillings out of a stiff's teeth, but they seem to be passing up the hard stuff nowadays. Maybe all them meat wagon drivers are coming out of Alcoholics Anonymous now. I don't know any other way to explain a pheenomenon of this kind."

"Me neither, Hank," I said, "and I was a police reporter once. By the way, our high-living benefactor carry any smokes?"

"Excuse please," Brother Henry said. "I clean forgot."

Reaching into another storage shroud, he pulled out a deck of Carlton 100s, only recently adjudged by the government's ferrets to contain the lowest tar content—0.5 milligrams—and lowest nicotine—0.005—of any coffin nail on the market. There was nothing I detested more than the Carlton 100, naturally.

"Is that all the bum had on him, Hank?" I asked. "This is the same as puffing on a Tampax."

"Sorry, my good man. This is your new brand for the moment."

Well, it could have been a Tampax at that. I would have smoked it anyway so long as it hadn't been used. The big guy lit up too but the tailor didn't and I asked him how come.

"It was that lung cancer garbage, Brother Paul. I was a three-pack-a-day man when the Surgeon General's report came out—around '64—and I quit cold. Picked up the lousy habit again about five years later but then they started talking up that stuff about the heart and emphysema and all that and I kicked it again even though that fat slob wife of mine kept puffing away even when she went in the bathtub, which wasn't too often."

"You did right, Hank, so how did you wind up in this sanctuary?"

"Shit, I was healthy as an ox after doing a stretch on a bum check rap, so what happens? I get run over by a fucking gypsy cabbie who couldn't have had a lousy nickel's worth of insurance and musta been high on coke or something."

"Funny you should mention that, Hank," I said.

"Why?" Brother Vittorio put in. "You didn't catch it from any spade cabbie. You got hit by your own bum ticker."

"I did indeed, goombah. It was the noble tailor's reference to that 'high' that tickled me, because that's just what I've got right now. I mean like I'm higher than Dolly Parton's jugs. You non-music lovers wouldn't know her. She's a hot singer now."

"You can't get any higher, pal," Brother Vittorio said, "on account of this is the top with or without the booze. The elevator don't go no higher. Now maybe you wanna quit swillin that rich man's gin. You got your rounds."

"Good thinking, Tiny," I said. "I can use some fresh air."

"Fresh air?" said the genial Sicilian. "Whadd'ya think you're takin into that skinny schnozz? Fresh air's all that's served on these holy acres."

"I have another question," I said. "How come you two are in such good shape? I didn't get that far ahead in here and we're into the second bottle."

"Who counts?" said Brother Henry. "You started out still kinda light-headed and you don't wanna forget the chow situation. It's gonna take you a while before you can hold good drinking whiskey on an empty stomach. Vito and I don't have that problem anymore."

"Brother Hank," I said. "You're a fine gentleman even if you did fall afoul of one of the sillier laws downstairs, and if you got a quill you can put that down as something pretty special because my own revered father also was a tailor—well, he was in the garment racket, I should say—and in truth he never was one of my favorite people."

My keeper tapped me as I was reaching for another one of those cancer-killing Carltons.

"That's what you call tough shit, because your old man happens to be among the inmates."

You could have knocked me over with a fly swatter if they had one on the premises.

"Vito," I said. "You wouldn't kid an old sinner on trial for his former life, would you?"

"No, *amico*. Your old man's not only here but you gotta pay a call on him. Them Mustache Petes ain't too happy with guys who don't show no respect for their parents. You could even say it's prejudicial to your case."

"Pretty heavy word for you. My hat is off to you, sir."

"What's so heavy? I musta heard that word in real courtrooms a hunnert times. Never seen a mouthpiece who didn't use it until it was coming out of my cauliflower ears. Wanna go see Papa now or wait till your head clears?"

"No, now is just about right. I couldn't talk to that guy cold sober. What'll we leave the innkeeper?"

Brother Henry had the answer.

"I'll just palm the change on the mahogany, Paul," he said, deadpan. "There hasn't been a big tipper like you around in a dog's age."

"Thanks, my friend," I said, since even in my condition nobody could make me believe there was either any mahogany or any change in the heavenly gin mill, "but I do wish you would dip into my roll for some spending money, like in case you need a new pair of cufflinks or something."

"Not tonight," said the tailor, surely prison-trained because I never knew any tailors who weren't either Italian or Jewish and this guy was neither. "We had a live one for this little party. Let's hang on to the cash till we have to start dealing with the black-market types like Vito here, so I don't hafta go back to writing any rubber and going inside again."

I never was a fighting drunk, but I could have belted out that non-union tailor for saying a thing like that about my tall friend, who by now had begun to impress me as a full-grown, dead Ernest Borgnine. I don't mean the bully of an army sergeant who made life so miserable for Frank Sinatra and Montgomery Clift in the movie made from James Jones's *From Here to Eternity* but the brave and good Borgnine of the recent TV version of Erich Maria Remarque's classic *All Quiet on the Western Front.*

On the way out, I brooded about that crack of Brother Henry's and prayed that he was only making a small joke, because I detested the notion that my man Vito was still in the rackets after the way he went out. I would take that up with him on another occasion, but right now something else crossed my mind.

"Hey, big Brother," I said. "We never made that lunch stop."

"Yeah, but you didn't miss much. All we got time for now is that trip over to your old man's place. Get your head workin straight."

It turned out that the kosher district, speaking of city planning, was only minutes away from the tailor shop. But what the hell. My father came from a ghetto in Galicia in what was then Austria into a ghetto in what was then the all-Jewish Lower East Side and was now literally aswarm with blacks, Puerto Ricans and even Chinamen, and here he was in a ghetto again. It figured. For a Hebe, I mean. The deck was stacked against my people from the very beginning back in the time of King Herod, and maybe before that for all I knew. I might have made editor of the whole giant Hearst chain or Scripps-Howard and got paid like an editor if I didn't have the mark on me.

Chapter 3 ••••••••••••••••••••••••••••

My father hadn't changed a bit in twenty-two years.
He was still too short.
He still had that heavy accent.
He was still on the flabby side.

Above all, he was still the same loving, heart-warming man.

"So it's you, *bummicke*," he greeted me. "Big editor. I hit you with my belt, even my shoes, when I caught you smoking before your bar mitzvah. I told you you should stay in school. Look what good it did you."

"Hold the line, Governor," I said. "Let's take one thing at a time. We're not alone. I want you to meet my friend and good shepherd. Say hello to Brother Vittorio."

"Vittorio, Schmittorio. You never had a brother, only three sisters."

"Right. Why don't you ask me about your daughters and the woman who had them and maybe even your son who went to work as a copyboy for twelve dollars a week and became a judge?"

"A judge too?"

"Right again. On a Pulitzer Prize jury. That's a big thing in my business. Even made *Who's Who,* which is only for the most famous people. How do you like that?"

"Who's who. Who's what. Who cares. Freda's still alive?"

"Pop, you've lost all sense of time. She'd be over a hundred now if she was still around. She only made it to ninety something. Died in a lousy nursing home on Long Island with the fortune you left her. Now ask me about Birdye if it isn't too much trouble."

"You mean that one you married, that skinny piano player?"

"Yeah, the skinny piano player. You were crazy about her because her father had a year-round job but played the numbers and suffered from the shorts even worse than you. Ask me about Birdye."

"So I'm asking you, you rotten kid."

"She's practically a neighbor of yours now. You never had a chance to look her up, huh?"

"I mind my business. She wants to see me, I'm here. I don't go any-place. I don't even go to the shop anymore to work for those cossack in-law bastards of mine. Anyway that Birdye must be living with the Christians. She went to *shul* like you—never."

"Thanks. You're running true to form. You're the same adoring fa-ther who took a hammer and smashed up a bike I bought with some money I made delivering orders for a drugstore just because I played hookey a few times. Ask me about my children. It might cheer you up."

"All right already. Questions, questions. So what about your chil-dren?"

"My son is one of the most famous doctors in the country. Surgeon.

Does heart transplants, kidneys, whatever spare parts anybody needs. People come to him from all over the world, and they don't have to be Jewish either. That boy helps everybody, even when they can't pay. And my daughter is president of a big college in Connecticut—first woman president those *goyim* ever had. Jimmy Carter—he's the President of the whole country—tried to get her to join his cabinet and she turned him down because he's just a peanut farmer and his brother's an anti-Semit. Besides, the job wasn't big enough for her."

"There's grandchildren now?"

"Just Leni's daughter. She'll probably be a model or a movie star."

In all candor, I wasn't putting that man on to make him feel good, because I knew nothing had ever made him feel good from the day he came out of steerage, like my Russian-born mother a fugitive from the pogroms. As a boy, around 1890, he went to work for two dollars a week in the sweatshop owned by my mother's family. Years later anytime he had a few extra bucks because the strike or layoff seasons didn't run too long, they all went to my sisters so they could marry doctors (the closest any one of them came was to a pharmacist, and that didn't stick). I could care less about running last in the family, as per my arrival on that dismal scene, but I did burn when the Gov ripped off the $235 my bar mitzvah coined, leaving me with nothing but the fountain pens, although when my brain began to work a little better I got over that because I realized that he needed it to help feed us all, not to buy beer. Still, despite the funny looks I was getting from Brother Vittorio, I owed Harry a few and I was having too much fun to stop.

"Ask me about your daughters. They're all alive in case you're interested."

"So I'll ask you. What about my daughters?"

"Pearl's old as hell and living in California near Arthur and Selma. Her husband Jack died right after you—cancer. Daisy's still married to that Christian drinker she left the druggist for. And Fay and Sam are retired and barely squeezing it out. Anybody else you wanna know about?"

"Who asked you about anybody in the first place? I didn't ask you about you. When did I ever see you anyway?"

Gently tapped on the shoulder, I turned to my keeper.

"What's wrong, Vito? This too rough? I came out of a funny family, mostly because this old grouch didn't like too many people. They had to push me into coming in from Washington, where I was on the

Pentagon beat and it was red hot then, to go to his funeral. I know it's not that way with your people, so I'm sorry if this rubs you the wrong way."

"It ain't that, Paul," and I hadn't seen the guy this grim throughout our now time-tested friendship. "But I think you're pullin a rock."

"Why?"

"Well, you know when it comes down to that commandment about honoring your father and mother—the father first, check?—you could be in hot water. I told'ya for all I know this hole could be wired."

"Thanks, Tiny, but I can't see that because I don't know where in hell they could plant the bugs. No walls, no light fixtures, no phones, no picture frames, no nothing."

"I ain't arguin, but I still say you're makin a mistake."

"OK, but I don't dig it because they don't call any witnesses—and if they called this guy he'd tell 'em to fuck off. Those were always his two best words in English. Still, you could have a point. Watch this quick switch."

"Pop," I said. "I'm afraid I've shown you some pretty bad manners because I've been kinda low since I came up. No sleep or anything. Tell me, how have you been? You know how much we've all missed you."

"How could I be?" the Governor shot back. "You can't even get a lousy bottle of Ruppert's or a salami sandwich in this rotten neighborhood."

"We might come up with some beer, Pop, but the deli could be a big order. Anything else you need? Smokes?"

"Nah. Those Murads I could do without, what they cost."

The poor old man didn't know his brand was a museum piece now.

"What else then? You name it and we'll do our best."

"A little hot chicken soup I would like. All the time I have colds."

Brother Vittorio shook his massive head.

"There's no soup in the kitchen either, Pop," I said, "and if there was it wouldn't be hot anyway. I'm real sorry about that but maybe we can wangle you a new shroud. That one looks like it has sprung a few leaks. That's probably why you're catching colds. Vito's got a line into the tailor."

"Wholesale?"

"Don't worry about the money. You're my guest. Anything I can get my hands on. You took care of me long enough, God knows. You just name it. I came up here loaded. Tell me, how do you feel besides the colds?"

"How could I feel? It's like a prison. I feel like that cousin of mine who shot somebody on the East Side over a few dollars and they put him in Sing Sing, that nogoodnik."

I put a hand on that flabby right shoulder.

"Pop, you're too intelligent to say a thing like that. This is not a prison. It's Heaven, where you belong because you were a good man. There's worse places. Mom didn't even make it up here, and she was good, too. Right, Vito? My mother's not here?"

"She ain't on the books, Paul. I checked it. Maybe somebody hung a bum rap on her. There's an awful lotta creeps around."

"Don't I know it," I said, turning back to my father.

"Listen, Pop. I've got lots of people to see because I have some legal business, but I'll check in with you again, and I'm sorry about what I said about Mom before. She had a good life. Birdye fixed her up a real nice apartment and we took care of her and all the girls pitched in until she had to go to the nursing home, which was the best one on the whole Island, and then she was on Medicaid and the government paid all the bills."

"Medicaid. What's Medicaid?"

"The government takes care of everything when you're old enough and don't have any money of your own."

"All *goniffs,*" the Governor shot back. "I never got a nickel from those politicians."

"Well, you kept working, Pop. I begged you to quit after you got sick because you had Social Security coming and we were fixed to help you with a couple of extra bucks, but you wouldn't do it. You kept dragging yourself down to the Garment Center even when there was nothing left of your heart. Don't you remember?"

"What's to remember? I'm here already a hundred years."

"No. You're way off. Look, we have to run. We'll get that new outfit to you. Meantime, take care."

"That switch was a beauty, Paul," Brother Vittorio told me out on the boulevard of fractured dreams. "You think pretty fast on your feet."

"Why not, Vito? That's all I got to think on. We haven't come to a single bench yet, but there is something bugging me. You know, we buried that sweet man in some kosher cemetery in Jersey and I never stopped paying the grunt for what they call the annual care of the grave. It's up to thirty-four bills now and good old Dad ain't even there. I thought you Dagos had a lock on all the rackets, except for a few of my people like Meyer Lansky in the old days, but I guess I was wrong. They rolled me all those years just to sweep the autumn leaves off an empty hunk of ground."

"You gotta know better, pal. There's all kinds of people and all kinds of hustles, so what's the big deal? I never knew of a loose buck that got away in all the years I was in my business."

"When did you enter your profession?"

"I guess I was twelve, maybe thirteen. My old man was a shoemaker but I didn't see nuthin in that. I started robbin lofts and rollin drunks and kept movin up. Now where we headed?"

"How far is the morgue?"

"The morgue? You kiddin me? There's no stiffs around here."

"I'm sorry, Vito," I said. "On the papers that's what we call the reference room, or library."

"Four, five kilometers. Close enough. Whadd'ya want there?"

"I need a Bible so I can check Exodus for those Commandments and don't get myself into the stupid spot you just pulled me out of—a deed, by the way, for which there is only one word in the entire language."

"What?"

"Infuckingcredible. That's the long form. Any questions?"

"No. Let's move 'em. You was smart to keep them sneakers. It's rough goin barefoot on this turf at the start."

"So I gather. How come they don't have golf carts or something like that? We put the astronauts up with a thing called a moon buggy."

"You pullin my leg?"

"Not at all. That was ten years back when we got four men up there on two different trips."

"Oh, they made it, huh? Gee, that's great. First I hear of it. I came down with the lead poisoning the year before that, right after that colored preacher King and Bobby Kennedy got killed. I don't imagine you fellas wasted too much paper on me, though."

"What was your whole name, Vito?"

"Vittorio Pascaglia, but I was better known as The Chin."

"How come?"

"I got it street-fightin when I was a kid—onny it didn't mean glass chin. That was a shot nobody ever put me down with."

"You did get some ink, Vito, now that you mention it, because you went out in rather spectacular fashion. Just down the street from Headquarters, right?"

"Yeah, onna button. I was parked on Grand waitin to pick up Joe Profaci's brother-in-law, Magliocco, who was in line to take over that

Family. I was his bodyguard then after doin some good work as an enforcer and he was havin lunch in the Villa Pensa on Grand Street."

"Why were you hit?"

"You won't believe it, pal. The imby blew it. He musta made the Caddy a few minutes late and thought we just pulled in and Joe M. was still inna back, because he took a peek in there before he started poppin at me. He hadda be an import. You know the way them contracts go. You farm 'em out and the hit man's back in Chi, or Detroit, or Cleveland, wherever, before they got you laid out in your Sunday suit."

"What a dirty business. Worse than the one I was in. How far to the morgue?"

"Just around the bend, but what's the rush? This is a twenty-four-hour operation, all daylight. Very good on the eyes. It's twenty-twenty all the way. Maybe I wasn't the best Catholic boy on my block but I really think you wind up here the way you started—everything workin real good but your tool. This place ain't all bad."

"I can't say I doubt it, but that courthouse is something else."

"Sure, but you gotta hang in there with 'em."

"Yes, Vito. All I have to do is clip twelve Peters to pay one Paul. I wouldn't let on to my wife, but I'm not too crazy about the odds."

The library didn't lift my spirits any. The gent in charge, sort of a Lon Chaney without the hump in his back, reminded me too much of the character who was head librarian on the *Post* when I started out. How I hated it when some deskman or reporter sent me back there for an envelope of clips, because I was always treated like some kid fresh out of a reform school.

"What is it?" came the grunt, and it was that same voice sure enough. "Since you are new, you had best bear in mind that there are many books proscribed here."

"I think you mean *not* here," I grunted back. "I just want the Bible, mister. I figured you would have that."

"Of course. In all the versions from the fourth century Greeks' to the one bearing the imprimatur of King Charles to fragments of the Old Testament drawn from the Dead Sea Scrolls to the Vulgate of Saint Jerome to Tyndale, Wycliffe, Coverdale, Thomas Matthew, Henry the Eighth, Breeches, the Bishop's, Douay, that recent New American Bible, even—"

I had to turn the old curmudgeon off.

"Look," I said. "I couldn't be more impressed but I'm not here to do a version of my own. If you don't have the one put out by Simon and Schuster—I'm talking about Ernest Sutherland Bates's *The Bible Designed to Be Read as Living Literature*—I'll settle for your handiest copy of the King James version if it's not too much trouble."

"You won't get any expression of opinion from this quarter, young man," muttered the keeper of the books as he reached back to an invisible shelf and handed me a cheap brown imitation leather Gideon Bible, the kind I myself had pinched out of so many hotel rooms.

"I haven't had a chance to apply for a membership card yet," I said. "OK if I take this out and bring it back tomorrow?"

All that drew was a scornful look at Brother Vittorio that seemed to say what kind of nut have you brought in here?

"This is not a lending library," I was told. "You may consult what you wish to consult and return the volume."

"Thanks, mister," I said. "You're almost as nice as someone I knew in this same field once, although he worked on a New York daily."

Dead silence, the only kind there was up there, of course.

I flipped to Exodus, chapter 19, skimmed the opener about Moses making that meet with the Lord on Mount Sinai, and hurried on to chapter 20 where my man spelled out the Commandments, which I knew were seventeen in number in the wordy original version but with the eventual consolidation shook down to ten. I thought about dipping into Revelation too, since I was having no trouble at all reading without my bifocals, but didn't want to blow the time because I knew I had no choice except to get the Big Ten fixed in my mind or have to prostrate myself before that miserable librarian every goddamn day. I took a wild shot first, asking my companion whether he might perchance have a working Papermate on him but he laughed and said no, he didn't even carry a pen when he had his own handbook. "I worked the pay phones and kept the action in my head, Paul," he said, "because that way you couldn't get bagged with a pocketful of slips and hafta take a fall. Anyway, where you figurin to write this stuff—on your sleeves?"

So I went to work with my head, pretty well cleared by now, and had it all stored away there in twenty minutes or so, reading and rereading, and handed the Book back to Lon Chaney's stand-in without bothering to thank him. Then I told my soulguard I was ready to blow those creepy premises but needed a few minutes to figure where I go from there.

"Well, there's one of them fast food stops pretty close," he told me.

"Whyn't we drag ass over there and have a snack while you're workin out your game plan?"

On the golf course, Brother Vittorio watched me chewing a handful of lettuce and some other leafy junk along with some green beans colored white and sensed a further dip in my spirits.

"Paul boy," he said. "If you're lookin for arugala or zucchini or any pimentos and anchovies with the house dressin don't knock yourself out. I told'ya what was on the menu. It onny takes a few days to get used to this garbage and you eat it with a little glow on you'll think you're in your favorite joint on Mulberry Street."

"I don't doubt it, Vito," I said, "but tell me something. How does all this stuff grow here? I haven't seen any soil yet."

"It beats me, pal. They could get it delivered. I keep hopin they'll come up with a vendin machine contract one of these days. You know, like soda pop, butts and snacks, stuff like that. There's a barrel of money in them machines."

"I know," I said. "And all tax free."

Back to work.

Who was around this ballpark besides Birdye that I could pick up some quotes from on how I had never done business with any of the "strange" gods damned in the First Commandment? It had to be a small army, because I had never spent nine seconds pushing my own brand of Grade-A nonbelief. Around me, you could have God coming out of your ears and it didn't make any difference. Each to his own in my handbook—and hers, too. Hell, after Angela walked I started going with an ex-Copa girl who really was something more like an ex-nun still carrying her card, and on Sunday mornings I would roll out of the sack in rain, snow or sleet and walk her up to Chelsea's St. Francis Xavier Church so she could go into the box with her favorite priest. Then one time I had a Jewish playmate who wore the veil, so to speak, and on Saturdays I would deliver her to some synagogue up on the West Side. The black babe, too; she was some kind of heavy in Adam Clayton Powell's Abyssinian Baptist Church and I would drive her to Harlem on command (in daylight only, that is). Even had one once who was into the Greek Orthodox bit and I would cheerfully walk her way over to Second Avenue where her church was. Live and let live, like I said. I'll stick it anyplace except into your faith. But why was I letting the sun dial run down on those women? There wasn't one I didn't have fifteen or twenty years on and they still had to be Earth people. Then I thought of a babe who did a society column for us once and happened to be a disciple of Norman Vincent Peale. Now I was rolling good, even coming up with a few male friends who had the old-time religion, and I started throwing names at Brother Vittorio.

"No problem," he said. "Let's run down that society dame first."

Nancie Courtney, a redhead who was more accomplished under the sheets than she was with a typewriter, did not stake me to any excessively effusive greeting, which figured. I dropped her column (and she dropped me, for some reason) after getting us into a libel suit with an unforgivably sloppy piece of work, and only a couple of years later she came down with something bad and she was gone, so young. Despite that old hurt, Nancie had no qualms about talking to me on the matter at hand. No, I had never put the knock on her thing with the Reverend Dr. Peale or any other reverend doctor in her memory. Better still, drawing upon her aborted career in the gossip trade, she proved quite helpful. Had I seen Helen Harrington, that high (both ways) Episcopalian TV actress from Hollywood I used to run with when she came East on promo trips? No. Well, she went out on a combination of uppers, downers and vodka—talk about poorly balanced diets—after her series folded and she was only down the road a piece.

"You're the same doll, Nan," I said. "I won't forget this. If they let me put out some kind of heavenly rag up here you've got your society beat back."

"Thanks, Mr. Editor, but I would have to pass on your gracious offer. Working for you once, day and night, was more than enough for me."

Helen Harrington, quite a package except that she had one of those high-fashion bodies without too much to get a grip on, couldn't have been more pleasant. She told me that if there was such a thing as an affidavit I could take before the elders she would be more than happy to attest to my unvarying tolerance. "You sold me everything but God, Paul, and then let me pay for that abortion," but I wasn't going to hold still for a rap like that with Brother Vittorio tuned in.

"Miss H," I broke in, "would you mind if I refreshed your memory? First, there was a double cross to start with, because you told me you had your diaphragm where it was supposed to be that night in the Warwick and you didn't. Second, when I offered to stake you to that abortion I didn't know you were going all the way to London for it with a grand tour thrown in. Is that gospel or isn't it?"

The long brunette with the bouffant hairdo and shimmering silk shroud (I guess she had brought a flock of her own, since she was always on good terms with the ousted husband who ran one of Beverly Hills more posh boutiques) spared me any rebuttal. Quite the contrary.

"Oh, I was putting you on, Paul," she said. "It's much too late—fifteen years?—for petty grievances. All that trip cost was about five thousand dollars and I knew you couldn't possibly have that kind of cash running your little tabloid. If they'll let me take the stand I would be delighted to give testimony for you as long as there are no television cameras out there."

Nothing but laughs, that nice lady. I would have given her a big kiss if my one true love wasn't in the same dorm. And speaking of Birdye, neither Helen nor Nancie mentioned her, so I assumed they were not in the same social set in Afterlife, Unltd. Hooray for that. There was plenty of rough sledding ahead with my best girl as it was, and I mean rough if you never had to go through any rough sledding with no sled and no ice. So a quick switch to the male preserve was indicated.

"You know if Toots Shor's around?" I asked my Seeing Eye man after thanking Helen Harrington for her gracious invitation to drop in for a make-believe cocktail or a few bennies any time I was in that neighborhood.

"He sure is, Paul. He hadda have some kinda fix in, but I guess he knew all the big wheels when he was goin good."

"Vito, if you'll pardon the expression, you're dead wrong. Toots was a Hebe married to a devout RC and made both churches with his sons and daughter. So he put away the brandy like the distilleries were all burning down and sent in a hunk of action now and then and fell behind in his tax bites, but Blubber was a good citizen in all the ways you're supposed to be good, certainly according to the standards laid down in this hotel."

Brother Vittorio simply nodded and told me we were in for a long hike. We walked for a good two hours (well, there wasn't supposed to be anything *bad* up there), running into so many people it was almost like being in midtown Manhattan at seventeen hundred hours when all the offices were disgorging the toiling masses into the carbon monoxide. I asked about that and my friend explained that all our earlier journeys had been confined to the side streets but we were now on a main thoroughfare like Broadway. Were we, indeed? We hadn't encountered a single black; every one was as white, or whiter, than his shroud. What gives, Vito? Another quick answer that would have floored me if there was a floor to fall down on.

"The spades have their own neighborhoods, just like downstairs,

Paul, and the PR's are in with 'em. Also a Chicano here or there or a Cuban or the guys with the slanty eyes."

I couldn't fucking believe my own ears.

Segregation in Valhalla too, even with the growing recent talk about God himself being a black man? My fellow traveler on the lily-white road sensed my utter bewilderment.

"It's no big deal," he assured me. "They all got the same things the rest of us have—no more, no less."

The old separate-but-equal bunk that Martin Luther King's civil rights revolution was all about.

Not for me.

"Vito, I won't buy it. If this is what the blacks have been dying for since the time of the slaves, since the Civil War, since things like the March on Washington and all the bloodshed in places like Mississippi and Birmingham and Selma in Alabama and those long hot summers in the sixties when whole cities like ours and Detroit, Chicago, Cleveland, Newark and even the capital itself damn near burned down, then something's out of whack real bad. Man, if they had a cable office up here you would see me pounding out some piece of copy."

While I knew there wasn't a shred of bigotry in that huge frame, all that came back was a shrug of the shoulders.

"Hey, you hear anything I said?" I went on. "I tell you it's one thing if the nonviolent types like Dr. King or A. Philip Randolph or Whitney Young are around here but you ever get the heavy hitters like Huey Newton or Bobby Seale or Eldridge Cleaver or any of that breed dropping in and try to shove them into any ghetto you're going to see some real action."

"Newton? Seale? Cleaver? Who're them guys? Pugs, or what?"

"They never fought with any eight-ounce gloves, Vito. They carried heat and knew how to use it, too. They're pretty quiet now because they've been busted too many times and Cleaver, for that matter, switched to the Born-Again Christian circuit, but tell me something. What are you so lighthearted about? I'm talking from my guts."

"Aw, it was only what you said about that cable office. I could do some business with a wire myself. Maybe run in a connection to get some cadavers headed this way with some dope on 'em."

"Jesus, don't tell me you're talking about hard drugs."

"Nah. I'd never get nobody hooked on that shit, but what is so wrong with the kinda grass a guy could smoke insteada what we're eatin in this trap? I wouldn't be lookin to make no bundle, just to get some action goin. You've already been here long enough to know this joint makes Atlanta, even Lewisburg, look like country clubs. You can live like a Rockefeller in them slammers if you're connected, and what have we got here except twelve months of daylight and good weather? An action guy could get bored to death on this tier if he wasn't already dead."

"I haven't thought of it that way, *paisan*," I said, "and I'm just going to make believe I never heard you talking about getting back into the rackets even if it's just pot, which is about to go off the books as a crime now except for the big dealers who never get nailed anyway, but this segregation bit's never going down with me. I didn't beef about finding my old man back in his kind of ghetto because he's OK except for that beat-up shroud (how would you like to be lounging around Heaven all day in a shredded shroud, friends?), but the thing with the blacks is too much for my insides. You know the First Amendment, don't you?"

"No. Just Number Five."

"Well, Number One has to do with free speech. I expect to keep using it."

"No kiddin? You better beat your trial first."

I was so burned about the race thing we walked the rest of the way in silence, almost like a pair of strangers with a language problem or maybe a maximum security con like James Earl Ray with a guard he wasn't talking to, but at long last the tall figure of Toots Shor, darling of the sports and show business world in his time, loomed before us. My innkeeper pal hobbled toward me, so I knew the left side permanently damaged when he fell and broke his hip while walking sober in a Washington hotel suite years back had not been the beneficiary of any Lourdes-type miracle cure since his fairly recent move to the Upper Room. Still, Toots was beaming.

"You crumbum," he roared. "You had to make this dry hole on your press card but you look better in that nightgown than those Western shirts of yours. When'd you get in?"

"This morning, Bernard, only it wasn't my idea but some kind of freak accident."

"That figures. You see Baby much after I got the call?" Toots was talking about his miniature blond wife, and I had never seen a look like that on the man in all the years I had known him.

"No. I did see Rory some in the beanery across from the Garden where they're still selling your name. He's holding his own."

"Good kid. I miss 'em all, but mostly Baby. What a dame—and what a dame you had, Paul. Always put a shine on the joint when she came in."

"She's here, Toots. I was with her a while today."

"Ain't that great? Anybody ever belonged here it was your Birdye, but a newspaper bum like you had to have a ticket for the other place. How's DiMag doin?"

"Only like a million. He's now the face and the voice of the Bowery Savings Bank and coining money in armored car lots. The hundred Gs he went out with on the Yankees has to seem like fishcakes to Joe now."

"Jiminy crickets, that's good to hear. The Dago deserved it, even if he bust out with me over some crack I made about that first broad he married. I guess he'll always be hung up on Marilyn, huh?"

"Well, he's still shelling out for the fresh flowers on that grave out there and he's still on any coast where Mr. Sinatra ain't. Never forgave Ol' Blue Eyes for not doing more for Marilyn when she started that slide on the vino and the pills."

"No. What happened to Cannon? He never showed in this ballyard."

"I don't know, Toots. My guess is Jimmy wouldn't go anyplace where he couldn't stay on the sports beat—and you can't even get the linescores around here. Remember the great crack he made about your cuisine one night?"

"What crack?"

"We were sitting around after the curfew—this was long after Jimmy went on the wagon—and you kept a man in the kitchen in case anybody got hungry. Then around five A.M. you offered to spring for some food and Jimmy looked up and said 'Mr. Shor, when I require nourishment I go to a restaurant. I come in here strictly for the club soda and the good company.' "

Toots laughed.

"Yeah, and I couldn't get mad at the Irishman. I never wanted eaters in the joint anyway, only drinkers. Wasn't that the night I laid all the overtime on that half-assed chef and Gleason made me send over to the Stage Deli so all you freeloaders could have something you liked?"

"It was indeed, Blubber. You were all class."

"Thanks, crumbum. All class and no loot. How about Lenny Lyons?"

"Hell, Blubber, if he's not around here with his notebook it's the upset of all time. He may have been the world's leading name-dropper but he never dropped the name of the Lord in vain and he was so orthodox he had to be a lock for this cuffo flophouse. How come you haven't run into him?"

"The legs, Paul. Can't get around, so I only see the guys who drop into this hall closet. You gonna check in with Lenny?"

"No. I've got better ways to use the at-bats I've got coming."

"I guess it figures. Earl Wilson was always your man."

"It wasn't just that. Mr. Lyons had a bad habit of putting the blast on me with the owner whenever I knocked one of his 'exclusives' out of his column because we had it in the news section three days before or touched up one of his boffo anecdotes so the customer might get the point, but there's one thing I'll say for that man. When Birdye got it he was on the phone in five minutes. Anything I wanted from the Runyon Fund or anyplace else he had a line into. That was class with a capital C."

"You bet. Joe Louis still hanging in?"

"The Champ's a wheelchair case now, Toots, although the Caesar's Palace crowd in Vegas still has him on the payroll in that greeter's job for the hayseeds. You know he got off the needle pretty fast but he's just wasting away."

"What a damn shame. You wanna talk about class you can't leave that one out. He had it to burn. I would have given an arm and a leg—I'm talking about when I had two good legs—to see the Bomber in against a loudmouth like that Ali. How's Gleason, by the way?"

"Oh, Jackie's the same fixture on the Florida Gold Coast, just clipping coupons and banking his residual checks when he's not rolling around in his golf cart. Hardly ever works in anything, but 'The Honeymooners' is still in the reruns, same as 'I Love Lucy,' so that map's in millions of living rooms still. It's just a shame Jackie's not on live. Art Carney's red hot in the movies."

"The fat man's too rich for all those fairies in TV. How's that rag of yours?"

"I took a walk in '77 when the Gray Lady grabbed thirty-one mill and peddled it to some kangaroo named Rupert Murdoch. I thought I'd rather get some more words down than knock myself out for another publisher while Uncle ripped off my paycheck and the Australian had write-offs to burn."

"More books, huh? Lemme fill you in, Paul. You wrote too many before you got here. If I were you I wouldn't go around without this big walyo. There's some parties around who might like to have a talk with you, like the Dutchman and Uncle Frank."

Toots was talking about Dutch Schultz and Frank Costello, of course. I had done a bio on Schultz and the *Post* had covered the activities of the former Francesco Castiglia with unrelenting intensity all through his long career as an up-and-coming hoodlum to his eventual eminence as the Senate-dubbed "Prime Minister of the Underworld." What in the name of Whosis were they doing in this sacrosanct hideaway? I didn't ask but simply looked over at Brother Vittorio, whose bland face revealed nothing. He was a cutie, that one. He was surely no stranger to the gentlemen just mentioned by the old saloonkeeper, but I had to get down to the larger business at hand.

"Blubber," I said. "I came over to ask you something. You ever hear me try to steer any of the believers—what few you counted among your clients, I mean—away from whatever God they might have been hung up on?"

Toots didn't need a second.

"Jiminy crickets, no. What brings that up? You in a jam?"

"That's the mild way to put it, Tootsie. I'm on trial up here—all felony raps."

"Oh, I get it. You shouldn't have any trouble the way you use the words, Paul."

"Thanks, but if you're still in action don't get down on it. How did you beat those beards with your tax thing and your happy times as a bouncer for the speaks and all that?"

"Aw, it was a tapout. Even those old men knew I was paying up when I went and the rest of it was harmless. I came out smelling like a newborn baby and I don't see why you shouldn't. The worst thing you ever did was run a paper."

"Yeah," I said, "and speaking of papers, while I hate to dun a guy who's not carrying, that reminds me of the little wager you never paid off on."

"What bet?"

"The time you beat Sherman Billingsley out of fifty large for saying some mildly bad things about you on his Stork Club TV show and we bet an even mill that your pals on the *Journal* would bury it so Sherm wouldn't be too embarrassed in his set. I sent you the nicest little note about the thing once when I was more broke than usual and you never even answered it. Remember it now?"

"Now that you mention it, I sure do. Got a blank check on you?"

"Tootsie, your memory's going. That was what you sued about—the reformed bootlegger and ex-con telling his vast audience you were a specialist in writing rubber."

"So he did, the phony, but that was a pretty good piece of paper I wrote with the forty grand I had left after Si Rifkind showed me all that class and only took ten off the top. The whole bundle went into a trust for the kids. What a laugher, huh? A crumbum like Billingsley setting up a stake for my kids? You just made me feel like the million I owe you."

It was the old, soaked-in-brandy Bernard Shor, no worse for all the wear and tear. Except for my time with Birdye, not counting the blue moments, this would be the best part of my first day away from home. For my soulguard too, by the way, because there was no doubt that he and Toots were a cinch to become thicker than even Billy Carter and those motherfucking Libyan Jew-haters.

On the march again and not having the faintest idea about the hour (know any way to tell when it never gets dark?), I wanted to stop and check my girl on my impeccable record in the area of religious tolerance, but that was ruled out.

"Too far back," said the old soldier. "You need all your strength so you can start goin count-for-count with them whiskers. Otherwise you're a cinch to get hit with the book."

I knew the guy meant the book I always spelled with a capital *B*, and that raised a question I hadn't thought to ask up to then.

More than one question.

• Does the verdict have to be twelve and oh, one way or the other, like downstairs? Yes, indeed.

• Any such thing as a hung jury? Not in my consultant's memory.

• And the big one. What if you beat some counts and lose on the others? You can guess the answer. "I ain't all that sure but I kinda think you lose one you lose 'em all, like you either come outta there with a clean slate or no slate."

I wasn't too sure of that, for all of the good Brother's street-and-court smarts, but I didn't want to hurt his feelings by challenging that answer or asking him whether there were any jailhouse lawyers up there who could help me. Instead I simply asked what a finding of guilty meant. What was the punishment that fit the crime? Like with Birdye, I drew what amounted to a no-comment and elected not to press that either, just saying I could use some shut-eye.

"Shut-eye?" Brother Vittorio said. "You must think you're back on your old stampin ground in Greenwitch Village all set to sack out with some skirt. Well, that ain't the way it is on this turf. You're now in the land of the Big Sleep, only you don't get too much and don't need it, either. You don't lay your old head down 'cause there's no place to lay it and you don't really hafta anyway. You ain't workin. You got your health and twenty-four hours in the day, every day. *Capish?"*

"I *capish,"* I said, and that brought something else to mind. I hadn't taken a piss all day, so I had to assume that all the more pedestrian bodily functions also were a thing of the past on the other side of the pale. But, then, I should have known that. There were no zippers on those shrouds and no drop-leaf arrangements on the other end. "So how do we kill the time?" I asked.

"I wish you wouldn't use that word, pal," Brother Vittorio said, not without good humor, "but we don't because there ain't that much left. We make the long haul back and then head toward the gate and rap a while and pretty soon it's eight A.M. and you're back on the stand."

Good God in Heaven, friend, new neighbor and landlord, where did those first twenty-four hours go?

I suddenly realized that I wasn't even tired, nothing like one of those around-the-clock grinds on the paper with a Kennedy or King assassination or an election night or Watergate or anything like that. Hell, I couldn't wait to take on the enemy. How come? There was no geezer in the late P. Sann. It was as simple as that.

Day II

Chapter 4 •

Sworn again, I asked my superpeers whether I could, pray, address the court.

"Gentlemen," I said. "I have been given to understand that a finding of guilty on any single count is tantamount to a finding of guilty on all counts. Is that correct?"

Peter the First tossed that one to the Peter on his far right, who fixed me with the kind of look you might reserve for idiots or, say, any bum you just don't like on sight. Contemptuous doesn't quite cover it. This had to be the resident authority on the stickier legal points.

"The petitioner," that longhair started to say, but I broke in.

"Excuse me, but I must object to that word as prejudicial, inasmuch as I do not squat before you in that posture, since I never was a believer in the second chance bit to start with."

"Mr. Sann, by those very words you have managed to prejudice your own case," came the frosty answer, and I was chilly enough in that flimsy sheet as it was. "Nothing in your opening statement suggested that you were disposed to enter a plea of guilty and throw yourself upon the mercy of this Tribunal. Accordingly, you are indeed a petitioner."

"Sir," I said. "I do not recall having been asked how I wished to plead in the first place. Moreover, I must point out that I was not accorded so much as a moment's time to prepare my opening and this leads me to another rather crucial issue, if I may go on."

More ice.

"You have put a question before this body. In your own self-interest, it would be advisable for you to obtain your answer before going on at any further length."

"Thanks."

"The answer is in the affirmative."

So Brother Vittorio had it right. What was the point in numbering the counts if what it came down to in essence was a single count? I mean why not toss the whole thing into one boiling vat and call in the cannibals and save time if the calendar was so fucking crowded?

I turned to the main Peter.

"Your Honor, where I came from yesterday—and by the way the last person I had occasion to dine with down there was a nun—the common practice to reduce heavy court dockets is something known as plea bargaining. Is such a practice in usage here?"

The ball went back to the far right, and—

Q. Would you be good enough to amplify for your judges the process which you have described?

A. Gladly. You see, there are vastly more men, women and children—yes, children—detained as accused perpetrators of crimes than there are prosecutors or even judges or courtrooms in which to try them. Or, for that matter, prison cells in which to put them if they are indeed guilty.

Q. Please come to your point.

A. That's what I was doing. I regarded that information as highly pertinent. Plea bargaining is a system under which, say, a defendant indicted on a felony charge is permitted to plead to a lesser offense, such as a misdemeanor. As often as not that may result in a suspended sentence or nothing more serious than a cash fine. Then there are other situations in which the accused has been detained without bail pending adjudication and the court rules that the time thus spent in custody shall constitute—wash out, you might say—any previously agreed-upon prison term.

Q. What is bail?

A. Why, that's entirely commonplace also. When the accused is brought into court, at times even in the most heinous crimes, the judge will set a fixed bond and permit the defendant to remain at large pending the disposition of his case. That bond can either be currency or anything of material value possessed by such a defendant, such as a home he might own rather than rent. Also, there are bondsmen who will post cash bail for one who is deemed a safe risk and in a position to pay a five percent service fee. That bond is forfeited to the state if the accused flees the jurisdiction.

Q. Your reference to "bond," I assume, is akin to your earlier utilizing of the word "cash." Would you define that latter reference, please?

A. Cash is money, currency, the dollar bill. One cannot subsist without it. It goes by many names depending upon where one may be at a given time—pounds, marks, lire, francs, krone, pesetas, gulden, yen, drachmas, agorot. There are also such slang expressions for it as clams, fish, green, bread, moolah, kale, gelt, cabbage, dough, beans. The list is all but endless.

Q. So I gather, and I would remind you here of the biblical injunction interdicting the worship of God and Mammon. But to go forward, how, pray, does one obtain such currency?

A. Barring the criminal element, and unless one's forebears had amassed substantial wealth and material possessions, by one's honest toil. The latter was not true in my own situation, sir. My beloved father, with whom I spent many deeply treasured moments yesterday, labored without end through his appointed years and left behind nothing of consequence, so . . .

Q. The petitioner strays, I fear. The answer to your question is that no such device as a "plea bargain" is available in this forum.

The enemy swung in his chair, or whatever it was that was supporting his frame, and peered at the prosecutor.

"For a person of your professional background and reputed intelligence, absent a proper formal education," came those sepulchral tones, "I must observe that precious time has been wasted on a patently irrelevant matter. What would it avail you if the practice you have described, which I for one find exceedingly repugnant, did exist here?"

"I'm not sure I follow that," I said.

"Well, then, I shall endeavor to clarify it for you. There is but a single, universal sentence imposed by this body. Does it not follow that any effort on your part to barter for a lesser penalty would constitute nothing more nor less than a plea of guilty. Do you wish to so plead, perchance?"

Peter the First fielded that one for me.

"That question requires no answer from this petitioner." Period, end paragraph. They didn't need any pleas in there.

My first book, back in '53, was about the Wild West. Now, my spirits dipping with the speed of an elevator in Manhattan's Twin Towers, I felt as if I had been transported back in time and was in the dock before another beard named Roy Bean, better known as "the Law West of the Pecos." That fat old stewpot, armed with a copy of the Revised Statutes of Texas of 1879, set himself up in the town of Langtry in a shack complete with a bar, poker tables, jury box and bench and ruled with an iron if not always steady hand for twenty years, even though the more decent elements in that forsaken burg named for the singer Lily Langtry eventually set up a cry for elections. Any problem on that score? No. "The Law" lost to a rival in 1896 when a count of the hundred-odd ballots showed him with more votes than there were live bodies in the town, but he kept on dispensing what passed for justice in his combination saloon and courtroom just the same. While Mr. Bean preferred fines to the rope because he liked money better than still another cadaver on Boot Hill, he could be somewhat ruthless at times. Listen to the lyrically boring rummy as he imposed sentence on a miscreant caught rustling cattle:

"You have been tried by twelve good men and true, not of your peers but as high above you as Heaven is of Hell, and they have said you are guilty. Time will pass and seasons will come and go. Spring with its wavin green grass and heaps of sweet smellin flowers on every hill and in every dale. Then sultry Summer with her shimmerin heat waves on the baked horizon. And Fall, with her yeller harvest moon and the hills growin brown and golden under a sinkin sun. And finally Winter, with its bitin, whinin wind, and all the land will be mantled with snow. But you won't be here to see any of 'em, not by a damn sight, because it's the order of this court that you be took to the nearest tree and hanged by the neck until you're dead, dead, dead, you olive-colored son of a billy goat."

And Roy Bean, by the way, was a softie alongside the Hon. Isaac Charles Parker, the ex-congressman the hung-over Ulysses S. Grant sent out to tame the lawless Indian Territory in Fort Smith, Arkansas. That Bible-slinger's injunction from the White House was to take a year "and get things straightened out," and he had so much fun straightening things out—necks, mostly—that he went down in frontier history as "the Hanging Judge." The bloodthirsty bastard had so much fun he stayed on an extra twenty years. No defendant ever went into his courtroom better than one-to-five to walk out and no less than a hundred and sixty-eight men and four women were hit with the whole book, which meant a trip to the scaffold in the yard where Hizzoner could watch the baddies twisting slowly in the wind. Only sixty-nine, all men, actually made that trip. Why, you ask. Well, after a while Isaac Parker's juries began leaning to not guilty verdicts because they knew that no matter how thin a given case might be the man was a cinch to point the felon before him toward his oiled rope. Beyond that happy circumstance, Mr. Grant himself commuted forty-three of the doomed and when the Supreme Court opened the door to appeals in 1889 forty-six other Parker candidates for the gallows were turned loose either as the victims of unfair trials or clearly innocent to start with and another fourteen got off with prison terms. I always thought Will Rogers summed it up best in 1928 in a talk to some high school kids in Fort Smith (you know the Indian Territory had long since become the sovereign state of Oklahoma): "I just got here this mornin and I've been looking around. I find that Fort Smith ain't as big as it ought to be because it got such a bad start in the early days—Judge Parker hung so many men that this town got behind the other towns in size."

I must say Peter the First was the soul of patience this day, because there was no effort from the chair, or whatever, to press me as I went on in my head to my own territory and time. I thought about Sam Leibowitz. Elected to the bench after a sparkling career as a lawyer for the defense with a record of more than a hundred capital cases in which not a single one of his paying customers ever went to the Death House, old Sam turned into a modern-day hanging judge. It was almost as if he was doing penance for all the killers, including his share of professionals in the field, whose backsides had been saved from those twenty-two hundred volts of Con Ed's juice in exchange for fat fees.

Then there was a judge I covered myself in General Sessions (sorry, no name; he did some earnest work in the Jewish community) who was apt to go for the harshest possible raps in almost any case newsworthy enough to draw us poker players out of our pressroom and into his torture chamber, because he wanted to be mayor and loved to see big displays in the papers showing the voting populace what a hard-nosed hombre resided under that silver mane. It got so awful after a while that all eight of us on the beat decided to boycott that judge's courtroom on sentencing days in the more piddling cases in the interest of seeing some poor bum get off a little easier, whereupon His Honor called all our city editors and turned us in as lowlifes who would rather play cards than see justice dispensed.

Well, I fear I digress too much.

Back to the business at hand.

"The clerk is directed to read the first count," I heard Saint Peter say, and did that flunky, holding a piece of parchment at least three feet long, ever read. I can only give you the top here because I was pretty shaken by then.

The Petitioner, one Paul Sann, known by no other name, facing this Tribunal in Case Number 478, 329, 234, 537 (the figure is an approximation; I was never good with numbers except when I was working out the payoff on an infrequent winning parlay on the ponies), stands accused of violating Commandment Number One, which reads as follows: *I am the Lord thy God; which have brought thee out of the land of Egypt, out of that house of bondage. Thou shalt have no other Gods before me,* etc., etc., etc.

"Do you understand that count, Mr. Sann?" the prosecutor asked.

"I think I do."

"You think so? The full text has just been read for the record." (What record? I asked myself.) "Nonetheless, I shall attempt to sum it up for you as succinctly as possible. What the commandment at issue sets forth is that one shalt have no *false* gods and, further, that one is forbidden to foist upon others any false gods of his or her own creation. Is that clear?"

"Yes, sir."

"Then we shall proceed." Now that mile-wide ledger suddenly materialized in what passed for the man's lap. "On your behalf, Mr. Sann, I am pleased to confide that the available evidence appears to be grounded on the barest kind of hearsay, which is perforce looked upon here with a modicum of skepticism. Be that as it may, I put it to you now whether there is anything which you yourself might wish to confide to this Tribunal on the count at hand."

"No, sir. I have searched my mind with diligent care and while I never was a properly observant member of my own faith I cannot recall a single instance in which I challenged the right of any other person to believe in any god of his own choice. To nail this down, if I may resort to the vernacular, apart from my visits to my dearly beloved spouse and my father, I found some time since my arraignment to visit with a fair number of individuals with whom I had contact in my other life—and I have reference here to men and women of various faiths—to put this very question to them. In each and every instance, I submit now, my record in this particular area proved to have been impeccable. That is my testimony."

Now there was a murmured conference initiated by the prosecutor and swirling all across whatever passed for the bench. Looking all the way up and straining my ears until I thought they would burst, I could not make out a single word until the Holy City's D.A. addressed me.

"I have no further questions, Mr. Sann, although you would be well advised not to draw any undue inferences therefrom."

Inference my ass.

I knew I had those twelve beards by their unused balls and won that first round on a TKO. Although the thing actually went the distance, or at any rate until Saint Peter looked up, presumably at the sundial which worked without sun, and said that since it was but minutes away from twelve hundred hours he would declare that session adjourned. Then he banged his gavel, in a manner of speaking, and that was it.

The attendant led me out to Brother Vittorio, who asked me how it had gone once we were a safe distance from that civil service hack.

"I got 'em cold in Round One, Vito," I said. "If it's a Garden fight the referee stops it."

"Yeah," said the reformed Mafioso, "onny you got nine more rounds to go. You check 'em on that lose-one-lose-'em-all detail?"

"Yes, you had it right, only I'm not buying it."

"Uh huh—and the hung jury?"

"I laid off that. It's my hole card. I didn't want to tip my hand by raising that one."

"Good thinkin, counselor. The first stop's with the bride, right?"

Who else? Wife or not, Birdye was always my best friend.

Chapter 5 ••••••••••••••••••••••••••

I needed only the barest glance at my girl to tell that while it hardly seemed possible her spirits had taken a precipitous dip from the day before. My companion had no trouble detecting that either, so he left us alone and said he would drop in on the tailor.

"Want me to bring anything back?" he asked. "These threads of mine have pockets. How about a taste for the little woman?"

"Only if Hank came up with some Scotch, Vito," I said. "That's all Birdye ever drank."

"Any smokes?"

"She won't touch those filters. Right, baby?"

"I don't want anything." This was on the testy side. "And I don't see why you're drinking when you need a clear head."

"Your memory's going," I said. "Gin is what kept my head clear most of my life—and so far it has saved my bottom with those beards for two days running."

Leaving, Brother Vittorio told me he would take care of that new shroud for my father.

"You have to deliver it yourself?" I asked him. "There's got to be an old Western Union boy up here somewhere, no?"

"No, pal, we're usin United Parcel. More reliable. Don't worry about it."

With that he lumbered away, if you can imagine anybody lumbering on air, and I turned to Birdye.

"What's wrong, kiddo? I expected to find you more cheerful today. I'm loaded with good news."

"Like what?"

"I beat 'em clean on the first count. They didn't have one leg out of the whole twenty-four to stand on."

"Paul, let's not be silly about this. You know that nearly every count is more serious than that one. I don't want to play any games when this means so much to us."

"All right. No games. Can I buy a little smile?"

"Please be patient with me. I've had a very bad time since you were here yesterday."

I thought I'd try a switch.

"OK, if I can't buy a smile can I interest you in a spot of lunch on me?"

"Oh, come. Do I have to tell you that the men and women here, married or not, don't eat together?"

"Yeah, I know. They don't even eat each other. It's very depressing."

"Can't you skip that kind of crack? Tell me about the trial."

"I already have, Birdye. The beards didn't have enough in their black book to get that item voted out of a grand jury downstairs. Tomorrow I'm going to try to push them into combining the next two beefs to speed this thing up because it looks like such a drag."

"I can't believe you would do that, Paul."

"Why not?"

"Well, for one thing I doubt if it's a very good idea to come on like a

Philadelphia lawyer with that jury, but there's something much more important. You don't want to shorten your trial. You want the whole ten days."

"I do? Why?"

"Oh, please, I'd rather not talk about that right now. Just listen to me if it isn't too much trouble for a change, will you?"

I thought that crack was uncalled for but let it pass because Birdye had the blues so bad. You ask yourself what the blues are up above the blue. Very dark.

"OK, I'll think about it, warden," I said. "Now how about getting on to something more upbeat? You heard me mention my old man. I spent some time with him after I saw you yesterday."

"So I gathered. You must have been thrilled the way you two always got along. I never knew a father and son who were so inseparable."

"Yeah. We couldn't separate fast enough. Remember that story I told you about the time when I was six and he was running a grocery store in Newark during one of those endless garment strikes and I toddled down into the cellar after him and got left behind in that pitch-black hole with the rats?"

"Of course."

"Well, that was no accident, Birdye. That fucker left me down there on purpose. I just know it, always knew it."

"Very funny. What about your mother? Did you find out if she's here?"

"No way. She spent the last fifteen years of her life sick all the time and cursing God in all the known ways. Never let up."

"What a shame, but I don't imagine you found Harry all broken up. He was no more crazy about her than he was about anybody except his darling daughters—not counting Daisy, of course, after she married that Southern gentleman. Who else did you see?"

"Oh, I'll get around to that. I'd rather talk about us, since they seem to be holding a stopwatch on me the way you have it, Birdye. Why can't I get the chill off you? If you've got some fresh squawks wouldn't it be better to spill them and clear this clear air?"

"All right, I will. You didn't tell me Richie served four months in that horrible prison in Mexico City on a marijuana charge and you didn't tell me Leni's marriage broke up and her daughter's been living with her father."

"Good Christ, how do you know all that? You sure played it pretty dumb yesterday."

"Leni told Becky and Becky told Peggy Flanagan, that's how. I didn't want to tax you with it yesterday but it's too painful for me to hold it in. Isn't it kind of late for family secrets anyway?"

Ouch. We were on the most precarious nonfooting now. What else did my girl know, especially about Leni?

"Have a heart, Birdye," I said, "I didn't want to hit you with any downers right off the bat. I couldn't figure out what was going on because you weren't exactly flying, you know. You ask me anything you want now and I'll lay it on the line, inch by inch."

I didn't mean that. It was the riverboat gambler in me. In all our time together I had never slipped anything past that woman but the tiniest white fibs. Now if she knew the whole scoop on her daughter I was in trouble. I stood there quaking in my sneakers waiting to get banged with that but if Birdye did know that horror story, the whole of it, she wasn't going to lay it on me. The doll was still more concerned about my insides than her own.

"I'm sorry, Paul," she said now, eyes downcast. "I didn't mean to make it any harder for you. I know you did everything you could for the children. I'm sure you would have remarried except that you didn't want them to have any other mother after me, so I have no complaints. It's just the opposite."

(Catch that remarrying bit? You have now met the real Birdye. If I had told her once I told her a thousand times that if I ever had a second chance I'd marry the first babe I ever met who was a nymphomaniac and owned a liquor store.)

I wanted to take that woman in my arms and hug her to death—no, I mean just hug her like crazy—but this session was something more like a long distance call, almost as if I were on an overseas assignment or somewhere in the sticks and checking in at home.

"You're just as wonderful as ever, baby," I said. "More than I ever deserved, and I mean that. It comes right from my former heart."

Birdye elected not to dispute that.

Instead, out of left field, she brought up the matter of that former heart.

"You had that attack four years ago and you were in the hospital twice with it and never did a thing the doctors told you after that, Paul. The ulcer was one thing but I thought you were too intelligent to fool around when your heart started to go."

"Well, I don't want to argue that with you, except to say that I just wasn't going to live like a fucking invalid. I did cut down on the booze, not that I could ever buy the three-ounce-a-day rule my doctor laid on me—a man couldn't fill his Zippo lighter with that much—and I did get some more sleep. And I was off cigarets for almost two years and later quit the paper so the grind wouldn't kill me and went home and settled down with my typewriter, but if I knew I was going to see you again I might have conked out even faster. I told you I didn't leave anybody down there that ever really turned me on all that good. Believe me, kiddo, without the kind of love we had a woman's just someone to get your rocks off with, not much more."

"Paul, please. I wish you wouldn't keep telling me that. It makes me feel so guilty."

"Guilty? What a word to use at this moment. The guilt's all on the other shoe—I mean sneaker—but I think we can leave that for another day when Number Six comes up on the docket. The adultery bit. There's no way I'm going to hold out anything on you and no way I'm going to hold out on those judges, or elders or whatever the hell they are, and it's not because I'm afraid of any perjury charge to go with the rest of this junk. It's just because it's too late not to spill it all and take my lumps. From them, from you, from Him if it comes to that, although I don't know whether He's available for any heart-to-heart talks. But the big thing, honest, is you. I owe you too much to make believe I was an angel."

"No, you don't owe me anything. We had a wonderful life together. I was a very lucky girl."

"You have it all turned around. You're looking at the lucky one. I'd still be shooting craps on the rooftops and schoolyards in what they used to call the Borough of Universities—it's a jungle now—if it weren't for you. You took me where I went. I never wrote a line except for you, never laid out a front page except for you, never cared who liked anything I did except you. I lost all that in '61 and never got it back, or gave a damn, for that matter. If you needed witnesses and I knew how to wangle a furlough I could produce them in carload lots but, then, I had no idea I was headed this way. There wasn't any line on it, and that reminds me of something which might lighten this thing up a bit. Remember when that lovable Big Sam let me off the hook for seven hundred so we'd be able to pay the landlord and also have a few cents left over for the kids' milk money?"

The first faint glimmer of a smile.

"Of course," Birdye said, "but that other tall man said he had pockets in his shroud, so I would imagine Big Sam does too, although I have no idea what a nut like you would bet on up here. You can't even bet on the weather, because it never changes, and that golf course is not for golf, which you never found a way to lose your paycheck on because there wasn't any betting on that sport. Besides, these courses are just floating lunchrooms for the vegetarian types. If they ever put in a kitchen I'll be the first volunteer."

"And I'd be the second, baby. I'd go on K.P. or even latrine duty just to be around you. I would forswear all sin and live like a church deacon just to have another couple of thousand years with you—in bed or out."

Now the smile went.

"Paul, your problem is not how many *years* you have but how many *days*. It's eight after today. Eight."

"Why do you keep banging me over the head with that, Birdye? You make it sound like I'm an outbet when I'm the first Jewish boy ever thrown to the lions. Why not give it a chance and wait till the jury comes in? Maybe the least I can do is hang up those beards."

"I don't think there is such a thing here."

"And I don't think you could be any wronger. I just don't see how they can have one set of rules in this place called Paradise with a capital *P* and another one in the lower case paradise downstairs. It goes against the most elementary sense of justice and decency. Listen, I'm counting on it. I've been looking around in there for one or two jurors who may seem a little on the friendly side. I figure to find me somebody like that and work 'em right down to the last day."

No response, and anyway at that moment Brother Vittorio, a teeny bit wobbly, strolled in and out came a hooker of gin in a Styrofoam cup and some of those disgustingly healthy Carltons.

"I'm sorry, lady," he said to Birdye. "Our connection's fresh out of Scotch and also Chesterfields."

"That's quite all right, Vito," Birdye said. "I told you I didn't want anything, but you're very kind." Then, turning to me as I downed a pretty good slug of Beefeater on my empty head and lit up with one of my keeper's wooden matchsticks by striking it against the metal fasteners holding the laces on my sneakers. "Have you asked Vito if he knows whether Ed's here?"

She was talking about Ed Flynn, the best friend of all our adult years.

"That's Edward Patrick Flynn, Tiny," I said. "Irish as Paddy's pig, six-two and better looking than Bugsy Siegel or even Tyrone Power, not to mention the current crop of pretty boys like the Redfords and Newmans and that crowd, which is the new breed. We were reporters together and went all the way up together. He loved Birdye and we both loved him. It was the cleanest triangle in history."

"How did Mr. Flynn go?"

"There was a fire in his hotel room and he jumped out of the window to try to make a roof one flight down across the alley but missed," Birdye said. "He should be here. He was buried from St. Patrick's Cathedral."

"I'll chase him down for you the minute I get a blow, ma'am. It's no big deal."

"It's real important, Vito," I said. "He was our guy."

"Check. I'll get right on it, Paul, but don't we have to get movin on some other calls? I mean if you're done with the little woman, of course."

"I'm afraid so," I said. "OK, wife?"

"Sure. I'll be here tomorrow. I don't waste any time on shopping trips or run around in the car anymore. I've really settled down, sort of like a matron who just knits or watches television most of the time."

At last, the first touch of the old humor.

I felt so good I could have kissed my girl on those luscious lips.

Hell, I could have kissed her all over—except for Brother Vittorio being around.

I was always terribly shy about that sort of thing.

Chapter 6 ••••••••••••••••••••••••••••

Walking down that waterbed road without any water, my unarmed soulguard said some nice things about Birdye and I began to blabber.

"Vito, you haven't even met the real woman. She was one of a kind. She wasn't even sixteen when we met and I was hooked even though she held me off for two whole years and then it was two more before we could tie the knot. I mean I had to get up to editorial clerk on the old *Post* with a big twenty-five-dollar paycheck before we could set up housekeeping. Damn, that kid went to work in a hat factory to help furnish the place. Then we bought a baby grand on time—fourteen bucks a month—and she started teaching piano. She owned a medal she won in a citywide competition for high school seniors, so she had no trouble finding customers. Then, once the children were bigger, she knocked herself out trying to help the whores and junkies in that women's can on the Square in the Village, went to some school for interior decorators and had a whale of a business about to explode when the Big C got her. You can't possibly imagine what kind of babe that was—still is, although the chill might throw you off."

"Nah. I make the spot she's on. She don't know if you're here for the long pull or just passin through. I could tell what you two had right off the bat. It was the same with me and my Rosario. That's what keeps me goin in this deadass joint, because there's no way she don't show someday and when that day comes the round man hauls some vino outta one of them shrouds he uses as filin cabinets or you're gonna see him walkin around with a brand new face."

"Beautiful. You have any kids?"

"Does the Man have whiskers? I ain't the kind to blow my own horn but our oldest boy's a lawyer—for the defense, naturally—and I got one daughter who came outta one of them good Catholic colleges and she was teachin parochial school when I left. And the older one got married to a square guy, an insurance hustler, and had two bouncing bambinos almost as beautiful as me. I got no complaints, pal. Maybe I was one of the boys but I ain't ashamed of what's down there bearin the Pascaglia name. All because of my Rosario. The funny thing is she came out of one of the other Families—that rat Genovese, no less—but she was Golden Rule all the way. For the kids, I mean. Just couldn't do a thing with her Vito. But, hey, you got work to do. Where you wanna head first?"

I had to think about that for nineteen seconds.

Birdye had taken something out of me, so I wasn't up to any pretrial labors for my next bout in the arena. To top that, I was pretty well burned at myself for having to be reminded about Ed. Where the hell— oh, that filthy word again—was my head?

"I'll tell you, Vito," I said. "The most I wanna do is hang around Brother Henry's a while and then maybe find my man Flynn. How's that sound?"

"No big deal. I'll drop you at the tailor's and check a connection in the warden's office—well, the Department of Records, I shoulda said— and dig the guy out and hustle him over there."

"You can't do that," I said, bordering on the morose. "Birdye didn't tell you the whole thing about Ed. He was a bottle baby much of the time. That's how he happened to go out that window. The fire—it was in '47—was nothing, but he must have had an idea that he was Super- man or something and could make a loft building a good fifteen feet away and went down seven floors. I died the same day, Vito, because his last bottle of Jack Daniels came out of a tenner I lent him after we left a party in our publisher's penthouse. Anyway, the thing is he was one fighting Irish drunk and hit like the old Joe Louis or the new Ali or even that murderous Rocky Marciano. Both hands, so I can't get him back on the hard stuff because he might bust some heads around here just for the fun of going against a ghost or two."

"OK, so we do it the other way. I'll find out where the slugger's stashed—he ain't in no drunk tank, that's for sure—and pick you up. How's that?"

"Only what I expected from an oversized angel like you. Let us hasten to the mahogany."

I wasn't in the Godly Issue Saloon and Boutique much more than an hour, going easy on the gin because I didn't want Ed to see me loaded and get any ideas, when the big guy came bustling back in.

"It's onny a short haul," he told me. "Wanna bring any smokes?"

"Ed would puff on a bar rag if he could get it lit," I said. "He has to be dying for some coffin nails, if that's the way to put it."

Then I turned to Brother Henry, already half in the bag.

"Got a whole pack you can lay on me?"

Out came another deck of Carltons.

"Put it on my tab," I said. "I don't want to abuse your kindness, Hank."

The tailor responded with what we used to call a no-comment when I was in the news game. Still, deep down, not that I gave a darn (notice how I'm talking better now?), I knew I wasn't on the cuff in there because that businessman, sure as God made green apples, or whatever He made, had to be using some other cuff to jot down the grunt. My only question was whether he knew the current market in the more commonplace afflictions, like eighty-five cents for a pack of cigarets outside the discount stores and a booster of gin running around a deuce in your everyday joint up to three or even four bucks in the fancier spots where they bruised it with a whiff of vermouth and threw in a hunk of lemon or an olive on the house. Beyond that, I had no way of knowing, and cared even less, how much that con man was throwing on top for his services.

Walking over to the sin bin reserved for Ed, Brother Vittorio asked me what was on the boob tube nowadays. Still running them good Westerns like "Gunsmoke" and "Bonanza"? I told him no, it was mostly cops-and-robbers stuff, like Telly Savalas as the kind Lieutenant Kojak who never laid anything harder than a lollipop or a touch of sarcasm on the bad guys, Robert Stack in his forty-ninth rerun as Elliot

Ness in "The Untouchables," and the new lady cops. Angie Dickinson in "Police Woman" and three other dames in "Charlie's Angels." Also, Jack Klugman as a combination medical examiner and amateur detective in a show called "Quincy" and Raymond Burr not only still nailing the ne'er-do-wells in that Perry Mason series in reruns but also, out of a wheelchair, no less, in a thing called "Ironsides." I told Vito I didn't really know the TV scene that well because I was into my writing so hard. What about the soaps? Still red hot, I said, and the reformed gorilla told me he used to get a real bang out of those shows and never fooled with the gangster stuff because his Rosario didn't want their kids seeing that sort of thing.

"I usta drop into a movie house once in a while to see what the life was really like where I come from," he said, "but they all seemed like comedy shows to me."

So I told him he missed a few recent good ones, like the two-part *Godfather* and *The French Connection* one and two, but not much else. We also dipped into the massage parlor and porn scene, both of them calling forth some very strong strictures from my fellow stroller on that road without potholes, and suddenly—

There was Ed, just as beautiful as ever, receding brown hairline and all and none the worse for that fall—no surprise because the embalmers at Mr. Campbell's store had exceeded themselves on that job.

"You're the one guy I never expected to show," Ed said with those steel-gray eyes glowing. "You come up with some phony papers from a Mafia connection?"

"Careful, old buddy," I said. "Brother Vittorio here was a card-carrying member of that fraternity, not that he's all that sensitive about it."

"Why in Christ should he be?" Ed said. "In some ways it was cleaner, let alone better paying, than the racket we were in." The man mountain just smiled benignly as the playmate of all my springtimes went on. "But let's skip the small talk. How's our girl?"

"She's here," I said.

"Oh, no. What happened, Paul?"

"The cancer in the family. You knew that story. Her mother with the breast bit, then the sister in the backside and the other one in the brain, only Birdye had the worst of them. A thing called Krukenberg after some early Nazi. You don't want the ugly details."

"When?" Ed seemed utterly shattered.

"Fourteen years after you left our happy family."

"How did I cash in? That old prick in the morgue doesn't stock any clips or newspaper files."

"You must have dozed off with a live butt and dropped it on the A.M.'s you were supposed to be checking to see what we were going to do with our first edition, Ed," I said, remembering the Carltons and asking Brother Vittorio to hand them over. "You went out the window even with the old widow in the room under you screaming that the fire trucks were on the way and the super about to bust in with one of those sprays. You were going for a jump an Olympic gold medal winner couldn't make without a running start."

"I guess I had to be in the bag pretty good, Paul. Why didn't I just stagger out my door?"

"Simple. It had a lock you turned the key on from the inside, right? Well, your door was locked but the keys weren't in it. You stuck 'em back in your coat and either forgot or couldn't get to it if you tried."

"I'm sorry I brought it up. Let's get back to our girl. Is she OK?"

"I wouldn't say she's bubbling over, Ed. She's got the shakes because I'm up against what passes for a court in this holy establishment."

"That figures, but how does the kid look?"

"Only like the same little watch charm."

"I'd drink to that if I hadn't joined the local A.A. outfit after I signed the Golden Register. I gotta see Birdye. I always loved her almost as much as the Jewish bride who evicted me just because I wasn't home enough of the time. And speaking of looks, you put some years on, Paul. You must have made all the stops once you were on your own."

"Where's your Irish head? Ever know anybody who got younger working in that sewer for our sainted owner?"

"I guess not. You stay in touch with Debbie?"

"Not enough, Ed. She was still in the Brooklyn Heights house and teaching school the last time I talked to her."

"How are Rich and Leni doing?"

I filled Ed in on that twin saga, whereupon he elected to switch to another item, like how were the less reputable types in our town and was it still SRO in the Death House.

"Those days are over, buddy," I told him. "The chair went out of style in '63, put in moth balls as cruel and unusual punishment for the disadvantaged who couldn't buy the good lawyers. Capital punishment's pretty much down the drain now, courtesy of the Nine Old Men, but more and more states are battling like mad to get it back, not that we need it so much in Olde New York. All we had was around seventeen hundred and fifty homicides in my last semester, no more than about five a day."

"Good Christ. Wasn't it only around six hundred a year when I was around?"

"No, more like seven, around two a day, but it's been picking up at an adequate rate—nothing to be ashamed of, anyway."

"Beautiful. What a town."

Then Ed asked me about the paper I went to work on after seeing Pat O'Brien and Adolphe Menjou in the Hecht-MacArthur *Front Page* and deciding that I wanted to be a reporter like O'Brien's Hildy Johnson. I told him I was boosted from city editor to his job as executive editor after a while, held it too long, and left when the Gray Lady took her hand off the throttle, getting a little shaky by then (the throttle, not the hand) because the paper that sold for three cents when I started had skyrocketed all the way to twenty-five and wasn't worth that much to enough people.

"What about my gal Irene?" Ed asked, referring to the fabulous secretary who was his some-time roommate after the booze wrecked his marriage. "She still around?"

"No, she went off with that phony she knew who managed Rita Hayworth in the early days and something went sour there. Irene went out on the pill-and-whiskey bit one night."

"Gee, I'm sorry to hear that. Next to Debbie and our Birdye I guess I liked her the most."

"Yeah, but you wouldn't stay dry for her either, you Irish bum. You wouldn't have stayed dry for Cardinal Spellman, although he gave you a send-off in St. Pat's like you were once a choirboy there. All the names turned out, especially the pols looking to get their pictures in the papers."

A laugh from that prince among sinners.

"I'm glad I wasn't there for that one," he said. "I could never have kept a straight face."

"You were there, all right, but I guess you didn't care for the accommodations with no bar or anything and didn't stick around very long once the obsequies were over. You made it here without having to go before those stone faces in what passes for a courthouse without barred windows and guards carrying thirty-eights."

"Of course. Why wouldn't I after leading a life of absolute probity?" Ed was puffing on another one of those filters now. "By the way, what is this thing I'm losing my clean breath on? I don't feel anything."

"It's healthier for you, Mr. Flynn," Brother Vittorio put in.

"Thanks, but who says it's a cigaret?"

"The manufacturer, Ed," I said. "It turned out in the sixties that we were all going to meet the Maker ahead of our time if we didn't quit the filthy habit, so the industry went real big on filters. Also made 'em longer so you could puff on 'em longer and die slower."

"What caught up with you, Paul?"

"Natural causes, or I guess you could say unnatural. I mean my ticker went bad when I started to reach the so-called Golden Years but I made believe it never happened, so it happened again and that was it."

"What a damn shame. You had to have a lot of words left."

"Yeah. That's what I had—words. I was pretty much out of live broads and mostly making love to my typewriter." Now I turned to the large one to change the subject. "Vito," I said, "would you believe this guy was a college boxer?"

"I guess he coulda been inna heavies. He's got the built."

"Well, *paisan,* you're nearly right, only Ed wasn't on the varsity because he never made the gym up at Brown. Did all his fighting in the saloons or on the campus and then floated around on three or four papers before I got him settled down on my rag. Wet or dry, though, you're looking at one of the great reporters. Tracked down a killer in a Brooklyn gin mill one time when half the cops in town were out looking for him."

"Hope it wasn't nobody I knew," Brother Vittorio said without a touch of rancor.

"No, Vito," Ed laughed. "It was just your everyday murderer. The heaviest job we did in the organized crime department—Paul here worked it with me and a baby task force—was on Handsome Joe Adonis when he had all the Brooklyn pols eating out of his big mitts in that restaurant of his. We blew the whistle on all the guy's rackets, even the legit end, like how he came up with the contract for all the over-the-road hauling in the Northeast for Mr. Ford."

"You stopping there, buddy?" I put in. "Why don't you tell my keeper who drew the real tough one when that series started?"

"I was coming to that. Paul was sent out to Joe A's house to see if he felt like talking. You know how many times his Birdye called me to see if he survived that assignment, Vito? Maybe ten."

"What happened out at the house?" Brother Vittorio asked me.

What happened. Memory Lane. I tap on that modest frame dwelling befitting a man sweating out a living off a little restaurant and picking up some change on the side in extortion, shylocking, narcotics and a few odds and ends like that. I weigh in at a hundred-thirty with arms like cue sticks and that door is opened by a gent about five-by-five (was that a bulge under his sport jacket?). I say excuse me, sir, I am a reporter from the *Post* and my city editor sent me out to see if Mr. Adonis cares to make any comment on that series we started today, and Godzilla says I better get the fuck off that street because Mr. Adonis don't talk to no goddamn reporters. So I drive around to a phone booth and call my commanding officer, who knows no fear, and he tells me to hang there all day in case our man has a change of heart and wishes to offer us a rebuttal. Yes, sir. I hung, but it wasn't all that boring. Some kids started a stickball game and I got my tennis sneakers out of my trunk and begged leave to join them, having been a two-, three-sewer hitter in that sport when I was a younger boy. No problem, they were short one guy, and where does my side put me? In the outfield—square in the sights of Mr. Adonis's curtained windows. You know the dopey notions you can get in a spot like that. You're settling down under an easy fly and just as the Spalding reaches your sure hands a buffalo gun's poked out of one of those windows and you hit the concrete before the ball. Well, I really wasn't that nervous, although it did occur to me as that game dragged on that it wouldn't be the worst idea for me to check out, go get a blast or two, call my bride, and then settle down, way down, in my Chevy parked across from Joe A's place. I did no such thing, of course, because when you were working for Walter Bartlet Lister Esq. the dumbest thing you could ever do was to leave the scene of what might be your last assignment. I mean you either died for that city editor or your life wouldn't be worth living anyway. And so I slouched behind my wheel until the never-more-welcome darkness settled over the Borough of Kings—proprietor Mr. Joseph Doto, a/k/a Joe Adonis to the man in the street, the cops wearing the blinders and the more highly placed thieves who needed his benediction to get elected to public office and fill up the tin boxes in their bank vaults.

"You couldna got hurt," said my soulguard when I wound up that only slightly overdramatized saga. "Nobody in our crowd ever laid a glove on newspaper guys. Wasn't the last one when Al Capone had Jake Lingle rubbed out because he was onna take and also puttin too much in his paper?"

"That lapse in your knowledge of history leaves me shocked, tall man," I said. "You have overlooked the time one of the less nice types in your set—Mr. Johnny Dio—had some lye tossed into Victor Riesel's eyes after Vic said some bad things on the Barry Gray talk show."

"Hey, you're right, I forgot that one, but maybe there's something you don't know about it. The messenger boy who put out Riesel's lights got wasted himself pretty fast because he done the job for a lousy five hunnert and then started screamin for five Big Ones when he found out your man was such a big-name columnist."

"No, I did know about that, Vito," I said. "Also, Vic wasn't my columnist when it happened. I just started him out. He was on the *Mirror* when he got his friend Dio mad. Now ask the Irisher about the time we had some poor bastard an inch away from the hot seat."

Ed roared.

"You recall the Easter Sunday murders, Brother?" he asked. "It was in the late thirties. Some nutty artist went wild and killed a girl named Ronnie Gedeon—we called her a model until it turned out that she just posed for cheesecake pictures—and her mother and then jammed an ick pick into a male boarder of theirs. I picked up a tip on some chauffeur in the neighborhood known only as Frenchy who was supposed to have the hots for Ronnie and we ran down the bag he was banging up there in the East Fifties. I fished a blood-stained ice pick out of her kitchen and my helper here dug out a pair of Frenchy's drawers with stains on them that suggested he might have had his jollies on that visit to the Gedeon place, so we passed our treasure along to a homicide dick we knew and the paper went to town with it."

"And you had the wrong guy?" Brother Vittorio asked.

"Vito, we had the wrong guy, the wrong ice pick and the wrong shorts. The police lab turned up red wine on the pick and just plain piss on the shorts, but we took it all back the next day and Frenchy—don't ask me why—never sent any lawyers after us. They could have walked away with our presses."

"Ed," I said, enjoying all this so immensely, "our friend had to know about Nick Montana. He ought to hear the Beverly Reynolds story."

"Only if you tell it, Paul. It might arouse a certain hunger in me I've been fighting all these years."

I told. Nick Montana was a whorehouse operator who had beaten two trials on hung juries and seemed to be home free because the D.A. then, a Tammany hack, said he couldn't find Miss Reynolds, his key witness, even with two of his very best assistants scouring the whole landscape for the lost hooker. So Mr. Lister put Ed and me on it and we tortured the phones among the higher-class types we knew and in no time at all the Irishman was in Chicago with the lady a willing prisoner in a flea-bag hotel and more than happy to fly back with him and expose her legs on a witness stand for a third time. The net: the vice lord who had exploited her charms and kept most of the take copped a plea and settled for a three-year term and the red-faced D.A. tried to get Ed and Mr. Lister indicted for obstruction of justice only to find that no grand jury would agree that a newspaper which had done his job for him could be assessed with any such crime. On top of that, the sleazy prosecutor had to dig into his own treasury to fly Miss Reynolds back to Chicago, where she had by then switched from selling her overworked body to slinging chili.

And so it went, into the night (if you had a watch, that is), with Brother Vittorio absolutely charmed by us two playmates. We touched every base from the days when Ed was on the *Journal* and I was on the *Post,* to our time together on the city desk and in the Washington Bureau before that and right down to the tragic end.

When we were just about out of minutes, Ed asked how he could find Birdye, saying he had never been in the women's dorm—an upset which could only have been made in Heaven, of course.

"It's too hard to chase down by yourself, Mr. Flynn," the tall man told him, "but if you want I'll run you over later when Paul's goin over the coals, onny I gotta be back at the courthouse by noon or blow this soft touch."

"That's fine, Vito," Ed said. "And would you take these empty straws back? I guess I'll stay off the butts if this is the way they're making them now."

"I wouldn't quit on it. Paul tells me you're a Lucky Strike customer and in this operation you never know. A carton of them could show anytime."

"Good enough, but how do I pay for them? I got here without a plugged nickel because I must have left that hotel room in my pajamas."

"It's on my tab, as usual, buddy," I said.

"You open up a charge account or what?"

"No, none of the retailers up here will go for the slow-pay bit. I happened to go out with my pants on and I was holding pretty good. What do you want to do about Mr. Shor?" I had mentioned that session hours earlier. "He can't get around on that bum leg."

"I'll check in with Toots after Birdye. Is it very far, Vito?"

"Small detour is all, but I can point you there. We gotta move now."

"Let's go," Ed said. "I just hope Toots didn't bring along any of the grunts I must have left in that oasis."

"It's not to worry," I said. "The retired innkeeper has the same interest in the coin of the realm as he always had. Zip. He's content enough to be among the living dead now, or is it the dead living?"

We left Ed with Birdye, who dissolved into tears at the sight of him, and pretty soon I was back in the star chamber, where the main Peter granted my motion to join the next two counts—"time permitting"— and the clerk was directed to do his thing.

"Thou shalt not take the name of the Lord thy God in vain; for the Lord will not hold him guiltless that taketh his name in vain."

"Remember the Sabbath day, to keep it holy."

The prosecutor:

"Do you fully understand the import of those two commandments, Mr. Sann?"

"I believe so, sir."

The other guy didn't look as if he believed so at all.

"Be that as it may, I propose to expand upon Commandment Number Two lest you are perchance unaware that it imposes upon all the children of God an absolute commitment to hold the name of the Holy Father in complete, total and unswerving reverence at all times. I underscore those last two words. What they connote is that one may not resort to swearing or blasphemy on the pretext of some special condition such as, let us say, anger, frustration, rejection, a setback in the achievement of one's life goals, financial reverses or what-have-you. We shall proceed now."

Time out while the man leafed through page after page of that monstrous ledger. I know I exaggerated its dimensions earlier, but this is something you could bet your own nightshirt on: it was no smaller than the blackboards the NFL coaches use to diagram plays for their sweating, filthy-rich charges. Even a little wider, indeed, and I had to marvel over the ease with which the prosecutor handled it, although for all I knew there might have been an easel under it, but now the assault was on.

"The record before me, Mr. Sann, literally abounds in instances—*ad infinitum,* verily—of the most clear-cut and specific situations in which you have used the name of the Lord in vain. While this Tribunal is not unaccustomed to encountering such lapses, I am impelled to observe that yours would appear to be a most special case even were I to put it in its mildest possible terms."

"Objection," I said, glaring at Peter the First. "That statement prejudices my case almost beyond repair."

"Overruled," the chair roared in a gentle whisper. "The petitioner will be afforded ample opportunity to enter his defense."

"Exception," I roared back, whereupon Peter on the Far Right opened up.

"Sir, you have amply demonstrated your quite remarkable acquaintance with the law for a person bereft of any university degrees in this field or, for that matter, any other [AUTHOR'S NOTE: wasn't that last fucking crack uncalled for?] and yet you appear to be unaware that exceptions may be taken only for purposes of appeal, whereas you have been advised that there are no appeals from the judgment of this the highest Tribunal."

Since the mother had kicked that door open, why not try to stroll through it?

"Thank you," I said, "but I do have some knowledge of Judaeo-Christian teachings, like when one is so fortunate as to be granted passage to this eternal sanctuary he is permitted to see the Heavenly Father face to face. Does that in itself not constitute an appeal which cannot be denied?"

The man in the Brooks Brothers sheet glanced sideways at his D.A.

"Mr. Sann," quoth that beard ever so dryly (and was I myself ever dry at that moment), "the knowledge which you have professed falls somewhat short in situations such as yours. You do not happen to enjoy any entitlement to an audience with the Supreme Being short of your formal admittance to the Holy City, and you are at this stage nothing more than a petitioner whose credentials are under challenge."

I remembered a time long ago when the Celtics set a new record by winning their first eighteen games and then blew a close one on the road and I called Auerbach to offer my solace. "It's no big deal," Red told me, although I knew he was only inches away from suicide. "Win one, lose one." So I took my fall with the most abject grace I could summon up from the depths.

"I'm sorry, I didn't know that," I said. "May I ask now whether you propose to read the citations you have glossed over so that I can deal with them individually?"

"I do not, and the reason should be starkly apparent to you. The commandment at issue applies with equal force to the members of this body as it does to any particular petitioner. The name of the Lord cannot be used in vain in this chamber any more than it can be used in vain elsewhere in His universe. Isn't that rather elementary for a man of your background, however irreligious?"

"Objection," I snapped.

"The petitioner will state his grounds," said Peter the First.

"This objection is twofold, Your Honor. If I cannot hear the allegations against me, chapter and verse, I fail to see how I can properly defend myself against them. Beyond that, I submit that the reference to me as 'irreligious' is clearly prejudicial without any foundation having been laid for it."

Pete slipped that one to the charmer on the right.

"Mr. Sann, the first part of your demurrer is so utterly fatuous as to be unworthy of discussion. As for that 'irreligious' reference of my colleague's, you yourself laid the foundation for it when you characterized yourself so glibly as a nonbeliever. Further, the rules in force herein require a petitioner to confront any allegations against him, explicit or otherwise, without resort to time-consuming legal technicalities."

"In that case," I said. "I will withdraw the second part of my objection but I must stand on the first as wholly valid in my own understanding of the law on Earth as it must—or should be, at any rate—in Heaven."

"Well spoken," said the smirking, self-assured sonofabitch with all the cards. "However, it might be well for you to bear in mind that you shall hear any number of specific citations—paraphrased, necessarily. Thus your fear of having to conduct your defense in total darkness is groundless. Saint Peter?"

"The multiple objection is overruled. The prosecutor may proceed."

And did that poisoned arrow ever proceed. This narrative would outweigh the *Encyclopaedia Britannica* (1974 edition, thirty volumes) if I so much as glossed over what droned forth from those frigid lips.

Just for openers, it turned out that I had very seldom moved a piece of less-than-perfect news copy or locked up a late edition without uttering one profanity or another or even coining a new one. Check. And shall we go back a step now, like a few decades? In Morris High I had been reported to the principal on at least one verifiable occasion when some math teacher overheard a certain four-letter word issuing from my mouth. (I always was better with words than math, you know.) But the heavy artillery was just being wheeled into place. The man had stacks of prose from my own books with which to clobber me. For example, there was that one on the twenties literally awash in foul language in my coverage of the gangland bloodletting during the Prohibition wars and all the other dirty linen in the decade in which the nation's morals began to sink into the morass. This was very deep water, so deep I had trouble staying afloat, although once I saw the way this beef was going I thought I had a quick out: wherever proscribed words appeared in that work of history, which I reminded my tormentors was on many college lists, they were not mine but rather direct quotes from the principals involved. Peter on the Far Right swept that under the rug, or whatever, with one swift sentence.

"The volume in question bore the name of this petitioner and no other person."

Stiffed on that score, I was belted with my recounting of the classic confrontation between the silver-tongued William Jennings Bryan and Clarence Darrow in the Scopes evolution trial in Tennessee in 1925, but what in the fucking name of G-- was wrong with that straight narrative? Oh, well, the words were not at issue, it turned out. The tone itself made eminently clear my distaste for the Bible-blathering Bryan and all but slavish admiration for the agnostic Darrow. Oh. Onward and downward, fathom by fathom. In my recreation of the Sacco-Vanzetti ordeal I had not only cited a verboten out-of-court reference ascribed to the Hon. Webster Thayer of the Massachusetts bench but even used it in the big type as the title on that chapter ("THOSE ANARCHIST BASTARDS"). Again, swimming against the tide when that never was one of my better sports, I submitted that I didn't say it, the judge did, and that went down the chute. Along the same booby-trapped line, my essay on Scott Fitzgerald as well as another on Hemingway in a later work carried not a glimmer of distaste for the explicit blasphemy writ by either of those towering novelists. What was there left to argue? Back to some things in the Darrow-Bryan category: my account of the rise and fall of Aimee Semple MacPherson evidenced nothing but contempt for the labors of a woman in the service of the Lord. Right, pal? No. I wouldn't hold still for that kind of rigged game. Brown bedroom eyes spitting anger, I reminded the heavenly lynch party that Sister Aimee herself had brought nothing but shame upon the Son, the Father, the Holy Ghost and her own parishioners when she slipped away from her International Church of the Four-Square Gospel in Los Angeles in 1926 with her congregation's hefty radio operator, made the motel scene for thirty-two days and then came up with a bogus kidnaping story to cover it up. How many of the Commandments were laid waste in that process? The counterpuncher took care of that:

"If the Tribunal please, I would suggest that the petitioner now be advised that Sister Aimee Semple MacPherson is not on trial in this chamber."

Check. Shall we now take up P. Sann's reportage in the matter of Father Divine?

My pleasure, gentlemen.

Was it not commonly known that Harlem's self-anointed savior had not only stripped the faithful bare of all their worldly possessions, refused to account to the tax man for the fortune amassed in that process and also casually discarded the first Mother Divine for a party a good deal younger and, er, more shapely while counseling his own flock against indulging in any amorous exertions within or without his assorted "heavens" whether lawfully wedded or not? How many Commandments shot down in that process?

The *consigliere* again:

"I am now impelled to submit that Father Divine is not on trial before this body."

And from Peter:

"Mr. Sann, you would do well to abandon your present tactics."

"I am sorry, Your Honor, but may I be permitted to interject an observation which this Tribunal might in its wisdom accept as relevant?"

"Proceed."

"Thank you. I have reference to a scandal commonly referred to as Watergate which led my own country to its worst Constitutional crisis a few years back. In the White House tapes made public at that time there were any number of explicitly profane references from the lips of President Richard M. Nixon himself and in the media I was among those who printed or broadcast those forbidden words. I raise this issue on the assumption that the prosecutor himself surely intends to bring it forth."

I expected the next voice to come from the far right, and I mean far, because I had that guy down as a Nixon-Agnew Republican who more than likely listed such GOP stalwarts as Ronald Reagan and Barry Goldwater as pinkos, but it was the prosecutor who stepped to the plate.

"Your Honor," he said, "for the purpose of expediting this proceeding I shall refrain from citing any instances of blasphemy flowing from the pages of this petitioner's journal."

I didn't count that as a home run off a Sandy Koufax (just an average Jewish pitcher, after all) or a Nolan Ryan, or even a basket laid in against the likes of a Bill Russell, Wilt Chamberlain or Kareem Abdul-Jabbar, but it did lift my sagging spirits. Oh, about ten seconds' worth, let's say, because the man—no busher, as previously noted—was about to lead me into a mudhole wider than the Grand Canyon:

"Mr. Sann, the record now amply reflects your affirmation that in the instances in which irreverent language appears in your works of history said language issued not from your quill but from the mouths of others. Putting that factor aside for the moment, I now wish to inquire into a volume of yours not factual in context bur rather in the fictional genre."

Ouch. Talk about taking one below the belt when you left your metal cup in the dressing room.

My only published novel, a top nonseller of the mid-seventies read by my editor, my son, the honey-tinged blond who was my weekend roommate at the time, my helper Helene who made me that connection with Sister Margaret Mary, Lisa Steele, one of my sisters and perhaps two or three strangers, was about a caper pulled off by some angry bookmaker to empty out the city's Off-Track Betting offices with homemade win tickets. The cast included one (1) pure Catholic girl violated by the bookie's Hebrew first lieutenant, a pair of dirty-talking hoods imported from Chicago to keep the necessary OTB coconspirators in line, two honest whores (were there any other kind?) and a tough Irish detective who talked like a tough Irish detective.

Were *those* all *my* words? That novel had my name on it.

Yes, sir.

Literary license? No. Instead I went to *nolo contendere,* which comes down to no contest reduced from the Latin.

Thanks, old chap. Now shall we go back a step to another P. Sann effort, circa 1967 and on the next Spring list in an updated edition? In a segment of that one I had dealt with the evangelical scene, led by the Reverend Billy Graham, on to the Armstrongs *père* and *fils,* on to the growing army of the Lord's modern-day Messengers hauling in the big bucks not with the old pass-the-plate method but with their enormously expensive television and radio huckstering, on to the Born-Again crowd. Here I was hit with some excerpts even with that revised version only in galleys and yet to reach the stores. Did that one not exhibit a clear distaste, even contempt, for the men and women valorously straining every fiber of their beings to bring people to Christ? Well, who reads what and how? Even with my sneakers in the flames, I had answers to burn.

Item: All the ducked questions over the gold pouring into the soul-savers' coffers.

Item: Herbert W. Armstrong's Worldwide Church of God pressed by a West Coast prosecutor over big bills suddenly moving in multi-million dollar real estate deals.

Item: Straight entertainment, just plain old show biz, all but drowning out the Message on that booming TV-radio circuit.

Item: How the incumbent president's own Sister Ruth had linked hands with the smut-peddling Larry Flynt when he embraced the Savior while he continued to cash in both on the pornography in his magazines and the kinky sex products of his own manufacture advertised therein.

Item: How the Reverend Sun Myung Moon espoused explicit anti-Semitic doctrine—the Jew as Christ-killer—while proclaiming the Second Coming and salvation for *all*.

Item: Had I not written in approving terms of the Reverend Oral Roberts setting up a splendid university in Oklahoma? Not wishing to see any fresh coals poured on the fire in that segregated haven, I skipped the fact that the Roberts educational factory sheltered very few black faces except on its basketball team.

Withal, borrowing from Mr. Nixon's cleaner terminology, it was perfectly clear that nothing was helping my cause, and now that crafty prosecutor, keeping me off balance with one switch after another like a prizefighter going southpaw on you between rounds, brought up my Auerbach book. You won't believe it, but the man cited an actual count on the bad words in that one—all quotes, of course.

I was on the point of tossing in a fresh objection when the bomb fell.

Referring to his ledger, the prosecutor read a memo I had written to Dorothy Schiff eleven years earlier:

> I have made my Decision for Christ. Please accept my resignation as of two weeks from this date.

I would have hit the ceiling in that open-air torture chamber even if it happened to be cooled by those antique whirling fans that could chop a man's head off. But, then, there was no ceiling.

"Objection," I thundered. "That memo was never sent to my publisher. It was nothing more than a piece of frippery which I filed away."

"Do you wish to deny that you committed that memorandum in mockery of the Son of God to writing?" Saint Peter gently inquired.

"No, Your Honor, just that it constitutes a personal document not admissible in this proceeding because its very acquisition violates a commandment we haven't come to." I was losing my steaming-hot cool now. "I cited the matter of illegal search and seizure on my first day here. I now dare to invoke another, even more reprehensible item: theft, simple theft."

Well, here comes Peter on the Far Right, scowling:

"Outraged almost beyond words, if the chair will bear with me, I submit that the petitioner is striking at the very underpinnings of this Tribunal."

And now, for the first time, a brand new voice.

The third Peter from the left:

"Your Honor, may I offer an observation?" A nod from the main beard. "I do believe that Mr. Sann appears to have a valid point. With this record already replete on the commandment at hand, does this body truly require the use of a purely collateral document unseen by the person to whom it was addressed?"

Saint Peter, blessed with a surprising silence from the right:

"The chair overrules both objections without prejudice to either side lest we become mired down in what at best appears to be a tangential issue, however distasteful its context."

Score one, and did I ever need it, for the defense.

The good Pete again:

"We are but moments away from the hour of adjournment, rendering academic the petitioner's motion to join Commandments Number Two and Number Three. I shall entertain a like motion on the morrow."

"Thank you, sir," I said, but I was looking at that beard way over on the left.

Outside, Brother Vittorio welcomed the dead Paul Sann as if he had just died again.

"What's the long face, pal?"

"Vito, I just got put through a working over you never could have dished out when you were taking your basic training as an enforcer. I mean both kneecaps. Any red stuff showing on my bedsheet?"

"No way. They got no baseball bats in there."

"Maybe not, but they really wiped the floor, or whatever, with what's left of this broken hulk. Believe me, they knocked the dead shit out of me this time."

"I'm real sorry to hear that. Where you want the remains delivered? Back to your pretty bride?"

"No, no. Let's see if we can break the course record to the tailor's. It's either that or the gas pipe for me."

"Don't blow any time hunting down one of them. Up here it's all what they call solar energy, whatever that is."

"I should have known, Tiny," I said. "Then it may have to be the rope."

"That's two other problems," Brother Vittorio came back, a broad smile creasing his creased features. "There's no belts onna shrouds except for the *capo di tutti capi* himself and no place to swing from, so let's cut it, huh? You'll feel a lot better once you down a couple and slide over to the little woman's."

That sweet Sicilian couldn't possibly have been wronger. Still, I liked him so much I was glad he had never come up against a courthouse killer like the fucker who had left me on the canvas with my former lifeblood dripping from my battered lips.

Chapter 7 •••••••••••••••••••••••••••••

The gin, and I'm not sure the slippery Hank wasn't cutting it with Perrier water in that speakeasy by now, didn't help me at all. Nor did a little surprise produced by our host. Dipping into his Top Secret stores, he came up with a deck of that Tareyton Ultra Low-Tar King, number five on the government list of the real goodies. Tar: 2 milligrams. Nicotine: 0.1. Menthol, no less, and passing over the 263,732 yellow memos dropped on my head by Dolly Schiff while I was the chief operating officer in her boiler room I couldn't tell you what burned me more. Still, a soldier sent into the front lines either takes what's coming to him or pops a few into his C.O.'s back and beats a quiet retreat, but I wasn't that kind. Standing over to the side while the two Brothers talked about the opening Wall Street prices or the ball scores, or whatever, I swallowed that menthol without letting loose a single oath as I fell to some serious brooding about the Fortunate Isles.

Fortunate Isles?

The way I had read it that meant a rent-free or surely rent-controlled getaway where the souls of us favored mortals—all duly blessed or we're bumped off that flight and left in the takeoff lounge with the bars all closed for the night—live happily ever after. No more scrounging for the buck, no hassles with those assles in Internal Revenue, no Ms.'s fleeing your hearthside in anger over some imagined grievance (why do they slam the door so hard when love leaves with them?), no more fears about strangers dropping in on you with a switchblade or a Saturday Night Special, no chasing after the richnik in the duplex because his rent check bounced again, no more dentists using triphammers and asking you questions with your mouth stuffed with cotton tabs and the saliva drain not working, no more fretting over whether some nut in the Kremlin is going to soak up too much vodka and press the button, no more dirty looks from the old couple at the next table who happen to know your cigaret is giving *them* cancer instead of you, no more tiptoeing around so you don't plant your boots into what the dog lovers left for you, no more concern over who's supposed to be making it with Jackie or Bianca Jagger or the runaway Mrs. Trudeau, or who has slung the new lasso around studs like Warren Beatty or Burt Reynolds, or whether Jimmy Carter has any overpaid helpers turning on behind his back instead of getting high on Born-Again holy water, no more senseless irritation because Roy Cohn picked up seven new well-heeled clients after the Godfather Gambino got blown away, no more sweat because cat food is beginning to cost more than people food, no more *Times* obit pages with too many good citizens on them that you knew (all younger), no more calls to the Sanitation Embassy to inquire whether the garbage is ever going to be picked up again or left for the rats, no more junk mail, no more sour taste because it turned out that Eleanor Roosevelt switched to the lesbo side after Franklin gave *his* heart to her ex-social secretary or Joan Crawford was the worst mother who ever lived or Errol Flynn was a switch-hitter and German spy on the side while he was killing so many Nazis on the silver screen that he made John Wayne look like a pantywaist in his sallies against the Indians, no more wasted seconds over whether the Jesuit Jerry Brown was really living it up with the high-flying Linda Ronstadt who was no stranger to the happy dust you take through your nose.

My keeper broke into that semipainful reverie.

"Don't you wanna roll, pal? We been here maybe an hour."

"Let us take our leave, good Brother," I said, but I was beginning to know my way around the misnamed Fortunate Isles and quickly sensed that he was pointing toward Birdye's stand-up boudoir. "If you're heading me for my wife," I told him, "we're on the wrong expressway. I don't want her to see me in this mood."

"What happens if you don't show? Ain't that gonna bug her even worse?"

"Yes and no. Maybe Birdye'll figure they started their own daily up here and Pete's got me running it. I wrote a few selling headlines in my time."

"Aw, quit it, Paul. You gotta get yourself outta the dumps. Whadd'ya wanna do—start your homework on the next counts?"

"I don't have no homework, teach."

"How come? You draw a postponement?"

"No, but it's only the Holy Day and the Mom-and-Pop junk coming up. There's nothing I have to do on those and I doubt if you could get faded on Number Five if you were looking for some action. I don't mean any reflection on the life you chose, Vito, but I never put anybody away except with my typewriter or a front-page zinger once in a while and I can't believe the sainted beards would bang me with a manufactured case in that department."

"You got that straight. They don't flake nobody in there. You either done it or you didn't."

"I'll buy that, goombah. They haven't hit me with a wrongo yet, although they did miss a whopper this morning when they were reading me back my own books with the naughty words X'd out."

"What was that?"

"Remember Virginia Hill, the mob's satchel carrier?"

"You don't forget a piece of tail like that, pal. You ever run with her?"

"Never got that lucky. The closest I ever came was with a reformed burlesque queen, size forty-four, who wanted me to write her bio and turned out to be the best mechanic I ever ran into. A pure barracuda."

"Did'ja write that one?"

"There was no way, Vito. Nobody but a one-way queer would leave that enormous round bed with the mirror on the ceiling to go play with that lady's old portable, but let's get back to Miss Hill. She mothered herself off in Austria around '66 but first she dropped a line to the IRS ferrets who had been on her ass for years and said 'Fuck you and the whole United States Government' and I quoted it in something they were reading to me in there but the Lord's D.A. either blew it or gagged on it, I don't know which."

"Shame. I always hated to hear a dame use bad words. So where we goin?"

"Well, what I wanna do the most is haul into the nearest pizza joint, or maybe a Nathan's, that has beer and a machine with real cigarets, but since we're both walking around short for the moment I have a few other ideas to ring in on you. There's some people I'd like to see— men people, that is."

"Like who?"

"Can we go uptown to the local Harlem?"

"If you got the legs. Who do you wish to see, master?"

"Mostly Martin Luther King Jr."

"Good enough. Hang a left here."

I was just making a small joke when I said 'uptown' but, man (and Ms. too), was that ever uptown. We must have walked three hours to get to the black ghetto and then lost another forty-five minutes or so before we could get anybody who would direct two honkies to Dr. King's heavenly ministry. I had never met the man, although we did have some mutual friends and he was always high on my paper.

"Dr. King," I opened up, "it is a privilege for me to meet you after all these years. You left an enduring mark on our society."

The minister, so different without his mustache, forced a smile plainly underlaid with a deep sadness.

"Yes indeed, Mr. Sann," he said. "I left my mark. I had a dream and when I actually did get to the mountaintop I found that Mr. James Crow had reached it ahead of me. You know the inscription on that massive crypt where they laid these weary bones when I was only forty-nine, don't you?"

"I do indeed, sir," I said. "Used a picture of it in a book on the sixties, in fact. It said 'Free at last, free at last. Thank God Almighty I'm free at last.' "

"So it did," said the little giant who had laughed in the face of death (and Mr. Hoover's wiretaps as well) for so many years. "And I have been asking myself ever since that spring day back home in Atlanta how wrong mere mortals can be. Is it even remotely conceivable to you gentlemen that not even an assassin's bullet can purchase a black or any of the other oppressed minorities the freedom for which so much blood has been shed?"

The ringing, melodious, stentorian tones were missing from that poignant statement, I thought, as I glanced at Brother Vittorio to see how that word "assassin" went down with him. The ex-mobster not only failed to wince but, evidently moved, stepped in with an answer.

"You got the short end up here, Reverend," he said. "That's for sure. I'm more of a long-termer in this place and I never understood this setup."

"Thank you, sir," said Dr. King, turning to me: "Mr. Sann, I assume you left that other vale of tears only recently. How was Coretta?"

"Only one of our country's proudest adornments, Dr. King," I said.

"I can't recall a single event of any social consequence—and I'm not limiting this to the color issue, you understand—to which that magnificent woman has not lent her support. I don't mean signing petitions and that sort of thing. I mean getting out there in the trenches—right down to the end with the Vietnam protests and the furor over a hush-hush war we were waging in Cambodia until Mr. Nixon and Henry Kissinger finally decided enough was enough in '73, into the brand new outcry over the nuclear plants poisoning the landscape, and all the stops in between. I don't know where she finds the hours or the strength. If you think my keeper here—I'm on trial now, by the way—is a tall man I make him a dwarf alongside Mrs. Martin Luther King. She's a one-woman movement for everything that's good and just."

"How very gracious of you to say that. I've been out of touch because I spend so many agonized hours here wondering whether it was all worth it. But," the minister hastened to add, "I would not want you or the good Brother to misread that. I have not given up the fight and never will. It is just so difficult when one is totally segregated and there is no public forum, no arena in which to build up the kind of ground swell which won us our mild successes in the civil rights revolution . . . . So difficult."

Overcome with emotion, I asked the man whether I could recite something he put on tape not all that long before James Earl Ray took the contract to kill him.

"You have that committed to memory, Mr. Sann? My, my, that is flattering."

"Dr. King," I said, "I can read you back some morsels from your Nobel Prize speech but that tape played at your funeral seems more appropriate to me right now. What you wound up with was 'I'd like for somebody to say that Martin Luther King Jr. tried to love somebody . . . that I did try in my life to clothe the naked . . . that I did try in my life to visit those in prison. And I want you to say that I did try to love and serve humanity.' Well, sir, I just want to say that you did all that and more and left behind a better America than you were born into—however imperfect to this day—and nothing can take that away from you. You were—are, I should say—truly a man for the ages. If they let me stay up here, you have a volunteer. I hope I'm not the first."

The minister took my hand.

"No, Mr. Sann, you are not the first. There are good people here—not the least of them John and Bob Kennedy and even Lyndon Johnson, who proved to be an even more dynamic advocate in the cause of equality—but as I mentioned before we are confronted with that all but impenetrable barrier. I am referring again to the total absence of any avenue of meaningful communication."

I was about to ask why he wasn't going one-on-one with the Almighty Himself but thought that might be either out of line or the rudest possible kind of prying, so I held back.

"Dr. King," I said, "I've been a gambler in my time. I would like to say that if I was still into that kind of nonsense I'd stake my mortgage on you no matter what the odds."

Now I got a smile without all that hurt.

"That is a most generous statement, my friend. I want to express my deepest appreciation to you for making the long journey to this ghetto to pay a call on me when your own time must be so precious at this moment. I happen to have some knowledge of the agony you must be enduring. Adam Powell and Paul Robeson both had to undergo the most soul-searching ordeals before that Tribunal—the Reverend for his style of life outside of his church and the great basso for embracing those godless Russians—but let me thank you for coming by. I don't have too many people dropping in on me these days."

I took that as a signal that our time was up but there was something I needed to tell the man.

"Sir," I said. "There are two items I neglected to mention. Outside of Montgomery today there's a road called the Martin Luther King Jr. Expressway—and that's the least of it. There's been a movement on for years now to declare a national holiday in your name."

The minister grasped my hand.

"How nice, Mr. Sann," he said, "but the last thing I ever wanted was my name on any streets or buildings or, for that matter, any national holiday named King. For me, the word was always freedom, not King."

"That's some kind of man, Paul," Brother Vittorio told me as we left. "I'm real glad you took me on this hike. Wanna hunt down them two he mentioned—Powell and that Robinson guy?"

"No, Vito," I said. "The Reverend Mr. Powell wouldn't be too thrilled to see me because I never let him off the hook when he was ripping off Congress and playing footsie in Bimini with one cunt or another on my taxpayer dollars, and I never knew Paul Robeson. The guy I'd like to say hello to while we're in this section of town is Louis Armstrong. That beautiful wall-to-wall face could cheer me up no end."

"You mean Satchmo, huh? No big deal. Them music men hang together just as if they was still playin. It's on our way back, in fact, but don't tell me you're really skippin the missus all day or I could lose my temper, pal."

"Sorry, not today. We catch Satchmo's act and then I'd like to check in with the brothers Kennedy."

"I don't know about that. You could need an appointment to see them two."

"No kidding. Well, my own schedule happens to be too tight for making dates, so I'll take my chances. Find me Satchmo first. He once did an album called 'Louis and the Angels' and I'm just dying—dead if you want—to see how that worked out for him."

Even at that moment we could hear a mighty chorus belting out one of my favorite spirituals, "Sometimes I Feel Like a Motherless Child," in a swinging, jazz style, and there was no question whose voice led all the rest. Mr. Armstrong himself. We quickened our pace and ran into perhaps as many as a hundred people banked in a circle and beginning to scatter as a voice rang out, "Take five." Louis. Who else? I went up to the corpulent music maker and presented myself as a long-time fan new to the Holy City and the Man without the Golden Horn beamed.

"Mighty nice of you to drop by with this short dude," said the old master, as jovial as ever. "I can't say I've seen too many white folks since I played my last club date seven, eight years back, but we gotta go in high. I give these cats more than five and they wander off on me. How's things in that other heaven?"

"Nothing to write home about, Mr. Satchmo," I said. "How are you doing?"

"Oh, I have no bodily complaints but I wish I'd thought to carry a horn. I still haven't come upon a single one of all those golden trumpets the Bible says they have up here. Can't you just imagine what 'Blow, Gabriel, Blow' would sound like in these green pastures?"

I didn't ask where the green was. If Satchmo said there was green, that was enough for me.

"I sure can," I said, "but I could also go for a few bars of 'Nobody Knows the Trouble I've Seen,' 'Swing Low, Sweet Chariot,' 'Didn't It Rain,' 'Hello, Dolly!' or 'Blueberry Hill,' but I guess you'd have to make that whiteberry hill in this concert hall. And I would give everything I have on me, which is only a pair of illegal sneakers, for that one about a kiss to build a dream on, or a few touches from 'Porgy and Bess.' You played that better than Gershwin wrote it."

"Hold on, stranger. Can't nobody truthfully say that. It's men like George made the music. All I did was put it in my trumpet and sing along some of the time. Who's around down there now?"

"In two words, Mr. Armstrong, no Satchmo. You were the last of the breed."

"It's mighty nice of you to say that but I was just one lucky black man. Happened to be down in New Orleans when the blues were born and it was all milk and honey from there on in. But then of course," he added in that familiar gravelly tone, grinning all across that great expanse, "the Good Lord blessed me with that soft 'n sweet voice of mine. You don't ever wanna forget that. I should have been one of those crooners, like Rudy Vallee or Bing Crosby. Easier on the old lips, you know?"

Now the heavenly Armstrong chorus was trickling back and he sang out, "Come on by anytime. There's no reservations and no cover in this club, not even on weekends."

Once again, I found the sentimental Brother Vittorio moved.

"Damn," he said. "I only seen that trumpet blower on the TV, never live. We gotta come up with a horn for him."

"Yeah, I'd make that a Number One priority, Vito, but I have to tell you something, much as I hate to knock the Bible with a properly devout person such as you, but you heard the man himself mention it. Revelation has this Upper Room practically swimming in trumpets giving off the most beautiful sounds and here's the greatest without even a used model to put those magic lips to. How do you figure that?"

"It beats the hell out of me, but don't you worry. I'll slip the word to Hank, although that punk could stick a pretty good price tag on one of them, new or used."

"No problem," I said. "Just put it on my grunt. Birdye would jog up here in her bare feet to hear Satchmo belting it out again. She was so hung up on him she used to throw a flock of his records on the turntable and play an accompaniment on the piano. Oh, what a sound that made. I just wish we had thought to bring along a big white handkerchief. Mr. Armstrong's just not the same without the horn and the hanky to wipe the sweat off his brow."

"Paul boy, you out of it again? There's no handkerchiefs and no sweat in this ballyard."

"I know, Tiny," I said. "I guess I lost what's left of my head. Which way to the Clan Kennedy?"

"South by south, but it crosses the golf course, so we can grab a bite. I'm starvin."

"What a pity. You'll be even hungrier after we stow away that organic garbage. No chance for a slice of pizza or some deli, huh?"

"Look, pal. There's an expression from the Good Book, or some book anyway, I used to hear when I was a kid in parochial school, like everything comes to the guy who waits. Somethin like that. Well, that's the way it is around here. You gotta take it one day at a time."

"Beautiful," I said. "One day at a time and I got seven left if I can't either beat those beards or go on the lam—or something. You're really a charmer, *paisan.*"

So we had our rabbit food after a while and dropped into the upstairs Hyannisport and—how lucky can you get?—found John and Bob Kennedy strolling along together just as if they were on that beach on the Cape in the family compound they both loved so dearly.

Following the indicated protocol, I addressed the President first.

"I'm sorry to intrude," I said, "but I'm Paul Sann from the New York *Post.* You may recall that you came in and had lunch with Dolly Schiff and me just before those debates with Dick Nixon."

"I do indeed, Paul," and I had no doubt whatever that the President was just being his old courteous self. After the Bay of Pigs, the Cuban missile crisis, his facedown with U.S. Steel ("My father always told me that all businessmen were sonsofbitches but I never believed it until now," he said in private after making that Goliath back down on a price boost in '62), let alone the day he came into the sights of Lee Harvey Oswald's $21.45 mail-order Italian rifle with the scope, how could he possibly remember that my owner sprang for roast beef sandwiches one day and her editor took him on a tour of the plant?

But I was dead wrong. Or is it wrong dead? I keep getting mixed up.

"I still get a laugh now and then out of something you said to me that day down in your city room," John Kennedy went on. "You told me the barefoot lawyer from Whittier would be a cinch for me in those four debates if I simply let him do all the talking. Looking back, you had it right. That con artist had a faculty for always sounding or looking as if he was hiding something. He made all those devastating Herblock cartoons look like oil paintings. You know Bob, by the way?"

"No," I said. "We never did get together somehow," and the shorter Kennedy, still with that unruly haircut, extended his hand as his brother went on. "Who's your friend here? I wish I had that kind of bulk around when I had my short lease on the Oval Office."

"This is Brother Vittorio," I said. "He's my personal Secret Service man, courtesy of our friends on the Tribunal, where I happen to be spending my mornings."

"That figures," Bob Kennedy laughed. "No journalist should be accredited to this beat without an extremely thoroughgoing examination. What this place needs is more infighters who really know how to go for the jugular, say like Joe McCarthy and the young Roy Cohn, to put your kind through the meat grinder."

"You didn't do too badly yourself," I said, "when you were working for the McClellan Committee and going after Mr. Hoffa."

"Whatever happened to my chum Jimmy?"

"You mean you don't know?"

"Somebody cut off our subscription to the Washington *Post*," the President put in, "so we're not always on top of things anymore." Knowing he was kidding, I turned back to his brother.

"Well," I said, "you do know the battling bantam dropped in at Lewisburg in '67 to do the stretch you stung him with in that jury fix and the looting of the Teamsters' pension fund. What you don't know, if you're not putting me on, is that he had a friend in the White House after LBJ walked away because 'Nam had him so far down in the polls he couldn't find his own name, so the gates opened for him in four years."

"You mean Tricky Dick found himself moved by that thief's plight?"

"Yes," I said, "but I'm not sure how much of a favor that was, because Hoffa would have been better off on the inside. He disappeared four or five summers ago, apparently in some jam with his business partners in the mob, and no *corpus delicti* ever turned up. The last thing we heard was that he's now the rear bumper on somebody's limo."

"I'll be damned," Bob Kennedy said. "That character was more fun when he was around. He gave some of us a purpose for living."

Now the President took me by the arm and we left his brother alone with my Brother.

"How are Jackie and my kids, Paul?" he asked, turning very somber.

"They're all great, sir," I said. "Caroline and John John have stayed off the gossip column circuit and Jackie's now an editor at Doubleday and the same highly respected lady."

"You ever have a chance to spend any time with her yourself?"

"I did, as a matter of fact. She started with Viking Press when she went into books and called me about doing my bio—you know, the whole long story with Dolly—but I wasn't going to spill all that, bleeding from every pore, so nothing came of it."

"That was all after the Golden Greek died, wasn't it?"

"Oh, sure. Only the people with the longest and meanest memories can remember that far back. To most of us that woman will always be Jackie Kennedy."

"To me, too, Paul," the President said. "You can't imagine how much I would like to do it all over again—but I had to go and make a goddamn political trip to Dallas. Tell me something, what about the Arab who killed Bob?"

"This one's got to hurt," I said. "You know what California regards as a 'life' sentence—like sixteen fat years. So Sirhan's due out in '85 or so and no doubt will find an army of literary agents, TV and movie guys at the gates of San Quentin waving incredible fortunes in his face for the inside story of his own travail. He could even turn up as a stand-up comic with a Las Vegas act for more loot than they ever paid Sinatra or Barbra Streisand—or maybe his own television show. That's a beautiful place we all left. The buck is still what it's all about."

"How right. I guess I learned all that at my own father's knees. How's my kid brother doing?"

"Well, before my name came off the voting rolls it looked very much as if he had his mind set on going against Jimmy Carter for the nomination this time."

"How did his chances look to you?"

"It was too early to tell." I wasn't going to bring up Chappaquiddick and the girl in the water. "The country's in a mess—home and away, but mostly home. Sky-high inflation, near recession, energy crisis, heating costs out of sight, gasoline up to a dollar and a quarter when you can find it, heavy unemployment. So it could really depend on what the peanut farmer at Sixteen-hundred Pennsylvania Avenue can do to turn it around before the convention next summer. I'll tell you this: if it gets much worse the Republicans could have a live chance."

"Who have they got?"

"I don't have to tell you Ronald Reagan still has his white horse saddled up. Reagan and your old backer John Connally were the front-runners, with a whole pack behind them—a young Senator from Tennessee named Baker, George Bush, General Haig. Also Bob Dole and a few no-names. And Gerry Ford's in the wings too, waiting for the lightning to strike. He could run and get elected just because he was nice enough to pardon Mr. Nixon so the bum could get a little richer writing books and doing a big-money TV shot with David Frost instead of facing impeachment by the Senate or maybe some time in a federal slammer."

"I wouldn't doubt that for a minute, Paul," the President said. "Our old country always was loaded with enough laughs to wash away the tears. Let's get back to Bob and your stunted friend." I had a feeling that there were some other things the man wanted to ask me but wasn't quite up for as he went on to say, "Love to see you again but I suspect you're pretty well tied up."

"Only up to both ears," I said, and now we were back with Bob Kennedy, who wanted to know how we were doing around the world.

"Oh, it's pretty hectic," I said. "Not worse than what you fellows had with Fidel Castro or Khrushchev but rough enough. The restless natives in Iran finally caught up with the Shah and he had to run for his life with nothing more than whatever billions he had stored up, and a Moslem lunatic—the Ayatollah Khomeini—came up with all the oil and the other baubles Mr. Pahvlevi couldn't fit into his getaway plane. Then last month Khomeini's revolutionary student legions grabbed our embassy in Tehran along with at least fifty hostages and it's been a time bomb ever since. They're talking about trying all our people as CIA spies, not that the CIA had any idea what the hell was going on there, and the thing was on the way to the U.N. and a sure Soviet veto on whatever we wanted to do about that mess when my number came up. It was all pretty scary."

"Bob," John Kennedy said, "how many times have we talked about why anybody in his right mind would want to be President of the United States and the supposed leader of the free world?"

"Not enough, Jack," RFK said. "Not nearly enough. Christ, I hope to hell Teddy's got enough sense not to try anything that dumb."

It was time to go, but I pleaded for the floor to set forth my own Top Secret, Eyes Only theory on Watergate: the whole thing was a setup arranged by a consortium of book publishers (hard and soft), *Newsweek,* movie producers and David Frost, with the actual burglars and a small army of the insiders—among them Poor Richard's tried and true attorney general, John Mitchell, and his storm-trooper twins, Bob Haldeman and John Ehrlichman—tricked into taking the fall.

Bob Kennedy, still more the A.G. or the counsel in a Senate investigation, thought he could trip me up on that one. He had two questions.

"If that's the way it was, Paul, why didn't you break it and collect yourself a Pulitzer and also get very rich? And who was Woodward and Bernstein's 'Deep Throat'?"

"Simple," I said. "I was saving the thing until the count was in on the tons of gold all the parties in on that deal coined, and I can't believe neither one of you doesn't know the other answer. Deep Throat was a night worker named Richard Milhous Nixon."

That left both brothers in a considerably more cheerful mood than we had found them in, so my 'round-the-sundial companion and I departed and I wondered how much time we had left before the bell sounded.

"No more than a few hours. Why?"

"Well, Vito," I said. "I'd just as soon kill them at Hank's sin bin."

"Be my guest. You done enough for me today. I wish my Rosario coulda seen me with all that class, and what a ball it woulda been for the kids."

"No problem, Tiny. They'll pick it up on the satellite. You wouldn't believe what those scientists can do nowadays."

"Pal, I'd be even more surprised if I knew what a satellite was. Sometimes I wish I had your education."

"You had more," I said, "but it was in a different field."

Day III ~🐝

Chapter 8 •••••••••••••••••••••••••

Climbing those endless stairs (I know, what stairs?) with a nice Beefeater glow on, I had a brilliant idea.

Make that two brilliant ideas.

First, in this go-round I was going to work like a pack mule on my own Peter (Peter on the left, I mean) and go all out for the first hung jury in the House of God and then try to get the enemy twisted up in the double jeopardy gimmick so they couldn't try me again. I knew you could invoke that only after an acquittal but thought it might play because the whiskers surely had never gone against anybody with my law-smarts before.

Second, I was going to hold down the chatter and see if I couldn't wash out the next three counts to pick up an extra session on that silly adultery thing and wheedle myself a wrap-up day for a summation.

I found Saint Peter rather coldly formal, as if he hadn't had a good night's nonsleep, and I was barely squatted and praying for a miracle, like the bailiff Wilhelm handing me a cup of steaming black coffee with some cancer-causing no-calorie sweetener, when the clerk read me Number Three:

"Remember the Sabbath day, to keep it holy."

"It is my intention to plead guilty on this count in the interest of saving your valuable time," I said. "Guilty with an explanation, that is, the way it is where I came from."

Peter on the Far Right objected, of course.

"Your Honor, are we to permit this petitioner to subject us to yet another filibuster?"

The good Pete ignored that cutthroat.

"You may state your 'explanation,' whatever that might be," he said.

"Thank you, I won't take but a minute. Once I was out of my teens and beyond the influence of my parents, who were Orthodox and observed the Sabbath, I was out of that scene altogether, but I ask you gentlemen to bear in mind that on the daily journals below the presses almost never stop, not even on the highest of High Holy Days in my own faith. In that respect, I wish to note that during the Yom Kippur War in the Middle East six years ago my people, however devout, did not call a halt when the sun went down on Fridays so we could all make believe the guns weren't going off and go to the synagogue. I can cite any number of comparable situations, if not quite that weighty, but I am content to cop out—excuse me, plead guilty—with nothing more than the passing observation that I myself have known scores of duly pious men and women who for one valid reason or another were not always in a position to observe the Sabbath." I was looking at Peter the Third all this time because I sensed something in those eyes. Maybe this was one of the few journeymen who worked for me in the old days and didn't go away mad. "I have nothing more to say on this point."

The clerk, so directed, read Commandment Number Four.

"Honor thy father and thy mother; that their days may be long upon the land which the Lord thy God giveth thee."

"Do you wish to have this commandment expanded upon for your guidance?" the prosecutor asked.

"No, sir. I feel no need to address myself to this count unless there is something in your ledger that may require it."

"There are no specifications here of any consequence," said Mr. Beelzebub's spokesperson. "Is it your wish to proceed?"

"Yes, sir," I said, wondering where the hell that black coffee was. The mother on the right again:

"I must observe that this is most extraordinary. Are we not about to set a precedent which might well come back to haunt this Tribunal on another day?"

Pete shook the guy off like Tom Seaver telling Johnny Bench no, he didn't want to throw the slider.

"The clerk will read Count Number Five," he droned, and I would have staked him to one on the house if he had had any bad habits and I had any good drinking whiskey in my shroud.

"Thou shalt not kill," the clerk sang out as if I had been a hit man for Murder Inc. instead of an editor paid only a little better than a union plumber on double time in the best of my wasted years.

"I have never taken another human life," I said, still basically addressing my own Peter. "Indeed, even in the face of some rather extraordinary situations in my allotted days I never dared to entertain such a horrendously lawless thought." I was thinking about the sleazy Mexican lawyer, furnished by our own embassy, who had emptied me out while supposedly arranging my son's one-two-three release from that pigsty called Lecumberri, so you can put that testimony down as a small fib.

The prosecutor didn't bother to consult his ledger.

"Mr. Sann," he said, trying without a smidgen of success to wrest my iron gaze from whence it rested, "this commandment is likewise not at issue in your case." Then he turned to the chair. "Shall we go forward, Your Honor?"

"May I speak on that point?" I interjected, and Pete nodded.

"I believe we're coming to a fairly critical issue," I said, since s-e-x was next on the agenda. "I would prefer to have a full session on the next commandment."

"So ordered," spake the gatekeeper who moonlighted as a nonpaid judge. "The Tribunal stands adjourned."

I did not rise with my accustomed dispatch but stayed put to see if I could catch the eye of Peter the Third as the jury filed out—and damned if I didn't. I cannot attest that I caught a sly wink but there was something there. Whatever, it warmed my insulted heart no end, and Brother Vittorio dug it at once.

"You musta killed 'em, pal," he said. "You look like a new dead man."

"No, Tiny, I gave them the Holy Day rap but beat 'em on the next two hands down. It's something else."

"Like what?"

"I found myself a pigeon on that jury."

"Aw, c'mon, I had my own coop when I was a kid not even six feet tall. There ain't any pigeons around here."

"No, seriously, I've got a gut feeling that I'm getting to at least one of those guys and can hang up those whiskers."

Clearly unimpressed by this development but not wishing to

dampen my spirits, the big guy let that one lay, simply observing that I figured to be "up" for a visit with Birdye.

"I wouldn't say 'up,' " I affirmed, "because I haven't felt anything stirring under this nightgown since I was poured into it, but you're right. I just can't wait to get to Birdye. Wanna jog it?"

"Let's not lose our heads, Paul. You told me you was workin out pretty regular. Also, you got the sneakers. So let's just walk it, huh?"

I walked so fast that even with his seven-league strides Brother Vittorio had trouble staying with me. Outside the family Astroturf, he asked me how long I was going to be.

"As long as my bride will have me, Vito. Why?"

"Well, then I might as well stick with Hank in case anything shows in that warehouse. You think you can find your way back there yourself?"

"Not without street signs, traffic cops or even meter maids in this village."

"OK. Suppose I come back like around dinner time?"

"Beautiful. What's for dinner and when?"

An impish look showed now on that angelic face.

"Whyn't we just play it by ear?" Brother Vittorio said while I wondered if he was holding something out. "I'll see'ya later."

And he was gone and I was with Birdye again. Was I in for the same kind of reception I had to hold still for that one time years back when I neglected to show in our own love nest?

No.

My girl, evidently feeling she had been too rough during those first two visits, was more like her old self again, not that she fell into my arms.

"Paul," she said. "I'm so glad you're back. You must have had a very tight schedule yesterday."

"Jam packed," I said. "Saw a whole flock of people, but we'll get to that. What time you got on your Omega?"

"It's not quite eleven. Shouldn't you still be in court?"

"Yeah, but I managed to wash out three counts and still draw an early break, only that ain't the half of it, Birdye. I think I've got something going for me now."

"What?" The tone did indeed suggest the warden I knew and loved all that time.

"A Peter of my own, that's what."

"Paul," Birdye said, looking stern. "Can't we skip the funnies today?"

"This is no funny, kiddo. I'm not talking about my schwantz. I'm talking about one of those judges. Worked on him real good today so he could be in my back pocket—I mean if they had pockets in these rags—before those twelve beards retire to their meditations."

Birdye could not have looked any more skeptical.

"Don't tell me you're talking about a mistrial."

"I sure am, and don't kiss it off because you may have heard it never happens in this saintly jurisdiction. There's always a first time—even in this hell-hole—sorry, I meant Heaven-hole."

"Well, wouldn't that just mean you start all over, Paul?"

"I don't know, but suppose it did? If I've got the old guy I think I have it's a hung jury. How much time you figure they're going to waste on a nobody like me when their calendar's jammed worse than Brooklyn's? Now let's get off it. Ask me who I saw yesterday."

"How many guesses do I have?" My girl was cheering up.

"None, baby," I said. "It was only Martin Luther King. You remember how he exploded into the national scene after that Montgomery bus boycott in '55, yes? And the brothers Kennedy—Jack and Bob. And Satchmo. How does that grab you?"

"Louis Armstrong? Oh, that must have been marvelous, Paul."

"Only a beautiful five minutes because he was working out with a chorus."

"I understand the others, but how does he come into this?"

"Shame on you, Birdye. Satchmo recorded almost as many spirituals as Marian Anderson. He's cleaner than a hound's tooth and also gives me a piece of color in this lily-white joint to go with Dr. King. I don't have to tell you how important that minister is, do I? He's right up there with the Kennedys in my book."

"Paul, I haven't kept up with things too well since you stopped bringing the paper home. I can understand why Louis Armstrong is here. He was getting on, but Dr. King and those two Kennedys were so young—younger than we were, weren't they?"

"Yes, Birdye, but John Kennedy was assassinated in Texas in '63 riding in a motorcade with the bubbletop on his limo down—and Jackie alongside him, by the way—and Bob Kennedy, who was running for president then, and Martin King got the same treatment within a couple of months of each other in '68. You have no idea how rotten it is down there."

"Oh, my God," Birdye said. "How awful. Were the murderers all caught?"

"Sure, but the sonofabitch who got JFK never had to stand trial because some screwball put a slug into him while the Dallas cops were moving him from headquarters to court. The ex-con who killed the minister is in maximum security down in Tennessee on a soft negotiated sentence, only ninety-nine years, but Bob's assassin had the good sense to do his business in Los Angeles and the California gas chamber went out of style years ago, so he'll be out in time to make a score with the story of his suffering and pursue his hobby, which is hating Jews. He's a jockey-sized Palestinian who decided the second Kennedy had to die because he was too strong for U.S. aid to Israel, but let's get back to us two, yes? You feeling better?"

"I guess so, dear, but I don't want to get my hopes too high."

"Good enough, Birdye, but look at it this way if it will help. Make believe I'm having a pipe dream and there's only six days left, all on the house. We can make a second lifetime out of six days—hell, I'll take six minutes when you're smiling against six hours with Liz Taylor, who's kind of hefty now, I should confess. Also, she's on her fifth husband, or he's on her. I don't really know."

The first full-blown smile, hazel eyes glowing like diamonds.

"Paul," Birdye said. "It's been so many years, but there's something faintly reminiscent about that little speech."

"Why do you say that?"

"Oh, only because that's the way you sneaked into my panties that night when we were baby-sitting for my sister Fay. It's pretty close, anyway."

"Is that a grievance or a passing observation, wife?"

"It's neither," the doll said. "It's only my way of telling you how much I love you, how much I've always loved you, how much I will always love you. God knows you've been bad in your time, but you're still the greatest."

God knows? So how come I'm sweating it out against twelve Peters and can't even see the Man? Christ, in my time I interviewed presidents and prime ministers and even Jayne Mansfield and now without my working press card I might as well be free-lancing and trying to nail the Pope for one of those plain-talking *Playboy* interviews. But here, drunk with joy, which as you know has fewer calories than gin, I got onto another track. Why the hell hadn't I talked Brother Henry into letting me keep that air travel card, which he had surely moved by this time for a hunk of change? The way I was wired up there—I mean with Brother Vittorio as my cornerman—I had the ecstatically wild notion that I could come up with one of those fly-now-pay-later deals and whisk my girl off to some place where there was nothing but sun and surf and a place to rest your weary bones (side by side, natch). Damn, I could pick up maybe three hundred Gs for my landmark brownstone and buy us a whole island or something (WARNING: THE ACT OF MUGGING ON THE ISLAND SANN IS PUNISHABLE BY THE SEVEREST PENAL-TIES) and really pound out the Great American Novel. I could make Judith Krantz and those other upstarts with their multi-million-dollar deals look like minor leaguers writing on space rates. I could . . .

"Paul," said the woman I was with, "are you still here?"

"I'm sorry. I guess I was daydreaming, but you were in it. Were you ever in it."

"Thanks, but I would rather be with you in the flesh. Now where were we?"

"You said you loved me the most and I should have said I loved you more but that wouldn't have been true, because you put it all out, baby. I'm tempted to say a thing or two about being fucked by the fickle finger of fate but I'm not because Vito tells me this place is probably bugged. Otherwise you would hear a few things about Him from this dirty mouth."

"Who, lover? Your tall playmate?"

"No, silly. The Him with the capital *H*. You'll never hear me put the knock on Vito. Apart from you and Ed that's the most lovable citizen I ever met."

Birdye lowered her eyes and I sensed that she was sinking back into the depths. How had I messed up this time?

"What's the matter?" I asked. "Did I say something wrong?"

The answer came in a barely audible murmur.

"Ed was here yesterday, Paul, and I'm not quite over it."

"I don't dig that. Be a big girl and tell me what gives."

"Well, of course I wanted to see Ed—more than anybody in the world except you, and the children, of course—but it brought back that damn fire and broke me up. I know it didn't do him any good either, not that he showed it, but it tore me into little pieces."

I took those strong hands that could knock out Mr. Liszt's Second Hungarian Rhapsody with the same authority as a Teddy Wilson toying with a simple standard.

"Birdye, I hope this isn't too harsh," I said, "but let's be realistic about this thing. You weren't around very long yourself after Ed, so it isn't as if you lost all the wonderful years you thought we had coming with the Irish terror—and now here we are in the same place together. Why not look at it that way?"

"I'll tell you why, Paul. It's the years *you* lost with Ed. You two were like brothers. He would have killed for you and you would have killed for him. You couldn't possibly have found another friend like that."

"You're wrong," I said, and this was just short of a white lie (that's all you could tell up there, after all). "I've got that Steele couple, Lisa and Robert, and there's Red Auerbach and the big Polak, Joe Lapchick, was around until a few years ago, back at St. John's after his time with the Knicks ran out, and, hell, better still, I've got a guy in Boston I'm nearly as close to as I was with Ed. Jason Wolf, Red's accountant. He kept me out of Lewisburg once I started to get into what Dolly considered the big money, like into the forty-Gs class, then fifty, then sixty. We're thicker than two straight cons in the same cell."

"Please, dear. Now you're talking about somebody in Boston you must see once a year when you make out your tax return and then I imagine one more time when you're audited. Don't play games with me."

"I'm not, Birdye. I was a regular on the Eastern shuttle before the lights went out. Went up there only a few months ago when Jay's middle son married a lovely Italian girl, and he's got some clients in town and a week-long seminar for CPA's at NYU every year, so you're wrong."

"Paul, that's fine, and I'm sure the same thing goes for Red, but how can you count that as the same kind of thing you had with Ed? You two were hardly ever apart for much more than five minutes at a time. I don't know how you managed to squeeze me in there now and then."

"I would have to say that's below the belt if I had a belt, baby. The three of us were together more often than not when Ed and I weren't working. Give me an even shake, will you?"

"All right, I take it all back."

"You're the same doll," I said. "What else did you and the *shikker* talk about?"

"Oh, all kinds of good things, all the beautiful years, but then he brought up something perfectly awful."

"What?"

"That night he called us when he thought he killed a marine in a midtown bar and you told him to get into a cab and come up to the Bronx. Then you had the office check the police and the hospitals and there was no dead marine anywhere and it turned out that Ed had just knocked somebody in a uniform unconscious."

"Oh, Christ. Don't tell me he also mentioned the time he was working out on one of our drunken printers in Jim Moran's and Jim called me over and Ed was so blind he wanted to go a few rounds with me when I pulled him off that guy. I survived that night, which I didn't think you needed to know about, only because another live marine, a nephew of Jim's, happened to be in that saloon and threw an armlock on my playmate and took him to his hotel."

"No, I guess Ed has blocked that out."

"Good. Then I'll remind him."

"Please don't, Paul. Let's stay with the good times."

"Yes, ma'am, whatever you say, but this has to be a straight trade-in."

"What do you mean?"

"It means from now on when that delinquent comes around you don't buy yourself the blues. Deal?"

"Yes, and by the way Ed told me he ran into Bill O'Dwyer and he asked about you. I never understood how you two ever stayed friends after the paper drove him out of town. Remember the dinner he gave for us in Mexico City when he was the ambassador there?"

"Well, I can clear all that up for you. Bill'O always thought that it wasn't P. Sann who wanted him out of City Hall and then fed the Kefauver Committee the stuff they killed him with later, but the higher seats of power. Besides, he knew it was Irving Lieberman's legwork—back to when he was the Brooklyn D.A. and his canary Abe Reles went out of that window in Coney Island with six of his own picked cops guarding him and Albert Anastasia beat the big Murder Inc. rap—that done him in. He told me in Mexico he harbored no grievance against me because it was that 'lousy little Jewboy' of ours who did the real dirty work."

"What? How could he have said that to you?"

"Birdye, you know I never looked Jewish like you."

"You never told me about that crack."

"No, I was afraid it would spoil that fun trip for you and I never got around to it later. Now it doesn't matter. Irving himself went out with a second stroke not too long before my heart hit me back."

"You going to see Bill?"

"I don't know. Until this trial's over I want to spend every available minute with a girl I used to know. Bertha Pullman."

"You're nice, Paul," Birdye said, and at that moment we had a visitor.

Brother Vittorio, with a rather substantial bulge under his shroud and the grin of an Italian Cheshire cat.

"Vito goombah," I said. "What's under the cloth?"

And out it came, once the reformed gunzl took a quick gander around all four sides of the compass.

One brimming plastic cup of Beefeater.

One brimming cup of Dewar's Scotch.

One pack of Camels.

One pack of Chesterfields in the long model.

Two hot pastrami sandwiches that weren't hot.

One plastic cup of coleslaw.

Two kosher dill pickles in another cup.

"You fucker," I said. "To what do we owe all these goodies?"

"First," came the answer from that battle-worn face. "I hafta ask you not to use any bad words around the little woman, OK?" I nodded. "And second, where I come from you don't go around spillin no professional secrets. Now will you and your bride dig into this here grub?"

Birdye took a swig of that Scotch—her brand, mind you—and nearly choked.

"Excuse me, Vito," she said. "It's so long since I tasted any of this, and I never had it except on the rocks with water. I didn't know it was that strong, frankly."

"Sorry, ma'am," said my good angel. "You can't even get ice in the winter in this playground. Just put it down kinda slow and it won't be no worse than cough syrup after a while."

"Thank you," Birdye said. "What are those cigarets? They were just tiny little things when I smoked." *cop. 2*

"They stretched 'em out, baby," I said, firing one for her. "It's just a commercial gimmick, and they hung a filter on 'em so they don't taste so rough."

Birdye took a long drag, blew it out, sucked another lungful through those tantalizing lips, and spoke. "I don't want to offend our benefactor, Paul, but I don't feel anything."

"Well," I said, "you have to get used to these kings. Want a drag on this Camel? I switched to something called MORE because there wasn't anything around called LESS but you know this old brand of mine's got the kick of a mule who smokes."

"No thanks, dear, I'll give this thing a fair chance. Let's eat."

I spread my pastrami sandwich open and turned to the figure up there in the nonclouds.

"No mustard, *paisan*? You ever see a Hebe eat delicatessen without mustard?"

"Sorry, Paul. Hank didn't have none in stock. Maybe next time."

Now a few minutes passed while my bride and I wolfed down those two sandwiches and the coleslaw like we had just come out of a Soviet labor camp after twenty years on black bread, water and some mush masquerading as soup. Then we washed it down with a few more blasts and lit up again before I returned to the attack.

"Vito, have I held out anything on you in all the years we've been cellmates in this dump? I've got to know at least two things, since I am still a journalist in my former heart. Make it three." I guess my engine was speeding on the gin by then. "One, at the risk of repeating myself, I have to know what accounts for our good fortune on this most pleasant evening above the stars. Two, how come this party's only for Mrs. Sann and me, since we're all family now? And three, what took you so fucking long to get here once this gusher hit?"

"You used another bad word, pal, but I guess I gotta level with you anyway the way you moved me up in class yesterday. *Uno,* the reason I told you I had to drop in on Brother Henry this morning was because a dwarf I know slipped me a whisper about a new shipment."

"Hold it, Tiny," I said. "I've only had the pleasure of meeting one very short guy here. Don't tell me you're talking about Brother Hector."

"Check. I didn't wanna lay it on you too fast, but Hector, not that he came up here with any yellow sheet in his diapers, ain't above doin a little business onna side. That's how you happened to keep them sneakers."

"Proceed," I said, borrowing a word from my pal Pete.

"OK. *Due,* I've been putting on the feedbag all afternoon and I gotta watch it. If I go over two-fifty I got trouble draggin around with an athalete like you. And *tre,* I thought you wanted as much time as you could have with the missus."

"Very generous, you mountain Guinea," I said, "but you went too fast on that *uno* detail."

"Paul, have a heart," Birdye broke in, no longer choking on the Dewar's or rapping that imitation cigaret. "You're not on the desk now spitting out orders to some tryout reporter."

"Try to remember who's in charge here, kiddo," I said. "Downstairs, it was you. The only real privilege I ever had was to take the garbage out to the incinerator without asking permissionl Up here, it's me—or is it I? I will thank you to let this small center answer the question on the agenda," whereupon it bubbled forth.

"It's no big deal, Paul. This was a head-on shot onna Jersey Turn-pike—some poor bum jumpin the road. Fog, I guess. Anyway, it added up to seven DOA's—I guess your bride knows that's dead on arrival, right?—and five of them was adults and the luggage showed with 'em, so Brother Henry struck it rich. There's more where this taste came from."

"Were the stiffs all my people?"

"No. Onny one car. The other one was my countrymen so there's enough to go around for all of us." Now the big guy reached into his shroud, produced a bottle of Château Villemaurine 1973, and drew the cork out with his massive, only slightly yellowed teeth. "I thought you might like to wash all this down with some vino. Wanna empty out them cups?"

Mine was emptier than the back pocket of a New Yorker riding a jam-packed bus. Birdye, mildly tipsy, had about two fingers of Scotch left but, her impeccable manners intact, put that away and our host poured the wine and helped himself to a gargantuan slug out of the long green bottle.

"I drink to your health and well bein," he said. "You're both my kinda people."

"Brother Vittorio," Birdye started to say, but I broke in.

"Look, kiddo," I told her. "Cut out the formality, you're not in any session at Twenty-one with those fat-assed rich broads intent on turning all the hookers into social workers or Salvation Army lassies blowing horns for a change of pace. This is still Vito you're talking to. Just plain, Vito. Got that?"

"Yes, master," Birdye said. "Vito, I just wanted to thank you for your kindness and ask you a very serious question if you don't mind."

"My pleasure." This was a bit on the slurred side, although I never dreamed there could ever be enough of the Demon Rum in the Godly vineyard to get anybody that size fried. "You ask, I answer."

The old Birdye. Like any wife. We throw her an absolutely spectacular party after almost two decades on a diet that would drive a church mouse into the streets and she's gotta get serious.

"Paul keeps saying he thinks he really has a chance for a mistrial. How do you feel about that?"

Brother Vittorio, may our elusive God bless and keep you unto eternity.

"Mrs. Sann," he said, and I knew this was straight off the cuff from a man who didn't even have a cuff. "It never happened before that I know of, but if your guy tells you he has a shot at it I would fade that bet. I don't hafta tell you them beards never coulda run into anyone like him before."

"Thank you, Vito," the little woman said, "and I wish you would call me Birdye. That 'Mrs. Sann' thing sounds as if we're strangers."

"You got a bet, ma'am, and I don't mind tellin'ya I'm flattered."

"Don't be silly," said the former Mrs. Sann, straight as a short arrow because she could always hold the hard stuff even without being any kind of serious, dedicated drinker. "We're all family now, like Paul said, so let's keep it that way."

"Sure thing, Birdye. Another touch of vino?"

"No, thanks very much, and I don't think Paul wants any. Why don't you finish it? It's a marvelous wine."

I had to put in my two cents worth here.

"I'm perfectly happy to have Vito kill that bottle, baby," I said, "but I don't cotton too much to being put on rations by Your Majesty, not in this semi-free country, anyway. No offense, you understand."

Birdye was not offended. There was obviously something heavier on that good mind (well, she finished high school).

"Paul," she said, evenly but with adequate affection. "Your next session with those judges is surely going to be the toughest and you'll need a clear head. Now will you please let me ask Vito another question I have?"

There went the cold pastrami without mustard, the coleslaw, the gin, the Camels and my best time since that marathon dinner with Sister Margaret Mary.

Birdye was laying the tough commandment on the festive table, the one where when the clerk gets to that boring oath an honest adulterer like me is apt to blow it and say "I did" instead of "I do."

All I could think of at that gut-wrenching moment was Rex Harrison in *My Fair Lady* singing that incredibly insightful Alan Jay Lerner line—*"Oh, let a woman in your life,* and you are up against the wall!"*

Well, I decided to cut my own Julie Andrews off at the pass—and oh, how I once wanted a taste of that gift from the Mother Country—even though I had meant to spend the whole night with my American love.

"You're so right, Birdye," I said, running a hand over her cheeks (the upper cheeks, of course) ever so gently. "The same loving doll. I know you'd change places with me if that's what it took to get me into this club but, look, we have to run now. I do need some time. We'll shoot over tomorrow right from court, OK?"

*Read "death" there, please.

"Of course, dear," Birdye said, buying the brush-off. "I've kept my social calendar clear for you."

What a beautiful day that could have been, I thought as we headed toward that disreputable tailor.

"Didn't that auto wreck sound like two families headed for some kind of Eskimo-style picnic?" I asked.

"I guess you could say that the way both them cars was loaded."

"Then there had to be some vacuum tins of coffee somewhere in that haul, no?"

"There was, Paul. I didn't think to bring none."

"That's OK, Tiny, on account of I'm going to need some of that—black—before this night's over."

"You're not gonna start beltin the sauce again?"

"No way. I'm coming out for the next round with my head clearer than the Bells of St. Mary's and Spiro Agnew's conscience."

"Aganoo? Who's that?"

"He was Dick Nixon's vice-president, or president for vice, and it turned out he was on the take when he was Governor of Maryland and even kept having those white envelopes—old markers, I guess—slipped to him in Washington. So they had him on a tax rap too."

"You tellin me a vice-president of the whole USA went into the clink?"

"Hell, no. The fix was in with the Justice Department so that shake-down specialist walked with a tap on the wrist and now he's cleaning up a fortune in one kind of business or another while punks caught with an ounce of marijuana in our own state are looking at fifteen to life. Anyway, I just want to settle down—or up, I should say—at Hank's and do some heavy thinking. You know this is the one that could settle my hash. I mean like it's the seventh game of the World Series and I either come out with that ring on my pinky or they shove it up what's left of my rear end."

"I don't get the tie-breakin angle, Paul. You're onny on Count Six."

"Vito," I told him. "This is not a numbers game we're in. Six is the one for all the marbles, because I never was any kind of model husband like you. I coulda been a contender but fell victim to the preys of the flesh."

Now we were at the tailor shop, where we ran into quite a scene. Brother Henry, obviously having dipped too deeply into that new shipment, was out stone cold on his feet and Hector, who couldn't reach that high, was trying to waft some potion into his nose. No problem.

The Gallo-Profaci delegate lifted the tailor like he was nothing more than an empty six-pack of Piel's Light and shook him back and forth until his bleary eyes opened, glazed with mortal fear.

"Hey, imby," Brother Vittorio said with ultimate authority but not a shred of meanness. "You gotta straighten up and fly right. This sorta thing don't look too good for the neighbors." Then he found Brother Hector down there. "Hecky," he said, "I got half a mind to change that ugly map of yours into somethin even uglier. I told'ya before not to let this fat slob soak up too mucha the new shipment."

"Brother Vittorio," said Brother Hector, a/k/a Hecky to his intimates, I knew at long last. "Don't lay this scene on me. I did the best I could but Henry paid me no mind."

"Arright, skip it." The enforcer turned back to the lush. "Dig out the java, dumbo," he said, "and pour yourself some. It's guys like you give this place a bad name."

Oh, how I loved that big bear.

"Vito," I said. "You are the very soul of kindness and concern for your fellow stiff. Let me tell you something. Whither I go from here, you goeth."

"Thanks. You mind fillin me in on that line?"

"Not at all. It means that if I blow this game and pick up a freebie going the other way I'm taking you along even if I have to carry you."

"You wouldn't hafta, pal, even if ya could. Any place you go I go on my own wheels."

And now a word from Brother Henry, replanted.

"What's alla mumbo jumbo?" he mumbled. "I needa pull myself together for the labors the dawn will surely bring."

"That's just super, imby," said the rebounder on the basketball team I was thinking of starting up there if I could rustle up any baskets. "Just keep your yap shut so our boy here can use his noodle on his business. Otherwise you're gonna hafta pay a call on some dentist you ripped off. Got that?"

"I guess so," said the tailor, his murky eyes closing again, and the midget spoke up.

"Brother Vittorio," he said. "Is it OK if I go get some of that health food shit? I went off my diet today."

"Sure," said that hunk of pure Sicilian gold, "and bring back some for Brother Paul. He needs to be at his top fightin weight, around the welters, for today's card. It's the main event comin up."

Day IV

Chapter 9 •

Man, talk about curve balls. Once the zinger was read and I rejected the customary offer to have it amplified as if I were a zombie who didn't know what he was doing when he betrayed his own wife, the next voice gurgled forth from you-know-who.

"If the chair please," the prick said, "I am constrained to interject into this session a matter inadvertently bypassed with respect to Commandment Number Two."

I came out aiming for the bleachers in deep center.

"Your Honor, I am not here today on redirect examination and I maintain that any such procedure would not only be grossly unfair but devastatingly harmful to my defense, My preparation from day to day must of necessity be devoted solely to the issue at hand. There are, after all"—and I was turning the old charm back on my own Peter now—"only so many hours in any day."

Did those granite heads know how I had been using some of those hours? I hoped not.

"Objection overruled."

"Thank you," said the other side's Peter. "I have reference to the questioning of this petitioner relating to profanity."

"Objection," I roared again.

The main man seemed a trifle annoyed.

"If it is the same objection overruled moments ago I would suggest, Mr. Sann, that you forgo it."

I forwent it, and my tormentor, without question a veteran either of the Spanish Inquisition or the Moscow purge trials of Joe Stalin's good times, went on.

"What I wish to cite is an incident in a facility known as French Hospital in this petitioner's place of residence in the Year of Our Lord Nineteen Hundred and Forty-seven. The petitioner was a patient there at the time. Does he wish to dispute that recorded fact?"

"No, he doesn't," I spit out. "I made a trip to Germany in that year with my country's Air Force for the purpose of demonstrating to our Russian allies that even with our old B-52 bomber we could deliver a full payload across the Atlantic and into their front yard if we had to, and while I was there I also covered the Berlin Airlift for my paper because the Soviet then was trying to choke off the supply of food and medical necessities to West Germany in violation of the Four Power Agreement which had divided that defeated nation into two parts, and—"

"Objection. My question called for a simple 'Yes' or 'No' and yet another delaying tactic appears to be in progress."

"Overruled," Pete said, and I went on.

"The thing is, I returned to the States from that assignment in a seriously weakened physical condition—I had only barely been over nearly fatal ulcer surgery—and was ordered into that hospital directly from the airport."

Another objection.

"Your Honor, is the petitioner to be allowed to make his defense presentation even before the charge is laid before this body?"

"Sustained," Pete said, and Genghis Khan went on.

"In that hospice maintained, I note here, by the Roman Catholic Church, were you not brought to task on at least one occasion by the Mother Superior?"

"No," I shot back. "It was not 'at least one occasion.' It was one, exactly one."

"Splendid. I shall accept that without cavil. Would you relate to this Tribunal what led to that remonstration?"

"You're asking me to testify against myself now," I said, "but I do not wish to invoke the Fifth Amendment privilege which I continue to believe is my right. What happened was that they wheeled in one of those hatracks to give me a blood transfusion without any prior notice and I lost my temper and resorted to a small profanity. It was nothing more than that."

"Was it indeed?" said Jack the Ripper. "May I refresh your recollection on a subsequent incident in that same hospice?"

"I'll save you the trouble, my friend. The army my doctor surrounded me with included a most attentive young nurse and once I was feeling a lot stronger I made a suggestion to that woman which I am willing to concede, and not without remorse, contained what was then regarded in many quarters as having a somewhat immoral tinge."

"Thank you. You anticipated my question and your candor is most gracious. I ask you now whether that 'suggestion' did not bring forth a second rebuke from the Mother Superior."

"It did not," I said, insufficiently warmed by the memory of that ultra-sexy redhead. "The nurse in question proved fully able to handle that situation all by herself. Now if anyone here would tell me how that thing constituted a violation of the Second Commandment I would be most grateful."

The prosecutor, plainly irritated over the needless intrusion by his colleague, stepped into the breech.

"I believe the oversight attributed to me has been adequately disposed of, Your Honor," he said. "Shall we proceed?"

"By all means," said Pete, and the run for the roses, with the petitioner trailing all the way, was on.

For openers—

"Mr. Sann, you entered into holy matrimony at a rather early age. Is that not so?"

"I was twenty years old."

"Twenty, and is it not a fact that you enjoyed an intimate relationship with the female of your choice some two years in advance of that time?" Brother Vittorio wasn't kidding. These guys had to have a tape on my thing with Birdye the day before when she made that crack about the way I sweet-talked her out of her bloomers. "That is indeed a fact, sir," I went on, "but we were pledged to holy matrimony well before that time."

"My question called for a 'Yes' or 'No' answer. I must admonish you to adhere to that procedural requirement, for this particular count may well require all the time available to us."

What a mild way to put it.

"Yes, sir," I said. "but I beg you to bear in mind that we are in a deeply emotional area. I have endeavored to spend every possible available moment in this holy sanctuary with my wife and in that process, inevitably, I could not but help subject myself to some very strong self-examination which has left me simply ridden with such remorse that—"

The headhunter on the far right—

"Your Honor, the petitioner concedes that a simple 'Yes' or 'No' is called for and glibly launches forth into another peroration. How much more of this are we to endure?"

"Sustained," Pete said, and the prosecutor picked up the bludgeon.

"Mr. Sann, is it not a fact that long in advance of the time you were financially able to enter into the marriage ritual you maintained a five-dollar-a-week room over a drugstore called Whelan's in your bohemian sector and on those premises dwelt in sin on occasion with the under-aged female of your choice?"

"Yes, sir, but I must enter a factor in extenuation here." I was working now on my own Peter, with whom I figured to spend most of that session. "There is an economic factor which seems material to me. Another young couple shared that cold-water room and so what it came down to for me was but two dollars and fifty cents a week, whereas to take the required vows and maintain a proper home I needed to be able to rent a suitable dwelling, which required more than my paltry earnings—fifteen dollars a week at that time—would have permitted. I think I should note here that our eventual union was consummated under the Orthodox auspices of our own faith."

"Most praiseworthy, and you were forever thereafter faithful to your duly wedded spouse?"

"No, I was not, but—"

"You have answered the question. We shall go on to some specifics in random order. Did there come a time when by the force of circum-stance you were separated from your betrothed for a period of three months?"

"Yes, sir. I was assigned to the staff covering the United Nations organization conference in San Francisco in 1945 and had to leave my wife at our home in Washington, D.C., because we had two infant children."

"Thank you, and would you here and now swear, mindful of the oath you have taken, that in the said three-month period you were able to observe the biblical injunction against adultery?"

"No, I would not, because that would be an untruth."

"Then it is your testimony that you indulged in extramarital affairs during the period under discussion?"

"Yes, sir."

"Did there come a time thereafter when your professional labors took you into far-flung areas of your native country for the purpose of witnessing political conventions and is it not a fact that on those occasions you indulged in extramarital adventures?"

"Some of the time. Some of the time I was able to take Mrs. Sann with me."

"Commendable. I now put it to you whether you were among the scriveners assigned to the so-called 'Crusade Special' when a General Eisenhower was seeking the presidency against a candidate of the opposition party named Adlai Stevenson?"

"I was, sir. That was in 1952."

"During that time were you able to observe your marital obligations?"

"Objection," and now I turned to the main Peter. "Am I to be subjected to an endless stream of leading questions—the word for it where I come from is 'fishing expedition'—or confronted with the factual evidence against me?"

"Overruled," Pete said. "You are directed to answer the question."

"The answer is in the affirmative."

"Then it is your testimony that you did indeed adhere to the marital strictures on that extended absence from your domicile?"

"That's correct."

The prosecutor dipped into his ledger and closed it in about nine seconds, obviously having run into nothing but blank spaces, but there was no change in the color of his colorless face.

"I shall accept that answer, Mr. Sann," he said, "and come to a moment brought up at the outset today in another connection—your journey with your Air Force. The record shows that your time was divided between the provinces of Berlin and Munich. I ask you now whether in that time you fell prey to the weaknesses of the flesh."

"I did."

"You had the services of a female driver furnished to you by the American Military Government, is that not so?"

"Yes, sir."

"Did you upon one eventide bid that person to your quarters in Munich for the purpose of fornication?"

"Yes, but nothing like that happened."

"Really? Perhaps my record is amiss in this one instance. Would you be kind enough to expand upon your response?"

"Gladly. That woman—a war widow and a former schoolteacher, no less—had a young son and I asked her how she was rearing him. When she told me that she had been lecturing him on what she termed the 'international Zionist conspiracy' which she said had brought their nation to its knees I invited her to leave."

"But there were others, I gather, whom you did not summarily dismiss?"

"Yes, sir."

"Very well. Now on two separate occasions before the demise of Mrs. Sann you were dispatched to the Middle Eastern regions on reporting assignments. Did you observe your marital obligations on those occasions?"

"I cannot answer that with a 'Yes' or 'No.' "

"May I inquire why?"

"Certainly, because the answer is both yes and no."

"Would you amplify that, please?"

"In the land of Egypt, where there was a strong antipathy toward my people, I abstained from any intimate contact with the other sex."

"Indeed, and in the land of Israel?"

"I cannot make the same statement, but may I offer some testimony in amelioration of that response?"

Do I have to tell you what happened then?

"If the chair please," harrumphed the Arab on the right (in English), "the petitioner has answered the question. Why then should it require any elaboration?"

Saint Peter, and I'm not all that sure he was too crazy about that nitpicker, had a whispered colloquy with the prosecutor and let the poor bastard wearing history's first male Scarlet Letter go on.

"Thank you," I said. "I merely wished to convey to you that in Tel Aviv the Chief of Police himself, whom I had interviewed on the subject of prostitution and related matters in the Jewish State, offered me the services—gratis or otherwise I cannot truly say—of a fallen woman of his own acquaintance and I rejected it out of hand as wholly reprehensible."

"Most admirable," Pete drawled. "Does that complete your statement in, as you have termed it, amelioration?"

"No, it doesn't, Your Honor. May I cite one other comparable instance?" Green light from the white whiskers. "I was in Petrograd once on a tour of the Soviet Union with John Vliet Lindsay, then the mayor of my city, when I received a call in my hotel room from a woman who identified herself as Natasha, simply Natasha, who volunteered to join me and I rejected that offer out of hand."

The prosecutor with the global vision and global plainclothes network, dipping into his ledger as I spoke, must have been waiting for me to stick my unwashed feet into that kind of manhole.

"Mr. Sann, I would counsel you against any further disingenuous or deliberately misleading testimony. Did you not accompany your mayor in the false guise of an urban affairs expert while surreptitiously probing the situation of the dissident Russians of your faith who were struggling to obtain visas to emigrate to the land of Israel and had been forewarned by certain informed sources that it might well be courting danger, exposure or even arrest for a person in your duplicitous situation to enter into any, shall we say, social adventures with Soviet females of any station?"

"That is so, except that I must rebut your use of the word 'surreptitious,' since the secret police over there, known as the KGB, had me under constant surveillance whenever I strayed from the mayor's official party."

"Well and good. The issue before us at the moment happens to be marital infidelity and you have introduced an incident which took place some twelve years after your wife's demise. We shall come to the latter stages of your existence below in its proper course. Now, leaving aside your journeys away from your domicile did you ever permit yourself any dalliances in contravention of your vows?"

"Objection. That's another leading question."

"Sustained," Pete said. "The prosecutor will confine himself to the specifics in his possession."

Any problem? No. The Executioner just tucked the ball under his arm and headed for pay dirt.

"Did there come a time when you employed a certain unmarried female to record the activities of the upper classes within the pages of your journal?"

"Yes, there did, but I hope we can avoid the use of names in this context."

"That, Mr. Sann, shall hinge upon your testimony. I ask you whether in due course you enjoyed a romantic involvement with the person under discussion."

Pretty good way for one of those ascetic types to put it, no?

"Very briefly," I said.

"Please refrain from qualifying your answers. Was there perchance an actress with whom you had a similarly intimate relationship?"

"There was."

"And did that not have extremely serious consequences?"

"I'm sorry. I don't follow that question."

"Perhaps I can help you then. Did not that particular female become impregnated as a result of your dalliance and was that child eventually aborted—denied the right to life—that is?"

What a thing to hit a guy with.

"Objection!" I was screaming as loud as I could with a parched throat, even apart from a slight discomfort I was suffering as a result of that illicit cold pastrami over at Birdye's pad, and didn't wait for the chair's response. "Am I on trial here for murder? I thought we covered the thou-shalt-not-kill item yesterday."

Saint Peter looked toward his lion tamer on the right, who, of course, had all ten toes on the starting block.

"The question under challenge goes to the very heart of the petitioner's moral character and could not possibly be more relevant."

"May I argue that, Your Honor?" I asked.

"Proceed."

"I have readily conceded the infidelities put to me up to this juncture, yet I am now being taxed with an event which may have flowed from a later involvement deemed illicit in this Tribunal's reading of the commandment at issue."

That voice again:

"If the chair please, we have all heard our share of non sequiturs in this chamber since the Creation itself. Now, lo and behold, a new standard has been set in that area. I hold firmly to my position."

"Mr. Sann, you are directed to answer the question," quoth Pete.

I was so muddleheaded now that I must have thought I was downstairs, because I started to ask whether the clerk would read that one back but then caught myself.

"The answer is yes. There was an abortion."

"Thank you. Did you ever enter into an illicit relationship with a secretary in your employ?"

One for my side.

"Sir, I had a male secretary for twenty-five years and it was never my thing to stray from the Good Book's mandate against homosexuality."

"Come now. Obviously I was not inquiring as to whether you had an involvement with any person of your own gender."

"Oh. May I interpose a question?"

"I suppose so," said the prosecutor, seeming a trifle weary, "there being no other objection around the table."

There be no other, so I plunged ahead.

"Just a while back I suffered a rebuke for citing an incident covering a period during which I was a widower. Am I now to be questioned at length about that very same point in time? I find this turn of events beyond my poor comprehension."

The celestial Roy Bean again, and didn't I ever know it.

"Your Honor, the petitioner spurned the routine offer of an amplification of the count at issue. I find *myself* impelled to suggest that such an exposition is urgently required lest we permit ourselves to become altogether bogged down in wasteful discourse. May I go forth?"

Why not?

"Thank you. Let the record reflect that the petitioner is now being advised that Commandment Number Six, while it contains nothing more than the five words *'Thou shalt not commit adultery,'* is not limited in any authorized and accepted text known to this body solely to the conduct of men and women united in holy matrimony; further that the word *adultery* is effectively consonant with the word *chastity* which need have no relationship whatever to the wedded state; further, that chastity in turn is consonant to purity and that, moreover, those two words taken together impose upon a man an absolute requirement to conduct himself at all times in the ultimate and most totally committed sin-free manner, observing each and every stricture of the Maker during the entire course of his existence from the cradle to the grave; further, that the doctrine I have enunciated extends well beyond the manifold perils of the flesh even to such elements as idleness, consuming alcoholic beverages to excess, reading—or, in the present instance, I should note—*writing* offensive literary material or, indeed, even so much as exposing oneself to any public lewdness which may be available in the community of one's residence."

Oh, brother. How would you like to count the units in that swift little sentence, even skipping a semicolon here or there? Man, I had trouble with some of the more obscure outpourings of William Faulkner in the all but endless saga of that cracker Flem Snopes in his mythical Yoknapatawpha County, not to mention Tom Wolfe and a few others I don't want to put the knock on here, since this is *my* trial. But Good Christ, I had just been hit with the kitchen sink in a place that didn't even have a urinal. Where the heck do I go from there with icicles beginning to form on my wrinkle-free forehead? Well, I knew one place I had to go. I couldn't let that reference to P. Sann's cloth-bound words go unchallenged even if the bum had me cold, and the main Peter generously opened up some crawl space for me.

"Mr. Sann, has that simple exposition set your mind at rest?"

"Yes and no, Your Honor. That reference to my own literary endeavors was gratuitous at best in the context of this hearing. After all, we disposed of my own books early on and I trust I was able to establish that any irreverences under my byline all but invariably stemmed from other sources."

"Except for that little novel," drooled the other Peter, and he had me there, so I shut my Ivory-white mouth and looked mournfully toward my own Peter in the manner of a sheepdog left out in the rain all night. Well, how much more can a man take, fellow workers? The prosecutor proceeded to go on . . . and on . . . and on and on. I'll try to set it down here more in Morse-code style to save time now that we all know there is no more precious commodity not only on earth but anywhere else. Most of this is post-Birdye, and it is exceedingly important to me that this be clearly understood by all Earth people who may stumble upon this heartrending chronicle on some remainder counter.

That divorcee who had the silver Caddy and the penthouse. Yes. That until-then devout RC in our house-lawyer's office whom I deflowered. Yes. That ex-model, no big name, I pinched from a rewriteman on my staff. Yes. That pretty daughter of the publisher I was seen with for a few times. Nay, nay, nay. A thousand times nay. The girl was properly married and I never laid a glove on her, so help me G- - (well, busting into Fort Knox would have been easier). The movie press agent who wanted to trade her body for some free ink. No, that would have violated my professional ethics. The kid from the chorus of *West Side Story*. No (not that I didn't knock myself out trying). That secretary to a Lindsay commissioner. Yes (news source, you know). That good friend of my lost wife who was on the town. No way, not even if she had been the last living dish on Hell's second level. That woman an ex-boss of mine (Ed Flynn, who else?) once had a thing with who dropped in on me years later. Yes. That bust-out married blond who was on a ninety-day tryout on the staff. Yes, but that was the only time like that because I truly regarded such behavior as inexcusable for an editor (and may the Good Lord have mercy on the soul of an infidel who commits infidelity). That statuesque brunette with the blazing headlights the Hearst honchos rang in on me when they were offering me the moon and the stars to slip 'em a little inside dope on Dorothy Schiff and her next-anointed spouse because she was suing one of their papers for a million or so. Shit, no (which isn't the way I said it, although it was gospel of the purest ray serene). The one I met at the Lion's Head in the Village who came home and played the piano for me, just the way Birdye used to. Yes. That aspiring writer who wanted a little newspaper experience to get her off the ground. Yes, but she never went on the *Post* payroll. That Japanese artist known for the wacky phallic designs made from macaroni shells or something. Yes. That henna-haired widow in our building after Birdye's lease ran out. No, she wanted a guarantee that I would get her to the synagogue on time. That girl I borrowed from another department when *Look* magazine needed a real-life city editor to pose with some actor starring in a TV newspaper series but didn't want to photograph me with a fat male secretary. No, her own boss had the lock on her.

Dear God, would this trip down the rapids ever end? Apparently not. I thought the prosecutor must have used up everything in his peashooter when he softly inquired whether I killed some idle hours in '64 with a lovelorn columnist coining huge sums (but without my paper's help) telling the girls how to keep their home fires forever aglow.

"I did, sir," I said.

"And what transpired on that occasion?"

"Well, when Mrs. X asked me to pick her up at her hotel for dinner I did not know that she was syndicating her body as well as her words of wisdom for the troubled, but I found her in a state of undress with the bath drawn for both of us."

"Come now, Mr. Sann. Are you asking this Tribunal to believe that you were the victim of an assault?* Would you simply tell us whether you and your companion proceeded to perform your ablutions in unison?"

"We did."

"And did the two of you proceed from the bath directly to your supper engagement?"

"No, sir. We went to bed for a while first, but as I have testified none of this was on any motion of mine."

Peter on the Far Right, just as fresh as he was on the first few laps in this marathon. "Should the petitioner not be reminded that the count at issue bears no reference whatever to the point he has so needlessly raised in two separate answers?"

"He is so reminded," said His Honor. "The sin of adultery does not take into account its origin or inception, just the *act* itself."

You could have made a necklace out of the italics on that word '*act.*'

"I am sorry," I said. "I thought it was pertinent."

In the fistfight business you can be saved by the bell when some

---

*It was a straight case of rape, in truth, but I was not one to lodge that sort of complaint against a woman.

other gladiator has rattled your brains, or a referee with a heart of gold can stop it before they call for the litter bearers. Where I was there was nothing between you and the reception area at Armageddon.

I was saved by that sundial on the stroke of twelve hundred hours.

You think I came off the rack that morning a thoroughly beaten man, huh?

You couldn't be wronger.

As rough a time as that was, put it down to eye contact or mental telepathy or what-have-you, I reeled away from that exercise in soul-washing with a strong feeling that I had sewn up my Peter. As that sweet man trooped out behind the main Peter (and you tell me where that man planted his staff as he walked) I thought I spotted a sly wink that said hang in there, you fun-loving bounder, you're still alive. Even if he hadn't come out of my own sin-ridden circuit my patsy must have had his jollies in his time, maybe even in Sodom or Gomorrah or some latter-day fleshpot, but somehow had slipped through the Linen Curtain. I'm not talking about payoffs, you understand, because that kind of sacrilege, and properly so, surely would doom me to that unpleasant fire-and-brimstone treatment in Gehenna. I'm talking about wit, sheer wit. I would have given anything for a few over at Brother Henry's with that gent but, then, jury tampering was the stinger Bob Kennedy initially got the hooks into Jimmy Hoffa with, and look where that martyr for the toiling masses was (Hoffa, I mean, not Bob Kennedy). In any event, I felt pretty good. That thing about latter-day secretaries of mine in skirts had been lost in the shuffle, not bad when you're playing catch-up, and the way I saw it the only immediate problem I had was with Birdye and I was ready for her. I had the four remaining counts—stealing, bearing false witness, coveting thy neighbor's wife or anything else he thought he owned—all listed as pieces of cake I could zip through like a small guard going in for a two-pointer after a steal. Throw out that sex stuff. I never was any worse than any other growing boy and they darn well knew it, so I had those whiskers by the short hairs. Stick with me, Sister Margaret Mary, I'm the fellow you came in with, or the one you sent, anyway.

Chapter 10 •

"They mop you up good in there?" Brother Vittorio asked.

"What else? They had all the cards. If they missed any time when I had fun with my clothes off I can't think of it myself, but don't count me out, Vito. I know I got at least one mark who can't be taking any of this too seriously. I just wish the hanky-panky hadn't used up that whole session. I had some points of my own to make."

"Like what?"

"Well, on the business of chastity and all that, leaving aside such things as unsavory company, since I didn't always run with leading citizens like you, I wanted to tell those hangmen I've never blown a minute on the raw sex on the new cable TV or the porn in the movie houses. You know, there's a couple that have been running for years—*Deep Throat* and *The Devil in Miss Jones*—you wouldn't believe. That *Deep Throat* is just what the title says. Some babe named Linda Lovelace is in it and they never found a stud that one couldn't eat. Well, her press agent brought her down to me so she could prove she was real and they weren't faking it on camera and I wouldn't even see her, although just between us I wasn't in the office at the time, but I had lots of other things to tell them. Like there's an ass-peddler named Xavier Hollander who had a book ghosted on her happy life called *The Happy Hooker* and I must have been the only guy in the world who didn't read it. Had something even better, too. You knew about Polly Adler, the greatest of the old madams. I was offered her confessional for half the take and wouldn't touch it, and that's not all. I told you they turned Times Square into one huge massage parlor—anything you want from a ten-dollar hand job to the works for a half or so. And there's live sex on stage in all kinds of joints I've never been near. That's all what the lawyers call mitigation, Vito. I could have looked pretty good, no?"

"Not the way I see it once they had'ya cheatin on the vows, counselor. I got an idea the worst is still to come. I don't mean inna courthouse. We're at the little woman's place. Want me to blow away in the wind?"

"No, come on in with me—at the start anyway."

My wife wasn't alone. Ed was with her so she'd have a shoulder to lean on.

"How did it go, Paul?" Birdye greeted me, so casual she might have been asking how I felt about the weather if we were in a place that had weather.

"Not so bad, baby," I said. "They had no more bum raps on me than you did when you were standing your twenty-four-hour watch."

"Really? I'm so glad to hear that—especially if I could believe it."

"That's not nice, Birdye," Ed said. "Your fella was always a model husband. I was the bad one in the family. You told me that a hundred times."

"I said some other things to him, Ed," the doll replied. "Not only after all those trips but even a few times when he wasn't away, and you must know it."

It went that way for a while, not all that heavy, and then my cornermen left and Birdye let it all spill out. She had no desire to hang all the stained linen on the line, of course. She was simply busted up over the beating she knew I had taken and what seemed to her the inevitable consequences, and nothing I was able to say could shake her. For the defense, however, I did press a few points.

"Listen, Birdye," I told her. "There are two damned important items you better listen to—and listen good. The first one is that most of that time with my sneakers in the oven had very little to do with the days we were together. And even as far as that goes I don't know what kind of ribbon clerks this highest branch office of the FBI uses to do its snooping, because they had me in with some babes I wouldn't have taken my pants off for if we were alone on a desert island and I had pants. You know, after you went all kind of well-meaning people, especially that little do-gooder friend of yours Rose Franzblau, made me the 'extra man' at their dinner parties and you can't imagine the kind of kosher meat they threw at me. Mostly widows or divorcées with loot to burn. This one had a chauffeured limo and a penthouse. This one had a co-op of her own on Gracie Square and some garment wheel's fortune. This one had a place in Scarsdale with her own tennis court—for guests, I mean. Her game had to be Mah-Jongg. This one split her time between her Palm Beach mansion and Fifth Avenue apartment. This one wanted me to quit the paper and just write and screw. Well, I ran like a thief. You know why? None of those man-eaters dripping with gold and charge accounts could hold a candle to you. I'll tell you something else, since I'm spilling my guts here. I wouldn't give a nickel for the marriages any of those sex-starved or no-come richniks had, because they didn't know a fucking thing. They just had some shmucks paying the grunt. There was a show on Broadway long after you were gone called *I Never Sang for My Father* that had a line in it that told me where I was. Something about how death ends a life but not a relationship like we had. I mean how the one who's left keeps punching away at the bag and trying to find the way back—I think the playwright called it a 'resolution' nobody ever finds. Well, that's where you left me, baby. You were six feet under, or I thought you were in that ground anyway, because I shoveled the first spade of dirt on you, but the fact is we were still together, and I did something about it. I took myself off my banker's nine o'clock shift and moved up to five to put out the first edition myself so I wouldn't be the hard-on on-the-town available for inspection every night."

"Oh, Paul, do we have to go through that junk again? You were a free man, period. You're insulting my intelligence now. You know your real problem with those judges is what happened when I *was* around, not after, so why not cut all this out? It hurts enough as it is."

"Birdye, I'm telling you this is no snow job. What they had in that book of theirs was ninety percent after '61."

"How lovely. So you only cheated on me the other ten percent of the time. How many times do I have to tell you it doesn't matter anymore? What matters is how your trial comes out. After that if I had something to bang you over the head with, like a tennis racket, I would do it. Now will you just hold me in your arms and not say anymore?"

I don't know how much time went by in that process—or how many tears fell—but it was long. Finally Birdye stepped back and asked me how I sized up what still lay ahead and I sweat blood trying to assure her that we were over the big one and it was clear sailing the rest of the way.

Another strikeout.

"Paul," Birdye said. "You know how much I'm praying that you're right but you've been thickheaded about this thing from the first day. You know what Walter Lister told you when you were starting out— how you had fine judgment for a kid but could get in trouble with those quick decisions of yours. That's what's happening now. Why don't we just let this run its course? The worst is over, and your problem is not with me but those graybeards."

"White," I said. "Ivory-white."

"All right, white. Let's change the subject, yes? Walter isn't still alive, is he?"

"No, baby. He got all used up in '67. I can even tell you the month— May. I was supposed to go to Philadelphia—he retired a while before that as managing editor of the *Bulletin*—and say a few words at the funeral but that was the day the *World Journal Tribune* went into the tank and we were alone in the evening field and the owner wanted an all-day council of war to see how far we could fly."

"What was that other paper you mentioned?"

"Oh, I forgot. You're a little behind. The printers went on strike toward the end of '62 and it lasted a hundred and fourteen days for everybody but us, because Dolly walked out on the Publishers Association after two months and we cleaned up. Then after a while the other papers started folding their tents and Hearst, Roy Howard and Jock Whitney put together that three-way combo and couldn't make a go of it, so the town came down to us in the afternoon and the *News* and *Times* in the A.M. Dream Street. We flew all the way up to seven hundred thousand but chiseled too much to hold it. We were selling more ads than news."

"Did you have fun, Paul?"

"Not much. I really should have hit the typewriter full-time after you went. I might have made a real score."

"How could you have done that? You had the children to take care of."

"Yeah, but I was in good shape—good enough to tangle with my Royal for a year or two, anyway."

"I'm sorry you missed Walter's funeral. He was your real father, wasn't he?"

"He was indeed, Birdye, and the greatest of all the city editors. They don't make 'em that way, anymore. Hell, they don't even call 'em that. Now it's a little fancier—metropolitan editor."

"How about Walter's wife?"

"Dorothy didn't outlast Walter by much, but the three boys are around, all doing real good."

Now those hazel eyes turned sad.

"And Rich and Leni?"

"Come on, baby, I told you they're OK now, and I left them in good shape. Can't say I had any fortune in the bank but I bought my landmark in the Village for a hundred and seven and the real estate market's gone absolutely wild, so that house is worth maybe triple now and there's less than sixty thousand left on the mortgage with the couple I have in the duplex upstairs paying more rent than that monthly grunt. We haven't got a worry in the world except us two, Birdye."

"Yes, Paul. I just wish that wasn't such a large order."

"Well, you keep saying that and I'll keep saying it ain't and we'll have us a Mexican standoff."

"Please don't ever mention Mexico, Paul. I don't want to be reminded about Richie having been in that dreadful prison."

"I'm sorry," I said. "Now can you spare me a small smile?"

I got the smile, real small, and at that moment our two buddies came back, the baby tank with a faint bulge under his shroud. He was carrying some cigarets and booze.

"Vito," I said, very sternly. "You didn't let the Irish lush have any of this medicine, did you?"

"No way, Paul. Besides, he didn't want none."

I looked at Ed as if I had just heard that he had checked into a divinity school on God's campus to go for the turned-around white collar.

"Did I hear that right?" I asked him.

"You heard it right."

"Well, I can't fucking believe it, buddy. You had to die to get on the water wagon and stay on it."

"You hit it on the head, Paul. I guess I found out that's the only way. Besides, I wouldn't want our girl here to see me loaded again and slapping people around. She had her share of that in the old days."

"Didn't we all?" I said. "I'm proud of you. Stick with the cigarets when you can get your hands—or Vito's—on them. For you, they're healthier, even though the larger brains have proved that mice who smoke too much wind up with their little lungs all shot."

Birdye was so pleased she treated the reformed A.A. dropout to a kiss.

And so we went through that afternoon until Brother Vittorio reminded me that it would be the worst possible manners if I didn't drop in on Arthur Flegenheimer and Mr. Costello, as per invitation, some time soon.

Birdye picked that up.

"You know, Paul," she said. "I've been marveling over how there's so little demand around here for an audience with you except from people like that. It's so hard to understand for a leading citizen like you."

"You're wrong on at least two counts, baby," I said. "Without a daily or any radios or the six o'clock TV news my presence on these ghostly (I meant ghastly) acres is known but to a very few people, and second I haven't tried to hunt anybody down, not even Walter if he made it, because I wanted every possible moment with you and Ed so long as I was out on no-bail. Any other questions?"

"No, lover," Birdye said, drawing deeply on her Chesterfield. "I wouldn't have time for the answer. This Scotch has made me drowsy. I think I'm about ready for a stand-up nap."

"Excellent," I said, "especially since that's the only kind there is in this hotel. Remember those huge beds in Vegas?"

"No, I remember the casinos better, because we hardly ever got to the bedrooms except to shower and change our clothes."

"Your memory's all shot, kiddo. You were always at your peak on the road, but sleep well. I'll go see the Dutchman and maybe Uncle Frank and Tootsie and get a good night of no-rest myself. They're all preliminary bouts from here on in."

"Yes, Paul, but you lost some money on those too when you were betting on the fights. How's *your* memory?"

"Bruised, doll," I said. "You have cut me to the quick—and you know what George Gobel said about that once."

"This some kind of private joke?" the Irish teetotaler asked.

"No, Ed," Birdye said with some relish. "Paul's talking about one night when we were all in Toots's after hours—Jackie Gleason and Earl Wilson and Rosemary and Cannon and some others—and Toots made a crack about how short George was and he said something like 'You have cut me to the quick, Mr. Shor, and you lack the intelligence to know what a great burden it is for a man who has to earn a small living making people laugh to go around the rest of his life with a cut quick.' That was such a fun night."

"I'm sorry I missed it, Birdye," Ed said. "I must have been in a preliminary bout myself in some other saloon."

"No doubt," I said. "Busting heads, not quicks."

"Paul, don't be so mean," Birdye said. "Now go ahead."

Chapter 11 ••••••••••••••••••••••••

I called my Dutch Schultz biography *Kill the Dutchman!* and expected to find him in a small rage over that bloody opus, but I should have known better. That hoodlum always enjoyed seeing his name in print almost as much as he enjoyed sending a pair of his more reliable helpers out to pop a few into some upstart or business rival.

"How's it goin?" he asked me.

"I won't know till the jury comes in, Arthur," I said. I knew that once the ex-Bronx Beer Baron made his real score after Prohibition went out, moving in on the blacks and Cubans to take over Harlem's twenty-million-dollar-a-year policy racket and keep it with the help of some heavy artillery buttressed by Tammany's powerful Jimmy Hines and a remarkably tolerant D.A., along with the friendliest cops in town and a weasly lawyer named Dixie Davis, he hated to be called by anything but his square first name. "I'm sure you dig that from the two tax trials you beat upstate."

"Yeah, but I can't say I ever sweat much. I always had at least one juror in the satchel and that's all anybody with half a brain ever needed. Know anything about Frances and my children?"

"Just the boy. He had his own photography shop in San Francisco. I looked all over the place for your wife when I wrote your success story seven or eight years back but couldn't find her or the other kid. I heard from the boy on the Coast after that bio came out but didn't have any occasion to follow it up."

"I wanted to talk to ya about that." The mean, mussed-up face with the twisted beak didn't look any meaner, so I wasn't apprehensive at all. "I heard about it from some punk around here. It wasn't too nice for Frances what you wrote about me hangin around Polly Adler's while I was on the lam for two years and that Fifth Avenue pad I had while I had her set up in Queens real nice for her own good."

"I'm sorry, Arthur," I said, "but the fact is I wasn't the one who ever connected you with any other babe. That stuff came out after you finally quit to that slug in the liver and some woman who didn't look a bit like Frances showed up at the hospital in Newark to stake a claim on your possessions which the law laughed off."

"How'd Frances come out?"

"I never knew. There was all kinds of talk about the five mill you were supposed to have stored away for a rainy day but if it ever turned up Uncle himself didn't know or he would have put the snatch on it."

The Dutchman laughed.

"Them fucks," he said. "I hope the big bills never did show, because the feds sure woulda got 'em before anybody named Flegenheimer. How's that editor of yours, the one I give the interview to in that chophouse the night before the firing squad dropped in? He was a decent fella."

"Mr. Lister? He's dead."

"Nice man. He kept his word with me—straight quotes. I guess that was the last thing I read—except for the policy numbers I was goin over with Lulu 'n Abe and Abbadabba before the guns started goin off. They all went aheada me, huh?"

"Yeah, but not all that easy, even though they had enough lead in them to open their own retail shop. Rosenkrantz lasted all through that night. Landau, who chased the guy with the forty-five and sawed-off shotgun clear into the street with blood pouring out of him like water, made it to the dawn, but that roly-poly Otto Berman went pretty fast. You hung on nearly a whole day and talked your head off with a hundred and six fever—not that the cops could ever figure out what you were mumbling about. Apart from all kinds of loving things you said about your mother it was all in some kind of code nobody could unscramble except for a few raps on Johnny Torrio."

"Nobody spilled nothin?"

"Nope."

"Good. It was Mendy Weiss and Charlie the Bug, wasn't it? I never seen Weiss because I was takin a leak when they bust into that back room, but I made out the Bug pretty good when he came in after me with his automatic. Imagine hittin a guy with no heat on him and his fly open? How'd those scumbags come out?"

"Weiss got off the hook. No case, but they had Workman so good he stopped his trial with a *nolo contendere* to beat the chair and he was inside almost twenty-three years. He was a little gray-haired man selling notions in the Garment Center when I did the book."

"Good for him, that prick. He was only doin a job, like you done yours and your big friend here." Brother Vittorio beamed. "My only beef, except for that fucker Tom Dewey who wouldn't leave me alone, was the Big Six that put the contract out for the hit on me just because I wanted to take that choir singer out myself. I know about Costello. He's a neighbor I don't pay no calls on. What's with the rest of them, Sann?"

"Meyer Lansky's the only one still among the living, Arthur. About seventy-five, pretty sick, and just walking his dog on the Miami Gold Coast. Your pal Dewey nailed Luciano on a prostitution rap and got him thirty to sixty and then let him out after about nine years when he made Governor, but Lucky's heart went around fifteen years ago when he was in exile back home. He made it past sixty-four. The mob itself took care of lover boy Bugsy Siegel for cheating too much when he was building them a gambling palace—the Flamingo—in Vegas. Lepke said his farewell in the chair on a Brooklyn murder and Longy Zwillman checked out with a rope around his neck on his Jersey estate but we never knew whether it was his own idea or somebody else's."

"Shit, every one of them bastards but Siegel sound like they lived to a ripe old age—and I never seen my thirty-fourth birthday. That shyster lawyer of mine also croaked, didn't he? And Jimmy Hines hadda do some time when Dewey went into the policy operation and he must be croaked by now too."

"That's right, Arthur. You led the whole lot of them. It's like what Leo Durocher said about nice guys finishing last."

"Don't put me on, Sann. You had me givin the order to waste Vinnie Coll in that drugstore phone booth down on Twenty-third and stickin a forty-five into Jules Martin's mouth just for goin south with twenty Big Ones in my restaurant protection business, which was a sort of legit operation when you come down to it. None of those traps, not even Jack Dempsey's, coulda lasted five minutes without me holdin the shakes down to something they could afford."

"Yes, but the cops had a pretty good line on the Coll wipeout and the Martin thing all came from the eyewitness testimony of Dixie Davis. If you wanted to enter any rebuttals now I would be more than happy for my publisher to reissue that book, only I can't get to him. I haven't even found a pay phone up here."

"Fuck it," the Dutchman said. "It don't matter to me no more what anybody said about me. I always took care of Frances and my mother and sister and made the switch with Father McInerney and spilled it all, which is how I made it here. I ain't got no squawks. Not with you, either. You made your kinda livin and I made mine. You find me anybody says I didn't give him an even split, even them smelly Cubans in their silk shirts and the chimney sweeps up there in Harlem, and I'll buy'ya a steak dinner."

"That would be very hard, Arthur," Brother Vittorio put in, "especially if you wanted hash brown and French fries with it."

"Yeah, I was only makin a small joke," Schultz said. "I never done any more than an overnight stop or two in any can but this place is tighter than a virgin's box. I'm not even sure I woulda let Father McInerney switch me, especially the way it hadda hurt my old lady, who was a real good Jew, if I'da known it was this rough."

"Arthur," I said. "You made the right decision. At least you're still around. All the rest of your playmates figure to be closer to China, except Uncle Frank, of course."

"I guess so, Sann. You gonna pay a call on that shithead Costello? He's been here six years now and probably thinks he's still the Boss of all Bosses."

I looked up at my man, who nodded.

"I expect to see the guy, Arthur," I said. "Any message?"

"Yeah. Tell that guy to shove it. He never went to bat for me with the Big Six even after Al Anastasia cased that Dewey layout on Park

Avenue and told 'em Dewey could be hit like a duck in a Coney Island shootin gallery."

"I'll tell him," I said.

Brother Vittorio, that cutie, knew the old don even better than he knew the Dutchman and introduced me as a newspaperman who never dealt any off the bottom or "didn't give us all a fair shake."

"Fair shake?" came the gravel voice attributed to a bad throat condition when Costello tangled with the Kefauver Committee in '51. "This fella did even better. I came pretty close to beating a tax trial with his help one time."

"How come you never told me, Paul?" the big one asked.

"Oh, it was nothing," I said. "Uncle Frank here was in the box and one of the jurors called in sick and some jerk on my city desk sent a reporter up to talk to him, so the defense moved for a mistrial and I was hauled in for contempt. The judge was a huge gent with a walrus mustache—Sylvester Ryan—and he chewed me out real good but the trial went on."

"Didn't it, though?" said the square-shouldered, scraggly-faced mobster. "And I come out on the short end just because my good wife was writing more paper than a businessman with the income that my accountant had me down for was supposed to have for spending money. It didn't matter that much—not that I was lookin for any forty-two months inside—the way things was. You must know, Vito. I was ready for a little peace and comfort by then with all them stupid animals like Genovese movin on me. And, Jesus, then later they get The Chin to aim a slug at my head that only scratched me and ruined my best hat."

The Chin? I felt a chill. Vito had told me that was the way he used to be known but I never connected him with the bungled rubout attempt on Costello in the lobby of the posh Majestic Apartments on Central Park West some twenty years back. The big guy sensed my discomfort and stepped right in.

"Frank's talkin about some nobody, Paul," he said. "Name of Gigante. Had a brother who was a priest in the Bronx."

"On the button, Vito," said the fallen Prime Minister, "but I let the jerk off the hook. Wouldn't finger him and he beat that case easy. He still around, Sann?"

"I don't know," I said. "The last I heard his own head went soft and he wasn't any use to anybody."

"Well, what's the difference? In my line you ran into all kinds of people, good and bad. It's too late to hold any grudges. I had my run, past eighty, and I lived a full and good life and was lucky to make it here. Didn't I used to see you around the Copa Lounge and Toots's and Gallagher's and them joints?"

"Sure, Frank. We even talked a couple of times in the Shor A.C. but never got that close. You know Toots is up here."

"Why not? That man deserved it. He was all heart. Staked more of them comics and busted old fighters and ball players than the Chase bank and never hurt a fly except once in a while some drunk he needed to throw in the gutter on Fifty-second, but, hey, I gotta get some rest now, fellas. This goddamn throat of mine is still killin me. The worst thing I ever did in my life was smoke them butts."

I let that modest self-impeachment pass in the nonwind, since it was never my practice to sit in judgment on my fellow man except on edition time or a book deadline.

"Could I ask you something before we go, Frank?" I said.

"Shoot."

"It was Vito Genovese who sent The Chin after you with that little twenty-two, wasn't it?"

"If *you* say so. I never talked and I ain't startin now."

"Fine, but tell me something. If Genovese got lucky and had a pass for this hideaway—you know he faded away in Atlanta about ten years back—would you look him up?"

"Hell, no. I shook off that pop gun incident but never got over the way the four-eyed creep put out a contract on that minor leaguer Joe Valachi in the slammer and made Bobby Kennedy such a big man with them hearings when Valachi turned to become a TV star. When was that?"

" 'Sixty-three," I said.

"Yeah. Better show than Kefauver's. What a cockeyed world. All the time I was around I never made out why our own guys did more for the feds than those stumblebums could do themselves."

"Good point," I said. "You remember what Bugsy Siegel said?"

"What?"

"He said 'We only kill each other,' and he wasn't far off, was he?"

"No, he wasn't at that. Drop around anytime, Sann. It gets awful lonely here."

"Thanks," I said. "I'll try, Frank, long as I got my man Vittorio here to keep me away from the bad elements."

Costello, between coughs, laughed softly.

"Uncle Frank mentioned Bob, Vito," I said as we started down the road without the golden streets, not to mention the Koran's delights of the flesh or Revelation's excellent cuisine. "How far are we from the Kennedys?"

"Only like from Mulberry Street to Staten Island, Paul. People like them don't live too near the Schultzes and Costellos. Don't them skinny legs of yours ever give out?"

"No way. I told you I was a jogger."

"Yeah. What about them sneakers goin?"

"Oh, I don't care anymore. You up for this march?"

"I don't have no other dates."

If I had thought to borrow Birdye's Omega I would tell you it must have been well after midnight when we got to Hyannisport II. But believe me, it was long after the darkness which had been reserved for the other place, the unmentionable one with the free steam heat. Bob Kennedy was by himself and didn't mind the intrusion at all. Indeed, he wanted to see me real bad, I suspected, because he asked Brother Vittorio if we could be alone for a while.

"Paul," the younger Kennedy opened up, "there's something that's been burning me which I didn't bring up on your first visit for reasons I'm sure I don't have to spell out."

"You can ask me anything, Bob," I said. "The time for being cute is gone for all of us."

"Isn't it, though? I'll come right to the point because Jack could show up any minute. I had almost forgotten about this thing until you came along but I've been simmering ever since. It has to do with Earl Wilson—your Broadway columnist. I heard that a few years after I had my accident he got a little richer with a book which made me and Marilyn Monroe a romantic pair—something about my running into her at Peter Lawford's house and losing my head. That's right, isn't it?"

"Yes."

"Well, what a thing for anybody to print just to pick up some royalties. Can you imagine what that had to do to Ethel and my older kids?"

"Of course, but I'm not sure there was any fortune in that book."

"That's not the point. The point is, why would anybody do a thing like that unless he was starving in an attic somewhere? Wilson ran in hundreds of papers and led the pack then, didn't he? He couldn't possibly have needed the money. Why would he have done it?"

"I don't think I can answer that, but you must know the story was around before Earl put it between hardcovers."

"Oh, I don't doubt it, and I have no grievance against you because all you handled was the man's column, but I was coming to a larger point. Wilson did another book after that, or so I've been told, and in that one it turned out Bob Kennedy wasn't the real love of the pitifully troubled Monroe's life but Jack. That's what really hurt, Paul. You know how many writers I knew along the line. I was surrounded with the literary Mafia, but how could the same guy chase the big bucks with that kind of thing about *me* and then turn around and go for another bundle by making my brother the man in the same woman's bed? It all seems so goddamned immoral to me."

"I can address myself to that one with a little more authority, Bob," I said, "because I had something to do with it. Earl and I were always very close—I broke him in on the *Post* rewrite desk when he was a hayseed out of Ohio via the Washington *Post* copy desk—and he was a little fretful himself about that hunk of his manuscript and asked me to read it. Well, I had an idea about how he handled it and told him I wasn't going to dry clean it for any kind of workout, so he bought that and I gentled the thing down real good even though the original version had been syndicated overseas by then. I'm not looking for any credits here, just telling you the way it happened, but believe me the hardcover version wasn't anywhere near as rough as the stuff that got printed for our foreign cousins."

"I'm grateful for that, but nothing can ever diminish the pain. You understand I don't care about myself in all this. It's Ethel and Jackie I keep thinking about."

"Do you mind if I ask you something that could hurt a little more?"
"Not at all."

"The word get up here about another female named Judith Exner?"

"Yes, Paul. I heard it but never told Jack. That was the slut who was the Chicago don Momo Giancana's mistress and John Roselli's and a couple of million others like that, I imagine—and the story was that Frank Sinatra introduced her and it went on and on from there until our friend J. Edgar invited himself to lunch and told my brother the score. Just between us, the fat bastard told me first, but that's neither here nor there. I simply can't bear to think what that mess must have done to Jackie when it hit the papers. The Exner woman cashed in on it with a book of her own, didn't she?"

I didn't have to answer that, nor even brood over whether I should try to soften the Wilson rap by bringing up the hatchet job Mr. Mailer pulled off later on RFK and poor Marilyn for a bundle of spending money, because the President strode up then.

"How are you, Paul?" he said. "You're becoming one of the regulars in this Rose Garden. How's that star chamber proceeding of yours going?"

"Two ways, Mr. President," I said. "One good and one bad."

"Par for the course, I imagine. When Bob was my attorney general he was never able to come up with anything quite as hard to beat as those Commandments, despite the impeccable religious upbringing all of us had with Cardinal Cushing at our side from the cradle to the early journeys Bob and I made to this retreat without wars, politics, television or newspapers. And speaking of newspapers, I had a rather disturbing visit this morning from another recent arrival, a New Yorker like yourself, It was about my wife and a columnist of yours, Pete Hamill. Have I got the name right?"

"Of course, and I think I know what's about to hit the fan."

"I don't doubt it. The man told me Hamill wrote an absolutely vicious piece about Jackie when she married Onassis and then turned up himself as one of her escorts after Ari went to his Maker—in some heaven he probably owned himself, I imagine. That so?"

"Yes, except that the column you're talking about never ran in the *Post*. I killed it, not because I was worried about libel but because of the bad taste. Pete really said some rough things about marrying for money and all that."

"But then after you left the paper, and while all the garbage writers had Jackie running around with Hamill, somebody down there dug it up and ran some excerpts?"

"That's right, and I'll never know how the Australian ever found that thing. I had the type dumped but somebody else, maybe more than one somebody else, must have salted away a galley proof. Pete was on the *News* when they started to run those tidbits. He called me but I told him I had no idea how the thing had turned up almost eleven years later. It's a good thing, too, because Pete's a pretty heavy hitter and would have reduced the party who leaked it to hamburger meat if he ever caught up with him. As it happened, his thing with Jackie was over then anyway."

"So I was told. I must say it made the whole ugly incident a bit easier for me to swallow."

"I'm glad," I said. "It was a downer for all of us, but at the least it never made the networks. Nobody picked it up from the *Post* that I can recall."

"Small consolation, Paul, but it helps. I must say I have never brooded as much about myself—since that autumn day in '63, certainly—as I have about that sort of thing, not that I'm taking any kind of bow here. It's just that nothing else can possibly matter anymore. I'm sure you must feel the same way."

"I don't have to, Mr. President," I said. "I never got the kind of ink you did. My guess is the *Times* recorded my farewell in about three paragraphs under a character who was once their own crossword puzzle editor or maybe some poet nobody ever read, but what's the difference? I was born to blush unseen—like a real poet said once—and you were fated to be known to billions of people around the earth."

"The difference is zero," the President said. "It still comes down to dust—not that I can say I've seen any lately—for all of us mere mortals. All I wish is that Bob and I and Joe, who died so young in the war that was supposed to end all wars, had a little more time. There was so much to be done—so much."

"There's even more now," I said, leaving to join my mammoth man-walker because we had such a great distance to cover before they rattled out the next count against P. Sann, pagan and infidel (in the wedded state, that is). On that score, Brother Vittorio came up with an afterthought.

"I was thinkin, Paul," he said. "Maybe you pulled a rock yesterday when you didn't plead the Fifth."

"No, *paisan*," I said. "The way it plays in there you can't plead the Fifth on the Sixth."

Day V
and Day VI ❧

Chapter 12 •••••••••••••••••••••••••

I'm putting two trial days together here because I'm hazy on how I killed the anxious hours in between. I know I spent lots of time with Birdye and Ed, but for one thing I think my head was going and for two others I was getting colder and colder up in that rarified air, so much so that I'm fairly certain I made no stops at Brother Henry's. I guess maybe I didn't want to drink or smoke on an empty stomach because of my old ulcer. I wasn't worried about my heart anymore, of course, because I knew that was altogether gone while the scar on my duodenum was still there and a doctor I once had told me if it ever perforated again once I was past forty it could kill me. I did pay a call on Bill O'Dwyer one night, but that's barely worth reporting. The Boy from Bohola knew I had seen Don Francisco and that evidently touched a raw nerve. In the Kefauver hearings, summoned back from his exile in sunny Mexico, he had to answer some questions about at least one visit he had paid to the don while he was on leave from the D.A.'s office in Brooklyn and serving stateside as a brigadier general in procurement. He said he had dropped in on Uncle Frank only because the less patriotic elements were pilfering too many things the boys in the front lines needed to keep them warm but that didn't go down too well and I guess the sight of my face brought all that back and turned Bill'O off, not that he wasn't his old courtly self when he gave me the brush.

Anyway, to move this thing into the courthouse, there were no hassles of consequence either over Number Seven *("Thou shalt not steal")* or Number Eight *("Thou shalt not bear false witness against thy neighbor")*. That bit about stealing, as you must know, went beyond pinching things into such mush as respecting the property of others (whateverthehell that meant), inflicting damage on same and accepting bribes—not to mention the fine distinctions between simple theft and the kind that might require the use of a touch of violence, say with a lead pipe wrapped in your favorite newspaper, a stiletto or maybe a German Luger. I'll reduce most of this to Q. and A. to move it along because it was all so piddling.

Q. (from El Prosecutor, who had that ledger in his lap) Mr. Sann, will you tell this Tribunal whether you ever violated Commandment Number Seven?

A. Happily, sir. In our sub-teens the other kids and I sometimes swiped potatoes off outdoor fruit stands so we could build a bonfire from which to draw some sustenance. You understand, we had no money with which to obtain those potatoes.

Q. And that manner of pilferage constituted your sole violation of the commandment at issue?

A. No, sir.

Q. Would you amplify that, please?

A. Objection. I am once again being asked to bear witness against myself.

Q. (*the* Pete, although I expected his flamethrower to put his thirty pieces of silver in here) Sustained.

A. Thank you.

Q. Did there not come a time when apart from your illicit incursions upon the fruit and vegetable emporia you began to make comparable visits to establishments maintained by other merchants?

A. I believe you have reference to a retail outlet such as Woolworth's, commonly known as five-and-dime stores in those years. Some of us did pick an occasional trifle off those counters, but . . .

Q. You have answered the question. Did you, Mr. Sann, ever perchance misappropriate articles of any monetary value from motor vehicles?

A. Well, sir, many of the automobiles possessed by the more affluent were open touring cars and now and then some of us reached into the pockets affixed to the doors and made off with such inexpensive things as a flashlight or a pair of pliers.

Q. To move forward—once you were in your latter teens and gainfully employed did you ever misappropriate any property belonging to your employer?

A. (why kill time with another objection?) Oh, I surely left the office now and then with a typewriter ribbon or soap eraser, not much else.

Q. Did you not on occasion leave your office with some parchment paper?

A. I think you're referring to waste newsprint cut down to letterhead size. It had no value whatever.

Q. (Peter what's-his-face, to the chair) Is this petitioner to be permitted to set a monetary value upon the thefts at issue here?

A. (Pete) Sustained.

Q. Did there not come a time when the 'waste newsprint' you have described was replaced by a more costly brand of parchment?

A. Yes, sir. Copybooks which contained carbons so that a given number of duplicates might be available to the numerous editors through whom a given story had to pass.

Q. And did you at times leave your place of employment with some of those 'copybooks' in your possession?

A. That was a common practice for those of us involved in outside literary endeavors.

Q. Thank you. Now the ledger in my possession reflects a dispute which involved a matter of disbursements claimed by you in the Year of Our Lord Nineteen Hundred and Sixty-one. Is that not correct?

A. Yes, it is. My publisher questioned an item of some twenty-four dollars and change, including gratuities, which I had spent on a lunch for a news source of substantial importance.

Q. And were you accordingly reimbursed?

A. No. I had a rather quick temper, and so while the trifling sum in question was properly receipted I elected not to pursue the matter and, indeed, never thereafter submitted any requests for sums due to me except on such outlays as airline fares, hotel bills and out-of-town meals.

Q. There was, then, no repetition of any similar dispute?

A. Quite the contrary. I waived many thousands of dollars in fully proper reimbursable expenditures in the years thereafter.

Q. Most touching, Mr. Sann, but irrelevant. I now ask you whether in the earlier stages of your career—as a scrivener, that is to say—you had occasion to perpetrate any thefts.

A. Objection.

Q. I shall rephrase the question. Was it not a common practice on the journals of your time to acquire by whatever means available certain materials desired by said journals?

A. Yes, sir.

Q. You may elaborate if you will.

A. A newspaper reporter, then and now, must of necessity obtain any relevant material—photos, documents, letters, for example—for the purpose of assembling a full and fair account of a given event. Thus in any situation in which the opportunity presented itself, almost invariably in the case of malefactors, I did appropriate certain things which were being withehld from public scrutiny either by the police or, more often, the particular persons involved. I did not regard this practice as in violation of the Seventh Commandment. It was a condition of my employment. There are journalists who have been awarded the profession's highest honors for stories developed through their skills in this particular area.

Q. Really? Well, then, let us go on to your companion career, in particular your tome on the felon Arthur Flegenheimer which I would assume required you to seek information from certain law enforcement agencies.

A. I dealt with the prosecutors in New Jersey as well as the boroughs of Kings County and New York in my own city.

Q. And those public officers cooperated with you fully and freely?

A. No, not quite.

Q. Then you found yourself impelled, I trust, to resort to other means to obtain the documentation which you required?

A. Objection. I am again being asked to impeach myself.

Q. The question is withdrawn. What was it that you sought in the province of New Jersey?

A. Records pertaining to the trial of the man eventually imprisoned in the murder of the aforesaid Mr. Flegenheimer.

Q. Were some of those records perchance of a confidential nature and not set forth in the trial of that person?

A. Yes, sir.

Q. And you were able to obtain them nonetheless?

A. Yes, I was.

Q. You are confessing to the Tribunal that you stole them?

A. I would prefer to say that I was able to get possession of them.

Q. A semantic distinction, at best.* And you followed the same procedure elsewhere?

*Look, I'm not saying they're antisemantic up there.

A. I did.

Q. Splendid. Now that same tome contained the complete transcripts of private telephonic communications between the Secretary of the Treasury, a Mr. Morgenthau, and the Director of his Federal Bureau of Investigation, Mr. Hoover, as well as the Mayor of New York, one Fiorello H. La Guardia, did it not?

A. Yes. Mr. Flegenheimer had long been a fugitive from justice on an indictment for tax evasion and Mr. Morgenthau took it upon himself to advise the gentlemen you mentioned that he thought it was time for someone to take the man into custody.

Q. Was the transcript in question reposing in the archives on the estate of a deceased president named Franklin Delano Roosevelt?

A. Yes, sir—at Hyde Park, New York.

Q. Much of it not open to public scrutiny, as I understand it.

A. That's correct.

Q. You obtained that document by theft then.

A. No, I myself was never in that library.

Q. How then did the material, shall we say, fall into your hands?

A. I am sorry, I cannot say, because that would violate a confidence which would forever after destroy my usefulness as a writer. The courts below generally tend to uphold that position.

Q. Come now, Mr. Sann. *Someone*—an accomplice, perhaps—*stole* that document for you.

A. I wouldn't put it that way, sir. Someone made it available to me. I cannot go beyond that.

Q. Very well. I believe the point has been more than adequately made and shall let it rest there and turn to a line of questioning prompted by your own reference to Mr. Flegenheimer's tax problem. Is it not a fact that you yourself quite recently had a similar problem?

A. "Similar"? I have to say it was as similar as night and day. Mr. Flegenheimer was charged with evading taxes on hundreds of thousands of dollars in illicit income. Mr. Sann's tax return for 1977 was disputed by the authorities over five or six write-offs which my accountant, a gentleman very highly regarded in his profession, had deemed entirely proper.

Q. And was that esteemed person's view upheld by your government?

A. I fully expected it to be.

Q. That was not the question.

A. But it was the only answer I could give you. The scheduled audit postdated my voyage here.

Q. I see. Let me ask you this, then. Is not the withholding of proper taxes subject to criminal penalties and thus to be regarded as concomitant with theft?

A. If you're talking about a felony prosecution in the matter at hand, the answer is no. At the worst if some of the deductions I claimed were to be disallowed I would have to do nothing more than write a check for a few hundred dollars plus an interest assessment of six percent. One might be subject to capital penalties, such as fines or even imprisonment, where no tax returns have been filed at all or where truly substantial amounts of money may have been involved. Unlike Mr. Flegenheimer, I never was in any such lofty income bracket.

Q. You never faced criminal proceedings in any tithing situation, then. Is that your sworn testimony?

A. Of course.

Q. So be it then, and I commend the petitioner for the all but uniformly forthright quality of his responses today.

How nice. If those "all but" forthright responses made me a common thief in that sacred place not without its complement of racket bums, murderers and friends of mine like Bill O'Dwyer then I was afloat in a waterless sea of hypocrisy. I stole a fresh glance at my Peter and happily noted that he seemed rather bored. Better still, the minimal participation of Peter the Wolf suggested that he might have lost his thirst for my blood. Turning all this over, I felt a slight draft crawling up my left leg and reached under my shroud, fearing the worst.

It was the worst.

There was a hole big enough to put a finger through in the sneaker on that foot, whereupon I silently cursed Red Auerbach. How could a man of his wealth and prominence in the sporting arena, collecting a royalty on every sneaker bearing his imprimatur, endorse a product that would go to pieces so fast in a place where there was no concrete and no hardwood floors? Did my old pal have no shame? Oh, well, skip it. I was still on the stand, or whatever, and the prosecutor just thought of something.

Q. A related matter comes to mind, Mr. Sann. Did you ever accept bribes in your capacity either as a scrivener or supervisory official?

A. In all fairness, sir, don't you mean to ask me whether I was ever *offered* any bribes? Your question reeks with an assumption of guilt.

Q. As you will. Were you ever offered any illicit funds?

A. I was.

Q. Would you describe the circumstances, please?

A. Yes, sir. The family of a young woman who had been reported to the police as a missing person confided to me that she had actually fled with a black—they were called Negroes then—and offered me fifty dollars to keep that story out of my paper to spare the embarrassment which would surely ensue. I rejected the proffered bribe but my city editor, a most humane person, chose to let that incident go unrecorded. On a later occasion, as an editor myself, a man identifying himself as a fur merchant called me and offered to furnish my wife with a mink coat if I would hire his daughter, a journalism graduate. I asked that party his name and rejected the fur. Another time I was offered two hundred dollars a week by a bookmaker in return for having the employee handling the race results in my sports department phone them to him as they reached our office. I spurned that out of hand even though the sum involved almost equaled my weekly stipend from the paper.

Q. That last recitation is rather confusing. Please elaborate upon it.

A. Well, a bookmaker with such advance information would be in a position to take advantage of gamblers calling to place wagers moments after a race already had been run and, better still, bet the winning thoroughbred himself with unsuspecting colleagues in his illegal profession. That was a practice known as past-posting.

Q. There were no similiar incidents during your career as a journalist?

A. Just one, a few years back. A city commissioner under investigation by my staff sent me a large gift-wrapped package—liquor, I assumed—which I did not open but had returned to him by messenger, whereupon the man called and asked if I would meet him for a drink. Suspecting a more direct offer of a bribe, I had a special state prosecutor equip me with a taping device affixed to the small of my back and controlled by a button in my trouser pocket. Beyond this, two of the prosecutor's aides were seated at a nearby table in the bar where we met so that they could bear witness if the corrupt official passed anything to me, such as an envelope or cash.

Q. What was the outcome of that incident?

A. There was no direct offer of a bribe, simply some professions of a complete innocence of any wrongdoing and a suggestion that the two of us had much in common and might enjoy a profitable friendship.

Q. Did your newspaper eventually print its findings on that officeholder?

A. We already had published some of them and went on to publish still others, which led to that commissioner's resignation and subsequent indictment both for perjury and evading taxes on illicit income. In another instance, if I may go on, as a young reporter on the police beat—covering the criminal element, that is—I was approached by two notorious underworld figures who sought to engage my services as their public relations officer in the hopes that I could remove the stigma attached to their names. Those men offered me thrice whatever my salary may have been—it was actually sixty-five dollars a week— but I rejected that because of my unswerving devotion both to the law and my profession.

Back among the dead, the worst Peter:

"If the chair please, the petitioner, under questioning on the issue of bribery, now regales this Tribunal with a tale not only beyond confirmation but clearly having no reference whatever to the acceptance of illegal funds. Therefore I request that the irrelevant portion of his testimony be stricken."

"Your Honor," I protested. "The line between bribery and a blatant effort by sinister elements to enlist one's services seems awfully thin to me."

"Let the record stand," the good Pete said. "Does the prosecutor have any further questions?"

"I did not until this latest colloquy, but since the petitioner himself has introduced what must be regarded at best as another tangential issue I would inquire of him whether he ever had occasion to visit an inmate sequestered in a correctional facility and there pass the coin of the realm to any such person."

Good Christ. Were they also monitoring contact visits in the slammers?

"I don't mind responding to that," I said. "I think you're talking about a young man who did some carpentry in my home and later was taken into the toils by federal undercover agents while selling them a proscribed drug known as cocaine. Shocked and repelled as I was, I thought that youth could be rehabilitated and so paid several visits to him in the prison in the province of Danbury, Connecticut. That's all there was to that."

"Oh, come now. My question was meant to elicit testimony as to whether you passed money to the miscreant housed therein."

"I did, sir, but an explanation is in order."

"Let us hear it, Mr. Sann."

"Federal prisoners then were permitted as much as thirty-five dollars a month from the outside for the purchase of such needs as cigarets, toiletries and additional sustenance from the canteens to supplement the prison fare (I didn't see any point in mentioning such other trifles as marijuana, hard drugs, life-sustaining weapons or protection from the more muscular inmates). This youth—a father of three children, by the way—came from a family not always in a position to remit those required funds to him, which is why I furnished them on two or three of my visits."

"This was in violation of the institution's rules and regulations as known to you?"

"I believe so."

"Really? You either believed it or you knew it. Which was it?"

"I knew it."

"Thank you. No further questions."

The next session went much the same way, except for a few wrinkles of small consequence. The prosecutor obviously had no ammo to suggest that I had ever turned in a neighbor but squeezed out some questions bearing on such related things in Number Eight as withholding the truth or, worse, telling lies or committing such bad things as calumny. Thus he asked whether as an editor I had ever willfully withheld any stories from my paper. That could have taken a whole deathtime to answer, since editors make decisions every minute on the hour affecting what goes into a given story and what doesn't for one reason or another, so I simply objected that the pole was in the water again and Saint Peter went along. That it? No. Had I ever been a defendant in a suit for libel, slander or defamation of character? Yes, by the score, like anybody else in the media, but during my stewardship the newspaper had never lost a libel suit of any consequence. Another piece of cake, huh? No. The enemy's water pistol was far from empty. At the time I left my gazette was it not a fact that three suits, two for twenty-five million dollars apiece and one for a trifling six million, all naming P. Sann as one of the defending culprits, were pending?

Yes, sir.

OK, counselor, let's see you wiggle off that hook. My pleasure.

"The litigation you're talking about all came under the commonly accepted heading of nuisance suits meant to gag newspapers. One twenty-five-million-dollar case you cited was filed by a congressman after we said he had pleaded the Fifth Amendment during an inquiry into his affairs when in fact he had invoked several other applicable amendments which amounted to the same thing: he wasn't talking. Well, under a landmark Supreme Court decision—*New York Times* v. *Sullivan*, nineteen hundred and sixty-four—public personages cannot collect any damages without establishing either malice or reckless disregard, both enormously difficult to sustain. So that one was pretty idle. The other big case was instituted by two immensely wealthy real estate men after we revealed that they were renting space to operators of so-called massage parlors which really were nothing more than legal brothels not employing professional masseurs but harlots. This again was in the classic mold—designed to get me to call off my reporters, which I did not do. That one lay dormant for years and I heard quite recently that the plaintiffs had elected to drop it. Now that six-million-dollar thing stemmed from a story of ours baring gross neglect in a nursing home for the elderly operated, I should note, by a man of the cloth of my own faith. The rabbi involved either failed to pursue it or it was dismissed on a simple motion. I trust that answers your question."

The prosecutor said thanks a lot, it did, and that was it on Number Eight and while I had no idea what time it was, a claim I couldn't always make downstairs either, the man in the expensive robe announced that although it was not quite eleven hundred hours he would adjourn at that point. Nice kid, that Pete, as I believe I indicated earlier. If I had paid counsel he would have been saving me enough in fees to go out and buy Birdye a damned expensive gift if there were any shops around—assuming, of course, that Brother Henry hadn't dipped too deeply into my roll.

Day VII ᶿᵛᶿ

Chapter 13 •

On my seventh day in the great void, Brother Vittorio and I were
hanging around the tailor shop late one night when Brother Hector
came bustling in.

"What gives, Shorty?" the tall man demanded to know, looking
down around his shins. "You oughta be in your crib by now."

"Hey, don't make cracks like that, Vito. You got no call to hurt my
feelings all the time. I came over here with a message from Mr. Sann's
friend Shor. *Urgente.*"

"What is it, Hecky?" I asked, downing some Beefeater.

"Something about a baseball player named Munstein."

"You mean Thurman Munson. He was the Yankees catcher. Got
himself killed flying a plane he had no right to fly. What's the problem?"

"I wasn't given any details. Mr. Shor only told me he had to see you
and Vito."

We made Toots's dry hole in good time, even with the decay in that
left sneaker and some growing wear on the other one slowing me
down, and found the old innkeeper bordering on the morose.

"Paul," he said. "Thurm Munson dropped in on me a while ago—
first time—and we gotta help him bad."

"*We* gotta help that guy, Blubber?" I said. "You know how he always felt about newspapermen. You told him I was part of that 'we'?"

"Yeah. Thurm's not mad at you. Just said the crumbums you had covering the team always gave him a hard time, so he wouldn't hold still for interviews."

"Look, every reporter who ever got into a Yankee locker room gave that guy a hard time just saying hello, but he made pretty good copy by *not* talking, so I never had any rap on him. It's a wonder you don't. He cracked up his million-dollar jet back in August and waited till now to pay a call on a citizen of your former eminence."

"Oh, that's Thurman, always to himself. I don't mind."

"What's his problem now?"

"Bad, Paul. They buried him with his first championship ring when he was playing for Billy and they blew away the Dodgers in six but he got clipped for it when he was moved up to this league. It's really killing the guy. I never saw him so down."

"He can't be down, Tootsie," I said. "Everybody's *up* here. Let us now open the floor for the enforcer. What about this, goombah?"

I had never seen Brother Vittorio so steamed. I'm not even sure his face wasn't flushed.

"That crooked sonofabitch of a tailor," he thundered. "I thought there was a funny look on his ugly map when the midget mentioned that baseball player. What in hell would he want with the man's ring when he can't wear it or even fence it?" He turned to Toots. "Where's Mr. Munson now?"

"He's checking back in with me soon, Vito. Went jogging to cool off and keep those piano legs of his in shape."

"OK. Hold him. We won't be long. And if I can't show because they bag me for Murder One or something Paul will shoot over here in the getaway car with that ring."

Next stop, Brother Henry's, and we were barely in the shop before Brother Vittorio and the little tailor were eyeball to eyeball, which is to say that the round man was once again in the arms of my buddy, and I quote:

"Lissen good, you two-bit thief. The onny thing I ever heard of that's lower than you is whaleshit, and that's onny because it's at the bottom of the ocean."

"What's going down here, Vito?" All but choking, Hank barely got that short inquiry out.

"What's goin down is you got about four seconds to come up with a certain ring that says New York Yankees on it and somethin about a World Series. Now you wanna ask any more questions or try for one more breath before I tear off your dumb Polack head?"

The tailor, set down and trembling, had no questions but simply reached into a spare shroud and withdrew a small object tenderly wrapped in a double piece of that cheap textile.

"Vito, honest, on my own mother's grave, may she rest in peace, I didn't know this came off any friend of yours."

"It didn't, creep. It came off somebody else's friend—Mr. Toots Shor."

"Jesus, I'm awful sorry. It was that baseball player. I didn't figure he needed it so bad because I knew he won at least two of 'em. That's God's honest truth, believe me."

"Bullshit. You woulda boosted a ring like that off your own beloved old lady that's restin in peace, you pickpocket."

"Tiny," I said. "Enough. Hank just never saw a piece of gold like that before. Let's head back to Toots."

"Thanks, friend," said the tailor, "but could you hold it a minute? I'd like to try to square this."

"Start pourin," came the command from above, "and it'd be real good for your health if you happen to have some brandy stashed. Mr. Shor looked very thirsty at me."

"I got brandy, Vito. Fine brand—Martell. Came in last night. What's that baseball player drink?"

The huge Italian, his temper cooled, looked at me.

"He was never much for the hard stuff," I said. "Beer mostly."

"I got none, Paul," the tailor said. "How about butts?"

"Not that I ever heard, but let's take some just in case."

"Yeah," the enforcer put in, "and while you're makin up this CARE package throw in some Chesterfields and a touch of Dewar's for Mrs. Sann. You could come out even yet if you do everything right, you grave robber."

By the time we made it back to the Shor GHQ the stubby athlete himself, minus that imposing mustache but just as grim-faced as ever, was on the premises and nervously pacing around. Handed his ring, he could have passed for a small boy on Christmas morning after Santa has delivered that first set of Lionel trains. I couldn't recall ever having seen him with a smile like that except maybe on the days when the Yanks wrapped up those Series with him behind the plate.

"I don't know how to thank you, big man," he told Brother Vittorio, "or you, Mr. Sann. Toots told me you had some class."

"Thanks," I said. "I believe that's the first time you ever said a thing like that about any old newspaperman."

"I never said it about a young newspaperman," the great catcher laughed. "I guess I bum-rapped all the sportswriters once in a while."

"Only after every game," I said, "and even during spring training if my memory serves me, but in this ballpark nobody's mad at anybody. Man, you did it all on the green playing fields, which is what you were paid for—and never enough, for that matter, in my mind." My helper was pouring for our host now. "Maybe Toots will let you have a sip of that brandy to celebrate today's win."

"Thanks. This ring'll hold me all by itself. I hardly ever tied one on—and damned if it wasn't your guy Maury Allen who put it in the paper the night Lou Piniella and I hung a beauty on after some road game. Remember that?"

"No, I can't say I do."

"Well, you should. The TV and magazines all picked it up. Lou and I were steaming over the way things were going with all that junk between Reggie and Billy, and Mr. Steinbrenner was on that trip, so we emptied the hotel bar and then went up and banged on the great man's door around two in the morning and he called in Reggie and before the sun came up all four of us were feeling no pain. Anyway, I don't need anything to drink right now. The ring's plenty, and I have to say this shroud covers it very nicely, thanks to these short arms."

"Smoke, Thurm? We've got some Chesterfields."

"No, I don't wanna break training." That one came with an impish grin. "If Mr. Steinbrenner made it here, which would be something like Charlie Finley ever winning it all again, he might hit me with a fine. How was that tiger Martin when you were around, Paul?"

"In the doghouse again. Belted out a marshmallow salesman in a saloon in Minnesota and George called off his last deal to bring him back. You know, that thing about conduct unbecoming a Yankee, so he's out fishing or running his Western shops and on the payroll for a hundred-and-twenty-five Gs for each of the next two seasons without having to haul on those pinstripes and go out and do battle with Mr. Jackson every day."

Munson turned kind of sad.

"I guess nothing ever changes," he said. He had the ring on now and was running a couple of those beat-up fingers over it. "Oh, how I wish I had that one more year I wanted, with or without Billy. Or Jackson or Mr. Steinbrenner either, for that matter."

"So did quite a few other Americans," I said. "You got some kind of send-off."

"That's nice to hear," the catcher said, "but when you come down to it what's the difference? All I ever wanted was the love of my wife and kids. That's what made me a jackass pilot. I couldn't see enough of my family. Maybe I never should have been a ballplayer at all but a farmer."

Toots, with about a third of that bottle stowed away and feeling no pain, broke in.

"Jiminy crickets," he said. "What the devil is this—an Irish wake? We all had our shot, even little Vito here. What's there to complain about?"

"You're right," Munson said. "I didn't mean to put any damper on this celebration, especially since it's my own party. I still don't know how to thank Mr. Sann and his clean-up hitter."

"You already have, bad knees," said Toots. "Now why don't you let 'em go? Paul here's got a woman he likes to spend his spare time with. You headed that way, crumbum?"

"Yes. We picked up a few blasts for Birdye, so it's a day for winners all around."

"There's only two winners here," Toots said. "Thurm and your strongman." He threw a flabby arm around Brother Vittorio. "You're a good human being and all muscles besides," he went on. "I ever open another joint you're my Number One bouncer. That way I won't need to spoil my own pretty hands on anybody. Just leave your home number with my secretary."

"You could have a deal, Mr. Shor, onny I don't remember the number it's been so long now."

"No problem, you wonderful Dago," the old innkeeper said. "I'll find you wherever you are. I'm loaded with friends in your old crowd. All you gotta do is stay out of jail if you can."

"I'll do my best," Brother Vittorio said. "Nice meetin you, Mr. Munson. Paul tells me you wasn't no busher."

"Hell," the catcher said. "All I did was go out every day and play my butt off because I hated to lose. I hope I'll see you guys again soon."

See what death will do for some people? This was the Thurman Munson nobody knew, letting it all hang out, but we weren't going to get away without having to answer two questions for the tipsy proprietor of that sidestreet saloon.

One: Vito didn't do too much damage to Brother Henry, did he?

"Well, he had something like that in mind, Toots," I said, "but I stepped in. We all need that tailor in one piece, real bad, even—or I guess I should say *because*—he has such sticky fingers."

Two: How was that last court session?

"Oh, not the worst, Blubber," I said. "They tried to make me out a thief but it was all kid stuff. You know I never would have had to stay on that rag all those years if I knew how to make an honest living stealing."

"You kidding me? What was that if it wasn't stealing, crumbum?"

"Tootsie," I said. "Nothing changes you, not even the ultimate adversity. We bid you a good day in the heavenly acres. And you, Thurman. Stay loose."

The kind of handshake exchanged by the catcher and my playmate left still a third question: Which one had the broken hand, and beyond that I had something I wanted to check with Munson.

"Answer me something," I said. "There's a story around that once when Catfish Hunter had the ball and was throwing more than his usual share of first inning home-run pitches Billy came out and asked you what the guy had and you said something like 'How the hell do I know? I ain't caught a pitch yet.' Catfish, who's a plain old millionaire farmer now, growing beer commercials on the side, tells it himself. That ever happen?"

"More than once, Paul, but I was only kidding," Munson laughed. "You know that before Jim settled down he threw me some a belter like Rod Carew or George Brett couldn't reach with a fishing pole. I had trouble reaching some of 'em myself or digging them out of the dirt but, Paul, I'd catch that guy for no pay—even today, and you can put that in your paper."

"I can't get the sheet on the phone," I said. "So long."

Walking over to the women's dorm, I found myself brooding over the segregation of the sexes in what has always been advertised as the universe's most prized piece of real estate, where there was no sex anyway, and asked my soulguard whether he could shed any light on that.

"It's over my head, pal," he told me. "I never ast about it because it didn't make no difference to me. I never double-timed my Rosario and wasn't lookin for any skirts when I got here."

"Well, I've been thinking about this ridiculous bit, Vito, and you know it doesn't make an ounce of sense. When I think of some of the devoted couples they've split out it burns my ass."

"You talkin about some friends of yours?"

"No, I never had too many friends like that. I only came across an occasional good man like you who never went and had a taste on the outside—not to mention a married lady or two, as far as that goes, but that's not what bugs me. I was thinking about some of the great couples down through the ages."

"Would I know 'em?"

"Some of them, yes. Take Clark Gable and Carole Lombard for openers. When she died in that crack-up coming off her War Bond tour Gable never got over it, not that he didn't tie the knot again. Take the author Scott Fitzgerald and his Zelda. The high life killed 'em both too young but that love affair was for the ages. Take Mary Pickford and Douglas Fairbanks. Even Hilter and Eva Braun. There had to be something there because Adolf kept that bag around even though he had no time for nonsense. And how about the Mormon boss Brigham Young and all his wives? And Adam and Eve, who started us all off on the best things in life. And then there was President Harding and his bride, not that he didn't cheat a little on the side with Nan Britton. And Ruth Snyder and Judd Gray—"

"Hold it, pal," Brother Vittorio broke in. "Them two wasn't even married. Didn't they whack out her real husband?"

"Vito," I said, "forgive me. I bow to your superior knowledge of the more unsavory events of our time. You no doubt know that when those two were headed for that overheated chair they turned on each other, but I always thought Madam Gray, who couldn't ever pop her cookies enough, really had a thing for her corset salesman. They made one helluva hit squad back in '27. Worked like horses over Mr. Gray. Tried poison and gas, even put knockout pills in his prune whip before they went to the sashweight. I have to figure if they had a second chance they'd throw out the little trouble they had in their trial. They've sure got a right to be together after what they went through to get here, don't they?"

"I guess so, but you sound like you're not holdin your gin too good. Who else you got in mind?"

"Oh, well," I said, certainly not holding my gin all that good. "I can go way back, like there was a couple named Hero and Leander in early Greek times—I mean long before they all opened beaneries in our town. Leander had to swim across a whole river to connect with that chick, something called the Hellespont, of all things, and one night he went under in the tide and Hero was so busted up she went into the water herself. You can't imagine how many like that there are in the books. The original Cleopatra—not Liz Taylor, of course—and Antony. The Irish writer George Bernard Shaw and his Mrs. Campbell, not that they ever actually made it together. Oedipus and his own mother, no less. George Sand—she was a woman—and Chopin, the composer. And another longhair music writer, Wagner, with a dame named Cosima something. Your guy Columbus and the Queen who staked him to that boat ride. The fat King Henry the Eighth and Anne Boleyn, even though he chopped her head off when that one went sour. Coco Chanel and the Duke of Westminster. Napoleon and his babe, although they say she smelled from fish sometimes, which is where the expression 'Not tonight, Josephine' comes from, Vito. George S. Kaufman and his Beatrice, not that he didn't get into a whopping tabloid scandal with Mary Astor, the movie actress. Ike and Mamie when he was stateside. George and Martha Washington. Cole Porter and his wife even if he did like boys better. Hell, I could go on forever. The thing is, what's the fucking sense of keeping people like that apart? You know I'm not trying to cop out for myself, because I don't belong here in the first place. We had that thing with Dr. King about the color line in this joint but I have the same feeling about the sex bit. I tell you it's just plain cockeyed."

"You got me, pal," Brother Vittorio said, "but what's buggin 'ya? You're seein your bride all you want anyway."

"No way, Tiny. I can't see Birdye enough. The only time I was able to go around the clock with her in that other heaven was on shore leave from the slave ship I worked on. Here I don't have to show in any goddamned office to pick up what's left of a lousy paycheck after the withholding bites and Social Security and Blue Cross and all that junk. Now I could be with her every minute if they didn't run this trap like it's the old Alcatraz. That's my point."

"Look, I ain't arguin, pal. I'm sold but you don't wanna do too much beefin. I told 'ya there's ears all over the place."

"Aw, cut out that garbage, Vito. Am I where I think I am or is this a branch of some more liberal slammer where somebody taps on the steel doors and whispers 'Pass it along, pass it along' and all the cons get the message or what?"

That one amused the big guy.

"Nah, nothin like that," he said. "It's onny that the word gets around, one way or the other. Don't ask me how, just believe me."

"Anything you tell me is gospel, *paisan,* but if that's so how is it the only word I get is that guys like the Dutchman and Uncle Frank wanna see me? I knew all kinds of people in my other life. Birdye made a crack about that the other day."

"You got me, Paul," Brother Vittorio said, and I thought about the issue on the table for a moment.

"Wrong, Tiny, I think *I* got me. I guess I really didn't run into too many boys or girls who figured to make it to this stop. There's always been a saying in my business that you meet all kinds of interesting people, but when you come down to it most of them are grifters or hustlers looking for an edge or a piece of space. You don't run into too many archbishoops—and I'm not passing over our duly elected officials. I remember once we helped a guy get elected borough president and then nailed him in some funny business on a Harlem tenement he owned, using the public treasury to make it a nicer place to live in and collect the rents, and he wound up in a cell very angry at us. Shit, go back to Tom Dewey and your soul brother Luciano. I still have my doubts about the way Lucky walked so fast on that thirty-to-sixty prostitution rap to go home to Naples and live like a prince. Dewey said it was because he helped us win the war against the Nazis and Il Duce by ordering the waterfront thieves to cut out the sabotage and then helped set up the invasion of Sicily, but I never bought all of that."

"You could be right. The word in the outfit always was that there was a little trade-in there, like the mob didn't do Dewey any damage when he ran for governor and then the White House two times, but I never stood in high enough to know if that was on the level. How come you never asked Dewey himself about it?"

"I did, but the mustache wouldn't look me in the eye. Just agreed to answer some questions by mail when I was dealing with that in my book on the Dutchman, only the answers settled nothing for me."

"What a pity," said Brother Vittorio, deadpan (what else?) as we got to Birdye's. "It's a shame there wasn't more straight-shootin types like you and me."

"Not me, big man," I said. "Just you. Except maybe for using a silver-tipped slug now and then, you lived by the Golden Rule. Mine kept getting tarnished along the line."

Chapter 14 ●●●●●●●●●●●●●●●●●●●●●●●●●

The first mistake I made with my wife was to steal a kiss.

"This seems like home, lover," Birdye said. "It's as if you just showed up after one of those long days at the office. I'm talking about your breath."

"Right again, kiddo," I said, "but this morning there's a reason. Vito and I went to a party over at Toots's place and we had a few at Hank's first. Catch on?"

"No, I don't. The one night you never found your way to Riverdale happened to be after a party—the annual office Christmas thing, wasn't it? And you had the gall to tell me you got so high you couldn't risk the drive home when I knew Dolly never furnished enough liquor at those celebrations to get anybody drunk who wasn't drinking with both hands. Now tell me what all this is about if you don't mind."

And so I started to regale her with that Munson vs. Brother Henry epic to keep it all light and lively. No luck. Never having heard of that catcher, since the men she had seen wearing the big mitt for the Yanks went back to such giants as Bill Dickey and Yogi Berra, that little bundle of no-joy cut me off around the second inning while enjoying a Chesterfield and sipping her Scotch.

"This is all very amusing, Paul," she said, "but I'd rather not waste any more time on it. You've barely given me any information on those last two days in your trial and I let you get away with it. Now I want to know all about them. I don't want to hear anything about fun and games."

"This wasn't all fun and games," I said. "Our man came very close to choking a second death out of Brother Henry before we got that ring back. Would have done it too, except that I threatened to get up on a ladder—if I could find one, I mean—and spoil that handsome face of his."

Brother Vittorio laughed.

Sister Birdye didn't.

"Paul," she said, "either cut it out or go back to your party. I won't stand for any more of this. I had enough in the other heaven."

My Birdye, not all that different from the bull-necked detective with fists like hams who has you under that hundred-watt pool hall light in the station house back room and you're either going to spill it all or (a) have all kinds of black-and-blue marks that don't show or (b) simply die of natural causes if you can't have a cigaret and a hamburger (rare, with fried onions, please, Sergeant) in the next ten minutes.

"Give me a break, will you, wife?" I said. "Those last two days in the courthouse were too trivial to blow any time on, that's all. The *Times* would have given them about one skinny graph apiece even on a slow day for local news. I did give you a play-by-play on the big one. Wasn't that enough?"

"No, it wasn't. I think you're holding something from me on purpose."

"OK, you win, as usual. But I tell you there's no way I can stretch this out."

"Then do the best you can. If I have any questions, I'll ask them."

"Who would doubt it, you little doll? All right. Here we go, but don't tell me you didn't hear some of this before in the short version. First, that stealing junk. You know I quit boosting things long before I had the great good fortune to get picked up by you. If those beards are going to count things like borrowing a sweet potato off a fruit stand or making Woolworth's thirty cents poorer so Barbara Hutton could only marry herself seven or eight limp wrists—I'm not counting Cary Grant, of course—and buy most of them off with whole barrels of money then nobody has a Chinaman's chance in what passes for Paradise."

"I'm so glad there's nothing Chinese about you except the odd name they wrote down for your father at Ellis Island. Paul, are you seriously asking me to believe there was nothing more to that session than that and yet it took the full four hours. You didn't get here any earlier than usual that day."

"Look, Birdye. I wasn't finished. You can have all the boring details you want. They got into garbage like swiping things from the paper and all kinds of trivia, so it dragged. You know the only thing I ever stole that was worth a damn was your fabulous body and you also know what it cost me to maintain over all those years."

"Your bookies cost you more."

"Yes, ma'am. Anything you say. The Seventh Commandment doesn't cover the theft of live bodies in any case, so that was it, period."

"You mean to say you didn't make a point of the fact that there are all kinds of people around here who spent their whole careers stealing and everything else?"

"You mean guys like Costello and Schultz and Vito here?"

"Hey, hold it, pal," Brother Vittorio put in, smiling. "Once I was growed up the worst I ever done in that department was to go out and help on a hijackin run once in a while."

"I take it back, Tiny," I said while Birdye seconded the motion with an affectionate pat on that shoulder she could barely reach. "I have no doubt whatever that you never stole anything except under orders which you were obliged to follow like any good soldier. Now, wife, to answer your question, I'm not in that courthouse to put the blast on any other dead soul. I'm fighting for my death and my death alone. I would only louse up my own case if I started banging those beards with embarrassing references that might cast reflections on their tireless labors. I've decided to hold back all the names, the good and the bad."

"I guess you're right, husband. I didn't think of it that way. What about the other count?"

"Number Eight? Well, if I can stretch that into more than one fat paragraph then I should have done a damn sight better with that novel. Did I ever bear false witness? No, I never bore false witness and they had nothing in the book to show that I did. Did I ever keep anything out of the paper? Sure, who didn't? You don't need that spelled out. Did I ever libel anybody? Well, one jerk or another sued every other day but the queen never had to hock the crown jewels. I didn't even bother to explain to the Grand Inquisitor that we bought off almost every suit that looked a little scary, not that we ever spent a helluva lot in that process except on the lawyers. Anyway, they finally belted me with the fact that there were fifty-six million dollars' worth of suits hanging fire when Dolly got out but I'm pretty sure I was able to satisfy them that those cases actually added up to fifty-six *cents* plus the legal fees. I should have mentioned that the three characters who hit us with those had to be walking around in their Jockey shorts after paying their own barristers but I didn't bother. That's the whole shmear, so help me Whoever."

"Then why should that session have used up a whole morning?"

"It didn't, Birdye. You didn't check your Omega when Vito and I got here, or maybe the sun was in your eyes or that watch stopped. If it did, I'll take it to the jeweler's for you. There's got to be more than one in this hotel."

"Very funny. Are you sure that's all?"

"Scout's honor," I said. "Now let's get back to what matters. Have you seen Ed?"

"He was here before. Didn't leave until after eleven. It was almost as if we had gone out to dinner together while you were out playing poker for more than you could afford or torturing your ulcer over the points in a Knick game—except that there was nothing on the menu tonight we really cared for, so we didn't eat after all."

"Good thinking, baby. You have to watch your weight anyway in case they put in a tennis court. You must have had fun kicking over old times with Ed."

The hazel eyes brightened.

"I guess we did, lover," Birdye said. "We were talking mostly about Walter and John Gibbons and Paul Tierney and some of the others. It was nice, except that I got the chills when Ed mentioned the time Walter sent you up to Sing Sing to cover all those executions."

Brother Vittorio, his delicate sensibilities evidently affected, stepped in.

"You went up there and seen some guys take the juice, Paul? Man, that musta taken some stomach. They couldn't get me in that place with a writ, only a conviction."

"Oh, it was nothing, you old softie. It was supposed to be five kids, which was close to a record then, back in '39, but Governor Lehman commuted two of them, so it wasn't that bad. Besides, there was some lousy dentist from Brooklyn who had a pass and was only there for the fun of seeing how efficiently that chair worked, and he got sick as a dog after the first kid went and that put my own queasy stomach in pretty good shape."

"Something else really did, Paul," Birdye said.

"OK. This was a gang of imbies who killed a detective—Mike Foley—in a tearoom stickup on the Lower East Side. There were seven of them but one beat it by turning for the D.A. and one managed to hide out for two years just about midway between the Clinton Street station, which had that case, and Headquarters itself. And then when the other five were in the Dance Hall up there on the river, steps away from the hot seat, Lehman let off an Italian dragged along on the lookout detail and a Hebrew who was supposed to have furnished the guns, although that had the smell of a frame because the cops didn't like him from another movie. Anyway, that left one other kid from your side of the fence, another Hebe and the Irish boy who killed the dick. He was the toughest and went last, as per custom when that more or less regular eleven o'clock Thursday night show was put on. I wasn't feeling too strong by then, to tell the truth, but that punk said something that burned my backside more than his, so I had no trouble knocking out my story."

"I ain't sure I get that," Brother Vittorio said.

"Well, the first two settled for a mumbled 'Goodbye' when the rabbi and the priest did their things but the Irish kid put the blast on the governor. Said something like if his name was Cohen and his nose was longer they wouldn't be sitting him down, so you can imagine how I reacted. I forgot to mention it but I had something to do with the commutation that other Jewish kid got, because I did a lot of work on that case and filled in Lehman's counsel on the holes in it."

"You put that inna paper what the mick said?"

"I sure did."

"None of the other reporters used it, the way Ed and I recalled it," Birdye said. "Is that right, Paul?"

"Ed couldn't have meant it that way. It wasn't the reporters. Nobody was going to leave a line like that out of his copy but Walter was the only city editor who let it run. None of the others had the guts. I guess maybe they thought it was going to start a religious war or cost them some Jewish customers. Who knows? They were all chicken in those days except Walter. He operated the way I did later, having sat at his knees so long. First he printed it and then he waited for the public or the publisher—you remember it was J. David Stern in his time, Birdye—to come down on his owl-faced head. Hell, you know he walked out on about six papers because he could never make up his mind whether he wanted to stay in the business or teach college English and starve, since he was starving anyway."

Birdye, all out of Dewar's but feeling good, came up with a laugh.

"I never told you, lover," she said, taking my hand, "but Walter told me you were the one who finally made up his mind for him about not using his teaching degree."

"Me? You kidding?"

"Not at all. Walter said that with someone like you around who was a dropout picking up his missing credits in night courses he could combine both his loves—teaching and newspapers."

"Thanks, kiddo," I said. "You know how to hurt a guy as much as that lovable meanie from Ohio ever did. What was the thing about John Gibbons?"

"Oh, Ed just talked about the way John pointed you toward the books he thought you needed to read and then came to that story about his last night on the paper when President Roosevelt died."

"Damn, what a story—enough to move a hard-nosed guy like Vito here. You know he's really a cream puff deep down except when he gets upset over a thing like Brother Henry putting the snatch on a World Series ring."

"Tell him, Paul."

"I wasn't there myself, Vito," I said, "because I was in Indianapolis digging into some funny business on an air force base where the brass hats were treating the black cadets as if they didn't belong with flyboys who had white faces. Anyway, FDR was killed by that stroke in Warm Springs in time for us to make it an extra on top of our final edition, only the stereotypers—they roll the news pages into the plates that go on the press—were scattered around the neighborhood saloons. So the big wheels all made their regular trains to their suburban mansions and this man Gibbons, who was the daytime news editor, hung in right through that night and put out the big follow-up edition practically all by himself."

"What about your man Lister?" Brother Vittorio broke in.

"He had left for a better job in Philadelphia. Anyway, the thing is Mr. Gibbons pulled off a small classic that made a whole page in *Life* magazine the next week. You know the casualty lists they printed in small type during the war, right? Well, the guy put the President at the top of that day's list of the soldiers dead in action. Roosevelt, Franklin Delano, Commander-in-Chief, etcetera. Man, that was a stroke of pure genius, except that the genius who thought it up also was dead in action for practical purposes. He had a bad case of high blood pressure and after he put that edition to bed he dragged himself the hell and gone to his home way out in Jersey's Asbury Park and wound up in a wheelchair. All finished."

"He didn't live too long after that, did he?" Birdye asked. "Ed wasn't sure."

"I forget too. Maybe three, four years or even less before the hypertension finished him. I know that was one funeral you and I didn't miss. Next to Walter, he was my other surrogate father."

I wasn't going to ask Birdye what she and Ed had been over about Paul Tierney because I was afraid I would have trouble keeping that innocent face of mine. The white-haired Tierney, a devout Catholic who was the *Post*'s managing editor in those same days and the man who first turned me on to the Bible as just plain good reading, was in San Francisco with our army on that U.N. assignment when that ulcer blew on me and he did something which bordered on the saintly. The navy in Washington bumped a young ensign off a military flight to get Birdye to my bedside and once I was out of the ether and a certified live one, thanks to the sulfa drug that washed out the gangrene, Paul got the keys to my room in the Palace and swept it clean of the female effects strewn around there (ever ask yourself why a woman would leave her contraceptive gear in a virtual stranger's hotel room?). The Irish bad boy knew that story, of course.

As it happened, it was Birdye who had brought up the golden name and she and Ed had simply talked briefly about what a lovely gentleman and splendid pro the guy was and how there couldn't be any doubt about that pillar of the church being around somewhere in our theoretically, or theologically, euphoric new home. There was some mention of the time I left part of my duodenum in San Francisco, of course, touching on the way Tierney took charge, giving all the orders, even to the surgeons, when I came unhinged.

"Hasn't Ed tried to run Paul down?" I asked Birdye.

"He didn't say so. He said he was going to ask our private eye here to do it."

"What took the bum so long?" I said, turning to Brother Vittorio. "It's Paul Aloysius Tierney Jr. You can't miss him because if they let him wear a beard he would look like God Himself."

"I'll get on it as soon as I can, pal, but I got an idea it's time for us to head for the torture chamber. Want a few minutes alone with the little woman?"

"No, thanks, Tiny," I said. "She hollers at me even more when you're not around."

"It's academic anyway, smartass," Birdye said. "It's ten after seven."

"Fine. Give us both a kiss good night and we'll scram."

I got the better kiss, as a proper married type like me has a right to expect, but even so I couldn't let my girl off the hook.

"I hate to mention it, kiddo," I said, "but now your breath smells like you've been drinking again."

"You're lucky Vito's here," came the answer. "Otherwise I would have something to say by way of a retort. Two words' worth, and they're not 'up yours,' by the way."

"You didn't have to tell me that, wife," I said.

Chapter 15 ••••••••••••••••••••••••

Strolling toward the Hall of No Justice, the best friend of my second life remarked on the bond between Birdye and Ed and me.

"You don't know the half of it, Vito," I said. "I never was the kiss-and-tell type but there's nothing I can hold out on you. You won't believe what happened in French Hospital one time. All I needed was a little blood and some baby food for my ulcer and I was strong as a bull—feeling like a bull, too—and before that week was out I was powerful hungry for the touch of my girl. Who do you figure worked out that arrangement?"

"Your buddy?"

"You bet. Stood watch outside one night so the tiger could crawl into that narrow bed with me for a few minutes. It would have taken the Mother Superior herself along with about six armed guards your size to get Ed away from that door until Birdye tiptoed out. Can you imagine a man getting it off—I mean with his own wife—in a hospital run by nuns?"

"Yeah, I guess, but only with someone like that mick around."

Yes, that mick—and that fire. With the ink still wet on Ed's obit our house lawyer told me there was a Mildred Weidenfeld on the phone who said Mr. Flynn had a wristwatch of hers and she wanted it back. Did I know anything about that or should he brush her? No, I did know about it. Ed never wore a good watch because he always led with his left in the saloons and tended to bust them, but I had met him for dinner at Shor's a couple of nights back and he was wearing one of those wafer-thin eighteen-carat Corums with a twenty-dollar gold piece for a face and a gold link band worth another small fortune. Was he stepping up in class? Ed laughed and said, yes, he was now selling what he had been giving away for so many years. He had run into a platinum blonde at Dinty Moore's the night before and after a few vodkas she suggested one for the road at her place. Forty or so, the woman had parlayed a healthy divorce settlement with some overaged tomcat into a considerably larger fortune both in the market and as an angel for Broadway shows. Her "place" proved to be a triplex penthouse on the Upper East Side and that "nightcap" lasted until Ed had to fight his way out of a queen-sized bed and head for the office. He had one foot out of the door when his lovingly insatiable hostess reached into a Ming dynasty bureau, drew out that Corum and insisted that he had to wear it because a man of his high position in the community shouldn't ever be seen with a five-and-dime Bulova on his wrist.

Keeping that saga to myself, I asked the lawyer to send the Corum down with a bonded messenger and tell the woman I had it on but would return it to her if she dropped down. Well, I was barely off the phone when she showed up—in a terrible hurry because she had an appointment with David Merrick and her chauffeur was concerned about the traffic. I took her into Sylvia Porter's empty office so she wouldn't stop the traffic in that bleak city room because while she wasn't any Lana Turner she was no rutabaga either. Would she care for a libation—coffee, tea, milk, booze? Thank you, no, Mr. Sann, she simply wanted to pick up that timepiece and tell me how utterly crushed she was over her friend Mr. Flynn's untimely end because he was such a dear. I didn't tell her that Mr. Flynn had not only misplaced her unlisted number but her triplex as well.

"You have Ed's watch with you, Mrs. Weidenfeld?" I asked.

A little fishing around in a suede bag that had to be worth another bundle and there was the Bulova.

"Oh, I'm so glad you reminded me, Mr. Sann. Your attorney told me you were Mr. Flynn's closest friend and you meant to wear the gold watch as a kind of memento, so I did think to bring his for you."

"That was very thoughtful," I said. "Can you spare another few minutes?"

"Why, yes. Is there anything you want to know from me?"

"Not really," I said, blinking from the glare of the heavy silver choker dressing up that remarkably youthful but surely retreaded neck. "It's the other way around."

"By all means," the woman said, patting her store-bought hairdo.

Now I needed a moment to get my head straight. Do I tell that cocksucker she never deserved the last shot at my buddy and ought to stick that Corum up her ass or drape it on the next properly hung stud who could go the distance with her or just cool it and be a nice boy? Well, you already know about my refined upbringing.

"Mrs. Weidenfeld," I said, "I just want to tell you a few things about the man who wore that very generous gift of yours for a couple of days, and I might mention in passing that you only got it back because the noble fire laddies overlooked it. Sometimes they boost the juicier stuff while they're dousing the flames. It's one of the fringe benefits not spelled out in their contract."

"Oh, I know about that, Mr. Sann," said the busy entrepreneur from Wall Street, Broadway and the high-quality mattress. "I lost some rather expensive jewelry when my ex-husband and I were living on Beekman Place and had a small fire. Speaking of that, how bad was that fire in Mr. Flynn's hotel?"

"You haven't read our story?"

"I'm sorry. I couldn't bear to go beyond the headline."

"Hmnn. Well, it was real bad. Ed never had a chance, but I guess I ought to get to the point, since you're so rushed. My wife and I go way back with that man. I thought it might comfort you to know that you got real lucky at Dinty Moore's."

"Really?" Those green eyes—or were they contact lenses?—lit up like road markers on a blacked-out strip of the Brooklyn-Queens Expressway as my guest rejected a Camel and inserted a Benson & Hedges into a long gold holder. "I'm not sure I quite follow what you mean. I take it you knew about our chance meeting?"

"Yes, Ed told me. You'll be gratified to know, I trust, that he did not identify you."

"I'm not in the least surprised. He was such a perfect gentlemen, and such good company. We had a most delightful evening."

In my mood, the obvious question would have been how many times did you get to heaven, baby, but I fought that too.

"That word 'gentleman' doesn't quite describe Ed, Mrs. Weidenfeld," I said. "They're a dime a dozen. He was a very heavy hitter in this business—you know he was only forty and had a long way to go—and also one helluva human being."

"I wouldn't doubt any of that for a moment, Mr. Sann. Was he married by any chance?"

"Yes, but bust out with his wife."

"Oh, how unfortunate." The swinger stole a glance at a diamond-encrusted wristwatch. "Is there anything else?"

"I guess not. As you must have gathered, I'm kind of emotional about this thing. Ed bought my kids their first teddy bears. I just wanted to talk to you because you were the last one for him."

"I understand perfectly, but I'm afraid I must go now. If you would care to get together some evening, your attorney has my unlisted number."

How nice. Much as I would have liked one of those Corums, I could not in good conscience sample the last piece of flesh in Ed Flynn's short life, so I just walked the nymph to the elevator, steering her clear of our foul-smelling men's room so the emanations wouldn't penetrate her mink. Then I stopped in that hole and flushed the Bulova down the drain. I had a passing thought about wearing it but knew I couldn't. It reminded me more of Mildred Weidenfeld than Ed.

The memory of that pain-wracked session, which I had never told Birdye about, was eating away at me as the man mountain and I stopped at the contrite Brother Henry's for a booster, and moments later I was facing all those beards again.

I opened with a motion. We were into the count that said *"Thou shalt not covet they neighbor's wife"* and coming down to the wire with Number Ten: *"Thou shalt not covet they neighbor's goods."* Since there didn't seem to me to be more than a hairline between those two, I asked whether they could be combined and got my knuckles rapped.

"Are you aware that you are proposing to curtail your own trial?" Saint Peter asked.

"This is the seventh day, Your Honor. It was my hope that if we could dispose of the remaining counts I might be granted an additional day for my summation."

"Mr. Sann, the chair is constrained to advise you that in this chamber there exists neither the time nor the need for summations on either side. Even beyond that, if this extraordinary proposal of yours were to be granted your presentation would be limited to a single session none the less. We shall proceed on Commandment Number Nine."

Proceed where?

Or was I reading that piece of fluff wrong?

Did "neighbor" mean the woman next door, or down a flight or so, or across the street—or any old wife anywhere you might want to cuddle up with? It turned out, and I surely deserved it for not doing my homework more diligently, that the word "neighbor" embraced the whole wide world, so we were really back on that perfectly sordid adultery count, which confused the dead H out of me, but the prosecutor must have had an early lunch date in his club or something, because he plunged ahead before I could wrestle with that development.

"Would the petitioner now describe to the Tribunal his relationships with the lawfully wedded wives of any other men in his time below?"

"I'm not sure I get that. In the session devoted to the Sixth Commandment I testified fully and freely as to my intimate relationships— and *non*intimate, I must note—both with married women and women living apart from their husbands."

I knew what—or who—was coming. It was the lonely end, or perhaps I should say the wide thrower, on the far right.

"Your Honor, is it so much as remotely conceivable that this witness needs to be informed that a person of the opposite gender who has taken the marital vows remains a duly-wedded spouse so long as that bond is not legally severed?"

"I would hardly think so," Saint Peter said, "but he stands so reminded."

Of course, and the prosecutor had his fishing pole baited.

"Mr. Sann, I put it to you now, since you have been duly made aware that the status of any marital situation into which you may have intruded yourself for purposes of fornication is irrelevant, whether you can recall any instances in this area which you may perchance have overlooked?"

"Would you rephrase that question, sir?" I said. "I got lost along the line."

"Happily. Suppose I discard the parenthetical reference and inquire of you whether you enjoyed illicit relationships with any wedded persons beyond those previously cited?"

Much as I loved that word "enjoyed" (from memory, that is), I had to fall back once again on my Fifth Amendment nonrights and Pete went along.

Time out while the man with the ledger dipped into its accursed pages, and what do you suppose happened next?

Back, back, back into the merciless record of that fourth day.

Was this woman wedded during the time of your illicit relationship? No. This one? No. This one? No. That one? I wasn't really sure. This one? No.

And so it went. If I unwittingly erred here or there, so be it. I couldn't see the beards impaneling another grand jury and going for a perjury indictment, and what if they did? If they were to impose two sentences on me, or three or four for that matter, they surely would have to run concurrently, so what the Hell (the capital *H* is on purpose here) could the difference be?

I answered 'em all to the best of my recollection, but not without throwing in an occasional observation that I was under double jeopardy all through this dreary session and having my ears bent with any number of sermons from the Far Right (and never wrong) Peter, until the bell got me out of that round.

Emerging with my head in my hands, I ran into the first really cutting chill wind I had encountered in my new abode.

Brother Vittorio wasn't out there, just the runt.

"What's up, Hecky?" I asked. "Where's my goombah?"

The answer couldn't have been more casual.

"He's what you call reassigned. There's a new guy on the way over."

"Don't make jokes," I said. "I'm not in the mood for it, OK?"

"I didn't make any joke. You pulled a new keeper, that's all."

I know it was stupid, since I was practically on the steps of the courthouse and exposing my sneakers, however ragged by this time, but I leaned down and put two gentle hands on the little fellow's shoulders. Sensing that he was holding out on me, I tried a sly piece of flattery.

"Stretch," I said. "You've always been one of my favorite people. What's this reassignment shit? I don't have to tell you what Vito means to me. Now spill it, will you?"

"Lean down some more." This was in a whisper. "All this is on the Q.T." I leaned until we were damn near head to head. Hell, I would have got on my knees if I had a place to put them. "The ginzo got busted," Brother Hector went on. "The tailor too."

"What do you mean busted?" I growled. "Busted for what, in Christ's name?"

"Watch your language, man. I don't know the whole story. You have to figure somebody squealed about the side business the old mobster was doing for you with Henry's help, so Vito lost his stripes and the tailor lost his shop. Happened this morning. That's the whole scoop, the way you might say it."

"Stretch," I said. "I could care less about Brother Henry, but I can't make it up here without the tall one. Now where the fuck do I find him?"

"You don't, but if I know Vito he finds you. You gotta wait it out is all."

"How long, friend?" I was bordering on panic. "What if they got him in solitary?"

"Forget it, there's no hole here I ever saw. Straighten up. You got a visitor. I'll blow."

The six-footer coming toward me, a hundred percent pure Aryan with a simply lovely blond coiffure and a military bearing, looked like somebody I had seen on the "Late Late Late Show" a few thousand times. Except for the shroud, I mean, since it had no epaulets.

"You are Herr Zahn, I presume?" I was asked.

"No," I said. "I am Paul Sann—s-a-n-n."

"*Danke*, Herr Zahn. I am Brother Wolfgang and you are now in my charge. I regret that you had to wait but my orders they were cut for twelve hundred hours and that is precisely the time."

Orders cut?

I was so right about that military bearing.

"Look," I said. "I couldn't be more pleased to meet you, but would you mind cutting out that Herr Zahn stuff? Just make it Zahn, or Sahn, or anything, if you want. Paul's OK too." Then I thought I'd throw the zinger. "So's my Hebrew name, which I believe is Pincus."

"You are non-Aryan then? *Juden?*"

"Then and now, Herr Wolfgang. I never change. What about you? We might as well get acquainted. I'm something of a stranger here. How long have you been around?"

"Nineteen-forty I came. I was a Kapitan in Herr Göring's Luftwaffe during the blitz but my aircraft was attacked by a squadron of Spitfires before the destruction of London."

"No kidding?" I said. "I hate to break chops, Kapitan, but you've got your history fouled up. London's still there, all patched up real nice.

Your blitz fizzled like a soda pop bottle left out in the sun."

My new keeper turned a pure purple—the only color I had seen since my arrival.

"This is the truth you are speaking, Zahn?" he gasped.

"Gospel," I said. "That's my strong suit. Your side blew it."

"You cannot be serious. Der Fuehrer is no longer the supreme ruler of the Third Reich and the conquered territories?"

"There's no Fuehrer, no Third Reich and no conquered territories, only a country called Germany, like it used to be. When your old allies from Russia came marching into Berlin in the spring of '45 Mr. Hitler swallowed some cyanide and then stuck a pistol in his mouth in his bunker under Berlin and Mrs. Hitler—you know she was on the *zahftig* side—had a low-calorie poison for dinner."

"*Mrs.* Hitler?"

"That's right. Adolf married Frau Braun just before it all hit the fan."

"This iss so sad to hear."

"What, that Adolf took a wife or lost the war?"

"*Nein,* Zahn. This whole terrible thing which you have related to me."

"Well, I feel pretty awful but you know you can't win 'em all. Maybe next time. Anyway, now that I've got you up to date, can you lay some information on me, like where I can find Brother Vittorio?"

"There iss no Brother Vittorio in my barracks."

"What a shame. You got a Brother Henry in there by any chance?"

"*Nein.* No Henry, but we do have a Brother Heinrich."

"He a tailor?"

"Please. He was commandant of a tank force in the Afrika Korps."

"How nice," I said. "You must be right at home, Kapitan."

"*Nein.* I have informed you of my service in the Luftwaffe. I had credit for sixty-six successful missions as a fighter pilot before I was reassigned to the Messerschmitt BF one oh nine E to fly cover for the young men in the *Luftflotten* program. That is how I vas shot down. It vas a surprise attack. Before then I held many decorations."

I wanted to say I hope you shoved all those medals, meathead, but thought better of it, since it looked like I vas going to need this dream-walking Nazi yo-yo for a while at least.

"Congratulations, Herr Wolfgang," I said. "Those kids in the RAF must have got plain lucky to take you out. Tell me something. How well do you know the layout this high up?"

"My orders list your authorized stops. It iss your general custom to call upon Frau Zahn first. This iss so?"

"Just about," I said, "but right now I would like to go over to the G.I. depot if it's all the same to you."

"There iss something *kaput* with your uniform?"

"No, with my noodle."

"Your noodle? This I do not follow, Herr Zahn."

"Hey, do you mind just making it Zahn, Wolfie? We're going to be together a lot, I'm afraid."

"*Ja*, Zahn. We go now to the destination you have requested."

Did my head ever swim on that brief trip. So the joint either was bugged or crawling with stoolies, like Vito suspected. Would I ever see the Dago again? I wasn't far from tears. Would I ever see that two-bit tailor and what was left of my spending money? I can't say I gave much of a darn about that.

What I encountered in the shop, which hadn't been redecorated or anything was a gaunt, gray-haired gent no bigger than my own father who was called Brother Sol. Good start. I was among one of my own, anyway. I don't mean just the name. You don't have to be Jewish to be named Sol. I had known a few gentiles who bore that fine biblical name in the long form, but this particular Solomon impressed me more like Solly. Had the nose and all.

"Got any idea where I can find Brother Henry, Sol?" I asked.

"You're talking maybe about the one who had this store before, Mr. Sahn?"

"It's Sann, like man," I said, "or at least it was until I hooked up with this beautiful Nazi here. I need Henry. You know him, yes?"

"No. *Vest nish* from any tailor like that, and from what I see if he was a tailor then I was David Dubinsky."

"I don't get that. Don't tell me you never had to drop in here all the time Henry had the shop."

"You are *meshugge* maybe? For what should I drop in? I can't take care of my own shroud? I was in garments before you were born."

"So was my father, Sol," I said, "and a whole flock of my uncles on my mother's side who got rich in the sweatshops and stayed rich even after the unions started, but that doesn't help me. I need Henry real bad."

"*Gournisht helfin,* Sahn. If I hear anything you'll come back and I'll tell you. You speak Yiddish, yes?" That came with a glance toward the blond.

"No, I can only catch on to some it. I wasn't too good in the Yeshiva."

"What a pity—how the children changed."

Der Kapitan was stirring about now, almost as if he had another set of orders cut for a fresh sweep over London, so I bid Sol a fond *zei gezunt* and put a question to the goose-stepping Wolfgang. Would he mind hanging outside while I saw Frau Sann?

"Das iss against regulations, Zahn. I am instructed to remain with you at all times."

"I know that, but you impress me as one helluva nice Nazi, and I've met quite a few of them in my time. I was over in Germany not long after your side got blown out. The thing is my other keeper let me have a few minutes alone with my wife once in a while. Wouldn't you want it that way if your own wife was up here?"

"I did not have a wife. There vas no time for *Fräuleins*. The Fatherland came first."

Who else came, Wolfie? Some other fly-boy? You know I didn't ask. My own position on the Gay lib crowd always vas if that's *their* thing let 'em go to it.

"I admire you for that, Herr Wolfgang," I said, "but have a heart. I lived with that woman the best part of my other life. What's so wrong if we're alone?"

Big deal, Zahn. Didn't I know any better than to try that kind of margarine (I had been watching my cholesterol intake for four years, remember) on a guy who no doubt had a uniform over his diapers and maybe even stood alongside his beloved Adolf in the aborted Munich Beer Hall putsch in '23?

The gorgeous aquiline-nosed new officer of the nonideological Tribunal speaks.

"What's wrong, Zahn, iss that anything is *verboten* which does not observe one's orders to the letter. Since you are in essence my prisoner, I shall follow all the requirements of the Geneva Convention even without regard to our respective ranks. Beyond that I cannot go under any circumstances."

Oh, how I would have loved to get that stiff alone in a soundproof room with Brother Vittorio Pascaglia or Brother Edward P. Flynn or even myself, for that matter, but that vas so idle.

"No hard feelings, Kapitan," I said. "I just thought I'd ask."

"*Ja.*"

Jarass, I nearly said. But now we were at Birdye's and the startled look on her face said it all. That girl knew a Nazi when she saw one, either in white, black or brown.

"What happened to Vito?" she asked me.

"I don't know, except I'm pretty sure he didn't get shot again. It looks like he drew a transfer, because he wasn't out there after I satisfied the honorable judges that I never lusted after the wives of any of our neighbors. This collar ad here was a crackerjack Luftwaffe pilot. Thought he came out winners too, Birdye. You can imagine what a wrench it was for me to have to tell him it went the other way."

"He knows what we are, Paul?"

"Of course. I told him. Why not? There are no ovens around anywhere, and he wasn't in that branch of the service anyway. How are you today?"

"I was fine until just now. When will we see Vito?"

"No sweat, baby. If they haven't got leg shackles on those big feet he'll find us."

"I do hope so, dear. You two have been so close. Can't we have some time together?"

Mein war hero, standing straighter than any wooden Indian I ever saw outside of a cigar store when I vas a kid, picked up that soft inquiry in his sub-zero tones.

"Iss against regulations, Frau Zahn."

Birdye went into a quick simmer.

"I am not Frau Zahn," she zapped the creep. "I am Mrs. Paul Sann. You call me by my proper name and I'll call you by yours."

"It's Brother Wolfgang, Birdye," I said, "but Kapitan turns him on better. I guess it takes him back to the days when he was zinging 'em into the limeys."

"I'll try to remember that. How did you say you made out this morning?"

"It was nothing. They didn't have anything and broke early, so I came out feeling like a million, since what's left is another tapout, but then I ran into this ramrod and it all turned around."

"You should have been here earlier. Did you stop to see if that tailor knew anything?"

"That's what I did, only there's a new shingle hanging out there, like Hank also got demoted—or whatever you get up here when you do a little business on the side."

"Oh, how awful for you."

"I wouldn't say that. Now I can finally get on that regime my doctor knocked himself out trying to stick me with. I just feel bad for you, because you don't have to live that way. Then there's Toots and Ed, too, and I wanted to surprise Paul Tierney with a little taste. He always had a martini before saying grace at dinner."

"I understand, but maybe you shouldn't say any more." Frau Zahn took a peek at my new custodian. "It might come back to haunt you."

"Good word for this place, Birdye, but heck, there's only a few more sessions with the whiskers and after that I'm on my own like any other free citizen on these spotless acres and I know my way around by now, so let's not sweat it on a splendid winter day like this. By the way, have I told you how smashing you look today?"

"Thanks. I wish I felt that way, Paul, but this is less than ideal. I couldn't be more worried for Vito or more ill at ease with this total stranger hovering over us."

I turned to the holder of all those decorations, which he wasn't wearing, by the way.

"Kapitan, can't you give us like *zwanzig* minutes? I might be in a spot to return a favor like that."

"*Nein*. Orders forbid."

"*Ja,*" I ja'd. "I wouldn't want you to lose your silver wings, or were they gold?"

"Gold, Zahn."

"Good, and I don't doubt that you earned them. It's a pity the air marshals on this base won't let you wear all that stuff."

"Paul," Birdye said. "Don't start anything. It's bad enough as it is."

"I'm only trying to make the ace feel good, baby," I said. "He already knows I harbor no ill feelings against his crowd because I'm such a tolerant and forgiving man. After all, he was just a hired hand doing his job, which was only to make the Mother Country disappear, right?"

"Of course," my Frau came back with the barest twinkle in her eyes. "I feel the same way. Kapitan Wolfgang does seem like a nice sort."

The Nazi couldn't have been more pleased, because he clicked his feet (ever try that barefoot?), made a smart military turn and announced that he would await me without—or wait without me—if I needed a few moments on any purely personal matter.

"Good girl," I said when shitface left. "I want you to cheer up. Vito's gonna find us or we're gonna find Vito. I'll drift over and pass the word to Ed and we'll lean on the superior skills he had as an investigative reporter before they hung that label on anybody who could cover a one-alarm fire or a press conference and get all the names right. If you can find Big Sam you can bet your locket and Omega on it. Is that a sale?"

"Yes, Paul. Whatever you say, but it's all so worrisome."

"Don't look at it that way, Birdye. It's only another cookout in this trial-by-no-fire. Be patient. We have a whole new life—or whatever—owed to us. Give me a little time and I'll have this Nazi all wrapped up. He doesn't know our side came in and did all that damage to the cause, so he's a soft touch. Here he comes. You turn on the old charm, yes?"

"I'll try, Paul."

It looked to me like a helluva long shot.

Chapter 16 •

Not knowing whether Ed had gone on my no-no list as a fellow user of contraband, I told the Nazi I had to see a former associate named Paddy Flint and knew the way there.

Ed's greeting demonstrated that his old skills were intact.

"Hey, I was expecting you, Paul. Who's your new walker?"

"Only one of Hermann Göring's better fliers, Paddy," I said. "Darn near wiped out London all by himself. He's my new gumshoe."

"He know about that communion of yours when you were thirteen?"

"Of course. I told him. What can he do to me—make me six million and one?"

"You're the same guy, all right. I heard you had a shot to get into the Arab countries from Israel one time and blew it because you put down 'Jewish' on those visa papers when you could have made yourself an Episcopalian."

"Wrong, Paddy," I said. "Israel wasn't the problem because I was carrying two passports—one without the telltale stamp. The thing was they all had the finger on me, Hebe or no, because of an explosive interview I wangled out of Egypt's strongman three years before, in '55, so all I cost the lady was one flight to Lebanon and one to Jordan and they both threw me out the same night and we didn't even have any hotel grunts. Don't you have something more current on your mind?"

I should have known that Ed wasn't going to plunge headlong into that "more current" problem.

"How's our Birdye?" he asked.

"Just great, but you ought to slide over there today. I didn't stay too long because of this new face, not she wasn't as nice as could be with Brother Wolfgang here."

"I figured that, Paul. Nobody ever made friends easier than that girl. You did OK with the judges this morning?"

"Yeah, it was a nothing session. Broke early."

"Seen Toots?"

"No."

"Well, you wanna skip him for a few days. He's pretty busy." Nice note there. So the brandy guzzler was on the proscribed list, which came as no shock. "Another old friend of yours came by this morning," Ed went on "and we talked a while."

"Who, Paddy?"

"That fellow you knew down in Little Italy. I never got his whole handle straight."

"Was he alone?"

"No, he had company."

"He leave any message for me?"

Ed let a beat pass, throwing a look at the Nazi.

"Nothing heavy. He said he was tied up on some other detail but would catch up with you along the line because he had something for you."

"That was all?"

"No, he mentioned a mutual friend. Said you'd know who he was because he's on the short side, like a very small guard in your game."

"What did he say about him?"

"Just that it might be a good idea to give that one a pass for a while. I didn't ask him why."

"Did he say anything about Hank?"

"You mean like where you could find him, Paul? He didn't know."

"Well, I guess we'll catch up, Paddy. I have to blow. I've got all kinds of unfinished business in the morgue. Anything you need checked in there?"

"No, thanks. I could do with some reading myself but that dump's useless without the dailies. I'd like to see how our old sheet's doing."

"It's a little changed now," I said. "The place is loaded with limeys and Aussies who could give you lessons even with your Hearst training. They've put the finishing touches on the art of knocking out a selling head and then getting some copy written to fit it, so when I left town they were about a hundred thirty thousand over the half million I left them and still flying. Except with the advertisers, that is. The paper's hardly fat enough to wrap a good sized herring in now, but the new owner's got about eighty-four other rags around the world, even Texas, not to mention the *Village Voice,* a magazine called *New York,* a sizzling national weekly, TV stations overseas, sheep ranches back in Australia and who knows what else. Just bought his own airline so he wouldn't have to stand in line in any airports. He blew ten million the first year on our paper but had it down to six point five the last time I heard, which for him is the same as you having to dip into your wallet for a fifth of Jack Daniels in the old days. But, heck, Paddy, this is no journalism class. I gotta run."

Rolling again, the ace wanted to know what vas that thing about a morgue. He didn't know from any mortuary, so I explained to him that I vas talking about a library and he observed that we would have to cross the golf course to get there. Would I care for a late lunch, perhaps?

"No, thanks, Wolfie," I said. "I'm watching my diet." Well, I couldn't risk losing the friendship of such a nice Aryan by telling him I would starve to life before I ever broke lettuce with a Nazi, could I? "You can stop if you want."

"*Nein.* I shall wait until we return to my billet."

So those fuckers had something going on the side, too. Who would have doubted it?

At the morgue I asked for the King James Bible again and the old bastard grunted that I had already consulted that.

"My compliments on your photographic memory," I grunted back, "but I didn't know there was a limit on how many times a subscriber could look at the same book here, especially the Good Book."

"There is no such limitation, Mr. Sann," came the reply as the man fished out the same moth-eaten Gideon model. "It is simply that I am sorely pressed for time here without any staff assistants."

With my summation in mind, I wanted to go over the relevant portion of Exodus again, dip into Deuteronomy in the same Old Testament and Revelation in the New and also check on Matthew, Mark, Luke and John.

"Make yourself comfortable," I told Herr Wolfgang. "We could be here a while."

That picked me up another *ja* and I went to work. I found nothing between the lines in Exodus and went on to Deuteronomy. I had always read that fifth book of my man Moses as the Bible's sexiest chapter—in awe, I should add, over its liberal tone. Like how procreation is not necessarily the sole purpose of the old-fashioned missionary position. How nobody got rousted for purely secular prostitution in the land of my forefathers. How Rahab, the whore of Jericho, won a commendation for her tireless labors. How Jephthah the judge was the son of a flesh peddler and never lost his robes. How the young were cautioned against getting clipped by the salesgirls but never threatened with having their things chopped off or anything like that. And how—mark ye this, for it has much bearing in this woeful narrative—adultery wasn't in the penal code as a capital crime either. Heck, the way Deuteronomy had it in my reading a wife had no ironbound claim on her husband's genitals and a husband who slipped away for a needed change of pace wasn't deemed to be guilty of anything worse than violating some other farmer's bride. And not only that, if you succumbed to the old lust without the license all you had to do was marry the girl even—mind you this—if you happened to have a wife at home living off your labors outside of the boudoir. Oh I know there was a small penalty, like both bedmates could get killed, for cuckolding a square husband and thus jeopardizing the family line, but still the general theme of that chapter was on the side of tolerance toward the citizens who leaned to the fuller, healthier and more varied lifestyle.

But excuse please. I fear I stray, if you'll pardon the double meaning.

Anyway, I moved on to the Revelation as set forth by Saint John the Divine, where the trail shifted a bit. There was Jezebel, and I thought John was awfully rough on that temptress: (*"Behold, I will cast her into a bed and them that commit adultery with her into great tribulation. . . . And I will kill her children with death"*). I guess I went to that windup chapter in search of some insights into this place I had been cast into, or up to, but that was no help. The Heaven described by John surely wasn't the one I was in, because it seemed like a helluva lot nicer place to be dead in. I wasn't all that troubled about the way Revelation struck out at the fornicators and whoremongers and all those other baddies but CH 20:12 did me no good at all: *"And I saw the dead, small and great, stand before God; and the books were opened; and the dead were judged out of those things which were written in the books, according to their works."* Ouch. The Man's own underbosses already had given me the old brass knuckle treatment over my works, so I went from that downer to my fellow journalists (all nonunion men) but that exhausting workout did no more than confirm what I had always thought about Matthew, Mark, Luke and John. Like any other four reporters, the best as well as the worst, they were so often miles apart on the hard facts. In all fairness, after all is said and writ, they were forty to sixty years late running down the story of the Son of God and got nowhere at all on the missing eighteen years in His ministry, no more than an army of modern-day reporters had gotten on the eighteen missing *minutes* in Dick Nixon's stint as the master recording technician of more recent times. But the big thing was that I knew it was sheer H when the desk sent you out on a hot one late and still couldn't quite write off the wild divergencies in the four Gospels. After all, those forerunners of mine didn't have to bump against the kind of deadlines Paddy Flint and I had battled in our time, so I thought they should have come somewhat closer to a more uniform set of facts. Closing the book on Matthew, I wondered why I had bothered in the first place. God, or somebody, had to know that P. Zahn vas not trying to pick up any kind of line on a Resurrection because he had no desire whatever to go anywhere without his Birdye.

I had no idea how late it was when I handed the Book back to that hunched-over misanthrope but I did notice a mildly interesting thing about Brother Wolfgang. He seemed to be half asleep on his feet, which set my mind going a mile a minute—faster, incidentally, than my normal speed in the place from whence, to my everlasting shock, I had made that lightning fast journey.

"You are finished now, Zahn?" I was asked.

"*Ja*, Kapitan," I said. "You seem a little shlepped out. I have a few other stops but if you're dragging I'll make them another time."

"*Danke.* We have covered great distances, and you are aware that I had no service in the Wehrmacht."

"I understand," I said. "Lead the way. How far is your place?"

"Thirty kilometers."

"I hope some of it is downhill for your sake, Wolfie," I said.

Vas I going to find myself in a whole nest of Nazis at the end of that trek? No. We were quite alone.

And that vasn't all.

We weren't there five minutes when my Nazi fell into a sound sleep marked by a most serene, even joyous expression. He had to be dreaming about how he dropped that last big one on London and was promptly summoned to Berchtesgaden, hung with the Iron Cross and another twenty-four decorations and boosted all the way up to Fatso Göring's second in command.

I had something else in mind and I didn't need the sleep.

I was just going to keep an eye—both eyes, in fact—peeled on all four sides.

I expected a visitor, because I knew the man mountain, with his vast experience both above and below, was going to find a way unless they had him surrounded by an army with comparable backgrounds, and in no time at all my ears were tickled by the sweetest, most melodious whistle I had ever heard.

I whirled to my left and there, some forty feet away, was my majestic friend. I snatched a quick glance at the sleeping ace (no less erect, of course) and bounded into a bear hug.

"Paul boy," my fallen guardian angel quietly rasped. "You're a sight for sore eyes. I been casin you and that kraut all day and I knew I had no chance unless you put him to bed back here."

"It was a tapout, Vito. I wore the Nazi down keeping him on the move and then driving him bonkers in the library. What the hell happened?"

"The midget put the finger on. He's one of *them* and I tell you I could kick myself inna butt for not smellin out that rat sooner."

"How can you be so sure it's him?"

"How? They had us all and turned the runt, which is why he's still on the courthouse payroll. You get any dope from Ed?"

"Yes, sir."

"How did you make him, Paul? He's on the shitlist too."

"I slipped one past Hitler's wunderkind. Used the name Paddy Flint and he fell for it."

"Nice goin, but I wouldn't try a stunt like that again. It could be too risky."

"OK. Ed said you had something for me. Is it what I think it is?"

"Yeah. I got tipped before the bust and shook down that fuckin tailor—and wouldn't you know he clipped you pretty good? There was onny a lousy fourteen aces in the shroud he used for a cash register for your Swiss bank account. I grabbed 'em but I could get a dustin while the heat's still on, so you better stash 'em."

The good Brother turned to plant his ample form between me and the sleeping beauty while I slipped seven spanking new C notes into each sneaker, observing that they were apt to take a beating because those Auerbach models were going so fast.

"It's OK, pal. You can Scotch tape 'em if they tear any worse."

"*Paisan,* I left the tape on my desk. What's with the dishonest tailor?"

"I don't know where they stuck that chiseler. He ain't our problem anyway. It's the fuckin midget."

"Tiny," I said. "All this profanity, which is so unlike you, suggests a six-foot-eight-inch rage that worries me."

"Forget it. You think I'm gonna waste that cockroach with my pinky? No way." Now a look of ever-so-pleasant reminiscence flooded those baby blue eyes. "You know, Paul, there's ways and ways. In the Family downstairs a guy crossed'ya you put the automatic in his ear and then ran some piano wire around his neck so he wouldn't suffer too much if he was still breathin, maybe stuck him a few times where it wouldn't hurt too much, and if you was real mad you cut off his mutton and rammed it in his mouth. Then you wrapped the remains in some rags and threw in a dead fish and left him in the trunk of his car or dumped him onna street where his own mob wouldn't have no trouble findin him and gettin the message. That's what you might call the humane way, only I don't want that mouse any deader than he was when he got here. I want him like he is so I can dish it out to him a little at a time. The last thing I'm gonna do is yank his tongue out so he gets outta the stoolie business."

"Vito, please. Why get yourself jammed up any worse?"

"How do I get in any deeper if the squirt can't use his ass-lickin mouth?"

"He can point, can't he?"

"Not this high, pal. You don't do no worryin about this. Now let's move it before Hitler's boy comes to life."

"Hold it. What happens to our supply line from the outside world? That tailor who took over for Hank sounds more miserable than my own old man."

"That ain't the half of it. They set up a new check-in system, somethin like the airlines done after all them highjackins when everybody wanted to go see the guy with the beard in Havana. I don't mean they brought up any of them fancy things to see if you're carryin a piece or anything but they're emptyin out the new arrivals before the tailor gets to 'em."

"Man," I said. "There's nothing they don't think of in this trap, but the hell with that. I meant to ask you if you needed any of these bills, but I guess it doesn't matter now, does it?"

"No, the store's closed tight. Look, I'll check in with Ed and maybe Mr. Shor too later on and then we go for the same bit tonight. You wear your mark down and I'll show here."

"I don't get it. Don't they have a guard on you around the sundial now?"

"Sure, but he's no problem. Decent guy. Worked in a bank and started takin some of the larger deposits home because he had a gamblin habit, of all things. Anyway, he took his last breath in Dannemora not too long back. Knew your name, in fact. Said he used to read your sheet when you had a column in it, so he's with us. Now I better shove off. You ain't got too long before court. Oughta try to get some shut-eye yourself."

"No way. I once promised myself that I would never lay my head— or even my feet for that matter—alongside any Jew-killer, so I'll stay up."

"OK. Take care, and give the little woman a hug for me."

"Why don't you drop in on her?"

"No soap. The spot I'm on that dorm's off-limits. Now lemme slip'ya two quick ones. You play it dumb with the midget like Ed told'ya, right?" Right. "Good. The second thing is when the beards bang'ya with this thing you lay it all on me, like I hadda twist your arm before you'd fracture the house rules. You could say you was scared shitless because you knew I had somethin goin for myself."

"Sure thing. There's no sense in my taking the fall when they've already got one noose around my neck. You know how much I hate to do that to you but, hell, if I don't they'll hang me by my balls—I mean if they can find them."

"That's good, Paul. I was afraid a stand-up guy like you wouldn't look at it that way. You're doin the smart thing."

"Maybe so, Tiny, but let me tell you something in front. It's gonna leave me even deader, because next to Birdye and Ed and my kids I love you the most, and I'm damn glad you got to this resort a few minutes before the other fuck knew you were on the way."

"Who?"

"The one with the pitchfork and the horns. You're too good for the sweatbox he's running."

"Jesus, Paul, that's the nicest thing anybody ever said to me in my whole life, even before I went bad. I better scram before I start bawlin."

Just imagine if that man had met someone like me in his formative years. Probably would have made the Governor's Mansion in Albany or even the United States Senate instead of going into a square trade and getting himself killed so young.

Day VIII ⸰ᴥ

Chapter 17 ●

There's nothing like a change in that boring daily routine when you're a defendant in a rigged trial, and it came—ever so welcome, like another hole in the head—when Wolfie delivered the body. Brother Wilhelm, waiting at the portals, directed me to present myself before the bench.

"Mr. Sann," spake Hizzoner, "you found yourself in the custody of a new trusty yesterday and surely do not require any enlightenment as to the circumstances which led to that eventuality. Quite the contrary, this Tribunal now requires some information from you."

The next man up was the prosecutor:

Q. From the moment of your arrival in this sanctified place, sir, you proceeded to engage in a variety of interdicted practices. Am I correct?

A. Well, much to my own deep regret. I—

Q. You will confine your answers to "Yes" or "No" except where otherwise indicated. You were able to avail yourself of certain contraband commodities?

A. I was.

Q. You are directed to enumerate what that contraband consisted of.

A. Some alcoholic beverages, cigarets and, just once, a small amount of food not normally available on these premises.

Q. Is that the full extent of your answer?

A. Pretty much, except that in the GI depot I was able to prevail upon the Brother in charge to let me keep my sneakers, which I value very highly for sentimental reasons.

Q. Your reference to value was in no wise pertinent. You will now name your accomplices in the other illicit activities to which you have confessed.

(Ridiculous, no? The counsel for the Un-American Activities Committee in God's own house was asking me to tell him something he already knew.)

A. I'm sorry, sir, but I cannot do that.

Q. You cannot or you will not?

A. I cannot and will not.

Q. How interesting. Early on the petitioner protested that he was being unfairly taxed to incriminate himself, albeit he is now doing precisely that very thing independently of any action by this Tribunal.

A. May I respond to that?

Q. By all means.

A. It happens that while I have no reservation whatever about self-incrimination in the matter at hand, I cannot bear witness against any other person or persons who may be facing punitive action as a result of my conduct. Throughout my life, regardless of any other weaknesses to which I may have fallen prey, I have held the most rigid and unswerving position on the issue of guilt by association. This is something so dear to me, so deeply ingrained in every fiber of my being, that I cannot stray from it. Again, irrespective of the possible consequences to myself.

Q. I take it, then, that you will not give testimony with regard to the forbidden aspects of your relationship with the Brothers Vittorio and Henry.

A. That is my position.

From the far right:

"Your Honor, may I respectfully suggest that a recess is in order?"

"The petitioner will be led out," said Saint Peter, looking pretty unhappy.

I don't know how long I was in the nonexistent corridor with Brother Wilhelm but there was one detail, fourteen clams worth, tax-free, warming the shredded remnants of my heart. Nothing had been said about my cash portfolio.

Led back in, I was addressed by Pete, as follows:

"Mr. Sann, you appear to have made a decision which, alas, passeth understanding. Withal, out of simple Christian charity, the chair extends to you a final opportunity to answer, fully, frankly and without reservation, the questions heretofore put to you with respect to the accomplices in the misdeeds currently at issue."

"I am duly grateful for that very generous offer, Your Honor," I said, "but, once again, and with all due respect, I must avow that there are no circumstances under which I would give testimony against a fellow man in a situation such as the one I now find myself embroiled in."

"So be it, then. You may be seated."

"May I ask a question, please?"

A weary shake of the whiskers.

"Do the events which have just transpired enter into this Tribunal's eventual verdict in the more consequential case at hand?"

"I shall respond to that in dual fashion. Your employment of the term 'more consequential' is inexcusably presumptive and the question itself is out of order. Your trial will now go forth."

The prosecutor did not reach into his bat bag as I resumed my yoga position and the clerk droned out: *"Thou shalt not covet thy neighbor's goods."* Nor did my tireless interrogator throw in the standard line about whether the accused needed any amplification on the count at hand, for now he was telling me, rather acerbicly, that the reference to "thy neighbor's goods" was only the tip of the iceberg in the Tenth Commandment.

"What is connoted by this injunction, for your elucidation, is that one is forbidden to take or without authority retain the possessions of other mortals and, beyond that, may not so much as entertain a shred of envy with regard to the material success of such mortals."

I had now heard it all, from the sublime to the dung heap.

"Thank you," I said. "I did not know until this moment that a reprise on the commandment dealing with theft was on today's calendar. Beyond that, going to the matter of 'envy,' I find myself totally bewildered. If there is a living soul on the face of the earth who has gone through his or her life without ever suffering that affliction it was never my privilege to meet them. I can address myself to this subject at further length if you wish."

"There is no need for that," the prosecutor said. "You have answered my question, Mr. Sann, and I have no others for the simple reason that, as in so many other instances, you have so graciously assisted me in my assigned task. Therefore, I shall rest the Tribunal's case here and now."

"We stand adjourned," Pete said, and he said it even quicker than you could recite that time-tested piece of wisdom which tells us that a lawyer who represents himself has a fool for a client. And didn't Peter Burger and the other whitebeards know the cast-iron truth of that one. I thought I felt a few drops of welcome rain falling but I guess it was nothing more than some droplets off my forehead, and I suppose that was just as well. How would you like to patter around in a soaking wet shroud in a preserve without a single one of those "1-hour" dry cleaning operations. How idle. It was like the time, on the very first day, I think, that I asked Brother Vittorio where the shower room was, since I had not had a moment to attend to my ablutions before my son dropped into my brownstone, and Vito said "You won't need none up here, pal, because you won't get no dirt on you no more." But let us go on, shall we?

Delivered to my new Nazi chum by history's smallest double agent, I told him we were heading for Frau Zahn's and after that I might make a few other house calls but would have to spend the rest of the day in the library.

"Late into the *Nacht* again, Zahn?"

"Very late, Wolfie. I have some heavy work in there."

"*Ja*. We go now."

Surprised to see me that early, Birdye wanted to know what had happened.

"Zilch, baby," I said. "Did you know it's a violation of God's law to hunger after anything any other bum has besides a wife? How could I take that kind of junk seriously when I never knew anybody who didn't value any damn thing he had, like say his car, his golf clubs, his secretary or even his favorite bartender, more than any old wife?"

"I love the way you put that, Paul, but I read it in your column about a thousand times, usually with little me as your patsy."

"Thanks a lot, but let me finish, will you? This time it wasn't for fun. There was nothing I could do but kiss off those characters in the newly pressed *schmattas*. Christ, they all walked the earth themselves once. What the hell could I tell them that they didn't know? Maybe there weren't any John Paul Gettys or Nelson Rockefellers around in those days. Was I supposed to confess that I never had the hots for any of the oil billionaire's army of wives but would have loved that castle of his in England with the pay phones for guests to keep the costs down? Or had no hunger for Rocky's first or second brides but could have used some of the no-pay loans he was forever laying on his inner circle? I guess you missed it, but Jackie Kennedy heisted that pint-sized shipping tycoon away from Maria Callas about ten years back.

Well, I never wanted a shot at Jackie because she was so skinny on top, but I would have loved a free ride or two on that Onassis yacht. OK? I'm telling you, Birdye, it's too ridiculous to blow any time on."

"I don't doubt it, Paul, but you've managed pretty well right here. Now maybe you can find some time for what I really wanted to know—what I've been torturing myself over since yesterday. Don't tell me you weren't asked about that business with Vito and the tailor."

"Of course I was. I told them to shove it."

"You're running true to form. How rough was it?"

"I don't know, baby. I did the only thing I could do and still look at myself in the mirror if I ever shave again, because if Tiny or that bedbug did anything against the eleven million rules in this operation, which is only a handful more than Dolly Schiff hung around my neck, then it was only because they had fallen under my immoral influence."

"Oh, sure. Who would doubt it? Would it be too much trouble for you to tell me what they said your heroic position on all this meant to your larger case?"

"They didn't. They just gave me one more chance to spill my guts and I said thanks a lot and was told to squat and we were off on that last count."

"Didn't you ask?"

"I did but Hizzoner told me I was out of order, as if it was none of my business because I'm only the shmuck on trial in there."

"Paul, I can't believe any of this. Didn't you even care about what might happen?"

"What was there to care about? Thirty days for contempt? I felt like I was one of the Hollywood Ten before the congressional Commie-hunters and couldn't have been any happier. You know how many canaries never drew another clean breath after they fingered all those other fellow travelers so they could stay on the studio payrolls and keep their swimming pools. I like it better my way, dead or alive. If it wasn't for the fact that Brother Wolfgang here never uses bad words I would say fuck 'em all."

That softened the kid up pretty good. I mean the Jewish kid, not the Nazi. She had never bucked me on a gut issue.

"I'm sorry I've been so harsh about this, Paul," Birdye said. "I knew you would never do anything to hurt Vito but why should you have cared about that tailor? He never did a damn thing for you he wasn't getting paid for, did he?"

"What's the difference, baby? It's too late for me to turn into a fink.

If this antiseptic ballyard is the font of all wisdom then they ought to set up their own informers' program like the feds and put out hard dollars to nail the guys they want, and they couldn't possibly have enough to lay on me because there ain't that much in the world. Rocky himself didn't have that much, which reminds me of something. Did I tell you he went out with his pants down and a young babe helping him shake off the day's tensions?"

"Please, I don't care about that. You always said that was the only way to go and I never argued that point with you except to say I never understood why it only applied to men and not women, but can we get back to the point? I'm so worried about what all this could mean when that jury retires."

"What in the name of J. H. Christ could it mean, Birdye? I'm on the grill on ten counts in another indictment. If they ring in my delinquent behavior on this planet I'll appeal it, that's all."

"Of course. I should have known, lover. You'll just go right to the top, as usual, won't you? You're nothing but laughs today."

"Why not? How many times did I tell you that if I hadn't kept laughing all those years in the jute mill after Walter went off to Philly and Ed was gone my ulcer would have bust with such regularity you could tell the time by it?"

"Enough, I suppose, but to use your own language this is another ballgame, isn't it?"

"It sure is, kiddo, and it's in the stretch. Why don't we wait for the score to come up on the heavenly board?"

"All right. I'm sorry to be such a nag. I'll get off your back. Tomorrow you sum up?"

"Yes. That's the ninth inning, and they don't go into extra innings in that lion's pit."

"Are you really in shape for that, Paul?"

"Well, it would be a little easier with a trial record to go over, or at least some notes on the cuffs of this bedsheet, but my head's clear enough and I'm going to spend most of the day in the morgue hunting down some things I can use."

"Good. You get started whenever you want. Ed said he would be around to hold my hand, but I haven't seen that other friend of yours. Have you had any word from him?"

Peeking at the Nazi to see how closely he might have been monitoring this session, I satisfied myself from his stupidly contented look that he was probably wondering where he was going to find room on his tunic for another piece of tin, so a small gamble seemed in order.

"I ran into him before court, Birdye. He's got his own gumshoe now but manages to get around."

"Will he come to see me?"

"Probably not, but his walker's a kindred soul who understands other innocents who've been wounded in action. Catch on?"

"I think so. Can you come back sometime today?"

"I'll try but I need to go for my Ph.D in the morgue because there's so much I have to commit to memory, and then my best bet might be to settle down and try to get the whole shmear in some kind of order. All I have is four hours to shoot the works, but I'll goose-step over here with Wolfie right after it's wound up and we'll go around the clock. He's a sweet Nazi and might even soften up and give us some real time alone. That sound all right?"

"Of course. Whatever's best for you, Paul."

I stopped at Paddy Flint's just to keep the ace on the move, always bearing in mind that he had no infantry training, but Ed must have been on the way over to Birdye's in a gypsy helicopter. Then it occurred to me that a trip uptown to say hello to Dr. King or rap with Satchmo if he wasn't in a recording session wouldn't be the worst thing for my flagging spirits.

"You are speaking of the Negro ghetto?" Wolfie asked, and when I said I was, Harlem North proved to be on Zahn's restricted list. Go figure that out. I finally make the half-fare and can't take the A train.

"I don't get that, Kapitan," I said. "I've been there before."

"Zahn, iss not on my orders."

"OK," I said. "I just thought it might be a nice change for you. The last thing I wanna do, like I told you, is cost you the wings you put your *tuchus* on the line for, so let's just head for the morgue, but you heard me tell my Frau we're going to be there a long time, *ja?*"

"*Ja.* We shall go there."

"Thanks. You might catch up on your own reading if you want. If you have any trouble with English they've surely got a few thousand books in your language."

"You think perhaps they would have *Mein Kampf?*"

"That's an outbet, *mein* friend. It's a book of history and there's no bad words in it, so it's got to be on the shelves."

"*Gut.* It iss many years since I have read Herr Hitler's words."

"Me too. Some fan of Der Fuehrer's borrowed mine and never returned it."

I don't have to tell you how glad that librarian vas to see me, especially when I started by asking for Adolf's bestseller. He produced it, clothbound, in a flash, but turned sour again when I handed that fairly recent Houghton Mifflin edition to the Luftwaffe delegate. I guess he thought I needed it more, and his grizzled head dipped a few more notches when I laid my laundry list on him—from Bartlett's to Mencken's *New Dictionary of Quotations* to the Oxford version to Clifton Fadiman's *American Treasury* and the one edited by Professor Bergen Evans, among a few others.

"My good man," he said, and you know he didn't mean it that way. "I cannot fetch you such an exorbitant list in one fell swoop, no less even remember all those titles. At the most, I will furnish you with one volume at a time."

"There's no need to blow your top, pal," I said. "That's all I can hold and read on my feet. Start with Mr. Mencken if you don't mind."

With all the digging I had to do, and you don't have to be told what a bitch it is to make your way through such haphazardly indexed minefields as Bartlett's and that Oxford thing, not to mention the effluvium Wolfgang vas into so happily, we burned the midnight oil pretty good before we started back.

"If you feel like putting on the feedbag, Kapitan," I said, "I wouldn't mind stopping at the golf course."

"*Nein*, Zahn, unless you require nourishment. I have not yet become accustomed to the food here."

What a cutie, huh? You can just bet the ace had access to some knockwurst and sauerkraut washed down with an excellent dark beer.

"Double *nein*, Wolfie," I said. "The few times I swallowed that stuff I came away like I had just had a nine-course Chinese dinner. *Faash-tait*? That's a joke where I come from. You eat Chinese until it's coming out of your ears and a half hour later you wanna go eat. Ever hear of a place called Luchow's in New York?"

"I have not."

"Well, man, I wish I could have taken you in there sometime. It's down near where I used to live and made to order for fellows with your tastes, and that's not all. There's a district in my town called Yorkville where a German with a normal appetite would need about six months to make all the good restaurants. All nice people, too."

I thought the guy's tongue would fall out, but it didn't, so I knew I was right in the first place. He wasn't missing a goddamn thing, loser or no. Probably had that delicious steaming red cabbage with every meal. I filed that away as a piece of information which might come in handy in due course, and after a while, a long while, we were back at his quarters and, presto, the scourge of London hit the sack. Straight up.

And then, moments later, that melodious whistle.

My anti-Fascist brother.

"How'ya doin?"

"Fine, Vito," I said. "I didn't have much of a bad time with the spooks yesterday."

Those huge mitts landed on my shoulder and I thought I saw something approaching violence in the man mountain's eyes but, then, how many of us know the line between violence and the deepest love two humans can share?

"No kiddin. Whadd'ya say we cut out the bullshit? I happen to know what you done in there. Picked up a fill-in from Brother Wilhelm, who ain't the worst dingbat around even if he does look like an undertaker's helper. You put your ass on the line, Paul, even though I told'ya they can't hurt me none. I coulda cut my throat when I heard what you done. You had no call to do that for anybody like me. . . ."

"Hold it, Tiny," I broke in. "If you wanna know the truth I didn't do it for you. I did it for *me*. I can't face my Maker, or un-Maker, whatever, if I turn canary for those beards. That too hard for an overgrown kid like you to dig?"

"Yeah. Way too hard, pal. I hate to think what a con man you woulda made if you went the other way, but I'll tell'ya this. I'll pay'ya back, one way or another. The only guy I ever knew like you was my own old man and my kid brother. The other one'd help a blind lady across the street and then leave her without a subway token in her pocketbook."

"Well, Vito, he probably fell into bad company when he was very young. I wouldn't be too harsh on him, and what's this about paying me back? You're insulting the best friend of your second life."

"Too bad. I'm still payin this one back, because you're some kind of man."

"Fine. Just stick the marker in my pants if you pass the tailor shop. The fact is I may need some help at that after the jury comes in, but I knew you wouldn't have to be asked."

"Yeah. On that one you can take the odds on what's in them sneakers. How was the little woman today?"

"Only great. Misses you a lot."

"You need anything? I got some fresh connections in the works."

"Don't tell me that with your fancy footwork you came up with a slice of pizza—I like it with the sausage and peppers, by the way—or maybe just a Nedick's hot dog or something like that."

"No, not yet, otherwise you'd see some bulges under my nightshirt, but things are workin. Like I musta told'ya more than once, it ain't all that different up here. There's always guys with one scam or another goin, same as downstairs probably."

"You must mean all the way downstairs?"

"Sure, inna hot place. You really set OK for the big one?"

"Good enough. It's all gotta come off the top of this beat-up head but I'll do the best I can and hope for the best. What else can I do against a marked deck?"

"Nothin, I guess, but my dough's on you."

My squadron leader, perhaps troubled by an empty stomach or a thirst for some suds, tilted a bit now and Brother Vittorio, facing him, noticed it.

"I better blow, Paul," he said.

"Sure, Vito, and God be with you if He's around and not on a sabbatical or anything like that, but hold the phone a minute. We've got a spot of business to transact."

"What kinda business?"

"The beards know about the sneakers. I could be a candidate for a dusting before all this is over."

"So?"

"What a question for you to ask me with your big head still on straight. I've got to dump these bills so they don't stick 'em in the cashier's cage in this casino of the dead or, worse, turn me in to the IRS. I got a tax rap going down there as it is. The ace's eyes still closed nice?"

"Yeah, and if he opens 'em he's gonna need to find himself a real good kraut doctor who wires busted jaws."

I bent down, got the money out and handed all but two hundred dollars to my former American keeper.

"You hang onto this in case the worst comes to the worst in this worst of all possible worlds, Vito," I said.

"OK, but whadd'ya holdin them two odd bills for? Ain't that risky?"

"I suppose it is, but I have an idea, like I might wanna tip one of the hatcheck girls or something like that."

Vittorio Pascaglia needed no elaboration and trundled away in the light.

Day IX

Chapter 18 •

I haven't mentioned it before, what with so much else going on, but there's no television in Heaven. None. Zero. Not even one old black-and-white set, but this is not any beef on the Good Lord's GHQ. For those of you with your entry permits stamped and a reasonable certainty that you won't have to go on the grill unless you were a newspaperman or author or did any other bad things, I bring it up here as a plus for the Fortunate Isles. To cite a single example, in my first nine days there, and you know by now that the word jock was practically invented for me (the athletic *fan*, I mean, not the athletic supporter), I never missed Howard Cosell. Think about that. I was an all-sports fan except for women's boxing, men's wrestling and mixed bowling and here we were in the heat of the NFL season—play-off time, that's all—and I had gone through two Monday football nights and I don't know how many fistfight telecasts and never once said to anybody in my higher-than-jet set, "I'll be hornswoggled. Howard Cosell's on ABC right this minute, *live* and in full color, and here we are sitting around playing with ourselves." Hell, the name itself never so much as crossed my mind except maybe one time when we were throwing down a predinner booster in Hank's place and it occurred to me that Heaven wasn't so bad at that because it was the only place I knew of where a man could get away from Howard Cosell. I remember saying to myself, Paul, you may be dead but you've heard the last of The Mouth.

But that wasn't the point I started to make.

What I missed, and this was so critical to my interests it needs no embellishment, were those Perry Mason reruns. Think of all the goodies I could have picked up from Raymond Burr, the only .1000 point hitter in the entire history of the law. Burr-Mason never had a client who didn't walk in the scene just before the last commercial because it always turned out that the real perpetrator either was the guy on the stand or that mope with the horn-rims sitting in the last row of spectators with the frozen smile of a gent who didn't have a worry in the world (not even a wife, say). You know that scenario. Burr-Mason's putting the D.A.'s star through a grilling that would make an F. Lee Bailey or an Edward Bennett Williams—or, H, even P. Sann—look like a first-year law student and, wham, that party cracks, points a finger, and the angelically smug citizen in the back row isn't a spectator any more. He's the new *defendant* and they might as well have that van with the wire mesh windows all revved up to whisk him off to the Big Q.

Well, you can't pull off anything like that in a courtroom without either witnesses or a section for spectators. I realize that it took me too darn long to get to it, and I'm sorry I dragged Howard Cosell in, so if you should ever enjoy the privilege of seeing the man off-camera please tell him I was only telling it like it was for me. I knew Cosell, even did a spot with him and Auerbach on Channel 7 once. Hopefully, he will understand the mental stress under which this segment was set forth.

You do dig what I've been talking about all this time, right?

What kind of shot did I have where I was?

Heck, where I was Raymond Burr himself would have come out looking like an ambulance chaser or telephone-booth lawyer waiting to chalk up his first win and open a storefront office. A bit edgy and in the Hall of No Justice a few minutes before the Justices themselves arrived, one behind the other and all behind Saint Peter, that's the sort of nonsense that was running through my mind on my biggest morning in the misnamed afterlife.

So much for that.

Court is now in session and the nonspectators will be seated.

"Your Honor and gentlemen of the Tribunal," I opened up. "May I start by expressing my deepest appreciation to you for extending me so rare a privilege and also beg leave to rise? I find this cross-legged position excessively uncomfortable, and beyond that I believe I might be heard more distinctly in a standing position."

"Rise," said good Saint Peter.

"Thank you, sir," I said, going directly before the bench. "I would like to preface my presentation by observing that I find myself at a rather formidable disadvantage on this most critical of days. Since it is my purpose to start with some essentials which I consider extremely vital to my case, I must note at the outset that while I have spent the best part of the past twenty-two hours in your reference room I am apt to stray here and there. Bereft of a trial record and also unable to commit my essential citations to writing I—"

Snake eyes.

The forked tongue on the right was up for the big one. Up mine, that is.

"Your Honor, I find myself confounded beyond measure by this petitioner's recitation of his labors in the celestial library. Does he not have to be instructed forthwith that he is obliged to confine himself solely to the evidence adduced in these proceedings?"

I didn't wait for Pete but came back swinging pretty good.

"If the Tribunal please," I said, looking way up there like a very short boy trying to make out the Star of Bethlehem atop that gigantic Christmas tree in Rockefeller Center, "I submit that it would be an outlandish travesty of justice to hold a defendant such as myself to the rules of evidence after eight days in which those very rules have effectively been in the discard."

"Precisely what is your point of reference?" Saint Peter asked.

"Very simply this: I have been denied the right of counsel, denied the right of producing witnesses on my own behalf, denied recourse to the well-established legal safeguards I sought to invoke in my very first appearance and, worse still, denied the right of appeal to the Supreme Being. With regard to that last reference, I hasten to assure you that I do not propose to intrude upon the wisdom of my peers in this chamber by invoking biblical citations so much better known to themselves than to me, but to go on I have repeatedly been asked to impeach myself—obliging the prosecutor, I should note, more often than not. Am I now to be confined to rules of evidence which the Tribunal itself has not deemed applicable in my case? This would constitute an irreparable blow to my defense."

A whispered powow with the prosecutor, and then the chair:

"This body, Mr. Sann, cannot, need not and indeed shall not accept as much as one iota of the statement you have uttered. Nonetheless, I shall permit you to go forth, but mind you this: the time which may thus be consumed is *your* time. We shall recess at our accustomed hour whether your summation has been completed or not. I trust that this is a factor which you have taken into account."

"I have, Your Honor, and please accept my most heartfelt gratitude for your kind indulgence."

"Proceed then." This came with a swift glance at Peter on the Far Right which seemed to me to say either "That's it, professor, let's get this show back on the road," or, G-- forbid, "Look, let this jerkoff hang himself."

"Thank you," I said. "I would like to start by citing first a distinguished American patriot, Patrick Henry by name, who made a formidable contribution to the Bill of Rights which I have mentioned here. Mr. Henry enunciated the view that all mortals are equally entitled to the free—and I underscore that word 'free'—exercise of religion according to the dictates of their own conscience and that it is the mutual duty of all of us to practice Christian forbearance and charity toward each other. This view, some two centuries later, is shared by veritable multitudes around much of the entire globe without regard, I note, to any particular race or religious faith. I shall come in due course to the reasons which impel this citation, and I go from there to the story of Job in the Old Testament. That man, surely out of his own incredibly grave tribulations, spoke of Heaven as a just and final retreat—I am paraphrasing out of necessity here—where the wicked cease from troubling and the weary shall be forever at rest. From my own experience, most respectfully and even without awaiting the finding of my judges, I say to you that the injunction of Job does not appear to me to be the order of the day in this chamber—and yet it is scripture from which countless billions have drawn solace down through the centuries. Once again, I concede that it is in the poorest possible taste for me to burden you gentlemen with citations from the Good Book and I shall rest on that single reference. Now I wish to call to your attention the writings of one Thomas Wilson, confessing that I do not know whether Mr. Wilson was a churchman or not, although I do know [thank you, Mr. Mencken] that he has been widely quoted on matters of piety since the eighteenth century. Mr. Wilson put it down that 'No man must go to Heaven who has not sent his heart thither before.' In all candor, I concede that I do not know whether that same wise man set forth any limitations or restrictions upon those covered by that reference, but I stand before you in the very posture he described and no other even having so readily confessed that I was not a person who followed any religious precepts past my thirteenth year in my terrestrial being. My point, reduced to its essence, is that I am here because I did indeed wish to be in this place and accordingly sent my heart thither, for there were loved ones in the Holy City with whom I wished to be reunited unto eternity. While I do not lack for further citations of consequence this is all I wished to say by way of a preface."

During most of that crisp peroration, I had more or less confined myself to Square One—directly in front of Saint Peter, that is. Now, according to plan, I began to move around on those rapidly decaying sneakers, starting with the baddest Peter to show that I harbored no animosity toward him but rather stood in awe of his dedication to his assigned labors, and then gradually moving clockwise until I was settled in front of my own Peter for the long haul that lay ahead.

"I shall proceed sequentially now," I went on, "to the counts in the indictment against me. With respect to the First Commandment, I believe I established my complete innocence beyond any possible challenge. I worshiped no strange gods and I remind you that your very diligent prosecutor himself spoke of the record on that count as based, and I trust that I am quoting him to the letter, on 'the barest kind of hearsay.' On the Second I found myself confronted with any number of profanities which had issued from my lips in moments of extremity basically flowing from the nature of the profession I chose. I say to you now that in my time below I had occasion to hear profanity, even blasphemy, uttered by deeply religious contemporaries. Moreover—"

"Objection," muttered you-know-who. "Is the petitioner to be permitted to take shelter at this late stage behind defensive references which did not occur to him when he was under interrogation on a given commandment? This is most irregular, Your Honor."

You think I held still for that guy?

No way.

I was flush under the chair before a single piece of sand fell in that sundial, wherever it was.

"Your Honor," I said. "I in turn submit that this intrusion on my summation is both unwarranted and unjust. I was on the point of citing—without using the actual language, of course—a profanity uttered in my very own presence in this sainted haven but a few days ago by a wholly pious man who once held one of the highest elective positions in the world below."

"The objection is sustained nonetheless, Mr. Sann," said Saint Peter. "Having exhausted the leeway you initially requested, you are now addressing yourself to the specific evidence in the record and stand enjoined not to go beyond it."

I said I would try my very best to follow that injunction, not that I wasn't going to keep skirting around it, and was told to go forth.

"Bearing on the same count, gentlemen," I went forth, "I say to you that I was unfairly taxed with published words under my own name which actually issued from the mouths of others."

What a dumbo. There was no way that was going to get past that wizard of a prosecutor, and it didn't.

"Mr. Sann," the man said ever so evenly, "even if this body were to concede some merit to that statement, I am constrained to remind you once again that one of the works in question was not of a historical nature but rather a fictional document and all of those words were yours, were they not? You so testified."

"I am sorry, sir," I said. "I did so affirm, but I believe I may have inadvertently neglected to call to your attention the literary license which is universally accorded to the novelist."

"You were advised only seconds ago that this is not a time for after-thoughts. Do you wish to further belabor this point or go on to the next count?"

"I suppose I have no other choice, sir. I did not observe the Sabbath. I did inform you that there were situations in which, in truth, I could not have done so even were I so disposed, but if I may borrow a word from your own lexicon I do not propose to belabor that point either. Instead, I shall proceed to the count stemming from the next commandment. Here, I believe I need say no more than that I never took another human life and no evidence to the contrary was produced." I had my eyes glued to my own Peter now because I was coming to the one that was warmer than H itself. "I now address myself to the adulterous conduct assessed against me and while I have no desire to go beyond any challenges I submitted during my examination I feel I would be remiss if I did not now set forth a point or two in extenuation. There are men here in Heaven, and women as well, who in the course of their own lives below also were guilty of violating the same commandment and—"

"Objection!" roared Peter over in right field. "The petitioner is once again going beyond the record."

I paid the chair a visit. What's the worst that could happen? I get disbarred?

"Your Honor, in all fairness I beg the Tribunal's indulgence on this most critical issue. I am addressing myself to entirely consequential references which I could not possibly have raised in my testimony without being ruled out of order. This fresh objection, I submit, strikes at the very heart of my summation."

"Would you expand upon that, please?"

"Thank you. I will not only be brief but impeccably cautious. It is not my purpose to impeach a single soul dwelling in the Holy City. I would not so much as mention a single name even if I were to be declared guilty as charged here and now, but I say to you that if I were to be denied permission to lay a passing reference in extenuation before this body then my defense is so riddled as to be unworthy of the privilege you have so generously accorded me."

"Objection overruled," good Pete said after a moment's thought. "You may proceed, but you are abjured, Mr. Sann, that it would serve your purpose best were you to abstain from abusing the chair's tolerance."

"Thank you, Your Honor. I cling to the belief that there is not a man among my judges who can fail to appreciate the deep anxiety which afflicts me as this session draws closer to its inevitable end, but I shall do my very best to adhere to your injunction."

Now I was on the move again, toward the left, and don't you ever listen to the sedentary types who tell you the legs go first. You know from my frank admissions to my Birdye, faithfully set down however embarrassing to a former sexual athlete, that there are some other things on the male beast which can go first in situations such as that of your narrator.

"There is a man on these premises, a much-esteemed gentleman of the cloth no less," I started out again, "whose self-incriminating admissions on the subject of infidelity were surreptitiously recorded on electronic devices by an agency mentioned earlier in this proceeding—the Federal Bureau of Investigation—whose long-time Director is undoubtedly himself in residence here. There are two other men I hold in the same high esteem, the Director not being one of them, whose infidelities were widely disseminated not only in the media but in published volumes as well and never put to rest in any manner even remotely persuasive, and I am speaking from direct, personal knowledge. There is at least one other person I have spoken to whom I myself taxed with indiscretions in a book of my own—and that man, mind you, did not challenge what I had reported about his adulterous conduct but merely chided me over it. As for my earlier reference to females in like situations, I would desist from any elaboration except to tell this Tribunal with all the candor at my command, however damaging to my own defense, that I had personal knowledge of their violations of the Sixth Commandment. I am of course fully aware that I and I alone am the defendant in this chamber and I am content to let it rest there with nothing more than a passing observation to the effect that I find myself impelled to wonder whether a double standard possibly can exist in Paradise itself. I ask your forgiveness, gentlemen, if that last remark may impress some of you as offensive. It was not so intended."

I thought my Peter seemed mildly amused over that one, but the prosecutor took the floor before I could suck in any solace from that observation.

"Mr. Sann," he said. "Without wishing to interpose a clearly indicated objection here, I am assuming that you have now concluded the portion of your summation dealing with the Sixth Commandment. Is that correct?"

"Yes, sir."

"Splendid. In that event I must remind you that you have gone from the first three commandments to the Fifth and Sixth without making any reference to the Fourth."

"I am deeply grateful to you, sir, but I believe I mentioned earlier the all but unbearable emotional stress under which I am laboring. Would you be kind enough to refresh my recollection on the commandment I passed over?"

"Happily. That is the one which deals with the honor one must accord to one's father and mother."

"I thank you again, sir. I believe I was able to establish my complete purity on that count. I paid all due honor to my parents throughout their lives and shall proceed now to Number Seven. On that score, I readily conceded the small thefts so commonplace to adolescents of the poverty-ridden class from which it was my fate to have emerged but noted that I outgrew that form of behavior at a very early age and thereafter never strayed from the commandment except in the most trifling ways, as in the matter of removing writing materials of small value from the newspaper which employed me."

"You did indeed, Mr. Sann, except that you have passed over the more consequential violations of this commandment in the years in which you were a scrivener."

"I'm sorry, sir. I did inform you that those acts of pilferage occurred as a condition of my employment, through which I was able to provide sustenence for my wife and children. I believe I may have failed to mention, however, that items so acquired—especially photographs— invariably were returned to their rightful owners."

"How nice to hear, even at this eleventh hour. May I suggest that you proceed with dispatch to the remaining counts inasmuch as there is but little time left?"

"I shall do so with but one detour of import. There are at least two gentlemen on these premises known to me—personally known—whose entire careers were spent in the most outrageous violations of the Seventh Commandment—all on the public record, I must note. And there is still another who held a high municipal elective position who had to resign that office and whose key subordinate was prosecuted and imprisoned for proven activities associated with theft."

"I remind you again, Mr. Sann, that the hour is late."

"And I thank you again, sir. I believe I can dispose of the last three counts in but a sentence or two. There was no evidence, not so much as a stray thread, to substantiate the remotest suggestion that I ever bore false witness against another man, nor that I ever coveted my neighbor's wife—at least to the degree in which I took that particular commandment to apply—or my neighbor's goods. On the issue of 'envy,' as I recall it, it is my belief that I saved this body precious time by electing not to expound on that most tenuous point. All of the preceding speaks for itself, but a related issue comes to mind which I believe may properly be brought before the Tribunal because it seems to me to bear on the Ninth Commandment as I came to understand it in this chamber, where I found to my chagrin that the word 'covet' was not limited to the act of sexual intercourse with the wife of one's neighbor but even interdicted such things as permitting a lascivious *thought* to enter one's mind. I cite to you now an incident of fairly recent date: the very President of the United States—a Born-Again Christian, no less—granted an interview to a magazine called *Playboy*, a publication so blatantly vulgar as to appeal only to the most base carnal appetites, in which he freely admitted that in his time he had lusted after females other than his own devoted spouse. Mind you, I am now making reference to one of the other world's most powerful and highly respected men—a model husband, model citizen and a shining example as well for the devout of all faiths. There are like instances in which—"

I was waiting for it, of course, and my gaze now was drawn from my own Peter (was that a halo I detected around his head?) to the far right.

"If the Tribunal please," said that Peter, "we now seem yet again to to be in an area of all but total immateriality and irrelevance as well notwithstanding the fact that this petitioner solemnly pledged himself to refrain from abusing the unprecedented courtesy extended to him today."

"Mr. Sann," said the good Pete, "while that observation was not put in the form of an objection I must express my complete sympathy with it. As it happens, alas, it is all but academic, for the hour is late."

"I am truly sorry, Your Honor, but I thought I was on material ground. May I now sum up, count by count, the case for my defense?"

"There is no time for that. You were cautioned earlier that you appeared to be in the process of exposing yourself to this very eventuality."

"May I, then, ask one more question?"

"You may," Saint Peter said ever so wearily as he reached for his staff and started to rise—in sections.

"Does the prosecution offer its own summation?"

"No, that practice has long since been deemed wasteful, needless and inefficacious. For your guidance, however, the record shall be reviewed in advance of your final appearance at oh six hundred hours on the morrow."

"Did I hear that right, Your Honor? Oh *six* hundred?"

"You did. You arrived here at that hour nine days ago. Therefore you shall hear the judgment of this Tribunal at that same hour on the tenth day."

Beautiful, let alone that word ineffuckacious. Only eighteen hours left to sweat it out when there wasn't even enough left of my Celtic sneakers to sweat in. I had to wonder why I quit writing and became a criminal lawyer.

Chapter 19 ••••••••••••••••••••••••

Outside, I told the ace I wanted to spend the rest of the day alone with Frau Zahn.

"*Nein,*" said the Hitler version of World War I's Baron von Richthofen. "This I cannot permit. Regulations."

"I know, Wolfie," I said, "but let me ask you something. Can you use any ready cash, like for a glass of schnapps or some sauerbraten or anything like that? Pig's knuckles, maybe?"

"You are speaking of reichsmarks, Zahn?"

"I told you there's no Reich, and there's no marks. I'm talking about the American dollar, which is what they're using in this country. Ever see a C note?"

"What iss such a note?"

"It's a hundred smackers. That could be like four millions marks or maybe even more. I'm not up on the current rate of exchange."

Brother Wolfgang managed to produce the first vestige of a smile since he met me and lost the war.

"*Ja*, Zahn," he said. "I am aware of the high value of United States currency here. You are in possession of such currency?"

"Double *ja*," I said. "All you have to do is face the Fatherland and you got it, Wolfie."

"Which way, *Bitte*?"

Like that *Bitte*? A dead-in-the-wool Nazi saying please to a Jew.

"You swing around. On the East you will see the part of Germany occupied by your former Russian cousins and on the West the part the good guys have the mortgage on."

Mein hero turned and I reached into my left sneaker and wrangled out a bill. Then I tapped the blond and held it in front of him while his violet eyes popped.

"Now look, comrade," I told him. "If you take this we have a firm deal. Once we get to Frau Zahn you float away till I'm due back in my own Nuremberg trial, which is something I'll fill you in on sometime. Maybe you can rent a Volkswagen and ride the autobahn or stroll along the Wilhelmstrasse to see what's in the stores now that you're loaded. Something like that."

"You make fun now."

"Just for kicks. What's the word in your former language that means you understand something?"

"*Verstehen.*"

"OK. *Verstehen?*"

"*Ja*, Zahn."

I gave the Nazi the bill, which he palmed without getting into any bargaining session that might have cost me the reserve hundred I had kept for such a contingency, and I must say the man's word was good despite his unfortunate background, because when I reached my girl I vas all alone.

"Where's your new keeper, Paul?" Birdye asked.

"AWOL. I shmeared him with a picture of Benny Franklin."

"How marvelous. You think of everything, lover. How did it go to-day?"

"Birdye doll," I said, embracing that little bundle of former sex. "Don't ask for a text on my summation. It felt like it was longer than Darrow on those fun kids Dickie Loeb and Nathan Leopold—and he talked for two days to save their asses. Honest, I'm too punched out for that."

"I know how you must feel. Tell me how you think it came out and I'll try not to be a nuisance."

"Good girl. I'm pretty sure I killed 'em on Numbers One, Four, Five, Eight and Ten and probably got a push on Seven, that stealing bunk. And I make myself a loser on the others, so it looks like five wins, one standoff and four bummers. Now if that isn't a hung jury I don't know what is. I get the verdict at six o'clock in the morning."

"Six? Why six? The court always starts at eight."

"It beats me, but I suppose they knock off their verdicts in the two hours before the next sucker goes into the missing witness chair. It's a break for us anyway. I'll come zipping back to this love nest nice and early. Iss good, Mrs. Zahn, *nein*?"

No, it wasn't.

I don't mean Birdye said anything. It was all in her face, so I pushed on.

"Look, baby," I said. "Between now and the time the jury comes in let's just have a good day and talk about all the fun times."

"I'm for that, Paul."

"That's my Birdye. Wanna go for a walk like we used to?"

"Where?"

"Wherever. We always talked good holding hands and walking. Why not head for the women's golf course and split some lettuce and things? The worst that can happen is some bitch turns us in but that's not going to change the verdict. The whiskers have too much to wrestle with as it is."

And so we were off on a perfectly delightful stroll free of any mishaps except that we passed Helen Harrington along the way, probably coming back from Lord & Taylor's branch in the Upper Room or Elizabeth Arden's, and my busted heart lost a beat or two. This did not escape Birdye's notice even though the elegant Miss H had too much class to show even a glimmer of recognition.

"Someone you know?" I was asked.

"Vaguely," I said, "like I might have run across her somewhere, but she didn't seem to connect with me."

Chalk up a small winner.

Settled down with food no self-respecting rabbit would eat, Birdye mentioned that Ed had been over.

"I love that new name you invented for him, Paul," she said. "He did too, because his father always called him Paddy and all kinds of people thought his last name was Flint when he used the phone on a story."

"Same problem I had before I became Herr Zahn. Remember? I was Paul Sand, more often than not, and after a while some TV actor made it with that name and I began to get all kinds of strange calls."

"Women, no doubt?"

"What else? I brushed 'em all, Birdye. If I had a number for the really beautiful Sand I would have laid it on them."

"Well, I'll buy that in my charitable mood today, you big skinny fibber."

"You're so nice to me. Let's get to the times when we were running around in genuine garments instead of these bedsheets, like tennis shorts and jeans and things when we were out on the town and you were all dressed up, low-neck so the cleavage would show."

"That was your idea, not mine," Birdye said, "because it made it easier for you to reach in while we were in the Olds. Where do you want to start? I honestly don't know. You're talking about more than thirty years, from high school and that Belmont Avenue corner all the way to this strange second honeymoon, if you could call it that. It was all good, Paul, every minute—well, almost every minute."

"Thanks, kiddo. That's very generous of you."

"Look, you taught me how to use the needle." A peck on the cheek came with that. "But I shouldn't have said it, I guess. We had so much fun together."

"What was the most?"

"It was all the most. From the cold-water room over Whelan's to the apartment we didn't have enough money to furnish on that street overlooking the Harlem River where we were the only Jews, to the two towns in Westchester after Leni and Richie came along, to Washington, to Queens when Walter made you night city editor and the drive from Hawthorne was too dangerous in the winter to that nice apartment on the park on Mosholu and finally to Riverdale. That was a palace, wasn't it?"

"You did it, but what else? You've locked us into New York and

Washington as if we weren't allowed to go anyplace else."

"Oh, not at all. I'll never forget those three trips across the country, driving all day, drinking in the cars, the drive-in movies at night."

"You forgetting something about the nights, Birdye?"

"Don't tell me, Paul. You had that crazy notion that it was very important for you to make love in every state on the map—and there were some we just drove through."

"Yeah, and quite a few where we stopped and I got stiffed. Want me to name just two?"

"I'm sure you will in any case."

"You bet. Intercourse in Pennsylvania and that town with the even better name in Colorado—Lay, L-a-y."

"Lover, there was always a reason. On the first trip we had the kids with us and couldn't always get separate rooms in the motels. Even then there were nights when you found a way, sometimes in the shower."

"That's right. You were often at your best with that nice warm water running over us, but you've still got us stateside. How about Aruba when our Vegas friends opened their casino down there?"

"That was a glorious two weeks. We even got in the water a few times when you weren't at the blackjack tables or shooting dice."

"No kidding. Where were you?"

"At the blackjack tables. I forgot to bring my knitting, but you know what I think about more, Paul? Havana before Castro came down from the mountains. You know, the afternoons with Papa Hemingway and his Mary after those two air crashes that almost killed him. And I often think of San Francisco and the political conventions you took me to when the children were older, and all those marvelous times with Helen and Milton at Kutsher's. I should have asked you about them before. I don't think we ever had two closer friends than that except maybe Earl and Rosemary."

"Well, that turned into a downer, Birdye, but this is no time to hash it over. It's too ugly."

"What do you mean? You stopped seeing the Kutshers? I can't believe it."

"Too bad, but something went real wrong after a while."

"You have to tell me, Paul."

"Only if you insist. This was meant to be a day for the good things."

"I do insist. I loved Helen and Milton so much."

"So did I, let's say for maybe ten years after you did me the incredible disservice of leaving me by myself. You remember when the Borscht Circuit boys built that trotting track in Monticello and Milton knocked himself out trying to lay some points on me at like four cents apiece and let me in on the ground floor and I turned it down because I didn't think a newspaper editor ought to own a piece of a dirty sport like that?"

"Sure I do. What's that got to do with all this?"

"Plenty, kiddo. There was all kinds of funny business in some of the races up there and I covered the guts out of it, Milton or no Milton. So in '71, courtesy of the male whore we had for an ad manager then, two hitmen from the Jewish Alps were privileged to sit down with Her Majesty and air their grievances about the way I was displaying their occasional embarrassments on our back sports page."

"I don't understand, Paul. What did that have to do with the Kutshers?"

"Practically nothing—except that the two gutter rats I'm talking about were Milton's own advertising genius, that sweet-faced Lipton kid, and Leon Greenberg, the track's president. And the way they put it to Dolly was that she either gets me off their backs or all the Catskills ads go—and that happened to be what we were living off then besides the high-rate take from the movies and Broadway to offset what the department stores were getting away with."

"This is still over my head. How does Milton become the villain?"

"Why not? Nobody could have gone to Dolly on that kind of mission without an OK from Milton and some of the other heavyweights up there. I know Paul Grossinger wasn't in on it, because he told me he was furious about the whole thing. Look, Lipton was the errand boy with the big bucks and that lightweight Greenberg was the track's foreign minister, but good Dolly gave me equal time after hearing out those executioners and I had no trouble at all making the case for the display I was giving to the fixes at that track. She wouldn't trade me in for the advertising loot, which kept coming in anyway because that crowd needed us more than we needed them, since we had the lock on their customers."

"Didn't you ever talk to Milton about it, Paul?"

"Just sort of. I was on the sun deck of a new Times Square hotel one day after a workout in the pool and he spotted me from some office across the street where he booked his club acts and called and said why didn't we get together, so I told him it was too fucking late for that because his emissaries already had their audience with the lady and failed to come away with my scalp and that was it. Christ, Birdye, you know the only guy that ever tried to get me fired before that was Mr. La Guardia when I was on the City Hall beat and broke that big housing story he was saving for the Sunday *Times*."

"Oh, Paul, I can't believe Milton was really trying to get Dolly to fire you."

"No, maybe they just wanted her to make me the composing room foreman or the clerk in charge of the returns, or whatever, but I wouldn't hold still for a move like that no matter who made it. There's nothing lower in the world."

"How awful, and it was never patched up?"

"Hell, no, but it had a few heart-warming postscripts. Not too many years later that sharpie Greenberg was looking at a federal judge for using the track's money—a lousy five grand, I think it was—to bankroll his son's bar mitzvah. The bum got off with a nine-thousand-dollar fine and court costs plus two years' probation when he should have gone into Lewisburg and run some trotting races for the honest cons. And what do you suppose the other Monticello directors did? They kept him on the payroll at his seventy-five G salary minus his royal title, so I had to figure he had kept his mouth shut about any other little swindles up there. And that wasn't all of it, either. Those two charming Slutsky brothers who had another fat piece of the track and owned the Nevele also had to pay a visit to federal court because they had neglected to send Uncle any money for a few years, so they drew five apiece and seventy-five thou in fines. All nice people. Blood brothers. I didn't mean to break your mile-wide heart with any tearjerkers but you were the one who brought up Milton."

"I'm sorry I did. I feel even worse about Helen."

"Don't. That woman stood up fine. Even called me when it was all over and begged me to come up—cuffo, anytime—but I said thanks, no. Anyway, I could never go back to the Jewish Alps with any woman whose name wasn't Birdye."

"Paul, it's nice of you to say that but what about that Italian I mentioned the other day? Didn't you ever take her to any place where we had been? I'm not bugging you, I'm just curious."

"Only Vegas, Birdye, but never in any hotel where we stayed. Look, I'll level with you, OK? I never touched the tall one—Angela Lauritano was her name and you met her one night at a screening—while you were still hanging in, never even saw the inside of her place until the day of the funeral. And that was a pure accident, by the way. I had my fun things written for that week but killed the whole column for one

on you. Angela came down to the office with me and broke up over that
hunk of copy and then we went to her joint, but I just had a couple of
blasts and went home to the kids. It was months before I made a pass
at her."

"Really, lover, I don't need to know any more about that woman.
Tell me what you wrote about me."

"Oh, it was a short one—not even half my space. I just told all about
our time together and what a helluva special person you were and how
the town was never going to be the same without you—not for me and
Leni and Rich and God knows who else. And it wasn't, baby. It sure
wasn't."

Tears? No, not from my girl the way I was hurting.

"How beautiful, Paul," she said. "That column must have touched a
few of your readers."

"A few? All I left in the house was a suitcase full of telegrams and
letters. If that piece of bloodletting had run before the funeral we
would have needed to hold the services at Madison Square Garden
instead of Campbell's."

"Campbell's? Not a synagogue?"

"No, Birdye. I wanted it there because we had the wake for Ed
there. I guess it sounds crazy but I thought it would be nice, like you
and the Irishman would be together again for one night after so many
years."

"What did you do about all the people you heard from? You couldn't
have answered all that mail. Did you say something in the paper the
next Saturday?"

"There was no next Saturday. That's when I junked the column. I
couldn't go back to my little funnies after that piece on you. I guess I
was all written out."

"Oh, what a shame. You never should have dropped it."

"Baby, I should have done that while you were sick, because the
secret about you and Dr. Krukenberg didn't hold up too good and there
I was with my smiling face over that page dishing out all those laugh-
ers."

"That's silly. You weren't supposed to go into mourning while I was
still alive. Would you tell me some more about Angela?"

"No. I told you it ran out and I told you why—you."

"You're so sweet, Paul. If you went first I'm sure the very same
thing would have happened with me. We started so young. Tell me
what else happened in those years."

"I don't know if it's worth it, and I'll skip the babes if you don't mind. I owe you that much, Birdye. I made the Pulitzer jury in '67 but lost my ticket of admission after that because the honorable trustees brought in a winner my national jury had never even seen and I blew the whistle. That touched off the worst national scandal those stiff-backed pantywaists ever had to sweat out and I wound up as the only newspaper bum who blew the Pulitzer both as a nominee—you know, the worldwide beat when Mr. Nasser told me through his own thick lips that he was going to annihilate Israel—and later as a judge, but I never brooded about it. Used it on the dust jacket of a book later, as a matter of fact. Do you want to go back to your place or have some more of this fabulous Caesar salad?"

"Did you say fabulous? I think Caesar would have had a rough time in bed with Cleopatra if he had to live off this slop. I'm ready to go back. Where do you suppose Vito is?"

"I have no idea but it's a good bet that he's dogging our footsteps so we're both all right."

On and on. Into the afternoon, into the night, into the morning. We talked a lot about the kids and the people we knew. About how the Arabs slipped across the Suez Canal that Yom Kippur night in '73 and I finally got to cover a war. About how Birdye's sister Pauline died of natural causes a while back and became the first woman in that fore-doomed family to beat the cancer rap. About all the fun we had on that slow-pay Steck baby grand after we were married, but on that score I caught some flack.

"You were doing so well, Paul," Birdye said, ever so sadly. "You really worked hard when you managed to keep your hands on the keys instead of reaching into my bra and you made it all the way to the opening of Tchaikovsky's First Piano Concerto and then quit. You could have been a fair classical pianist."

"Sure, maestro. With a tin ear and no sense of time. Wait till you hear what happened later, right after you stopped playing. I moved down to the Village while Rich was in college and Leni got that husband and a place of her own and I was in the Embers one night and they had a young guy at the piano who turned me on like crazy, so I asked him whether he did any teaching. He told me he had a studio over on Eleventh Street near the river and did it all with numbers—on the left hand with chords, that is—and I used to walk up to his brownstone from the office. Well, I worked like a dog at it—the way you tackled the boogie-woogie during the war because I was gonna go and you had an idea about picking up some small change in the jazz joints. The way this fellow taught you knocked yourself out on a piece all week and then sat down with him and played a duet. I got to 'Moon River' and Erroll Garner's 'Misty' and a few of the easier Gershwin and Cole Porter pieces and then something happened that was so awful I considered throwing myself into the Hudson or taking the gas pipe, except that I had an electric oven."

"What could have happened that was so terrible, lover?"

"I got to my professor's place early one day and he had someone inside with him and I thought he was working out with Count Basie or Duke Ellington but there was a woman about forty in the sitting room and she told me my guru was in the middle of a lesson with her son. I figured she was talking about a grown-up who started taking lessons in his crib. That's how good the sounds were, only it turned out the boy was twelve and never had a lesson, just a feel for the ivories, so when that concert ended I couldn't go into the studio. I wasn't only ashamed but burning. I told the jazz professor that if I ever came back again and ran into that kid I might strangle him so I was going home and play with my typewriter all by myself—no duets. And what did I do? I wrote a novel in eight weekends, not even stopping on the one when Jack Kennedy was assassinated and I put in about eighty-eight hours that Friday and Saturday and the best part of Sunday on the phones after Lee Oswald got wasted, and I never touched that piano again. In fact, when I moved out of my floor-through on Ninth Street into the brownstone I sold the Steck to make room for more bookcases. Right now I couldn't play 'America the Beautiful' if they had a piano in this trap, Birdye."

"Oh, Paul, that crazy head of yours. The way you worked you could have played the standards better than I did with the boogie."

"No kidding? Don't put yourself down, baby. I still have—well, I left it back home—the disc we made in one of the Frisco joints after you came out to see if I was alive and kicking. Got it on the original seventy-eight and tape, too. You were only sensational, so don't put me on. I went to the typewriter where I belonged, only it was more fun when you were doing the manuscripts on the first two."

"That was such a good time," Birdye said. "I would love to buy that back, except for one thing."

"What thing? Start swinging."

"It was the column, lover—the most vicious thing you ever said about me."

"What was that?"

"Don't tell me you've forgotten. You were writing about some record-breaking divorce settlement, maybe Bobo Rockefeller's six million or whatever it was, and you said you had done some quick arithmetic in your own situation and it could never happen to you because you had already lavished a small fortune on me—four thousand dollars for each favor in bed." Birdye was having more damn fun now. "You made up that number, didn't you?"

"How could you say that, wife? We talked about it after you cooled down that Saturday. I had those numbers worked out real well. All I did was add up my earnings in all those dreamy years together and divide it by the number of times you let me assault you and it came out to four thousand per in round numbers. I couldn't have been off by a helluva lot."

"Oh, of course. All you left out were a few items like the times we weren't even married, the times when you weren't even home, the times when any woman is entitled to a few days off and a few million others that must have slipped your little mind. Remember the kind of mail that piece of slander got you?"

"I sure do. You came out winners. I heard from quite a few of my female clients who were fans of yours and had the quaint view that even if you did cost that much in the hay a man who would put that in his newspaper didn't deserve a wife like you, and I wrote every one of them and pleaded guilty, but I will confess something to you now, doll."

"Spare me, please."

"No, I can't. I have to get it off my chest. Remember the day that old doctor gave me my discharge papers on the Coast and I solemnly promised never to drink any more red-eye or smoke a cigaret?"

"Of course, and then you took me to the Top of the Mark in that hotel on the hill and you drank bourbon and milk while I had my Scotch and you kept stealing my Chesterfields."

"And after that?"

"You tell me, Paul. It was a thousand years ago."

"OK. We got a cab over to the Palace and you made me undress and even with that damn bandage around my midsection you delivered me unto the only real heaven in the world—the one on earth reserved for the select circle of dream husbands like me. I think I forgot to count that one when I added up the numbers. Also a few times on the City of San Francisco, on that glorious train ride back to New York."

Birdye's face lit up but it was apparent that this was not a time for rekindling that kind of fire. She looked at her watch.

"On that note, lover," she said, "much as I hate to bring it up, we're running out of the other kind of time. Let's go."

218 ·

My Nazi bloodhound, clutching that C note, had kept his part of the bargain and was at a respectful distance from Frau Zahn's pad when we got back and ran into a guest—Paddy Flint.

"How come you're roaming in the middle of the night, Ed?" I asked him, and he said he wanted to check in with me before I went to pick up the verdict.

"I've also got a few bulletins," he told me. "The big guy dropped in. He tells me Toots is also on your no-see list now, Paul."

"That's no problem," I said. "The ace out there is a setup and I've bought what's left of his soul, if he ever had one, for a hundred bucks. He'd take me to see Al Capone if I wanted. Scarface has to be here if Costello made it. What other hot news have you got?"

"The good part. Vito has a line on Paul Tierney too—and a surprise to go with it. Walter is in residence as well."

Birdye received that bulletin with a show of pure ecstasy.

"This is getting to be a pretty nice place to live," she said. "I'm beginning to feel more at home every day, lover. With Vito's help we're putting the old crowd all back together."

Really? Was I one of them? I had not told the girl about the very dark reason for that early court appearance, how the ten-day tour ends on the button for the condemned. Uneasy now, I said I had to run and Ed promised to stay with Birdye until I got back.

"Thanks, Flint," I told him, "but no hands. You tried that in our other life a few times when you were in the bag and this tiger fought you off."

"I did? Don't tell me Birdye turned me in. I would never believe it."

"Nah, she never said anything bad about you. What are friends for?"

"You have a point there," Ed said. "I was loyal to both of you in my best days and my worst."

"No argument," I said, starting to go when Birdye put in an objection.

"Take another minute, Paul. I never got around to asking you how Richie made out on the Lafayette basketball team after his freshman year."

Why not lay it all on the line with the sundial tolling for P. Sann?

"He didn't, Birdye," I said. "I could tell you the kid went on to the NBA, like with the Celtics, as the smallest guard in the history of the pros, or pretty close to it, anyway. But the truth is his marks went into the sewer after you got sick and he was on scholastic probation by the time his sophomore year came up, so all he could do was win a couple of titles for his fraternity in the intramural competition. Then he went on to coach some fancy prep school team on the East Side after his three years in my trade—and then a Hippie trip and Vietnam heating up. Rich wouldn't go and kill any strangers, so I got him into the National Guard, which is where he was, or was supposed to be, when he got into that marijuana caper. But he's fine now, like I told you, and so is Leni. She went to court last month and got the family name back because she wasn't too comfortable with her husband's monicker, so there are two Sanns down there, both yours, and they'll be around a while and make it good. Now I gotta run. Can you spare me a little kiss?"

It was a big kiss. Might still be going on if Herr Wolfgang didn't goose-step over to remind Herr Zahn that the *Nacht* was running out.

Day X ❧

Chapter 20 ••••••••••••••••••••••••

I didn't have to put Der Kapitan, the wealthy Nazi, back in his stand-up Murphy bed that morning because I had only a few minutes left to get to the abattoir (and you can put that down as a pretty soft word).

Brother Wilhelm did not point me toward my squat but instead, holding my right arm much too firmly, I thought, led me before the chair.

"The clerk will read the verdict," Saint Peter said.

And the clerk read.

Three little words.

"Guilty as charged."

Big deal. To me that was about the same as picking up the *Times* in the lobby of the courthouse and finding that those Iranian fuckers weren't budging another inch on our hostages or the Russians were playing some more of their kind of game or the Knicks had lost another one on the road and dipped under that critical .500 mark. Or the sun wasn't coming out tomorrow like Andrea McCardle sang it in *Annie* but there were snow flurries on the way with sub-zero temperatures.

I wasn't through by a long shot. I wasn't even taking it squatting. I was on my two good feet and ready and fit to throw an appeal at those *goyim* with hearts of pure stone who never heard from appeals. Still, I was burning. I had never been hit with a yellow memo from Dorothy Schiff that stung quite as hard as that. I was so burned I didn't even look over at the Peter I thought I owned and skipped the prosecutor as well because now I dug that whole scene a lot better. That gent and the low-blow artist on the right were nothing more than the heavenly version of the good guy-bad guy detective team, one serving you tea and crumpets and the other one swinging the rubber hose.

"May I address the court before sentence is imposed, Your Honor?" I asked Saint Peter, who didn't seem to have much stomach left for many more of my poor words (I know, Pop, I should have stayed in school, like you told me).

"You may," came the answer, "but briefly. The Tribunal has other matters to which it must attend before the start of the next regular session."

"Thanks," I said. "I assume that I will be accorded the privilege of polling this jury before I make my statement. Is that not so?"

"Yes, Mr. Sann, it is not so. Indeed, I do not quite follow what you have suggested."

"I'm sorry about that. More shocked than sorry, in fact. In the judicial process below a convicted felon's counsel enjoys the right to ask each juror how he voted if he wishes to do so."

"That is a most edifying piece of intelligence, Mr. Sann, and my colleagues surely must appreciate it as much as the chair itself. Be that as it may, the practice you have just described does not exist in this Tribunal."

"May I argue it, sir?"

"You may not, since it is without relevance. You are not in your own province now. Please proceed with your statement with as much dispatch as possible."

"Thanks again," I said, speaking with all the anger-muddled force I could summon in a situation so upsetting. "I stand before you now, figuratively, that is, with a crown of thorns bedecking my poor head. I hope and trust that this is not to be regarded as blasphemy, because that is the furthest thought from my mind, but I submit that for practical purposes I have been nailed to the cross in this chamber. I am addressing these remarks to you with a spear in my heart and the Walls of Jericho collapsing upon me. I do not propose to point the finger at any Judas on this honorable body, although in truth I have had no question whatever since my first day here that I was in a room with more than its share of Doubting Thomases now going under the name of Peter—all named Peter. I say unto you one and all that I have been grievously misjudged, and I say once again that your denial of a direct appeal to the Heavenly Father violates every precept of the system of justice which all of humanity has been led to believe exists in this place. Saint John the Divine in Revelation spoke of one in his final extremity 'standing before God.' That is a direct quote, but I do not appear to be regarded as one adjudged worthy of a privilege supposedly available to all other mortals. This I must protest, even sensing its apparent futility, with all the vehemence at my command. I have been denied true justice but I am without rancor. However, I wish—"

Time out.

"Mr. Sann," and I thought Saint Peter was glowering now, "you have not only let forth a veritable flood of unspeakable blasphemy but dared to go so far as to demand a private audience with the Almighty, whereas throughout your entire life below—surely beyond the year of your communion—you steadfastly denied His very existence. The chair finds itself grievously offended by your arrogance. Henceforth, this Tribunal shall tolerate nothing beyond any remarks you may wish to make bearing solely on the case in which you have been adjudged guilty on the evidence as presented and buttressed by your very own testimony. With this remonstration in mind, do you have anything further to convey to your judges before sentence is pronounced?"

"I do, Your Honor, and I offer you my most abject apology for any blasphemy which I may have uttered in my deeply troubled state. I shall speak solely now to the case at hand. I submit that I was able to establish my complete innocence on no less than five of the Commandments as well as a strong case for reasonable doubt on still another. That leaves a finding of certain guilt on but four of the Commandments. Thus in my reading of what has transpired here I emerged with the scales more than adequately weighted in my favor. Assuming that to be correct as drawn from the record, sir, I respectfully ask you how an adverse verdict possibly could have been arrived at by a jury with such overwhelming experience and, I had a right to believe in this holiest of all places, a sure sense of compassion?"

"A most interesting presentation," came the voice from the rafters. "The chair finds it singularly remarkable how your eloquence manages to sustain itself even in the face of the ultimate adversity." A glance across the entire bench, left to right, and then the crusher. "Mr. Sann, let us assume for our present purpose that your assessment is entirely correct, shall we? Are you not aware that you have conceded that a finding of guilt on no less than four of the Commandments is in fact beyond challenge? Do you not understand—the chair would find this almost beyond belief—that one adjudged guilty on a single commandment is perforce guilty on all ten Commandments? Is that even remotely possible, sir?"

So Vito was right. You lose one, you lose 'em all, but that knucklehead Zahn, nee Sann, wouldn't buy it.

"Not at this point, Your Honor," I said. "My celestial education now appears to be complete and so I can do no more than raise a question of overbearing importance to me. I ask you whether even in the face of the adverse verdict I dare hope that this esteemed body may with Christian charity grant me leave to remain in this haven among my loved ones in a condition of penitence and forever pledged to an existence wholly free of all sin."

"That is a precedent which this Tribunal has no intention of setting. Is there anything further you wish to say?"

Did I? Only with both barrels smoking.

"Your Honor, it is at this juncture all but too clear that anything else I might have to say could only fall on deaf ears* in this chamber. I do, however, have this to declare to you: I expect to get everything which has transpired here in these ten days—this whole shameful travesty of justice—on some printed record by whatever means may be available to me. That is a professional obligation which I hold in sacred trust and must carry out at all costs—even, I might add, if I have to give my very life once again."

Here my Peter raised his hand.

Had I finally rolled a seven?

Nein.

"If the court please, these particular 'deaf' ears have now heard an open threat of blackmail so contemptible as to have debarred this petitioner from any further utterances. I for one find myself shocked beyond words."

Well, now hear this:

That was not—repeat not—the voice of *my* Peter. The one other time he had opened his yap it was in a firm, forceful, moderately youthful tone. Remember I said he might even have been a guy who worked for me once? Well, what had just issued forth came in a voice so high-pitched, squeaky and halting that it had to belong to some gent no less

---

*I know. Caution to the winds, but I was thinking about that old Hitler gag. How mankind's worst mass murderer turns up alive and someone asks him what's on the drawing board, Fuehrer, and he says, "Vell, the first thing is no more of this Mr. Nice Guy shit. That vas the mistake I made."

than five thousand years old, give or take a few thousand semesters.

So it was the old shell game—in Heaven itself—and I thought I had seen every last hustle known to man in my time.

Can you believe any of this, fellow workers? They had led me down the garden path so I could never get a lock on any one Peter while going against a trumped-up case with enough holes in it to build yourself the world's largest Swiss cheese.

So much for that. The court will come to order.

Saint Peter, plainly more grim than the federal judge who had chewed me out in the Frank Costello case:

"Mr. Sann, the time for any further procrastination is beyond us. The bailiff is instructed to return you to the entry point, from whence your instant departure from the Holy City shall be executed forthwith."

"Instant" departure? Not so much as a quick stop for some instant coffee? You could have knocked me over with a stray whisker from that floor-length beard, which I now noticed for the first time had some streaks of black in it and took to mean that this political appointee was even older than I had thought.

"I'm not quite sure I heard that right," I said, skipping that "Your Honor" junk. "Am I to be denied so much as the few minutes it might take me to say my last farewells, not even to my own dear wife and beloved father? I find that utterly beyond reason and comprehension as well. Now I can't believe my own ears."

And the last words of Peter the Good to Paul the Bad:

"My friend, you are abusing the patience of this Tribunal beyond endurance. You have been fairly tried, extended every possible courtesy, found guilty and sentenced. Shall we leave it at that?"

Why not, Pete? The time for quibbling is past, and the past is history.

I was saying that to myself as the cadaver Wilhelm pointed me toward what I had to assume was the Land without Promise but all the warmth a thin man could hope for while the Arabs and our own oil potentates were pushing fuel costs for homeowners to sky-high levels.

Between and betwixt this kind of solid economic thinking, I was cursing myself for that single day I had skipped with Birdye, let alone my failure to hunt down Walter Lister and Paul Tierney, two guys I owed such large debts.

Did I say cursing myself?

Hell, I was also cursing twelve other guys.

If I may resort to my normal tongue once again, I had been fucked. Royally fucked, just another mark for the upstairs Murder Inc.

There's a moral here, and I take the time to put it down only because I feel I owe it to my fellow man and, for that matter, even the Ms.'s. If you do happen to make it to the upper H leave your good bad habits behind. I mean things like drinking and smoking, cutting corners, looking for edges. Etcetera, etcetera, etcetera, to borrow Yul Brynner's best lines from *The King and I*.

End of sermon. The only thing holding me together was that my ass had been burned so badly nothing could burn where I was headed. That and the rock-hard conviction that the double-dealers I had just left would never see me again even if they sent a hired limo with a built-in bar and a No Tipping sign on the glass shield separating me from the driver in the white uniform. They had themselves a hombre with the know-how to set them up with a p.r. operation that would have packed that hotel with no room service and they blew it. They were never, but never, going to have to hang out any SRO sign. Talk about robbing Peter to pay Paul. The Peters had robbed Paul and screwed themselves. I felt pretty good once I had all that worked out.

Chapter 21 •

Who do you suppose was at the swinging door known to the innocently pious legions as the Pearly Gates?

The only brother I ever had.

Ever see a guy six-feet-eight with a scarred and busted face that could throw terror into a kids' Halloween party crying like a baby? There were enough tears streaming down Vito's map to float a rowboat in.

"C'mon, Tiny," I said. "Get a grip on yourself. This ain't the end. It's another beginning. All those hangmen did was switch my zip code from one thousand and fourteen to five zips, which is so much easier for people to remember."

Nothing but jokes, down to the last roundup, but it didn't help a damn.

Wracked with sobs, Vito seemed to have lost his tongue, but he found it fast enough when the Nazi, into whose care I had been deposited by Brother Wilhelm, said something about how his orders showed no time for farewells at the de-portals. This was a mistake on the ace's part, because all it got him was two hands around his delicate neck that would have wasted anybody in the world who wasn't already wasted.

"Lissen, kraut," Vito rasped, holding back the tears for this purpose, "if you wanna stay healthy in this concentration camp you shut your cocksuckin mouth. You got any trouble with that?"

There wasn't an ounce of fight left in that *fagele* sent thither by the RAF. After all, his specialty was dropping bombs on women and children, not striking other men in anger with his manicured hands.

"*Ja*, Herr Vittorio," he managed to gasp, "but iss no time. My orders they were cut."

"That's tough shit," Herr Vittorio responded. "You shove 'em, kraut, or somethin else could get cut if you got any."

"*Ja*, but Herr Zahn he has to go now."

"I know that, fuckface. You just hold your water."

The ace held his water—or his beer—and the man mountain took me in his arms, fresh tears falling on my shroud as I looked up and thought I saw a very dark cloud passing over us.

"You got jobbed, pal. I never seen a dirty deal like this where we came from. I don't wanna stay in this bedbug joint without you, and we had a hard deal. You told me somethin like wherever you go I go too."

I wrestled myself free, which wasn't all that easy.

"Tiny," I said. "There's no reason in the world—*any* world—for you to go where I'm headed. You led a proper life, home and away. I'm a small horse of another color. Besides, you've got work to do here."

"What work? I blew the job with them two-timin whiskers."

"I didn't mean that. I need you to keep an eye on Birdye and Ed, and maybe Toots or my old boss Lister. And, oh yeah, I almost forgot. You have to come up with that horn for Satchmo."

"What about your old man, Paul boy?"

"It's real nice of you to think of a detail like that," I said, "but you don't need to kill any time on him. He's just as happy or just as miserable as he was in his other life. You bootlegged him that new shroud. If you can't come up with any chicken soup, forget it. You've got just about my whole list."

"OK." The sobs stopped here. "I put the little woman first. She's the most. Nobody ever reminded me of my Rosario like she did. Nobody in my whole fuckin life."

"Good, Vito. Get yourself squared away so you can roll over there with this bulletin and see what you can do to hold her together. She's gonna take it real hard, but Ed's with her. Between the two of you she could be all right after a while. That's one tough dame. I don't wanna sound like Jimmy Cagney in one of those old Warner Brothers movies where he's headed for the green room, but I wish you'd tell Birdye and Ed I went out on my own two feet. You know, how I didn't have to be carried off screaming and hollering like there was any dog in me on the last mile."

"You got it, Paul, and I'm already squared away good. I spread a few of them bills around yesterday. Like I told'ya at the start, it's no goddamn different than any place else. There's always a palm waitin to be greased."

"That's super," I said. "It makes it so much easier for me. Man, I wish we could do it all over again and all be together—you and me and Birdye and Ed, all doing our things. You haven't got yourself messed up over the midget, have you?"

"Nah. I'll get around to that asshole in plentya time, nice and slow. That chiselin tailor, too."

"You can't mean it, Tiny. What do you want from Hank?"

"Onny a few bills back, that's all. That pickpocket dipped too good into your stash."

"Have you seen him?"

"I didn't have no time to waste lookin, but don't worry, he ain't gettin away. I onny kept casin you and made that stop with your pal Paddy Flint."

"Good, Vito, now listen to me, will you? You've got to let the midget and the tailor off the hook."

"No way. For all we know that was the rap that done you in. Personally I think you coulda come out winners except for that."

"You couldn't be wronger. Listen some more. There's two items here. One, if the whiskers put the shackles on you so you can't look after our little family that's pure murder for me, OK?"

"Yeah. What's the other one?"

"Something heavier for you. There's got to be an Immigration Bureau up here, since they've got damn near everything else, and the last thing you want is a deportation case, *capish?*"

"Aw, cut it out, Paul. I can't see that."

"That's too bad. Don't write it off—and if they bang you with one of those you go see Uncle Frank. The immigration wizards downstairs knocked themselves out going against him, so he knows all the angles on that shtick."

"Whatever you say, *amico*. I'm sold, all the way."

The Nazi was pacing around now and I thought I heard a whirring sound, like a NASA space ship or maybe a UFO with its motor idling. Or—why not?—William Shatner with the long-eared Leonard Nimoy and the house medic in their old flying machine and a few of those luscious babes from that old TV show on hand to make my last flight somewhat more relaxing. I always had the hots for those broads in the skintight outfits.

"Tiny," I said. "I better split. I just wish I had my stuff back. I hate to go where I'm going in this bedsheet—and, by the way, the crapper I'm headed for wouldn't even be there except that this crowd threw out a couple of guys named Satan and Lucifer and they set up their own joint. They might take me for a Bowery bum instead of a famous newspaperman, author and lawyer."

"No problem." The Sicilian polar bear ignored Der Kapitan as he reached under the back of his shroud and produced all my gear, right down to the Knickerbocker socks.

"How the hell did you come up with this?" I asked.

"Whatsa difference? It's all here, ain't it?" Now the tears again but I found a way to shut them off.

"You didn't throw in a hack saw or a nail file so I could cut my way out of whatever's out there, huh?"

"I tried, Paul. Honest I tried. I just couldn't come up with nothin like that. Even went for a piece but they gotta have them planted pretty good. Did'ja tell me all I needa know?"

"All I could think of, Vito, but hold it. I've still got another bill on me. I better lay that on you."

I started to bend down but was gently hauled back up.

"No good. You hang onto it. For all'ya know you could need it where you're headed. Like I always say, you'll sure as hell find some bum on the take."

What a way to put it.

The Nazi, edging closer, staked us to such a pitifully nervous look that I felt a little sorry for him. After all, for a lousy C note he probably didn't even need that loser had given me the best day of my whole death. Alone with the woman I had always been true to in my fashion.

"Vito," I said. "We've really abused the privilege this war hero so graciously extended to us. Can you get over to Birdye's right now?"

"Know anybody who can stop me, pal?"

"You told me it took a magnum in the other place."

I shouldn't have mentioned that, because now the man mountain looked as if he was tasting that garlic again but, happily, he wiped his red-rimmed eyes with his sleeve, gave me another shroud-bending bear hug and turned and left without another word. I guess he was choked up.

My German friend, needless to say, was plainly delighted to see such a rough-hewn type taking his leave.

"Zahn," Göring's boy said, taking me by the arm. "Iss time now."

"Thanks a lot, you Nazi prick," I said. "I'm gonna miss you."

The beautiful Aryan offered no rebuttal, nor even a *danke,* and walked me about ten steps.

I guess that scene with Vito had messed up my head pretty good, because I wasn't able to make any mental notes on the kind of vehicle I was led into. It could have been that boat from the River Styx on its return trip for all I knew.

I do remember my last words up there, though.

"Mephistopheles," I said. "Here I come. It can't be any fucking worse."

Chapter 22 •

Now, once again, I was in the Coronary Care Unit at Beth Israel Hospital in Manhattan and Ira Cohen was at my bedside.

"You did it again, Paul," my cardiologist said. "How do you feel?"

"Pretty good," I mumbled with that oxygen tube in my nose. "How long have I been here?"

"The police brought you in early this morning."

"How come?"

"You had a seven o'clock breakfast date with Richie and when he couldn't get you on the phone after you failed to show up he went around to the house and found you drenched to the skin and passed out."

It was only then that I noticed the I.V. in my left arm and felt those things on my chest that had me wired into the cardiac monitor.

"What's showing on that screen behind me, Ira?" I asked.

"Oh, you're doing as well as you should at this stage."

"That's nice, but I'm awful thirsty. I could use a beer and it doesn't even have to be cold."

"Paul, you're not in any bar. You're back in Beth Israel—on your own choice—and everything you need at the moment is in that needle. The profession hasn't started to use beer in heart cases yet. You can have a sip of water to go with your glucose."

"No, thanks, doc. Water was always hell on my ulcer. The aorta went again because I wasn't living like you said I orta, huh?"

Small chuckle.

"Of course. Why should that come as any surprise?"

"It doesn't. How long am I in for this time? I got a red-hot new book I have to bang out."

"Let's not go that fast, author. First we do all our poking around and then we know where we stand."

"Hey, hold it, fellow jogger," I said. "Don't tell me they're shoving another one of those horse needles into my groin for that enzyme test or whatever the hell it is."

"Oh, I don't know," the doctor said. "There's no need to rush things. You appear to be nicely stabilized, and that's our primary concern. All that's happened so far is that you've made a mess out of my weekend. We were going to the country to beat the snow when Richie called me."

"I couldn't feel worse about that. What else is new?"

"Well, Paul, why don't we start with your social life? There are too many people out there even now—and this time you're going to listen a little better."

"Listen to what, you murderer?"

"You have at least five or six days here in the CCU and I'm going to start you off with one visitor for ten minutes at a time every two hours. Any questions?"

"I guess not. You're the same generous guy I've come to know and love. I met a Nazi the other day who reminded me of you a little, except that he wasn't a Hebrew and he was better looking. I wouldn't say he was quite as nice as you though."

"Thanks for the compliment."

"No need, Ira. You know enough to tell me anything, like how long this whole sentence is?"

"Not quite, but you can safely figure that once you're in your own room you'll be on our excellent kosher diet for two or three weeks and then need a quiet month or two at home. You won't need the sneakers you came in with much before that."

"Celtic sneakers?"

"What else would you wear, my friend?" Ira, a rabid Knick fan, detested anything with the Auerbach name on it.

"I'm sorry about that," I said, "but I never could turn down a free pair of sneakers."

"Maybe you should have turned those down. They don't look as if they're wearing too well."

"You kidding?"

"Yes, I haven't had a chance to examine them, Paul. I've been concentrating exclusively on you."

"That's very decent. Now about that book I mentioned. I can't lose any time on it. That would be the worst possible thing for my health."

"Oh, I wouldn't say that. The worst possible thing for your health is the way you live."

"Problem solved, Ira," I said. "I just about kicked the cigarets in the last two weeks, and the booze, too."

"Really? That's good to hear. You may be coming to your senses finally—and not a minute too soon. You do know there's a limit on how many coronary incidents most men are supposed to have."

"Sure. Always have. Now what about me and my lover—the IBM?"

"You can go back to that when you get home, but not in your around-the-clock style. A few hours here and there and back to bed."

"Beautiful. Richie here?"

"Of course. He's back in his usual function as your usher and master of ceremonies. Let me get him."

My son with the black beard, such a pleasant change for me, bounded in and took the hand without the I.V.

"How do you feel, Dad?"

"Ridiculous is how I feel. I hear I blew a breakfast date with you."

"That's right."

The doctor gave my pulse a quick check and stepped out, threatening to come back in a second.

"Rich," I said. "My sneakers in that closet? Ira says I came in with them."

"So? You running today?"

"No, I think I had some C notes in them."

The kid got the sneakers, which proved to be in splended shape but bereft of any currency.

"Jesus, Rich, I think I've been clipped," I said. "I had a pretty good stash in there before whatever happened."

"Dad, you had two thousand dollars in your pants from that bet on the Steelers, but I got to it before the cops. What's your problem?"

"I'm not sure," I said. "Maybe Ira knows. Here he is now."

"I heard that question, Richie," the doctor said. "Your father knows his problem as well as the rest of us. Now I'm going to run uptown and have lunch with my wife and I'll stop in this afternoon. You have a splendid resident, Paul. Dr. Ciardi."

"Thanks," I said. "Give your wife a kiss for me."

Now Rich took the floor—and this place had a floor, thank the good Lawd.

"How come you didn't try to call me, Dad? You laughed off that first heart attack for ten hours, so I imagine you were up a while before this one."

"I don't think so. This baby must have hit like a sledgehammer, because I know I had no time to make believe it was indigestion. Who's out there?"

"Lisa, Helene with some nun and your sister Fay with Sam. Leni's taking the next bus. Besides them all I called was Red and Jason and Mrs. Schiff."

"Good. My favorite T-shirt in that locker?"

"You had it on, Dad. Did you figure the cops grabbed that too? I don't get any of this. You sound more like you O.D.'d on gin."

"Oh, it's all very complicated, Rich. I thought I got ripped off for a lot of stuff but now I remember I got it all back."

"Man, I don't know whether your heart went again or your head. Look, you have to rest now. Ira's real tough this time. I'm sending everybody home and telling them to check me tonight about when they can come in tomorrow—in shifts."

"No you don't, kiddo. Not so fast. How's that gizmo behind me read?"

"The ball seems to be bouncing nice and even."

"That means I've made a full recovery. What's going on?"

"Where?"

"In the world, bonehead. They free the hostages? Ali still retired? Teddy running or just driving broads around? Our team still rolling?"

"Jesus, Dad, I gotta get out of here."

"Fine. Send in Lisa and don't argue. And keep one of those bills if you're short. You were very helpful this morning. No man ever had a better son."

"Yeah, and no son ever had a wackier father."

Pretty as a picture in those long tresses but a wee bit heavy because she was almost eight months pregnant with her first child, Mrs. S swept in with the most glaringly tender and unforgiving look in her eyes.

"Well, you did it again. God knows you tried hard enough."

"You couldn't be righter, Lis," I said. "Not only that but you look great. You haven't put on an ounce since I saw you last."

"Paul, that was the other night. Are you all right?"

"Never better."

"You mean since that last attack, don't you?"

"I guess so. Where's Robert?"

"Waiting for me to tell him when he can come down. You've already been told that this isn't going to be another social event, haven't you?"

"I have indeed, angel of mercy, and you know I'm one guy who always does exactly what the doctor tells him," I said, and at that moment a trim, red-haired nurse who looked about fifty came in to replace the bottle on that hatrack holding my new intravenous Weight Watchers diet.

"Good morning, Mr. Sann," the lady said. "I'm Mrs. Flannery, your day special."

"How nice. Say hello to Mrs. Steele and tell me something. You ever work in French Hospital?"

"French? No. That's closed now, isn't it? Why do you ask?"

"Well, I was in there a few years back and had a nurse almost as good looking as you except that she didn't wear glasses and her hair was longer, more like Lisa's here."

Mrs. Flannery, nearly as shapely for her years as that French Hospital dish who got me in trouble in my trial, shook off the flattery.

"We have to get down to business," she said, looking at the watch strung from her neck. "It's eleven fifty-five. Your son may come in if you need him for anything but you cannot have another visitor before two o'clock. Those are Dr. Cohen's orders and Dr. Ciardi will be in very shortly."

"I'll be here, Mrs. Flannery," I said as Lisa pitched in with a request for a couple of minutes alone with me and ascended the pulpit.

"Paul, I hope this is it for you. Do you think you can come to your senses finally and live like a normal human being who has a reason to live and wants to?"

"That's a tapout. You're looking at a model boy now, all out of bad habits. Would you do me a favor?"

"What?"

"See if that skinny red wallet of mine is in my pants."

Mrs. Steele did as directed, moving with the grace of an un-pregnant woman.

"Why do you need this?" she asked. "You going out for a three-martini lunch and need your American Express card?"

"No, Lis. Just check it and tell me what's in it."

"It has your credit cards, your I.D. for Robert's office, your library card, a two-dollar bill, two blank checks, your half-fare ticket, your Blue Cross and Health Insurance and a color snapshot of some woman."

"She look anything like you?"

"Oh, come. Do you mind telling me what this nonsense is all about?"

"Got no time. We're up against a goddamn curfew. By the way, I checked in without my wristwatch, unless the cops boosted it while Rich wasn't looking. Can you lend me yours?"

"Mine? This is your watch, the one they gave you when you left the paper. I'm wearing it because you won't be seen in any public place without your Celtic watch. Why in heaven do you need one now?"

Heaven? *Oy vay*. What could you keep from that Yalie?

"So I don't get cheated on any time," I said. "Will you come back tonight with Robert?"

"Certainly. Do you know Helene's out there with a nun?"

"Yes."

"You're not thinking of converting, are you?"

"Not in a million years, Lis. I happen to know too much. That nun's just my new best girl. She's not married like you, or I should say not living with her beloved."

A brawny young doctor dropped in before the lady could deal with that one.

"I'm sorry, ma'am," he said, "but you'll have to go now."

Lisa bent down and kissed my ice-cold forehead (I must have brought that chill down with me) and I asked her to tell Helene and Sister Margaret Mary to go have lunch and come back.

"Mr. Sann," said my new visitor, feeling my pulse and glancing at my chart at the same time. "I understand you've made this trip before."

"Yeah. Four years ago. It was a laugher."

"Was it? I guess that's one way to look at a coronary, but Dr. Cohen tells me you had a touch of arrhythmia after that. Was that also a fun thing for you?"

"Of course. I never stopped laughing, doctor. That's why I'm still among the earth people."

"Hmnn. I think you stopped sometime during the night myself. Now I'm going to need some blood and—"

"Hold it. You don't mean with that long needle, do you?"

"No, not today."

"We could be good friends," I said. "What's next?"

"Oh, just a few tests and lots of rest. You want to sleep for the next few hours. Take this pill."

Sleep? After what I had been through? Why the hell did guys go to college and spend fortunes to become doctors when they never knew the real score? I swallowed the pill and lay there like a mummy—a pleasant change at that—and Rich peeked in a few times and that lying redhead nurse came in at least twice. She surely was that one from French Hospital. She couldn't fool me. I never forgot an ass unless it ran to fat. Anyway, after what seemed like nine years that *Post* watch showed fourteen hundred hours (that's navy time, you know) and in came my other two girls, little Helene looking like death itself, not even warmed over, and Sister Margaret Mary the very soul of serenity and good cheer. And why not? That lady knew this was one bum who was never, but never, going to be all dead. Yeah. She just didn't happen to know as much as I did but I wasn't ready to let on.

"We'll only stay a minute, Paul," Helene said. "Are you all right?"

"Never better. All I need is a few minutes to figure this thing out. I had no right to get belted again the way I took care of myself all these years."

Both women, parked on either side of my railed-in bed, looked awful skeptical, but they weren't going to push me around like that Steele dame.

"What is there for you to figure out, Paul?" Sister Margaret Mary asked. "You've been talking about another heart attack for years and, indeed, working most strenuously at it, as Helene tells it."

"I don't doubt it, Mimi," I said. "That's why I left the paper. This kid was bugging me too much about my way of life."

"Paul's right, Mimi," Helene said. "I was a terrible nag, and worse. There were mornings when I cheated and didn't put enough gin in his martini."

"You can say that again," I said.

"There's not enough time," said my ex-secretary. "Did Lisa tell you she thinks Mimi's converting you?"

"Yes, but she doesn't know anything. There's no way I ever abandon the faith I've been so devoted to all my life. Mimi, how have you been?"

"Just fine, except that I didn't expect to see you in a hospital so soon after that lovely dinner. You told me you were going to take me to that restaurant again very soon."

"So I did, but I had no idea there was somebody waiting at the house for me with a baseball bat."

"Well, you'll be all right soon enough if you do what your doctor tells you."

"Don't ever doubt it. I'm a new man now. The most they're going to find is some fresh damage to the cardiac muscle and blood in my gin."

Rich came in with a telegram and Helene read it.

DEAR PAUL: ISN'T THIS THE FIRST TIME YOU'VE BEEN IN A HOSPITAL WHEN YOU WERE SUPPOSED TO BE ON VACATION? GET BETTER. ALL MY LOVE. DOLLY.

"What does that mean?" the nun asked.

"Oh," I started to say, but Helene broke in.

"Save your breath. You see, Mimi, Paul had surgery for an ulcer when he had some time coming with his family before he was supposed to go off to World War II and he had his first heart attack while he was on vacation. That's what Mrs. Schiff is referring to."

"The lady has it right, Mimi," I said. "My former employer never forgot an executive who got sick on his own time instead of hers. It didn't matter with the union men in our jute mill because if their bodies failed them on their paid sabbaticals it was still owed to them just the same."

And here comes the other beard.

"Time's up, ladies," Rich said. "You know this guy will never chase you out."

Two fresh kisses and those two nice women left. Rich had sent my favorite sister and her husband back home to Queens. I entered no objection but said I did want to see Lisa and Robert that night.

"OK," said my new keeper. "Leni and them and that's it for today."

"You sure you were never a drill sergeant in the marines?" I asked him.

"Yes. I was something less than a grunt in the National Guard, but I'm not going to let you knock yourself out on this trip and get sent back with any damn extra heartbeat. You need anything from the house?"

"Pajamas, I guess, and a robe and slippers."

"Lisa said she's buying pajamas for you."

"Good. I hope she knows the left sleeve has to be a half inch shorter."

"Sure, Dad. Any other dizzy notions?"

"No. I'm thinking of trying for some sleep. Haven't had any for ten days."

"Hmnn." I think I was driving the black beard a little nutty. "Well, you always said you never needed much shut-eye."

"So I did, but I'm dozing off now. Don't tell 'em at the desk or they'll come in and give me some blood or take some piss or who knows."

"Fine, Dad. I'll be back later."

"Good, Rich, and thanks for coming over this morning. I hate laying around the house in my clothes."

"I dig that," Rich said, leaving. "It's not neat."

And so I slept.

Between visits, that is.

The resident.

That lying Flannery woman and the blue-clad nurse's aides I had no previous acquaintance with.

Ira.

The ones with the pills and the bedpans and the glucose refills.

The waste basket emptiers.

Some old guy hustling the Australian *Post* when I didn't have a quarter to my name (Sann, that is, not Zahn).

The way I sized it up they were treating me like any other guest in the CCU, but I had the most charitable attitude toward all those innocent toilers. How could they have known that I died and went to Heaven only to be forcibly evicted as a bounder beyond redemption. Hell, I knew more about death than the whole lot of them but I never was one to push my superior knowledge on anybody. I let them have their fun. Two EKGs. The portable X rays. The blood tests every two or three seconds, especially if I happened to doze off again, because Ira thought he had to know the extent of the fresh damage to the heart, not to mention any possible effect on the old kidneys which I had put no strain on whatever during my leave of absence. I had no beefs and on the second day I was enjoying the I.V.s more than what the Christians were dishing out upstairs. The only trouble was that I had to wait another two days before good Ira, faced with a flat refusal to let them plunge that horse needle into my wilted groin unless the visiting rules were loosened, finally said I could have a few hours alone with my favorite nun.

That was no easy contract, by the way, because my lay guardian angels kept demanding to know why I was so stubbornly intent on a special seance with Sister Margaret Mary and I wouldn't tell those heathens. Lisa was the worst of them, banging me over the head twice a day, morning and evening.

"Look," I told her. "I got something special with that nun. She was my last date—no hands, Mom—before all that stuff you and Robert have been telling me about my lifestyle came true. Now you quit bugging me, Lis. It's not fair to a well man. Try to think of this as sort of parishioner and priest or lawyer-client relationship, OK?"

"If you insist, Paul, but then you would have to do something for me."

"Of course. Want me to jog uptown and walk the beast or what?"

"No, silly. If you're going to marry that nun please wait until my daughter is born, because that's something I wouldn't want to miss and I don't want to buy a gown I can only wear once."

The beautiful brunette wasn't even smiling when she said that and left. Oh, brother. There's a woman with one of those rare husbands committed to that big commandment, an heiress en route, a gunmetal blue Great Dane puppy with more breeding than any human being I ever knew, six cats with framed papers attesting to their pure bloodlines, a townhouse in Manhattan and a farm outside of Saratoga—and she's miffed because I've got this thing with Sister Margaret Mary. Well, that's the way most of them are; nothing about the other sex ever surprised me. I had 'em all down cold because I knew my friend He made only one like my Birdye. Anyway, the summit was set, so appropriately, for Christmas morning, and Richie borrowed Robert's Caddy so that Sister Margaret Mary wouldn't be ripped off for her prayer beads or penny-poor purse on the IRT.

You think the good Sister needed to be told why I had called for that summit? Don't be ridiculous. She surely had her own pipeline to the Fortunate Isles but couldn't possibly know quite as much as I did about the place, which is perfectly understandable if you've come this far with me.

"Paul," the nun said as she drew a chair to my bedside, "I have a strong suspicion that there is something rather pressing on your mind."

"That's the mildest way you could have put it, Mimi," I said.

"Well, I'm here and ever so eager to talk to you."

"Thanks, you're nice. In fact, you're the nicest of all the nuns I've ever known, which is exactly one. You remember the sales pitch you made to me about the hereafter and all that, right? Well, I've been there, good lady, and you're the only one down here entitled to know that."

Sister Margaret Mary took my hand and staked me to the warmest smile of my second life.

"I suspect I am about to be treated to some more of your humor," she said, "but there's no way I would rather spend my Christmas morning, Paul."

"You've got it wrong, Mimi," I said. "This is all dead serious, and I mean *dead* serious in italics or capital letters. After that splendid evening of ours I went into another one of my title bouts against my IBM and I didn't just have a little coronary they fix up in here with needles and kosher food. I died and went to Heaven, which is where you told me all the deserving go, right?"

"Of course," said the nun, brushing a blond wisp of hair away from her forehead and leaning closer. "This *is* going to be a fun time, isn't it?"

"No, ma'am," I said. "I tell you I went to Heaven and Saint Peter was waiting for me at the Pearly Gates almost as if you had sent word up ahead of me. Only after that I found myself on trial before the highest court in the whole universe."

"Really, did you?" Sister Margaret Mary obviously was going along with this whole exercise in semimadness. "May I ask what a good man like you would have been assessed with?"

"Come on. It was a ten-count felony indictment and I don't have to tell you what those counts were, do I now, Mimi?"

"Of course not, Paul. Would you like me to raise your bed?"

"No, thanks. You can't imagine how badly I need to stay stretched out. The accommodations in the Holy City were not too elaborate."

"I'm sorry to hear that. I can hardly wait to hear the rest."

"Mimi, this is not a put-on—and if you hear the faintest suggestion of sacrilege you speak up and I'll try to blabber with more discretion, but right out front you might as well know you're not going to hear any knocks from this quarter on the true believers."

"That's nice to hear but hardly a surprise. I had no question whatever about your tolerance the night we talked. You said nothing worse than that *you* were not a believer, and I understood that perfectly."

"Well, you had it right. That's a rap I beat. I mean the one about not worshiping strange gods or intruding on the beliefs of any other mortals. Perhaps I shouldn't put it quite that way, though, because the fact is that in the heavenly Tribunal you have no way of knowing what you win on and what you lose, and anyway if you're guilty on one commandment you're guilty, period. To me it seemed a helluva way—excuse me, Sister—to run the highest railroad in the world."

"Well, we're all privileged to hold our own views on ethereal levels. I would not want to speculate on the Commandments you may have been deemed guilty of violating. To put it somewhat closer to biblical terminology, Paul, thy name is legion, but I for one will never believe that there are any conceivable circumstances under which a person like you would be denied the afterlife we talked about."

"How kind."

"I'm not being kind. I simply know from all the things Helene has told me and from what I have heard in this hospital from your son and Mrs. Steele and so many, many others that you have done your share of good works and more. You are never going to need any special benediction to be admitted to the hereafter. Never, because you are not the nonbeliever you so freely profess to be."

"Good, Mimi," I said. "I might be ready to buy a few shares in the Heavenly Father but I'm not too high on his helpmates up there. I was roughed up pretty good, believe me."

"Of course, but here you are. I suspect that you have had some kind of spiritual experience in these past few days which in the long run will prove to be very profitable indeed."

"Maybe so, Mimi, but the 'experience' you're talking about wasn't all that great. It was rotten, in fact. I won't burden you with the ugly details but I will say this much: there's quite a few things missing upstairs that the Bible tells us are there, like the golden harps and the trumpets—Louis Armstrong himself doesn't have one of those and you know that in the Bible in Judges there's something about how 'the Spirit of the Lord came upon Gideon, and he blew a trumpet,' let alone all those references to the endless delights of the flesh and whatnot. Honest, this is eyewitness testimony. You must have read *Pilgrim's Progress,* where Bunyan said the glory of the other world would never wear out. Well, it wore out for me pretty darn fast. You must take my word or it. I was *there.*"

The nun did not fall off her chair.

"Paul," she said, "I have always had a high regard for the philosopher Santayana, who spoke of the Bible as literature, not dogma, but there cannot be any question that Heaven is an eternally safe harbor where the righteous may enjoy eternal bliss. Didn't we talk about that?"

"I guess we did, although it seems so long ago now, but I didn't quite fit into that category, and, believe me, please, I ran into a few other people who were anything but righteous and did not get thrown out like me. But, look, I came back without a grievance against a living soul. I was a loser because I went up there without my dues paid, that's all."

"Well, you'll never make me accept that."

"Of course. Anyway, Mimi, the fact is that I could not be more grateful for the way I was treated on the Day of Judgment. After all, they could have sent me to the other place instead of letting me come back home to get a few more words on paper and have some more time with the people I love down here, like you."

"You truly are something special," Sister Margaret Mary said, eyes aglow on that handsome face. "You had a glorious dream because you earned a glorious dream. Now listen to me, Paul. There is indeed a hereafter and in your good time you are going there and in your case, trust me, there will not be a second trial."

"I know that. They can't put me in the dock again because that would be double jeopardy. Incidentally, I had to defend myself. There's no Legal Aid branch up there. Next time I'm taking along some gent with a law degree now that I know the score."

"By all means. That's very sound thinking." Here my confidante reached into her purse and drew out a pocket-sized New Testament bound in red leather. "May I read you something before I go?"

"Mimi," I said. "Can I have one guess as to what you've got that ribbon turned to?"

"Of course."

"Matthew?"

The nun looked positively dazed.

"It happens that I do," she said. "Now I suppose you're going to tell me the chapter and verse as well, aren't you?"

"Well, I could be wrong but I think it might be the Lord's Prayer, since I don't know anything in the Good Book that befits this top-secret summit any better."

"Dear me, Paul. That is precisely what I wanted you to read with me."

"No need, Mimi. I can read it to you without the Book."

"Are you serious?"

"Dead serious, or let's say live serious. I've had that piece of Matthew fixed in my head for a long, long time—as literature, not dogma, by the way—and I've just come through a most elaborate refresher course on that aborted trip of mine."

The nun closed the book.

"Would you mind very much if I asked you to recite it?"

"Not one bit.

"*Our Father who art in Heaven, Hallowed be thy name.*

"*Thy kingdom come. Thy will be done in earth, as it is in Heaven.*

"*Give us this day our daily bread.*

"*And forgive us our debts, as we forgive our debtors.*

"*And lead us not into temptation, but deliver us from evil: For thine is the kingdom, and the power, and the glory, forever. Amen.*"

Dr. Ciardi came in as I reached that last sentence, did a quick turn and left, or perhaps fled is the better word.

"Oh, dear," said Sister Margaret Mary. "That poor young man must have thought you were undergoing a conversion in this of all hospitals. Shouldn't I go after him and call him back?"

"No, Mimi," I laughed. "Let the kid sweat it. It might just make him treat me a little better, since he knows what an irreverent type I am."

"Please don't ever say that, Paul. You are only denigrating yourself. What just happened in this room has overwhelmed me almost to the point of tears. I honestly cannot recall anything quite like it in all of my forty-four years, so many of them in the convent."

The young doctor, evidently unwilling to set aside his Hippocratic oath even if his side was in the process of picking up a recruit, now returned.

"I'm sorry I broke in before, Sister," he said, "but it's time for this strange patient's medication and a few checks. Dr. Cohen is talking about letting him out of this unit tomorrow if he promises to behave himself, and I think I can now testify that he is."

"Dr. Ciardi," said the nun. "I would say that no one need have any concern on that score. This 'strange' patient, as you put it, is one of God's chosen children—not that you will ever hear him admit that, of course."

The resident broke into a wide grin.

"Ma'am," he said. "You've got me there. I've had seven years in this profession and I have to admit there's nothing in my training covering this kind of man, and I'm saying that on four days' acquaintance. I have an idea you've known Paul much longer."

"Not really, doctor," Sister Margaret Mary said, rising, "but you are most observant at that."

"Thank you, Sister, but I'm afraid I've got to start punishing our patient for a while now."

"Would you raise me up first, Gino?" I said, and the doctor turned the crank.

Halfway up, I drew that woman to me and kissed her on the cheek.

"I hope that's not out of line, Mimi," I said. "I just had to do it."

"I would have been furious if you hadn't done it, Paul," the nun said, reaching for her cloth coat. "I want you to have the very best Christmas of your entire life."

Then she handed me that pretty little Bible.

"Please take this," she said. "It is my present to you."

And she was gone—before I could say thanks.

"You two sure make a funny couple," the doctor said as the curtain closed behind the nun.

"There's nothing funny about it, Gino," I said. "We happen to be on two separate wavelengths which bumped into each other, that's all."

"I never doubted it, Paul." Now the bed was coming flat again. "Turn over, please. You've earned yourself the rare privilege of a rectal reading by a resident instead of a nurse."

"I couldn't be happier, doc," I said. "We'll call this your Christmas present to me, because there's nothing I hate more than any female poking that thing into me, especially when it's that redhead Nancy or, even worse, one of those young ones."

Dr. Ciardi sweated over me for fifteen minutes, taking blood and all that, and then said Ira would be in around three and very likely write my early parole from the maximum security CCU. The resident was barely gone when the kosher lunch I didn't want was brought in with Richie and Lisa about a half step behind it. Lisa was carrying a smuggled bacon, lettuce and tomato on rye (without the lettuce, as per my request) for me.

"How did it go in the confessional?" she asked with a dab of sarcasm.

"Only terrific, Lis," I said. "Too short, that's all. How could anybody with a dossier like mine spill it all in one session in the box?"

"That answers itself, Mr. Sann," said Mrs. Steele. "What else is new?"

"Oh, now you want the good news, huh, meanie? Well, young Dr. Welby tells me I might get sprung from this cellblock tomorrow for the luxury of a ninth-floor room—hopefully with a Frigidaire."

"Hey, Dad," Rich said. "If you're thinking of having any tin cans of your martinis smuggled in there you can forget it."

"It's no problem, Richie," said the lady, whose husband happened to own a worldwide security agency. "I'll have Robbie put guards in your father's room on three shifts, and then we'll do the same thing at the house when he's discharged."

"Hold it, mother," I protested. "I don't mind any of those gun-toting giants of Robert's in this joint but the house is out. I got a new book to write and I'm gonna need total solitude."

"A new book? What about the novel you had half finished before Richie and that patrol car brought the body in? You've been telling us that was a Book of the Month, *Reader's Digest* excerpt, movie—and how many millions for the paperback rights?"

"I forget, but it doesn't matter, Lis. I got a better idea a while ago. This one's a true story—not the nonfiction fiction form invented by Truman Capote or Mailer's new fiction-nonfiction on Gary Gilmore. It's such a surefire blockbuster I'm throwing out those Persians as soon as all the deals are wrapped up and getting myself a Great Dane bigger than your Mr. Condor."

"Really? That won't be easy, Paul, because there is no Dane bigger than Condor."

"No problem. I'll have one made."

"I suppose there's no point in asking what this new gold mine is about, is there?"

"Lis, if I told you once I told you a thousand times—Papa Hemingway told me you never talk about a book, you write it."

"It was more than a thousand times," Mrs. Steele said, "but I won't tax you with that. I came down to thank you for solving the problem we had about your Christmas present."

"What problem? I haven't done any shopping myself—had no time."

"Oh, sure. Anyway, we bought you the IBM Selectric Two with the eraser and all those things but I decided to keep it for myself, because Robbie had a better idea."

"Better than about twelve-hundred bucks, Lis, What?"

"A psychiatrist who makes house calls. Robbie will have him driven down with his own couch, since you don't have any."

"That's real nice," I said. "Try to make it a shrink who smokes, will you?"

The lady some people suspected was pregnant turned to the black beard.

"You did throw out all those awful MORE cigarets, didn't you, Richie?"

"No, I put them in the fireplace. They make a real good fire, even better than wood except for the smell."

"Good," said the woman in the color print that had been all the way up to Valhalla and back. "And the first time you see another pack in the house you call Robbie and there'll be a guard there in ten minutes. The one you've met."

"You mean Little Mark?" Rich asked. "He's no more than six-eight and three-hundred-seventy-five pounds, isn't he, Lisa?"

"That's about all, but he shouldn't have any trouble with your father considering the weight he's losing in here."

I quote my rebuttal in full, from the record:

"Don't lose your head, mother. I happen to have a newly acquired friend who made his bones in the Mafia and is not only Mark's size but in much better fighting shape. He's been on health food for a good twenty years and he's all muscles, no fat. Name's Vittorio Pascaglia if Robert wants to check his yellow sheet with the men in blue."

"Richie," Lisa said. "Would you come out and buy me a drink? I'm not supposed to do that with the baby coming but I can't fight it another minute. My Dane makes more sense than your father."

Once again, I elected not to throw in any objection. Let 'em go. What the hell (small *h*) did they know? What did anybody know except Sister Margaret Mary and the former Herr Zahn?

ABOUT THE AUTHOR

Paul Sann likes to think of himself as a *summa cum laude* graduate of the school of hard knocks—some of which still hurt, by the way. He meant to be a lawyer but stumbled into the hands of an extremely mean city editor on the old New York *Post* who, on the pretext that a rich and glowing career lay ahead of him in the newspaper trade, talked him out of going to college at night. And so, alas, he wasted the best of his appointed years doing all the things that a man could do in that sometimes honored estate without paying dues to at least ten unions. He was executive editor of Dorothy Schiff's *Post* for twenty-seven years before quietly withdrawing to get some more words between hard covers. Pressed, he will tell you that he has been a loser both as a Pulitzer-Prize nominee (for international reporting) and a Pulitzer judge, having been disinvited after 1967 when he exposed the august Columbia University trustees for proclaiming a winner which his national jury had never had the pleasure of reading. This is his ninth book and second novel. Independently poor throughout his twin careers, he doesn't write for money but just to keep off the increasingly perilous streets of his native city.